GROWN AND SEXY

GROWN AND SEXY

Phillip Thomas Duck

sepia™

GROWN AND SEXY

A Sepia novel

ISBN 1-58314-525-7

Copyright © 2006 by Phillip Thomas Duck

www.kimanipress.com

Printed in U.S.A.

Book I

Judges

Prologue

"Can you get away?"

She had two-toned eyes: sandy brown dominant, then, in bull's-eye position, a fleck of burnt-toast brown. Exotic eyes, made even more startling in contrast to her dark chocolate skin. Eyes you noticed, had to notice; eyes that pulled you in, lulled you. They'd forever been her best feature—what set her apart, what folk talked about when they mentioned her.

"I want to spend some time with you," he added.

"Can't, Lincoln," she said finally, blinking those eyes sexily. "You knows I gotta be gettin' home to my baby."

"Which baby? Daughter...or your man?"

She smiled. "Daughter. Why you wanna go and say something like that?"

"How it is," Lincoln replied. "I'm borrowing you. I accept it."

"I love being borrowed," she cooed.

"Come with me, then."

She blinked those pretty eyes a few more times and pursed her lips. "Gotta be done with me by seven, Lincoln. I mean it. He'll start to wonder if I keep coming home late."

"By seven," Lincoln promised. He took her by the hand toward his vehicle, a shiny black Navigator with leather seats and a state-of-the-art sound system he used to crank out classical music.

Lincoln, to be sure, was a different type of brother, which was the reason why she'd fallen so hard for him even though she had a man at home who had, until Lincoln stepped hard into her life, satisfied her completely. Now, of course, she made excuses and truly had begun to believe that her man never did satisfy her.

"Close your eyes," Lincoln said as they pulled up in front of a large warehouse building.

"For?"

"Only way you'll find out is if you close your eyes," he told her.

She closed her sandy brown and burnt-toast brown eyes right away.

They were on an elevator soon after, very creaky and old-fashioned, from the sounds of it. She kept her eyes closed, as Lincoln directed, and that left her wide open to thoughts. Lincoln. The things he did to her. Things that made her lick her lips, moan, and quicken her breathing.

He was sexy. Exciting. Made her experience things she would never forget.

"Okay, we're here," Lincoln announced, his deep voice breaking Lita's thoughts. "Keep your eyes closed."

He took her wrist and directed her into what she could just tell was a wide-open space. His voice had traveled for what felt like miles before the ensuing echo brought it back to her ears.

"I'm going to sit you, Lita. Keep your eyes closed."

"Lincoln, this is—" The touch of his finger against her lips quieted her thought.

"I'm tying your wrists; don't be alarmed. Keep your eyes closed, Lita."

She could feel his fingers on her face, then tracing the outline of her jaw. On her neck. His touch sparking some kind of electric reaction in her as he moved to her shoulders.

"I'm ready, Lincoln. Do me," she begged.

Her words halted the action. His hands moved from her shoulders.

"Open your eyes, Lita," Lincoln said.

Disappointed, she opened her sandy brown and burnt-toast brown eyes.

They were simply eyes, and eyes were for seeing. She wished they weren't; wished she didn't see this. The three wild badasses watching her, not saying anything, undressing her with *their damn eyes.* Encircling her as she sat, hands bound behind her, short skirt hiked past the decent point of her thighs, in a creaky chair she feared would fall apart.

"Y'all gonna rape me?" was the first thing she thought to ask.

They didn't answer, but she noticed a subtle upturn on each of their faces, a tiny trace of a smile.

She thought of her daughter at that moment. *Saw* her daughter, no doubt lying on the floor of their living room propped on her elbows, sitting too close to the TV set. Her plastic SpongeBob SquarePants tumbler nearby, filled with Kool-Aid. Dora the Explorer holding the child's rapt attention.

She also *saw* her man. A good one, even though something tickled his throat into a cough every time she brought up diamond engagement rings. But sheeit, he cooked for her and Samantha. *Cooked.* Fried chicken was his specialty. He was probably in the kitchen now, brown paper bags spread out on the counter of the island, two-ply paper towels atop the brown paper bags to aid in soaking up the inevitable grease. Standing at the sink plucking out feathers, his forehead creased in concentration. Earl.

Why had she ever stepped out on him? Especially with this psycho, Lincoln. Because Earl didn't drive a Navigator and listen to classical music? Stupid.

Lita's heartrate ratcheted up as she eyed the three wild badasses. Samantha and Earl. God, she loved those two.

She closed her sandy brown and burnt-toast brown eyes and entered darkness. Didn't like it there, so she opened her eyes again.

The three badasses still circled her, their dark eyes taking in her round breasts, full lips, and then settling, as expected, on her eyes. She didn't know which one frightened her more. The one staring at her from a curtain of thick black dreads, the end tips of which held the tint of brown highlights. The one she took to be the youngest of the three, with an unfortunate tattoo on his neck— P.I.M.P, the lettering in Gothic style. Regrettably, the biggest too, with that angry hip-hop scowl, dressed in a wife-beater T-shirt, baggy shorts, his oversized feet stuffed in charcoal gray Timberland boots. Or Lincoln, who'd calmly taken her by the crook of her arm as she left Macy's after a foot-weary eight-hour shift. He'd been his usual fine and persuasive self, helping her angle her way into the front of the Navigator that idled by the curb outside the mall, not gripping her arm too tightly as he did it. He was dressed nice, and smelled even better—a tailored suit, Just Cavalli Him cologne. But those hands: Lita'd wondered about them but never questioned Lincoln. Hands you'd expect to see on a man that laid concrete foundations for a living.

Why had she fallen for Lincoln's trickery? She had a

man. This was just karma. That's what it had to be. She'd been weak; she admitted it. But Lincoln had wooed her so hard, with such persistence. Why? she now wondered. For this? She'd been so wrong about him. So wrong.

She glowered at them. A-holes. Why didn't they say something? Why did they have to stare at her so intently? She turned her gaze away to take in the building, a former paint factory that hadn't churned out any semi-glosses or flats in close to ten years. A film of dirt and other particles caked the large frame windows of the abandoned structure. She couldn't see outside, which meant no one could see inside. That thought made her pulse race, made her mouth go dry. *Do something, you three! Get this crap done with!*

Besides the chair she sat on, the only other "furniture" in sight was an overturned plastic milk crate that supported a leather portfolio briefcase. The milk crate was black, the briefcase blacker. It had to belong to Lincoln. What was he? In her lust, she hadn't taken the time to find out. Stockbroker? Why'd he have to get into this type of crime? All the stocks he could mess with, corporate books he could cook, and he chose to walk into her world.

"Shall we convene?" Lincoln said, noticing her gaze had landed on him and stayed there.

"What y'all want with me?" she asked. "Why you doin' this, Lincoln?"

Lincoln's masonry hands were the color of rich coffee grounds. He moved to her, put a hand on her shoulder, and squeezed it softly, like they were lovers *and* friends. Then he stepped back in front of her and told her what they wanted, said a name that made her mouth drop open—her cousin's name.

"What?" she said. Had she heard that right? Had this Lincoln, this trifling ass nigga who'd twisted her mind and morals up with a long downstroke invoked the name of her cousin?

Lincoln didn't offer her an answer. Instead, he clasped his hands together in an almost praying position. "State your name for the record? Make this official."

"What kinda drugs are you on, Lincoln? You know me."

"State your name for the record," he repeated.

"Lita Grimes," she stammered. This was getting too weird.

"Duly noted, Lita Grimes," he replied. "And just so you know, my name isn't really Lincoln Rhyme." He grinned, shrugged. "I'm a Jeffery Deaver fan. What can I say? I picked the Lincoln Rhyme name because, one, I like it, and two, I didn't think there was any chance you read his books."

"What is all of this, Lin—?"

He ignored her and pointed to the dreadlocked man: "My brother, Anthony." Then the hip-hop one: "Nate." Himself: "And I'm Dante. Collectively we're known as the Ruffin Brothers."

The Ruffin brothers. This was bad indeed. They didn't usually show their faces. To some they were an urban legend. Lita would have thought so herself if they weren't now standing before her. A trio with a major "drug corporation" that funneled product through North Carolina, Virginia, and Maryland. Rumored to be behind several murders, but never caught—too clever for the authorities.

Now it all made sense to her. Now she knew why Lincoln had asked for her cousin. They wanted revenge. She wouldn't help them. She wouldn't.

"What do you want with me?" Lita barked, angry.

"I think you know, Lita. We—"

"I don't know a thing," Lita lied.

Dante Ruffin frowned. "Please don't cut in, Lita

Grimes. Decorum is of the utmost importance during an undertaking such as this. You understand?"

"I don't understand none of this crap," she spat. "Psychos."

"I think you do, Lita Grimes. I think you know what we want. We'd like your help in locating your cousin. Obviously, his early release from prison caught us off guard. We weren't expecting him home for another six months, but that is unimportant. My brothers and I believe you can help us find him. Where is he, Lita?"

She wouldn't help them.

Nate, the hip-hop brother, rocked on his Timberland soles. The dreadlocked brother, Anthony, stood impassively. Dante stroked his chin. Lita thought of her cousin. Memories flooded her: picking crab apples together when they were younger, finding fun in the simplest things, rolling worn tires through the secret dirt trails they'd discovered in the woods. Like siblings. Something her cousin had needed—a sibling.

"He did his time," she weakly eked out. "Stood tall and did his time."

"Not for Warden Ruffin," Dante told her.

"Why won't y'all leave him 'lone?"

"*He* stepped into our lives, Lita Grimes. *He* infringed upon our family. Our sister. We didn't go seeking him out. We're a peaceful bunch. Until…" Dante let that thought go, avoiding that dark place that could force him to do something, well, crazy.

"I don't know where he is," Lita said. She went to cross her arms, and realized she couldn't. The bonds, which bit at her wrists, prevented it. She closed her eyes. This wasn't happening. This was DVD stuff, something you picked up at Blockbuster and viewed on a Saturday night with a tub of popcorn, yellow butter painting your fingers.

"Look, Lita, we've been waiting patiently for his time served to end. We'd like to *discuss* with him our hurt, our grief, our pain. Some people believe jail time was justice served for him. You've read the newspapers, maybe. You know how this all ended, in any regard. Jail time isn't justice. You can understand that, can't you?"

"I can, yes," Lita said. But myriad images jogged through her mind. The newspapers—she hadn't read them, but folks talked about it. She knew about the Ruffin girl that was no longer of this world. Suicide. They were blaming her cousin for that, though? That was a reach. That Ruffin girl had problems.

"Where's your cousin, Lita Grimes?"

"I don't know." She closed her eyes. They'd kill her cousin if she told. She wouldn't.

It grew quiet, still, eerily still. She opened her eyes. The three of them looked at her, wordlessly.

"I wish I knew where he was," she said, grasping. "I'd tell you, I swear." Dora yelling, "Swiper no swiping" now. Chicken grease pop-popping. Lita wanted to get home to her family.

Dante raised a hand dramatically, popped the top button of his starched white shirt loose, wriggled his neck, took off his jacket, draped it over the chair Lita sat in, and looked at her. "I was hoping for straightforwardness from you, Lita Grimes. My brothers and I will be just as disappointed with you as we are with your cousin if you don't provide us with his whereabouts. You know what he took from us." He cracked his knuckles and sighed. "You can imagine we'd be very interested in some get-back."

Nate, the hip-hop brother, pulled something from his waistband, stepped forward, and tapped it against the palm of his hand. His eyes were narrowed and trained on Lita. He wasn't looking at her with appreciation, either.

Lita looked at his hand; she didn't know the maker of that thing—Colt, Magnum, Glock, or whatnot. She knew one thing and one thing only. It was a gun. Guns caused death.

"You need to be putting that away," she managed. She couldn't help but look at that tattoo on his neck: P.I.M.P. Pimps had a reputation for smacking women. Lita's gaze dropped to the gun again. She could take a smack, considering the alternative. "I most definitely ain't any help if you go and shoot me," she told him.

Dante nodded to Nate. Nate glowered at his brother, then, reluctantly, put the gun away. Dante then turned his attention back to Lita.

"You assault my ears, sister," he said, sighing and shaking his head. He moved close to Lita and lowered his voice to a soothing, comforting register. "But this isn't about how poorly you speak. I apologize for my brother. Nate is just a bit high-strung. Thinks life is a gangsta rap video. Rat-a-tat-tat for that ass. But let's forget that. Where's your cousin, Lita?"

Lita's mind was a VCR tape on fast forward: Dora and fried chicken...Samantha and Earl...crab apples and worn tires...her cousin. "I ain't—I don't have anything for you," she replied.

"I'd hoped you wouldn't go this route, Lita Grimes." Dante turned his back to her, his shoes clacking on the cement as he moved to the briefcase resting on the overturned plastic milk carton. He picked up the briefcase, flipped it open, and pulled out a sheet of pink construction paper. He moved back toward Lita, the paper flapping in his hands.

"Take a look at this, Lita Grimes," he said as he reached her. "Are you certain you don't know the whereabouts of your cousin?" He gently placed the paper in her lap.

Lita looked down. A breath caught in her chest. She

could feel her eyes start to sting and burn, then water. Then clops of her salty tears fell in her lap, sprinkling the construction paper. Dante quickly moved forward and rescued the paper from a drowning.

"Don't want to mess that up," he said. "She's very talented."

Lita closed her eyes, her emotions folding in on her.

"Lita? Lita Grimes?"

"Try his girl," she said softly. "She's his heart. He couldn't wait to get out and get to her." That was all Lita would give.

"His girl is…?" Dante asked.

"Myshelle Maxwell."

Dante frowned. "She stopped visiting him in jail, stopped writing him. I thought they were kaput." The information they'd gleaned from their CO on the inside, but admittedly, same dude that hadn't known their boy was springing early. Faulty intelligence.

"She was stressed, needed a break from it all," Lita said, softly. "He's been in touch with her. She knows where he is."

Dante focused on Lita. "I truly hope this isn't a cold trail, Lita Grimes." He waved the sheet of pink construction paper as he said it.

"He's not a bad man," Lita said. Her wet face flashed hot. The tears continued to wiggle down her cheeks. "He's trying to be better. He found Jesus inside, ya know."

"Jesus?"

Lita looked down and nodded. " 'Swhat I heard." She added, "A while back."

"You think it's real?"

"I wouldn't know." Lita shrugged, which took some effort. "I hope it is. I think it is."

"You a praying woman?" Dante asked Lita.

"I tries to be," Lita answered, wondering how a praying

woman could ever come to the situation in which she now found herself. Karma. Messing with this man she had no business messing with.

"*Try to be. Try to be*," Dante said.

"I try to be."

Dante shook his head. "No praying woman should mangle the language as you do, Lita Grimes. It's an affront to God. I mean, goodness, Lita Grimes. Have some reverence, some respect for yourself."

"I'm sorry. I'll…try better."

"Please do."

"What y'all planning to do when you find him?" Lita wondered.

Dante smiled. "Now, Lita Grimes, I *ain't* think I'd have to explain that to you."

Lita swallowed and tried to raise her arm to scratch her face, which burned with an itch from the tears, but couldn't. "I gave you what you wanted. Can I go? I want to get home to my baby."

"Which baby?" Dante asked, laughing.

Lita didn't answer.

Dante stepped forward and set the sheet of pink construction paper on Lita's lap. Then he moved around to her back and untied the bonds. She let her arms move free, wiggled them to get the circulation flowing, and rubbed her wrists, then picked up the pink paper and held it tight. Artwork her daughter had drawn…artwork that had been hanging in the hallway at Samantha's school. A message from the Ruffins: they could infiltrate any aspect of Lita's life if they wanted.

"Meeting is adjourned," Dante told Lita. "This Myshelle Maxwell better lead us to your cousin, Lita. In the meantime, you're free to leave. Give my regards to your little *artiste*. And Earl, too."

Lita grunted, then stood, pulled her skirt down, and skip-walked away, gripping her daughter's artwork to her chest.

Dante turned to his two other brothers. "Our boy's been born again. What does the Bible say? An eye for an eye?"

They nodded.

1

The Jeremiah Correctional Institution had been my home for two and a half years. I went in as one man and came out as another, leaving quiet as a rodent living in the eaves of some Baptist or Methodist church. During my exit processing, they gave me the jeans and sweatshirt I'd worn that first day thirty months prior, my Sony Walkman, and a check for eleven dollars and thirteen cents that I'd earned mopping floors. Thirteen cents an hour. Now that's minimum wage.

I passed through the doors to the outside, a different man.

I'd found the love of He's Sweet I Know inside. He's Sweet I Know, or, From Whom All Blessings Flow, the names I used to reference the Creator. I'd grown up hearing my mother sing those two gospel songs and even more secular songs as she did chores around the house. I'd never heard her say the words "God," "Jesus," or "Lord." We weren't church folks. We had a Bible, but it lay dusty and unopened in a cluttered corner of our living room. Needless to say, I grew up ambivalent to the Almighty of those two songs my mother sang. But jail changed that. I was now a believer. Tried my best to be one, I should say. I still had my moments of doubt, weakness, and failure.

Like at that moment of my release.

I was released, and at the same time, needed a release—a sexual release. Fornication, that sin of the flesh that men couldn't seem to resist. Some of my "Milkshake." My girl. Myshelle.

On the inside, I'd been used to getting that Milkshake every morning, some time after four when the COs would stroll by to make sure some despondent inmate hadn't turned his six-by-nine into a death chamber by hanging himself with his bed linens. After the COs passed, I'd either pull out my Milkshake's Polaroid, or simply muster up thoughts of her as I yanked on myself. It wouldn't take long for that warm feeling to travel up my legs, settle in my groin, and then spout milk on my fingers and belly. Well, being that I was out, and early at that, I needed the real Milkshake, and not some Polaroid version of her, either. The real thing was what I desired, needed, as much as I needed the air I couldn't see. As much as I needed From Whom All Blessings Flow, whom I also couldn't see, but could only feel, his presence a cape over my shoulders.

If asked, I'd have told anyone that my Milkshake and I had that weak-in-the-knees-R & B-record love that everyone hoped to find once in life. We even had our own anthem, Kelis's "Milkshake," a song I listened to repeatedly in my Walkman's earphones that morning of my release. An infallible love. One of kind. Forever. Soulmates.

I should have known better.

The air outside was hot and sticky that July morning I got out. I stood there at the gates of JCI, which the inmates called "Jackie" to soften the harshness of the prison. I stood there, outside, and squeezed my fingers around the air. It was that thick. But I didn't linger long. I took off on foot to the surrounding town and bummed a ride off some college-age white boy filling his tank at the Texaco that bordered the town. He was wearing a Nirvana T-shirt, high-top white Converse sneakers, and baggy skater shorts. I was on a mission to rebuild my budding family.

"Where to, dude?" he'd asked me.

I told him.

"Cool beans," he'd said. He reached forward and cranked the volume on his Hyundai's stereo system. Music flooded my ears that if played backwards would probably have told me to kill the white boy.

We didn't talk much during the ride. He was busy flinging his head wildly to the music, his long blond locks flapping down into his face. A quick swing of his head in the manner of a woman and the locks would move from covering his eyes. I thought of all the inmates I'd encountered during my two-plus bid that would have found the long hair sexy, this white boy even sexier, a surrogate for the women they couldn't have. Thankfully, I'd escaped that added burden of having that homoerotic impulse take my manhood and stomp it out like a cigarette.

All I wanted was my Milkshake. My weak-in-the-knees-R & B-record love. My time in prison had been hard on Myshelle, I knew. She'd be so happy to hold me, kiss me, without the prying eyes of COs standing up against the wall around us.

As the road passed by, too slowly for me, I must admit, I realized it would be only a little bit longer and we'd be together forever. We'd recorded the A-side of our R & B love; now it was on to the B-side.

Since my release, I'd made my moves stealthily, to keep eyes from watching me. Didn't have anyone pick me up at JCI; picked an anonymous white boy with a heart of gold to do me the solid and drive me. I was okay. Everything was right with my world.

When we arrived at Milkshake's little bungalow, the white boy pulled his Hyundai to the foot of her driveway. I looked over at my beaten-down Toyota parked carefully on the blacktop. The tires were sparkling, windows tinted. It didn't look beat up any more, to be honest. She'd taken good care of it, had held me down, had it looking better than it had when the blue boys took me away in handcuffs.

"This is it," I told my driver, the heart-of-gold white boy.

"Cool beans, dude."

"Not much," I said, handing him my Sony Walkman, "but all I can offer you."

"Nah, dude," he said. "I can't be taking that from you."

"You sure?"

"Did Kurt Cobain blow his brains out?" he asked, grimacing painfully at the tragedy of the Nirvana front man's suicide. A personal tragedy to this white boy and millions cut from his same ilk.

"Thanks," I said, touching his shoulder. "You'll be blessed."

"Already am, dude. Already am."

I stepped out, shut the door, and smelled the rubber of his tires peeling off down the road. He's Sweet I Know had been like that for me since the day of my conversion, bringing people like the white boy into my life to offer me the support I needed. Angels, I believed these anonymous souls to be.

I moved to my Toyota. A Playboy model air freshener hung from the rearview mirror. I couldn't remember if it was the centerfold I'd left dangling those two-plus years ago or not. I touched the hood. It was warm, just like the day.

The sun smiled down on me as I paused by my car,

a sign of good things to come, I imagined, and some birds chirped in the distance. I could smell burning firewood that tinted the air with a rich aroma. It felt good to smell something other than the smells I'd become accustomed to for the past three years. You know: urine, musty armpits, rotting teeth, and on bad days, blood.

I moved past the car and down the sidewalk path to Milkshake's front porch. I strutted up the steps and rapped a knuckle against the door. The main door was open, but the screen door was locked tight. I hadn't told Myshelle I was coming, but kept this whole release thing a secret. I knew that was my best bet. The letters I'd been getting in prison, threatening letters, had me on guard.

I heard her footsteps, slippers scraping across the hardwood floors. I got my smile ready. Ready to record our duet for the B-side of our R & B-record love.

But Milkshake didn't appear in the doorway. Some man stood before me in the screen, half my size, double my skin shade, and nappier about the head. In boxers and a T-shirt, and big fluffy slippers you wouldn't catch me in when death came knocking. Chewing on a chicken wing.

"Myshelle in?" I asked him, trying to catch which features this man shared with my Milkshake. One of her cousins, I figured. She had so many. Folks here in North Carolina, but also in Virginia, Maryland, and out west in Oakland and Sacramento. And a few that had found their way to New Hampshire, of all places.

Milkshake's cousin slid the chicken wing from his mouth and twirled it between two fingers stained the color of soot. "Onliest thing you got claims to here, nigga, is that Toy-yoda out there. I fixed her up for you. Couldn't be driving Melly around in a bucket, ya heard."

Melly?

He wasn't a cousin. I didn't know him. But he knew me.

"I need to see Myshelle," I insisted. I could feel my hands fisting. I tried to open my fingers but couldn't.

"She's buck naked at the moment," he said. "Waiting on me to finish this here wing. And you know you ain't seeing none of that."

I reached for the screen door and pulled on the handle, hard. It didn't budge.

"I ain't stupid," he told me, grinning, stray pieces of chicken lodged in his teeth. "Melly thought you might try this surprise route, seeing as those Ruffin boys got you all shook. We've been waiting on you to get out. It's hot so I got to keep the door open. But I make sure I keep the screen door locked. I know you been getting all Arnold Schwarzenegger for the past two years while I've been getting my fingers greasy and black with motor oil. Sweatin' my little ass off in that garage. Uh-uh. You ain't getting in this house, nigga."

I didn't like him. He talked too much.

That chicken wing morphed before my eyes to a plastic cup emblazoned with the Dairy Queen insignia, its contents a thick milkshake. I blinked my eyes a few times and tried to make that image disappear. Or maybe, tried to keep my eyes from watering. Weak-in-the-knees-R & B-record loves weren't supposed to crash and die like this.

I gripped the screen door's handle again and jiggled it, harder. It still didn't budge. The man I desperately wanted to be Milkshake's cousin chuckled at me.

"You can have the Toy-yoda back," he said. "That's only right. And I ain't touch a dollar in that shoebox you got in the trunk tucked by the doughnut. Melly told me that's cash from your dead mama and I don't believe in messing with a man's money anyhow. But you ain't getting nothing else on this here prop-per-ty, ya heard? Keys under the driver side mat, *Governor*." He slammed the main door shut.

I knocked but then gave up that ghost after several failed attempts, walked around to the side of the house, and peered into a window that overlooked the bedroom. It was just a screen but held those bars people used to childproof their windows. Those bars made me recoil briefly, but then I remembered that Milkshake was inside, my R & B love, with some other man. I peered in again. I couldn't see anything through the darkness, but I could hear muted voices. Couldn't make out words, but did hear someone cackling. Him.

Then I heard the creak of the bed's joints. Grunting. Moaning. More grunting. Louder moaning. I smacked my hand against the screen in disgust and collapsed there, crushing some flowers Myshelle had planted on the side of the house. Didn't care.

After some time, I found my way back to my feet and stumbled to the Toy-yoda. Chicken Wing was true to his word: the keys were under the mat and my shoebox of cash was still in the trunk, undisturbed.

I drove off in a daze but called the next day around noontime, figuring Chicken Wing was working. Myshelle, I knew, didn't work Mondays at the beauty salon.

"Hello?" Her voice was husky, a-pack-of-Newport-a-day husky. A bad habit we'd argued about constantly. I couldn't think of anything else that was a source of friction between us. So why had she done me this way?

"I'm at a YMCA over in Fayetteville," I told my Milkshake. "Come see me. We'll talk this through."

"Nothing to talk through," she said, matter-of-fact with her tone.

"I'm not going to beg," I said, emboldened with pride.

"Good. That would hurt me to hear."

She hung up. I called back. And called. And called. Gave up calling after two weeks of that nonsense, and sat around in my pay-by-the-week room trying to figure out a way to move on with the next phase of my life. Counting the money in my Nike shoebox, I convinced myself I hadn't been burned. I'd gotten my ride pimped, after all. That accounted for something.

But I couldn't get my mind truly away from Myshelle. Where had we gone wrong?

Prison.

I shook my head. Prison. So many of my hopes and dreams had withered away in the belly. Prison had killed the old me. It had destroyed my weak-in-the-knees-R & B love, too, and had turned my life upside down. No way, having faced that, I couldn't be a bit bitter. *A bit bitter* was a mouthful, but where I was just the same. From Whom All Blessings Flow kept me from being worse, from taking out my frustrations on the society that had put me away to begin with. So I talked to Him incessantly, and thought.

A knock came to my door at the YMCA on one such day of reflection. I was on my knees, praying. The knock made me pause and turn with my ear craned. A second knock came. I stood and moved hesitantly across the thin carpet, and peeked through the YMCA's thin pink curtain. Milkshake was on my porch, melting in the scorching August sun.

"No second chances," I told her as I cracked the door open, trying to be hard. But knowing I'd have a chocolate mustache within minutes if she'd have me.

"Ain't looking for one," she shot back. "Here. Somebody put this in my mailbox for you."

I took it carefully.

"Anybody follow you?" I asked her, trying to usher her inside while I scanned the lot.

"I know you worried about the Ruffin Brothers," she told me, shrugging aside my hand. "I got sense. I went to another place first, dropped a fake envelope in somebody else's mailbox, made sure everything was clear, then came to you."

"Thanks," I told her, settling down.

"They took Lita," she said.

"What?" My heart started to pound. Lita was my favorite cousin, and now that Myshelle was no longer in my life, my last true ally. I hadn't called her since my release, because I was unable to conjure up enough strength to explain, for the thousandth time, how I'd let my life fall apart. Lita always asked, refusing to overstand any of the reasons I gave. "Samantha wonders, too," she often said. "How do I explain this to a kid?"

I didn't have an answer for that.

And now, they'd taken Lita, an innocent in this war. I felt myself leaning sideways, and then caught at the last moment by the door frame.

"She's okay," Myshelle offered. "They let her go. She had a coworker call to warn me. She was worried they might have her phone bugged or something. Crazy, I know. But then, you never know with them three. The drugs around here are getting worse. It's turning into Baghdad out on these streets. Those three is like Uday, Qusay, and Saddam wrapped into one."

She was right; you never knew with those three.

Again I said, "Thanks," but noticeably weaker.

"Thanks?"

I nodded. "For letting me know."

"You brought this into our lives," Myshelle said bitterly.

I apologized and thanked her for the caution she had taken in coming to see me.

"Them damn George Pelecanos novels you got me reading," she said. "Got me thinking like a criminal and shit. Fucked up."

I frowned at her language. I had been trying to cut that from my life, and had succeeded, for the most part.

"Oh, I forgot you turned to John the Baptist or some shit," she said. "You don't like me cursing, right?"

"Not a good look for a woman," I told her. "Or anyone, for that matter."

"I'm doing me," she said.

"Doing somebody else, too," I replied.

She nodded. "That I am. He might look small, but he's hung so low his mama could have named him Seabiscuit."

That description made me frown. "I'm not hurting in that department," I reminded her.

"No, you're not," she agreed. "But he's got a good job. Treats me with respect. Never been to jail. Especially for…" She quieted, shook her head.

I let the comment drift as well. Watched her, admired her beauty.

Something was different about her. I couldn't place it. Eyes? Still brown. Makeup? Just a touch of lipstick, a little mascara. Hair. She had it styled in two ponytails. She looked like a schoolgirl. Like she was ready to go trick-or-treating at R. Kelly's house.

Two ponytails. Two long ponytails.

I reached up, took one, and softly tugged at it. Her head jerked in the direction of my tug.

"Heck is wrong with you?" she barked.

"Longer than ever," I replied. "All yours, too."

"Yeah and?"

"You said during our phone calls that you couldn't

come see me anymore because the visits stressed you out. That your hair was falling out in clumps. It was really this new guy. Wasn't it?"

She didn't reply. I looked up at the sky. A sun-filled sky. Despite the orange glare and the heat it cast off, my weather forecast called for a deep chill and rain showers.

"How long?" I asked her. "This guy."

"Two," she said.

"Months?"

She shook her head. "Years. It wasn't anything serious for the first year and a half, though. Sex 'bout it."

That didn't comfort me.

"Okay, no use me hanging. Be safe. Those Ruffins ain't a joke," I heard Myshelle say. She wasn't my Milkshake anymore. I had to accept it.

I turned my gaze back to her. "Listen—"

But she turned away, making her way toward the lot.

I looked to see that apple ass of hers doing its stroll down the path. I could relate to Adam—could overstand him biting into that forbidden fruit Eve dangled in front of him.

After Myshelle disappeared inside a little Ford pickup truck that must have been Chicken Wing's, I opened the envelope. I heard the Ford engine kick in as I pulled out the slip of paper inside the envelope. Heard Myshelle give the Ford gas and back from her space as I unfolded the slip of paper. Heard the Ford move from the lot, and then the tink of the motor fade, and swallowed my fear in a gulp as I read the note on the slip of paper.

Breach for breach, eye for eye, tooth for tooth: as he hath caused a blemish in a man, so shall it be done to him again.—Leviticus 24:20.

Heard you caught religion in the belly. You're going to

need it. Make no mistake—prison notwithstanding—your
debt to us is still unpaid. Judgment Day, soon come. Best,

The R's

It took me exactly twelve minutes to pack the few items I'd picked up since my release. I timed it. Angry I couldn't get the job done in ten, knowing those two minutes could have cost me my life. I bounced from my pay-by-the-week room and hit the highway in my pimped Toy-yoda, deciding that my new life would take shape in New Jersey, as far away from North Carolina as my limited experience could envision me going. I was violating my probation, running out without getting in touch with my Probation Officer to get his approval for the move, but so be it. It would be hard for him to keep me on the straight and narrow if I ended up dead in a ditch somewhere. So, Dirty Jersey it was. I told myself I picked Dirty Jersey at random, that it didn't have anything to do with the other letters I'd received in prison with a sender's address somewhere in the Garden State…from my father. That it had nothing to do with the man I'd grown up wanting to be like, basking in the approval he gave me, but for some reason withheld from my brother. Selfishly loving that approval. I flashed on a memory of my father standing over the toilet, his urine shooting off in two different sprays. One spray caught the toilet bowl, the other, the wall, staining the flat white to flat beige as it slid down the wall to the floor like golden tear streaks. My father had turned to see me watching him, wide-eyed.

"A dick is the closest thing man ever gets to having magic in his hands, boy," he told me. "It'll be one of your greatest joys when you get older. You'll see."

He laughed, as he did when he listened to those Redd Foxx albums in the basement he thought I didn't know about. Miss Ma'am would have to take care of the urine later. My father was too lazy to flush after himself, so Miss Ma'am would do that. And my father definitely wasn't cleaning the urine off the floor and wall. Miss Ma'am would do that, too.

I learned about love from those two. A father who could be so cruel to one son, driving that son to hell. And taught no lessons of value to the other son, driving him to prison. A mother who made my brother and me call her Miss Ma'am because it softened the biggest blow of her life— she had two sons and a husband to care for, so she wouldn't get her chance to be a famous jazz singer. No one would ever compare her to Ella or Lady Day.

Like Mary J. Blige sang once, "My Life." No one else had to row my boat. It was mine. I accepted it. He's Sweet I Know gave me no choice. But, as I had learned since my conversion, if He brought me to it, He'd also bring me through it if I believed in Him, remained faithful. And thinking on those lost episodes of my life, I knew that He was more than generous, for He'd brought me through everything while I hadn't been particularly believing in Him, or faithful.

Around Washington DC I decided I could take a break from my great escape. My stomach had started to growl and I needed to urinate. Still, I didn't stop until I'd reached Delaware. I got off at an exit that mentioned food and lodging, and came upon a twenty-four-hour diner with eats and a restroom. I slid out of the Toy-yoda. The once azure sky was now black as a computer monitor, sprinkled with white stars, a large pearl hanging on its canvas: that large pearl a clear and full moon.

I went inside the diner.

Did my gig in the bathroom to thundering applause from my bladder, then settled into a booth.

"Evening, handsome," the waitress said to me. She handed me a worn menu. "You look this over, but in the meantime, can I get you something to drink? By those muscles you got, I imagine you'd like a protein milkshake or something. 'Fraid we ain't got that, though, handsome."

Milkshake, she'd said. That comment made me flinch. "Iced tea?" I asked.

"Sweetened?"

"Only way to go," I told her.

"Sweet," she said, eyeing me. "Yes, sweet, of course." She shook aside some feeling and moved on, bouncing on her once white, now dusty tan sneakers, pushing her way through the kitchen doors.

I scanned the menu for breakfast specials because I had a craving for eggs. I figured the *Spoon-Fed 24-Hour Diner* could scratch that itch, even though they were the home of the "best country-style soups in the county" and the menu made nary such a claim about any of their other offerings. I looked forward to the eggs, though, which would be my first that didn't come powdered from a carton in close to four years. Eggbeaters were the rage at JCI. Made from real eggs, so claimed the manufacturers, but they could sell that one to the Devil at a discount.

The waitress returned with my iced tea, sat it on the table, wiped the moisture she'd gotten on her fingers from the glass on her apron, and pulled a pad and pen. She chewed her gum vigorously and looked at me just as intently. I imagined what she could do with that mouth of hers, those strong jaws. But I quickly closed my mind to that imagery.

I mean, prison time or not, she wasn't that good looking.

Her blond hair came from a bottle. One that must have

sat on the shelf past its sell-by date, because her hair had
no life whatsoever, so dull, so dead, no sheen. Her skin
was equally pallid, acne pocked around her chin, and of
no complement to her one good feature. Her deep blue
eyes. Bluer than my mood when Myshelle's Chicken Wing
stood before me, letting me know that he'd be the only
one slurping milkshake through a straw.

"Scrambled eggs, cooked brown," I told the waitress.
"Hash browns, two slices of toast, nice and brown. And another iced tea."

She finished writing and tapped her pad with the pen.
"You like brown, too, I see. That's my weakness also." She
winked. "You got it, handsome." Then she sashayed away,
through the doors that separated the back from the seating area, where she placed my order on a clip by the
reach-through window for the kitchen. She stepped back
out with a damp dishcloth and sashayed to another area
of the diner where she wiped off a just departed cus-
tomer's table. I have to give it to her; she moved her hips
like a song. Ella. Lady Day.

The front door of the diner opened; the bell stringers
on the inside handle jingled. A chill traveled down my
spine, an eerie sensation that kneaded the small of my
back like dough. I touched my nose. Suddenly it burned.
My eyes started to water as a sickenly sweet smell of chocolate invaded my nostrils. I looked up just as darkness covered my light, praying it wasn't three ridiculously large
dudes with venom on their breath standing over me.

It wasn't.

"May I?" the haggard woman asked me. "I'm rather superstitious and this is my booth." She had a mass of
crooked fingers pointed toward the empty seat across
from me. It looked at first glance like she had two hands'
worth of fingers on that one hand.

I was cautious with her. Prison had taught me this lesson. Life outside, with those three after me, reinforced the lesson. I looked her over: she looked safe enough. I nodded that the seat was hers for the taking.

"Thanks," she said. "I looked at you when I came in, and I thought to myself, 'there's a kind soul who would let me sit with him.'" She removed the colorful woolen hat that was too hot for this weather, and shook a mass of white curls down into her face. A bag lady, I found myself thinking.

"Name's Swizz," she told me as she made herself comfortable.

I smiled.

"Talkative one, aren't you?" She waited a beat and when I didn't answer that, she whispered, "I'm making you uncomfortable. I can get over my silly superstition for one evening, and find myself another booth."

I could feel From Whom All Blessings Flow shaking His head at me. "No," I told the woman. "I'm sorry. My mind isn't where it should be, that's all. This booth is definitely big enough for the two of us. Stay."

"Yeah?" She smiled; her teeth were whiter than I'd have figured. "Good. This booth has been good to me. My second husband left me the night after I ate some chowder in this very booth."

"That's good?" I asked, thinking about my Milkshake.

Swizz smiled. "When it came to Roy, yes, that was very good. Saved me from being his punching bag, spared me the embarrassment of one day catching one of the dirty sex diseases he was bound to get with one of his street harlots."

I looked away.

"But that's news as old as Lincoln's assassination," Swizz said. "Thanks again for your kindness, young man. You made an old lady happy. Darlene—the waitress here—she's always getting on me about disturbing folks for this booth. But as I said, superstitions are hard to die. But Darlene, that's a good young gal, there. She's like you, very kind to an old lady, even with all my foolishness."

"My name is LeVar, by the way," I told Swizz. Immediately, I thought of my youth: of toy trains, G.I. Joe action figures, Transformers. Then, a silver-dollar-size hole that bled despite my fingers pressed against it…my brother. I shook the thoughts aside and turned my attention back to the old lady. Swizz.

She nodded and looked at me as if I were a movie screen and she already knew my story before we reached the end credits.

"What brings you out so late, *LeVar*?" she asked. She had a confidence in her tone, as if she could pull out confessions. But I'm nobody's Catholic, so it wasn't happening.

"I'm moving actually," I said.

"All by yourself?"

"Self is all I have."

"*Really.*"

The way she said *really* chilled me, just as I'd felt my spine cool when she first walked in. It was as if the old woman knew of the strain in my life, knew of the tragedy that had me sipping iced tea and waiting on eggs at midnight on an August Monday turning to an August Tuesday. I made a mistake, I wanted to say, but those three won't accept that I paid for that mistake. Spent two and a half years making sure I didn't suddenly catch feelings for some man's booty hole, making do with a cot and three square meals. But they won't let me be, those three. So I ran. And I'll keep running because if they find me…

"Me, myself, and I," I ended up saying instead.

"What of your parents?"

"What?"

Swizz smiled. "I'm sorry. I'm being nosy. My children act as if I don't exist. Embarrassed that I don't quite fit their expectations. When you said you were all alone, I imagined my children saying the same thing when questions about me came up." She paused, a look of hurt on her face.

"I'd figure you for having lost your mother," she went on. "You've got that look young men get when their mother isn't around to help them shoulder this tough world. But I'd bet your father is still alive."

My body shook. I wondered if Swizz noticed. Wondered if she could see Miss Ma'am sneaking in the bathroom to smoke one of her coffin nails, and then tossing the spent butt down the toilet so my father wouldn't find out. I wondered if Swizz knew about the day Miss Ma'am started coughing up phlegm with an auburn tint. Could she see my father on I-95 years before my mother's daily vomiting, fleeing from his family? Could she see me come home one day to find my mother inconsolable, having gotten the divorce papers while I was in school?

"Oh,"—I concentrated hard in order to speak—"I'm sorry to hear about your children. But both of my parents are, in fact, dead." I didn't know why I was lying to her. Same reason I'd been lying all these years, probably. It was easier to lie than tell the truth. That I'd lost my mother when I was younger, that my father had left years before Miss Ma'am started puking so loud I thought I'd find her insides swimming in that toilet. Maybe after I caught up with my father, in Jersey, things could be different. In the meantime, I reasoned that folks didn't have to be six feet under to be dead.

"My condolences for your parents," Swizz replied. She smirked when she said it. Face not matching her words.

"Thanks."

"You've got a look in your eyes," Swizz said. "Like life hasn't been too kind to you. Like you've been through some things that would break most men down."

"Yes," I said. "Yes, I have."

"You think you can run from who you are and what you've done in Jersey?"

"What?" I made a quick motion that knocked over my iced tea and a saltshaker. A mound of white quickly formed on the table surface between us. My tea was swimming toward the table edge, the floor. I jumped up, glanced at Swizz, and went to get Darlene for napkins.

"I've got a spill, Darlene," I told her as she came through the revolving doors of the kitchen. "Can I have a few napkins to wipe it up?"

She smiled at me. "Ooh, you know my name. Spying my nametag, huh. I'll get it, handsome."

We returned to the table, Darlene immediately moving to wipe the surface. Swizz was gone.

"What happened to that crazy old lady?" I wondered aloud.

"What crazy old lady?"

I turned my head to look around, but didn't see Swizz anywhere. I turned back to Darlene.

"Swizz," I said. "The woman who always sits in this booth. Too superstitious for her own good. Looks like a bag lady. Gives you a creepy feeling. Place started smelling like a chocolate factory when she walked through the door."

Darlene stood to her full height and frowned. "I know all the regulars," she told me. "We ain't never had nobody name of Swizz come through here. And what's that about chocolate?"

I looked around, puzzled, and realized for the first time, that chocolate aroma that had been so strong in my nostrils was gone.

2

Russell Sykes stood in the kitchen intently watching the toaster oven. He hurried toward it once the two slices of white bread popped up. Then he pulled the toast out with his thick, callused fingers, dropped them on his plate, and blew his fingers cool. A glass of orange juice was in place at the table, a coffee cup ready for filling, and a jar of strawberry jam was on the counter. Russell picked up his plate, grabbed a knife, and held the jar of strawberry jam steadied under his neck as he tiptoed across the kitchen. He sat down at the table and massaged the jam over his toast. Then he poured himself a black cup of java. The steam from the cup wafted up into his nostrils, a rich aroma that made his eyes drift closed for a moment. But then he opened them just as quickly. Time was of the essence when you were in a hurry. He began devouring the food and drink at a breakneck pace.

Normally he read the entire newspaper, but today he just skimmed the sports section and breezed over the front page to see what major news dominated the world. Oil barrel prices were forecast to continue rising, the stock market was doing its impression of the Scream Machine at Great Adventure, and the Yankees were in the midst of another dominating year, thanks to their two-trillion-dollar-player payroll—business as usual. Russell placed the newspaper back on the counter, gulped the last drops of his coffee, and wiped the few stray breadcrumbs off the table and into his palm. He dropped the crumbs in the garbage and set the plate in the dishwasher rack with special care. The kitchen clean, he moved toward the front room, tiptoeing again.

He was just steps from the door when he heard the familiar voice beckoning him from upstairs.

"Russell!"

He contemplated leaving without answering. When he returned home later, he could say he hadn't heard her calling for him.

"Russell!"

He glanced at his watch. *Thirty more seconds*, he thought to himself. *Should have skipped reading the paper; could have gotten coffee at the 7-Eleven.*

"Russell," his wife called again.

He walked to the bottom of the stairwell that led to the second floor of their handsome home, rolled his eyes, and called up to her, "Yeah, baby?" The last thing he wanted to do was continue the argument from last evening.

"You weren't leaving, were you?" his wife called out.

"No," he lied.

"You promised you'd go with me to church today. You weren't going to sneak out and leave me sleeping, were you?"

Sure I was.

"Russell?"

"No, baby."

"Come up," Bevolyn said. "I'm straining my voice yelling."

He sighed, placed the briefcase by the foot of the stairs

like luggage for a long trip, and headed up to talk to her, feeling as if he were lugging something heavy on his shoulders as he ascended the steps. This was sure to be interesting. All of their exchanges were.

"I left a note," he said as he appeared in the doorway to their bedroom. The best defense a strong offense, his game plan.

"Thought you weren't going anywhere," she replied.

He had said that, hadn't he? She'd caught him in a lie. So much for his strong offense. He stood wordless.

Bevolyn looked at the pillow next to her, and strained without her contacts to make out the scribbled writing on the napkin he had left on her pillow like a hotel mint. She picked up the napkin, pressed it close to her face, and sniffed. Checking for some other woman's perfume etched into the napkin like ink. Russell wasn't too careful about covering his steps. It was easy for her to catch him in little lies, little discrepancies. She was a pro at that.

"I love you," he said, helping her to read the words.

"That what it says?" she asked. "Sure it doesn't say '*buck off*'?"

He moved toward her, took the note from her hand, and read it. "No, it says 'I love you.' "

"I guess you forgot about last evening?"

"No, Bevolyn. I just choose to move on, that's all." He backed away again, finding his spot by the doorway.

Bevolyn emerged from the covers and stretched. She sat up on the side of the bed, her nude light brown body a bit soft through the middle but toned everywhere else. Her large breasts lay heavy against her chest, her nipples and areolae noticeably darker than her skin. She grasped her ReNu contact case. A compartment was molded in plastic for each eye's contact. She twisted the cap off one side, removed a contact, and put it in her eye, then did the same with the other side.

"Must be nice to just *move on*. I wish I could do that," she told her husband as she turned and caught focus of him. She didn't notice his appraisal of her body. She didn't see the want in his eyes. She seldom saw the want anymore—she had convinced herself ignoring his want was her only remaining area of control in their relationship.

"You could move on, but you just choose to dwell on shit," Russell said. He ran his gaze across her hair, the long tresses tied together in a Scrunchie. Her hair had a touch of red tint, courtesy of the summer sun's rays and not a salon. She was as attractive as the day they had married, and yet so much had happened since, so much ugliness between them that soiled their relationship.

Bevolyn shot Russell a look. He looked good in black—Kenneth Cole. She could smell his cologne: woodsy, distinctly masculine. Just a dab he put on his wrists and neck. The women he slept with must like his scent understated, she figured.

She looked at his jaw line, the goatee he kept so neat and trim, his hair cut close, a little salt forming at his temples now. Looking good for a man who'd soon reach forty. Those full lips. Handsome on the outside, but so ugly on the inside. How had they come to this?

"The hell you looking at me like that for?" Russell barked.

"What did I tell you about talking like that?" Bevolyn asked. "You can't even mind your tongue on a Sunday, Russell?"

"You know me," he said. "Headed to hell with gasoline drawers on."

"Couldn't have put it better myself," Bevolyn replied. She finally noticed his eyes, probing her nude body, and pulled the covers around herself to cut off his view. "Now, do you care to discuss last evening with me? It'll serve you much better than running off like a coward."

"I'm not running off."

"Where were you last night?"

Russell looked at his watch. "Bevolyn, I haven't got time for this. I have to deliver these blueprints before ten. I have a full day's agenda. I need to be in my office right now working on—"

"Sunday is the Lord's day, Russell."

"He's not paying our bills," Russell retorted. "And I've yet to see His name signed on my performance evaluations. Maybe I wouldn't have to work so hard if it was. He's so compassionate and merciful. Maybe He would cut me some slack that my boss now isn't. But until that day…"

"I won't even dignify your blasphemy," Bevolyn said. "Talk to me about

last night. I want to know where you were."

Russell moved closer to her, placed his left hand on her right shoulder, and patted it twice. It was the same gesture he greeted his dog with when he came home, except with Demon he enjoyed the touch. He knew Demon would appreciate it, maybe reciprocate by licking his hand. Bevolyn wouldn't give an inch. No matter how much Russell begged, she wouldn't warm the chill between them. And she had the key to warming it, too: intimacy. Let him touch her, make love to him. Didn't the Bible she loved so much say that was one of a wife's duties?

Russell squeezed Bevolyn's shoulder, the squeeze, unlike the pats of a moment ago, sincere, loving, and caring. His olive branch to her. "I promise we'll talk at length tonight, over dinner. You can pick the restaurant. But I really have to go." He watched her eyes, noticed them shift down. That gesture still had the same effect on him as it had sixteen years ago, when they first married. It weakened him. "It's like I said, though," he added, "I didn't realize I'd hit POWER OFF on the cell phone and I got so bogged down reading over those...papers."

"Reading papers," Bevolyn said. "Now see, you're lying. You said last night that you'd stopped by the bank. You can't keep doing this, Russell."

Yep. Stopped by the bank. Read papers. All the same. He wouldn't tell her this, though.

"Can't keep doing what?" Russell asked. "Every time I come home late I'm branded with guilt for something I haven't done. That's nonsense, Bevolyn, and I'm sick of it."

"*You're sick of it?* How do you think *I* feel?"

Russell looked around at their bedroom, gazing at all the lavish accessories and designs with wide-eyed amazement. "I'll trade places with you in a second," he said. "I'll sit around on my ass all day while you work. I'll go off spending your money, and complaining all the time as if life has handed me some cruel punishment. I'll let you troop off to work, trying to shatter that glass ceiling while I continue to shop and complain. I'll cut off all affection with you and pretend it isn't sucking the life from our marriage." He raised his hands for her to see. "I'll let you rough up your hands doing a freaking list of household fixer-uppers that I demand you do during your free time. I'm a good husband, Bevolyn. You're sucking me dry. And not in the good way, either. Not in the *biblical* sense."

Bevolyn ignored that nasty talk, that sucking nonsense. "I was going to be a lawyer," she said. "You wanted me home taking care of the house, raising kids, so don't go throwing that shit up in my face."

Russell smirked. "Shit? Who's the heathen, now?"

"The devil in you brought out the devil in me. I'm not immune."

Russell nodded. "Sure…and for the record, home was the best place for you. School didn't suit you well at all. I can't believe you'd have the gall to even bring that time up."

She couldn't believe she had, either, considering what had happened in those early years.

"And as of yet your womb hasn't spilled forth an ounce of fruit," Russell added. "Won't, either." She'd be forty herself in a couple of years.

Bevolyn crossed her arms. "Afeni is—"

"Not your child," Russell cut her off. "A *foster* child"— he added with a sneer—"you took on, against my wishes."

"No," Bevolyn said, "you're right. She isn't my child."

They sat silent for a bit. So much bad history between them.

"You've got it good," Russell said, breaking the silence.

"Having a serial adulterer as a husband, you call that good?"

He sighed. "Don't go pinning that rap on me, Bevolyn."

"Truth hurts."

"No truth in it."

"When's the last time we made love? You're getting it somewhere," she said.

"It's been a while," he admitted. "All your doing, though, because I'd love to get up in you more than I do."

She placed a hand on her chest. Russell smiled. Once again, he'd gotten a rise out of her. It was difficult living with a bona fide saint. Ruffling her angel wings every so often was Russell's only enjoyment. Seeing her flustered almost made up for the disappointment that was their marriage.

Bevolyn lay back on the bed and muttered something Russell couldn't decipher.

"Come again," he said.

"Forget it. Go ahead and finish your eighty-hour workweek. I'm not letting you steal my joy today, Russell. I'm used to going to church without you."

Russell wasn't about to let her off the hook so easily. He moved closer to her. She smelled of Dove soap and Herbal Essence shampoo…the only woman he had ever known who didn't lose her scent over the course of a day, or night. But he wouldn't let that distract him.

"What did you say before?" he prodded. "You said something under your breath about my comment, 'wanting to get up in you more often.' "

"Once wasn't enough, huh, Russell? Had to go and use those sinful words again."

He inched forward another step, right up on her now, and grit his teeth. "What did you say, Bevolyn? I'm not going to ask you again."

She peered up at his shadow. She could see his hands balled in fists. It was best she answer him. She didn't want to add physical abuse to the litany of problems they endured. "I said maybe if you brought me the joy the Lord brings me, instead of your couple minutes of hump and slump, I'd make love to you more often. Now back off. And rein in that temper of yours."

Something ticked inside Russell. Their tepid sex life was a major issue of discontent and Bevolyn knew it. Bringing it up in this way wasn't productive; it was down right instigative. Picking a fight—that's what she was doing—picking a fight. Russell, fed up, was game for one himself.

"Hump and slump, is that right?" he asked. He nodded, undoing the belt buckle of his pants. Enough was enough. He'd show her hump and slump.

"What are you doing, Russell?" Bevolyn's voice cracked.

He unzipped his pants, wiggled out of them, and left them in a crumple on the floor in the center of their bedroom.

"Russell," Bevolyn said again. "Don't do anything you'll regret."

Russell pulled off his shirt and then his boxers, and slid out of his loafers. His penis fell flaccid against his thigh. He moved toward Bevolyn, massaging his penis to life as he walked. As he reached her, his penis was harder than the gray patio blocks Bevolyn had made him lay in their backyard the month before.

"You're so into your religion," Russell said. "I'm gonna make you scream God's name today if it kills me."

Bevolyn reached for the Bible on their bed stand. It was thick enough to knock some sense into her fool husband's head, she hoped.

Russell snatched the Bible from her grip and tossed it aside. Bevolyn tried to slide off the opposite side of the bed. Russell pulled her back and took his place on top of her. "Hump and slump, huh?"

"This is the Lord's Day, Russell; please don't do this. I'm sorry. I was trying to get a rise out of you. I admit it."

He gripped her by her wrists with one hand, spit in his other hand, and rubbed the saliva over his stiff penis. Bevolyn's eyes bugged out as Russell plunged his hardness inside her dry folds. Shocked, she didn't resist. "Call His name, Bev," Russell said, grunting, that Dove soap and Herbal Essence mixing with his cologne, and hopefully soon, their salty sweat.

Bevolyn bit her lip.

"Call on Him, Bev."

Moments in, she could feel her body responding, wetness taking hold of her middle. She found her hands wrapped around her husband's waist, pulling him hard toward her. It felt good. She wished it didn't. But it did. She was a woman with needs, she realized at that moment, needs she'd kept herself from having. Needs she hadn't met for him, either. No wonder he did what he did—lying in women's beds that God hadn't sanctioned. *If* he did it. Bevolyn had to admit she was a bit paranoid, that she had no solid evidence that Russell cheated on her. Experience, though, had taught her that people, no matter how sound, struggled with fidelity. That experience saddened her.

"Oh yeah, baby, take this in, baby. Bring me deep up in you," Russell said.

She wished he would shut up. His words made her feel dirty, made her view this not as lovemaking, but as a violation. She didn't want that to be her view. She wanted her needs met, lovingly. Wanted to meet his, lovingly.

"Take that, take that," Russell grunted. "Call His name, Bev. Let Him know you're thankful."

That, she wouldn't do. She wouldn't bring God's name into this mess.

"You still think all I'm good for is hump and slump?" Russell asked through gritted teeth as his flesh pounded hers.

"No," she answered, moaning now. "No, Russell." She could feel her legs going tingly, her breasts mashed against his chest, the hairs on his chest rubbing her nipples raw. He had his hands gripping her ass, pulling her to him as he pushed himself toward her, a tango. She really liked that.

"Yeah, baby. You woke something up in me, baby. I love it inside of you. Love it," Russell groaned.

Shut up, she wanted to say, but all that escaped her mouth were more moans. She gripped his buttocks as he did hers, and pulled him harder toward her. A breath caught in her chest as he went in, came out, went in again. Nice little rhythm he had going. Making her feel like a woman was supposed to feel. She clasped her feet around him, locked them together by the ankles. An unbreakable bond.

"Let it out, baby," he said. "I love you, Bev. Let it out. Please, Bev, baby, let it out. I need you to let it out. Tell me I'm the only one you love, ever will."

She did let it out—not the words he needed as affirmation, but a long and throaty moan that sounded as if he'd tortured it out of her.

Her orgasm inspired Russell. He bucked like a horse within seconds of her release, pulled his penis out, and squirted his hot white juice over her chest. His desire for children, an early obsession in their marriage, was no longer a burning flame. And he couldn't trust that she faithfully took her birth control pills. Some women, he knew, said as much but didn't take their pills—tricked men. And men, gullible as can be, fell for it. Not that Bevolyn would do that. Russell knew she didn't want children.

Russell fell back on his side of the bed, breathing heavily. "That's religion," he said after some time. "That's something I can believe in. You made a believer out of me, Bev. Praise you."

She didn't reply, but got up and stalked to the bathroom with his hot white liquid running a trail toward her belly button.

Inside the bathroom, she scrubbed her V with soap and rinsed with warm water. Outside in the bedroom, he wiped off his penis with the napkin he'd written her the note on and quickly dressed. He smiled at the bathroom door instead of walking inside and letting her know he'd enjoyed the warmth of her body, how much he'd missed her in his arms. That was one of their biggest problems, a lack of communication.

Bevolyn splashed water over her face, took a deep breath, and came back into the bedroom. Russell ran his fingers over the corners of his lips, wiping away the drool that had escaped when his mouth hung open as he nutted on his wife's chest.

"You're still leaving?" Bevolyn asked Russell.

"Nature of the beast," he said. "I have to work twice as much as the white boys; you know that."

Bevolyn plopped down on the bed. "You know Afeni could have walked in. What if she'd have heard you doing…what you did?"

"Making love to my wife?" Russell smirked. "Maybe she would have thought we were normal."

"You call what we just did normal?"

Russell waved her away. "Go tithe my money, Bev. Get us both a blessing. Maybe things will change one day."

"Still thinking about Afeni," she said. "She could have come home."

"I didn't ask for her to be here," Russell reminded Bevolyn. "And if my wife wants to give me some ass, for a change, I'm not worrying about who walks in. The Pope could come in with Jesus and the Disciples and I'd still try to get my nut."

Bevolyn nodded. "I think you should go."

"Baby, look—"

"Just go, Russell."

He eyed his wife for a moment, then nodded to himself, gathered his jacket, and left, thinking, as he descended each step, that he should go back and talk things through. He was sick of the gap that separated Bevolyn and himself, that whole Mars and Venus disconnect that he had scoffed at originally, but had come to realize was real.

But he never turned around. Instead, he reached the bottom of the stairwell, grabbed his briefcase, and stepped out, pausing briefly to look back once before closing the front door behind him. He found the UNLOCK

button on his keychain and moved toward the SUV
parked in the driveway. The power locks clicked open as
he hit the button. He looked up at his bedroom and saw
the curtains flutter, then sighed and got inside the SUV
he put in such long hours to be able to afford. The SUV,
the house, their investment portfolio. Long hours. And
Bevolyn didn't appreciate him. No one did. He'd probably never see his name in the newspapers. Damn!

He backed from the driveway, pulled the transmission
tree to DRIVE, and moved up the road. Something moved
inside his stomach as he saw Afeni walking slowly up the
street, Demon on a leash, Afeni's thoughts seemingly elsewhere. Afeni had on Capri pants and a small T-shirt that
showed off her midriff. Russell swallowed hard as he realized that men would soon be beating down the door to
get at Afeni. He knew the inevitable heartache and drama
that would follow. He didn't want it to happen, but knew
it would, and soon.

He pulled to the curb. Afeni, so deep in her thoughts,
almost passed by. Russell tooted his horn. She looked up,
smiled, and moved toward the SUV. Russell powered the
passenger side window down.

"Working?" Afeni asked as she leaned in.

"All I do," Russell said. He had to admit he cared for
the girl, but had a difficult time talking to her.

"Bet she isn't happy about that," Afeni said, nodding
her head in the direction of their house just up the block.

"She'll live," Russell said of his wife.

"Okay," Afeni said, using the word as a bridge to end
this strained dialogue. "I better get Demon home."

"All right," Russell said.

Afeni smiled and moved from the window.

"Hey, Afeni," Russell called to her.

She turned back and leaned in again. "Wassup?"

He felt his throat tighten. Thoughts were swimming in his head. "Stay outta trouble," were the words that came out.

Afeni nodded. "You too." She turned and walked on, Russell looking in his rearview mirror as she moved up the block.

When Afeni was no longer in sight, Russell pulled away from the curb. But his thoughts were home, on Bevolyn, on Afeni. Family.

The steaming cup of coffee went down smooth. Russell swallowed the last drops of the java, crumpled the Styrofoam cup into a ball, and tossed it toward the small wastebasket in the corner of his office. Plastic, black, the standard type of wastebasket found in offices everywhere. About a ten-foot distance from where Russell sat in his ergonomic leather chair. Unfortunately, his makeshift ball hit the lip of the can and skittered to the floor—shot missed.

"Hmm, boss. That was ugly."

Russell looked up. Rachel Sosa, his administrative assistant, stood in his doorway shaking her head, a smile of disappointment on her smooth Mary Jane candy-colored face. Her shocking blond hair was shorn close, in a spiky fashion, a style that wouldn't work for most women of color, but to Russell's frustration, fit Rachel like the proverbial glove. Her striped blue slacks did nothing to hide the strength of her thighs and the flare of her hips. Her white button-down blouse had a similar problem with her toned arms and two handfuls of breasts. The blouse was unbuttoned one button too much as far as Russell was concerned, that one button allowing an eyeful of the white lacy bra that tried with its best effort to hold in her full breasts.

"Bad angle," Russell defended. He swallowed and focused hard on keeping his eyes level, homed in on Rachel's face. Only her face. "I normally sink that, no problem."

"I figured as much," Rachel replied, letting him off the hook for his poor shot. "Your form was good. Not like Shaquille O'Neal shooting free throws."

Russell raised an eyebrow. "You know basketball?"

"Played."

"Really?"

"I was a tight end," Rachel acknowledged. "One of the best, I might add."

Russell smiled and leaned back in his chair, comfortable. "Don't know how to tell you, Ray, but that's football. Tight end."

Rachel shook her head. "I have to tell you, boss. That was basketball, too, when *I* put on *my* shorts. Trust me."

Instinctively, Russell's gaze dropped down to Rachel's waist and that firm round ass he couldn't see from this angle but knew existed. He caught himself quickly and looked up with embarrassment. The knowing smirk on Rachel's face shamed him.

"I can't thank you enough for coming in on a Sunday," he said, moving on.

"No need," Rachel said. "I *am* being paid. Overtime. Besides, I like working with you without everyone here. We seem to get more done."

Russell nodded. "That we do."

Rachel stepped into the office, letting the door glide shut softly behind her. Russell wiggled his shoulders and placed his hands on the desk. Rachel found the seat in front of Russell's desk, sat, and placed one leg up on the other. Flexible woman, Russell found himself thinking.

"So," Rachel said. "You want me to take it off?"

Russell's jaw muscles tensed. "Excuse me?"

"The contractor's expenses for the Baldwin project. They showed up on the wrong spreadsheet. Remember?"

Russell shook his head and snickered to himself. "I'm sorry, Ray. Yeah, take them off."

"Something else you wanted me to take off, boss?" Her eyebrow was arched, a smirk on her face.

"What?"

"We have to always play this tennis. I hit it to you. You hit it back to me. Now you know you heard me," Rachel chastised. "I ain't stutter."

"I did but—"

"You're a happily married man," she cut him off. Using the words she knew he would use.

"That's correct," Russell said.

"You haven't seemed happy, boss. Trust me. Your secretary, excuse me, administrative assistant, knows you probably as well as any other person in your life, wife included. You're not happy. Not coming in here on most Sundays and working these insane hours. Why are you working today instead of snuggling on the couch with the Missus?"

The Missus doesn't want to snuggle, Russell wanted to say, but didn't. He heard Bevolyn's voice in his head just then. "Hump and slump. Hump and slump."

Russell sighed. "You're a beautiful woman, Ray, Rachel."

"This I know."

"But, I couldn't do it. Can't do it. You understand that?"

"I do."

"You accept it?"

"For now, boss. For now." She stood. "I better go take them off...the contractor's expenses. You know what I mean? I'm sure you have a lot to think about." Her eyes flashed then, a sparkling light to them—the light a woman gets in her eyes when she knows she makes a certain man weak, knows that man wants her so badly he can't stand himself.

Russell didn't say anything. Rachel smiled devilishly, pivoted, and strutted from the room. Russell, despite himself, watched her go. When the door closed her out, he plucked the picture of Bevolyn he kept on his desk and pressed it against his chest. He sat back in his chair, closed his eyes, and whispered something. Some would call it a prayer. Russell wouldn't. He just hoped what he whispered became a reality.

3

"Something wrong?" she said to me from the motel bed in that soft voice that just hours before, had me feeding her dollars as if she were a snack machine. She hadn't spit out a bag of Cool Ranch Doritos or salty peanuts, either, as I pumped her with ones. I knew right away she was feeling me, the way she looked down on me from that stage, her eyes narrowed. How she pulled her breasts to her own lips every time she came within a few feet of me. How her long tongue snaked out of her mouth, flicked at her nipples, and danced across them when the light of recognition shone in my eyes.

The Devil is a liar.

But I wasn't.

I wasn't lying to myself. I was feeling her, too. Despite the strength I'd found in He's Sweet I Know, I was a man, with a man's desires. At that moment, my faith in From Whom All Blessings Flow wasn't squelching those desires.

I wanted, check that, *needed* this female.

She wasn't my Milkshake, didn't have that history Myshelle and I shared, but damn, she had a couple of other things—namely those jugs she kept pressed against her lips—that would make this work.

"What time does your shift end?" I'd asked her.

"Fuck you think this is? Wal-Mart?" she asked, without a hint of humor in her voice or expression. "This is the G-Spot. *A strip club.*"

I smiled at her. She got lost in my handsome face, I could see. Found her way again at my muscular shoulders, I noticed. Got lost again.

"My shift ends at two," she told me, relenting from her earlier position, her voice coated with lust. I knew the tone well.

"Can we chill together?" I asked. "When your *shift* ends?"

She nodded.

I'd found my way to Dirty Jersey, what the hip-hop kids called The State. Should have found my way to a church home…hadn't even looked yet. But I'd come upon another edifice where you could put money in the collection plate—the plate here known affectionately as a G-string.

If not church, I should have found my way to the address on the letters I had received from my father, but I hadn't done that either, and I wasn't sure if I ever would.

"Hey," my private dancer called out to me then. "Wassup, you handling this or what?"

I sat on the edge of the motel bed, trying to place aside those thoughts from earlier, my back to her. She lay naked behind me. I shut my eyes tight, to think.

"Coming to the stage," the DJ at the G-spot had said earlier, "Aloe."

Aloe.

Damn.

I knew I was in trouble before she climbed that pole, before I saw her calf muscles accentuated by those clear heels, before I saw her playing peek-a-boo with her breasts. The name alone intrigued me, especially when all the other girls had the usual black stripper names: Cocoa, Cinnamon, Honey, Coffee.

"Yo. You hear me talking to you?"

"Thinking maybe I shouldn't do this," I told her. I could smell her vanilla musk. As I turned and eyed that mound of nappy black pubic hair between her thighs, I tensed my jaw muscles and searched my memory bank for a verse of Scripture. Something I'd read in my Bible about the travails of lust—how to circumvent it. I think it might have been in I Peter. Maybe. I couldn't concentrate with her so near, so naked.

Aloe touched my shoulder, spider-walked her soft fingers across my back to the nape of my neck, and drew a circle between my shoulder blades. I'd done the same thing in Debra Cummings's palm when I was younger. That drawn circle in Debra's palm let her know I wanted to stick my thing in her. A circle was a territory marker, letting a pretty young thing know my hormones were raging out of control and she was my only hope in settling them.

"Don't," I told Aloe. I moved my back from her touch, from her drawn circle.

"What's the problem?" she asked. "You was talking all this crap in the ride over. 'Bout how you were gonna do me. So do me. Now."

"This isn't a good look for me. Overstand?"

"What?" she asked. I could feel the mattress sink, her body shift. "You're not feeling me all of a sudden?" There was concern in her tone.

I turned and reclined in the bed, my gaze on the ceiling. I couldn't find any answers in that popcorn paint surface, either.

"LeMar?" Aloe asked.

It felt strange hearing that name come off her tongue. I'd changed the *V* to an *M* when she'd asked my name earlier, to protect myself, but still, it brought thoughts I couldn't quite handle.

My childhood.

Toy trains, G.I. Joe action figures, Transformers. Then, that silver-dollar-size hole that bled despite my fingers pressed against it. I couldn't make it stop bleeding. I tried. But couldn't. My brother dying in my arms.

"It's my stomach, isn't it?" Aloe said, breaking my thoughts. "Doesn't look as flat here up close as it did when I was on stage, under them damn lights. You think I got a pouch, don't you? It disgusts you, doesn't it? You wishing I was still on that stage, with those damn lights, so I could still feel like a fantasy?"

I had to smile. Even strippers had body image issues.

"Oh, dang. You laughing at me," she said. "This is effed up."

"Has nothing to do with your stomach, Aloe."

"What…my boobs?" She quickly covered them with her hands. Her shoulders slumped. She had no idea how much I wanted to lick her chocolate, taste her vanilla. No idea.

"Nothing to do with them, either," I said.

"I have you know I look younger than I am. I'm over thirty. I'm doing well, I think."

I nodded.

"So you just ain't feeling me?"

"Of course I'm feeling you," I told her. "What man wouldn't? You've got those…" I'd started to run down her list of physical attributes. But then I thought better. Why challenge temptation when I knew temptation would have the last laugh? Why dig my grave deeper, put myself in a position where I would be seeing fire on Judgment Day unless I brought along Johnnie Cochran to plead my case at the Golden Gates?

If he didn't touch her tits, you must acquit.

"I've got those what?" Aloe pressed me.

Breasts like two large scoops of Jamoca coffee ice

cream, I wanted to say. Tight round butt that, with one touch, would make a blind man insane with frustration at not seeing. Two tattoos: a rose and a black panther. Smell like vanilla, but so, so, so, chocolate. Hmm.

"I've accepted His word," I told Aloe, looking heavenward. "I need to obey."

"You want to obey?"

"Yes. I do, Aloe."

She licked her lips and spread her legs. "Get on me, LeMar. Obey that. Don't say anything, or think anything, just get on me."

I hesitated. But then my gaze dropped to the moist spot between her legs. I sighed, jumped from the bed, and moved to the other side of the small room, keeping my stiff, hard erection at a safe distance.

"You just gonna walk away from this?" Aloe asked me, pointing with a slender finger to the spot between her thighs. "How you gonna do that?"

"My Bible tells me—"

Aloe raised a hand and halted me before I spread the word while wanting to spread her. "Stop right there. I get it," she said. "You're like the woman looking after my daughter—one of them Jesus freaks."

I shifted. "I wouldn't say I'm a freak. I try my best to love the Lord who loves me."

Aloe smirked. "I'm sure He's walking on water He's so happy you put all them dollars in my G-string, then talked me into coming here with you, and now you trying to fight the feeling."

I ignored her and went for the emotional instead of the physical. "You said you have a daughter?"

Aloe looked away.

"I bet she's beautiful just like you," I said. "Tell me about her." I was trying to walk myself down from the ledge.

"Nothing to tell," she said. She fell back against the motel's thin-as-paper pillow. I could see her lying stiff in the bed. I could smell her vanilla—her sex, moist, warm.

"Come on," I insisted. "My mother was always saying how much she wished she had girls to go with me and my bro…" I let that drift. I'd spent too much time lately thinking about my brother. I had to stop. That was a route to madness. I started again with, "My mother always wanted girls. She said there was something special about mothers and daughters."

"She was wrong," Aloe shot back.

"No, she wasn't. Tell me about your daughter."

Aloe wriggled in the bed, wrestling something deep within. I knew the feeling. She settled finally and pounded the mattress with a fist.

"Afeni," she said softly, her eyes still avoiding me. "My daughter, gonna be a poet one day. Fourteen and taller than me already. Chest bigger than mine, too. But she's gonna use her head to get ahead."

"You sound pretty poetic yourself. Maybe she got it from you."

Aloe smiled in appreciation but eventually shook her head.

"Who's the woman looking after her?" I asked. "You mentioned a woman. Called her a Jesus freak."

Aloe's smile faded and she turned her back to me. Our good vibe was lost again. She pulled the floral print cover up to her neck. I moved from my corner of the small room back to the bed and sat on the edge. My eyes quickly caught the green cover of the Gideons' Bible on the dresser. A latex condom sat atop of it. I cringed, looked away to Aloe, and pulled her by her shoulder to face me. She didn't resist. Her eyes were misting.

"Aloe?"

"My name is Diane," she barked. "I hate that name. I ain't nobody's damn Aloe."

Pheromones, the scent of sex, drained from the room. Lion's breath—the odor I imagined emanating from the predator's mouth—heated our little spot. Hot, musty, angry…yep, the breath of a lion.

"Diane," I said, speaking tender, trying to get back the vibe we'd had. "What's the story with you and your daughter?"

That brought back the pheromones. She moved back to her best defense mechanism. Sex.

She said, "You could be busting a nut. We got to be out by eight A.M. Clock is ticking." She tapped her wrist as if it held a watch. The way she looked and danced, it definitely would be something high class, expensive. A Movado.

"I'd rather have this conversation," I responded. That had to have been my help from the heavens talking because truthfully, as Aloe had put it herself, I could be busting a nut. I *wanted* to be busting a nut.

Aloe-slash-Diane threw up her hands. "My daughter's with a family named Sykes. Bevolyn Sykes, Afeni's"—she cleared something from her throat—"foster mother is like you. Spouting stuff about the Lord this, Jesus that, God this."

"How long has Afeni been with them?"

Aloe-slash-Diane rolled to the side, her back to me. Pheromones gone again. "Late last year, just before Christmas."

"What happened?"

"Had a little problem with my veins."

"Varicose? Phlebitis?" I asked. I'd read up on so many things during my time in the belly. Had all kinds of useless knowledge swimming in my head. I looked at her but didn't see any bulging blue veins anywhere on her. I couldn't imagine a deficiency anywhere on Aloe-slash-Diane's body. Her body was the ambrosia Zeus, Apollo, and all the other mythological homeboys craved.

"Heroin," she said sadly. Said it in two distinct syllables, the *o* in the second sounding more like a *u*. Her. Ruin. And it appeared it had been just that: her…ruin.

"Heroin? People still messing with that? I thought crack was the rage."

"Diesel?" she said. Diesel, the new name for heroin on the streets. "Hell, yeah, people still messing with it. Heroin ain't never left. Ain't never gonna leave." Aloe slowed her roll once she realized she was coming off like a Public Service Announcement for the drug.

"So how did you get involved with it?" I asked.

Aloe-slash-Diane rolled back to face me. "Stop asking me so many questions. Questions make me sad. You wanna get your jimmy wet or what?"

"You shouldn't hold sadness in. You should let it out. I've got a feeling you've never talked to anyone about this."

"I fell off the stage," she said, huffing. "Broke my ankle. Got on OxyContin. A legal Diesel if there ever was one. Even costs more. When I hit the streets again, my Oxy-Contin prescript nulled out on me. I gatewayed to Diesel. End of story. Now, you want to get your jimmy wet or what?"

"I better not."

Aloe-slash-Diane shook her head. "Your type kills me."

"What type is that?"

She leaned on an elbow, propping herself up so she could look me eye to eye as she disassembled my spirit. "Afeni goes to church with…with…"

"The Sykeses."

She shook her head. "Not the husband. Just the wife." She swallowed, frowned.

"Okay?"

"The church they go to, they done ran through two associate pastors since Afeni been going. The first pastor got some female up in the choir pregnant—married woman he had no right touching. They ran off together. That ho left behind her toddler and a husband. Husband drove his car to the park and ran it in the river right after his wife up and left him. He's taking a dirt nap now."

I shifted, uncomfortable. I didn't like to hear stories of people tearing down the temple of He's Sweet I Know that was loaned to them for a short lifetime. Not after the Ruffin girl—her suicide—sparked, the Ruffin boys believed, by what I'd done to her. Can't say they were wrong about that.

"The second pastor," Aloe-slash-Diane continued, "was also a teacher at the high school. Got caught trying to give a banana to some of his female students. And I ain't talking about fruit, if you know what I mean."

"What's that have to do with me?" I managed, still thinking about that scorned husband who took his Volvo or whatever for a swim in the river, knowing that bad boy didn't have a bit of Janet Evans or Greg Louganis in it.

Aloe-slash-Diane looked at me hard and smiled. I braced myself for the poison tip of the dart she was about to throw. "All you so-called Jesus lovers got sex issues, I swear. I could see you running off with that man's wife."

And him killing himself because of what I'd done. I looked down to see if the pain in my arm were the tip of that dart from Aloe's mouth. Instead, I saw that I'd reflexively dug my fingernails into my skin. I let my self-inflicted clamp loose.

"Jesus can wash their sins, and mine, white as snow," I said halfheartedly. I believed it, wanted to believe it, needed to believe it.

"Sure, whatever," Aloe-slash-Diane said with a hand wave.

"Has the church found any suitable replacements?"

"Nah."

My mind started churning over an idea. A ridiculous idea, but it wouldn't let go—it hung in the air like the pheromones and lion's breath from before.

"They better, though," she added. "Afeni told me the pastor is really looking hard for someone. He needs some help. Reverends do a lot of shit besides talk shit to the flock."

"What's his name?" I asked, quickly forgiving her for the two sugar-honey-iced-teas she'd sprayed on me in gunfire succession.

"Reverend G.H. Walker. Fellowship Baptist Church," she proudly stated. You'd have thought she was a member and that she walked around on clear heels every Sunday morning and dropped crumpled G-dubs—one-dollar bills to the unhip—in the offering.

"I hope they find someone," I said. That idea of mine still was perfuming the air.

Aloe-slash-Diane took a long, hard breath and tapped that imaginary Movado on her wrist again. "You gonna screw me or what? I had enough of this lollygagging. If I wanted to talk, I could go back to the G and yak with some potbellied lawyer that's too ashamed to ask his wife to suck him off."

I offered up a quick prayer of forgiveness for what I was about to do.

And I got on Aloe finally, no longer able to fight the feeling.

It was an acrobatic thirty-minute affair.

When we finished, I fell on my back, panting.

Aloe stood and started to quickly dress, the imaginary Movado on her wrist ticking down.

"You're a good dude," she told me as she pulled her sweatshirt on. Sex converts a non-believer better than some guy wearing a hot suit and standing on a corner selling bean pies.

"Am I?"

Aloe-slash-Diane stopped and smiled. "If I wasn't so caught up in this life, I think we'd be good for each other."

"I think I'd like to be a preacher if I ever got myself together," I told her. My idea had come back. Sex could make lips loose, too. Somebody needed to bottle sex and sell it at Wal-Mart.

Surprisingly, Aloe-slash-Diane didn't laugh at me, didn't smirk or "yeah-right" me to my fiery torment. She nodded. "I could see that."

"You could?" I sat up, my shoulders strong.

"Get yourself a line. Can I get a witness? Something like that and you'd be all in."

"It's not that simple," I said.

"Sure it is. Half the preachers ain't real, anyway."

Cynical, this Aloe. But truthful. Half of the preachers weren't real.

Can I get a witness? I hoped so, as my idea grew in my mind.

4

Instead of God, Sela Wheeler had her mind on a fat Dutch Master cigar, its tobacco innards discarded and replaced with what looked like crushed oregano leaves but wasn't. Those crushed leaves would soothe her in the same manner God soothed her sister, Bevolyn. And she wasn't about to get William Jefferson Clinton with her Dutch, either. Nuh uh. She'd light that sucker, inhale deeply, and let those crushed leaves go to work.

Smoke.

Sela's mind drifted to the warmth that would come to her chest, the pinkish red that would paint her eyes, and the bags of potato chips she'd devour with ferocity, her fingers coated afterward with crumbs and oil. She looked over at her friend Zelda, wanting this meeting over so they could get their "smoke out" on and popping. Zelda had her eyes clamped shut and her head bowed like all the other women. Sela couldn't help but smirk. Her girl Zelda was good at fitting in. She had even gone out and gotten a new dress, a lavender-colored spaghetti strap getup that didn't show a quarter of an inch of cleavage. She looked nice in it, though. Sela wasn't taking this that seriously. Wasn't buying a dress just because she had been baptized a few months ago, and was now fellowshipping with her sister and the other church ladies. Nuh uh. Matter of fact, she had missed quite a few Sundays since her baptism.

"Lord, we thank You this evening for the boundless wisdom and strength You've allowed to fall fresh on us," Bevolyn prayed. "We also thank You for the peace that umbrellas our lives, the peace You've brought to our individual doorsteps. We're forever thankful for all the blessings You have bestowed upon us. Thankful for our health, our families, for waking us up another day. I personally thank You for my sister's presence, and that of her friend—two more to add to Your number. And finally, Lord, we ask that You continue to bless the Women's Fellowship, and the good work we faithfully try to administer on Your behalf. Amen."

"Amen," a chorus of female voices echoed. Eyes opened and heads rose. Sela noticed that Zelda was looking at Bevolyn with something akin to wonderment. *Dang, girl,* she thought, *you are playing the role fierce.*

The women sat around in a circle in Bevolyn's living room on furniture the color of red wine. The color of the blood of Jesus, if you asked Bevolyn. The carpet was beige, as were the lampshades that canopied black bases carved of various Afrocentric designs. Several prominent paintings by black artists clutched the walls. Bevolyn knew how to coordinate; Sela had to give her sister that.

"Oh, I jumped the gun," Bevolyn said. "I forgot to let you all know how successful the baked chicken and beef dinner sale was." Bevolyn nodded to Truce Johnson, the treasurer.

Truce's gray-streaked brown hair was cropped close to her tire-round head. Her nails were painted in a striking shade of red. Her brown skin didn't have as much life as usual, for she was battling several ailments: diabetes, hy-

pertension. She made sure she had a black general prac-
titioner so she wouldn't constantly have to explain why
her body weight couldn't be found on the expected
weight-by-height charts that befitted only skinny white folk
with small bones. Despite her problems, she was always a
happy, exquisitely dressed woman with arguably the hand-
somest husband at Fellowship Baptist Church. God was
truly good to that sister, truly good.

Truce consulted her notepad ledger. "Bevolyn, Women
in Christ," she began. "After factoring in the expense for
preparing the dinners, I'm pleased to say we made a profit
for our King of four hundred thirteen dollars. Our goal
for the event had been three hundred and fifty dollars,
so we can surely see how good God is. Also, I might note,
we are now ahead of the financial goals schedule we put
together at the beginning of this year. Praise Him!"

"Hallelujah," Bevolyn exclaimed. "Our focus, our direction, is much improved from years past. I am proud of
all of you and the effort you put forth. It is indeed an
honor to be your president." She looked to her left. "Sela,
did you have anything you wanted to say? Any questions?"

"No," Sela said, shaking her head. She felt out of place
amongst these women, craving that smoke while they
thought of Scriptures and were a minute from breaking
into some gospel song. They wanted to lick the devil. Sela,
she wanted to roll a blunt, *lick it* tightly shut, then smoke
that sucker to an inch of its life.

"Sometimes the joy of finding Him is so overwhelming
no words come to mind," Bevolyn said in answer to Sela's
lack of a meaningful response.

"You can say that again," one of the sisters echoed.

Sela snickered to herself. Bevolyn could always find the
positive spin to put on any situation. That was her gift and
curse. She was a walking poster for all the dumb shit folk

got on shows like *Oprah* and said, life-altering mottos they draped around themselves: "If life hands you lemons… make lemonade."

"What about you," Bevolyn said to Zelda. "Did you have anything you wanted to say? Ask? My sister told me you grew up in the church but drifted."

Said she'd been to church before, Sela found herself thinking. See, Bevolyn's spin again. And good luck getting a word from Zelda. Nuh uh. Zelda wasn't about to say anything in front of all these strangers. She was too quiet, which was why Sela liked her as a friend; they balanced each other.

"I'm just looking to grow in faith," Zelda replied. "I can't say I have that foundation. But I hope to get it and learn how to worship Him correctly."

What in the heck was that about? Sela cocked her head to the side and examined Zelda from crown to heel. She *looked* like Zelda. But it couldn't be.

Bevolyn smiled. Why didn't her sister have the sense Zelda had? How did those two ever become friends anyway? They didn't seem to have anything in common. "Developing a personal with Him," Bevolyn told Zelda, "is the most wonderful experience you'll ever have."

"I know it," Zelda said, nodding.

Sela furrowed her brow. What was up with Zelda? Grow in faith, worship. A Dutch Master cigar, split, filled with what looked like crushed oregano but wasn't, and licked shut: that's something Sela could worship.

Bevolyn clasped her hands together. "Oh, sisters, I almost forgot. I have the cutest thing I have to show you. You'll get a kick out of this." She stood and headed toward the kitchen.

Sela leaned toward Zelda and whispered, "Sorry for this. But you're doing well. We'll laugh about it later while we smoke."

"It's good," Zelda whispered back. "I've enjoyed it. And I think I'll pass on the smoke."

"What?"

"Your sister is grounded. That's important. I need that."

Sela plopped back in her seat. Bevolyn this, Bevolyn that, the story of her life. Now Zelda was falling under Bevolyn's spell. Sela was Bevolyn's younger sister by nine years, a wild child who listened to hip-hop and R & B music like it was going out of style. The Roots for their down-to-earth spirit, Jay-Z for his cleverness, Nas for his poeticism, and Nelly because she liked to shake her ass. Her R & B tastes were a bit more eclectic. She'd croak before listening to a full Ashanti song. Mariah Carey gave her migraines. No, throw on some Jill Scott or Heather Headley. "He Is" was one of Sela's favorite songs ever, though Sela figured she'd never find a "he" as spectacular as the one Heather sang about. She had forever been unlucky in love. Elijah Turner, her last boyfriend, came to mind. She really needed a smoke. Now.

Bevolyn reappeared in the room. Sela shot her a gaze of fire that could burn down a brick house.

"Isn't it cute?" Bevolyn said. She held up a tiny sweater with an image of a black Jesus embroidered along the front.

"I know you're not trying to squeeze your stuff in that," Sela said.

"It's for Demon, Russell's dog, Sela."

"You're gonna put a sweater with Jesus on it, on a dog named Demon." Sela chuckled. "You probably do have a better chance of converting Demon, getting him to go to church, than you do Russell, though."

Bevolyn scowled at her sister but said nothing.

"And where is your superman lover?" Sela asked, consulting her watch. "It's awful late. Most offices have been shut down."

Bevolyn opened her mouth to respond. Nothing came out. Where was her husband?

"Who'd you go to dinner with?"

Russell looked up from his magazine. He was reclining comfortably in bed. Bevolyn stood in the doorway, hands on hips, anger in her eyes, in her posture. She had a small sweater in her hand, Russell noticed. A black guy with a thick brush of Afro and a beard, wearing what looked as if it could be a white laundry bag with a cutout for his head as a shirt or something. A shining sun was at his back. Russell's mind flashed on Rachel earlier, standing in his doorway at work, and the obvious difference in demeanor between Rachel and his wife. The divide saddened him.

"Told you, coworker," Russell said. He dropped his eyes back to the magazine.

Bevolyn was over him, gently taking the magazine from his hands: an issue of *KING* with Gabrielle Union on the cover in a black bikini.

"I was reading that," Russell told Bevolyn.

Bevolyn looked at the cover of the magazine and pursed her lips. "Insist on pushing me, don't you?"

"Just reading it," Russell defended.

Bevolyn waved her hand. "Which coworker?"

"Rachel," Russell admitted.

Bevolyn sighed and sat on the edge of the bed, her back to Russell. Russell moved to her and put his hand on her shoulder. She allowed it.

"Nothing is going on, Bev. Nothing."

She didn't reply.

"Sixteen years, you think I'd throw that away by cheating?" He knew the words were unfortunate the moment they left his lips.

Bevolyn turned, as he expected, and glared at him.

"Mistakes happen," he said. "Remember?"

She turned away.

"I'm not cheating, Bev," he went on. "Trust me." He flinched somewhere deep inside of himself. *Trust me*, something Rachel would say.

Bevolyn's voice was soft. "Your magazines. Dates with coworkers."

"Dates? We had dinner. My way of thanking her for all her hard work. Strictly professional."

Bevolyn shook her head absently. "Pushing and pushing and pushing."

"Listen—"

But then a pop sounded and black bathed them: a power outage. They'd been having quite a few of late. Needed an electrician to check on things. Russell stood, and, hands in front of him, found his way across the bedroom to the dresser. He picked up the flashlight in the plastic organizing tray and flicked it on. Using the light to guide him into the hallway, he stopped at Afeni's room, knocked at the slightly parted door, and stepped in without getting an answer.

Afeni sat by her desk, staring in shock at her dark computer monitor.

"You okay, Afeni?" Russell asked her.

Afeni turned. Russell could see in the beam of the flashlight that her eyes were blank, wet. "Was just finishing this poem," she said in a robotic monotone. "Everything went black. I didn't get a chance to save it. It's lost. Forever."

"You can't write another?" he asked.

Afeni's gaze dropped. "Doesn't exactly work like that. But yeah, I guess I could."

Russell moved to Afeni, not knowing what to do. She immediately rested her head against his stomach, sobbing softly, but enough that he could feel his shirt warming, her shoulders moving against him. He held a hand up, thought about it, and then, awkwardly, patted her head. She continued to sob, louder now, but he got the feeling his embrace was comforting her. Jeez, what had Bevolyn gotten them into with this? Afeni had endured so much in her life, had so many disappointments, heartaches. What good would he and Bevolyn—two broken souls themselves—bring to Afeni?

Russell turned at the creak of the bedroom door and flashed the light from his flashlight in that direction: Bevolyn, eyeing him comforting Afeni. Bevolyn paused for a moment, something indecipherable in her eyes, before she turned and walked away from the door.

You wanted this, Russell found himself thinking. You wanted this. He knew he should go and catch Bevolyn, explain himself further, let her know more vehemently that he wasn't cheating. Loved her. Wanted her. But Afeni's sobs held him in place.

He'd fix things with Bevolyn later. He had no idea that later, as uncompromising as it could be, might be too late.

5

I found He's Sweet I Know on the inside. Typical, I know—probably a dozen of the other ex-cons who added that *ex* to the *con* the same day as I did would make the same claim. Doesn't matter. Everybody has religion: something they worship even though there are some deep mysteries surrounding it. For some it's sex. For others it's amber-colored drinks that take away their ability to walk a straight line with their arms raised. For the wise, it's the real thing. From Whom All Blessings Flow. That's my chamber, where I fall in the scheme of things. What I choose to believe even when I backslide. Even when I slide. Slide in women like Aloe-slash-Diane.

We had sex. Sweaty, gymnastic, creative sex. Afterward, as I shrugged myself into my pants and watched Aloe-slash-Diane do the same with her clothes, I came to the overstanding that there was no use dwelling on what I'd done. It was finished. And from that point on, I'd make steps, serious steps, to continue on the path I'd started in prison: the path of the faithful.

"You know where I am," Aloe-slash-Diane had told me as we stood outside the motel. "You ever get the itch again and need it scratched."

I'd nodded politely, smiled, and tucked our experience away as a card in my mental Rolodex. A card I might pull out from time to time, mentally speaking, but never again physically. Sexing Aloe-slash-Diane again would be the road to torment.

I'd made too much spiritual progress to allow that to happen.

Skip back a pace to my spiritual rebirth.

I learned about He's Sweet I Know from "Lucky" Luther, a standing-tall inmate doing hard time for so many different offenses I won't even bother naming them. He got the nickname "Lucky" because the judge didn't give him the death sentence for his crimes. I assume I don't have to say any more. But anyway, my man Luck was forever comparing religion to something, trying to make it more palatable to the non-believer.

It was my first few days inside JCI. I was next to Luck, walking double file down the gallery with another group of inmates from our block. We had our hands in our pockets as required. The CO was behind us, barking out orders. I didn't have to turn my head to see him. The COs at JCI were a clear vision that would come to me even in my sleep by that point. After just a few days inside, I had most of the routine down. Inmates dressed in prison-issued green, COs in gray. COs kept a radio holder on their belts, which also held a latex-glove packet, a two key-ring clip, and a baton on a ring. I hoped I never had to experience that baton sliding off the ring. Never.

"Church is like football," Luck told me as we shuffled down the hall. It just so happened to be Super Bowl Sunday.

"Yeah," I'd replied, eyeing him. He'd been one of the few inmates to talk to me during that time, extending his hand and friendship on my first day in. A big gamble on his part, for inmates were rightly suspicious and extremely guarded and tightlipped. He looked like a pumped-up Malcolm X with prison tats on each chiseled arm, a thick beard flecked with gray, reading glasses covering his eyes even when he wasn't reading, and a Negro nose wide as the Motherland that had spawned our people.

He licked two fingers and then wiped them on his green prison garb, a habit of his I never would overstand. Maybe the knowledge in his hands was so hot he had to lick those joints, cool 'em off, before passing that hot potato to the next man. Maybe.

Anyway, he licked his fingers, then quickly pocketed them again, and told me, "That's right, church and football are practically synonymous. Take for instance your blitz…that's the congregation rushing off to Denny's after the service ends."

I laughed.

He went on with, "Staying in the pocket…folk putting a dollar in the collection plate but keeping that crisp twenty in their wallet."

"Yo, you crazy," I told him.

He wasn't finished.

"Instant replay…pastor loses his notes and starts preaching the sermon he preached week past."

My smile threatened to break my face. I started coughing.

"Sudden death…what happens to the congregation's attention span if the preacher ain't wrapped his sermon up by ten to one."

The CO, big ugly dude, caught up with us. You could look at his black shadow void of his features and know, "That is one ugly motherfucker." I was still cursing at that point.

The CO said, "You two keep cackling I'ma have to go

outside and get my Colt AR-15." COs weren't allowed to carry amongst the general population. Only got their heat if something big broke out. I didn't envy them. It was a tough job.

"Shooting yourself ain't gonna make you any prettier," Luck told the CO without smiling.

That was Luck for you.

But Luck's wit wasn't the deciding factor in getting me to cross over and roll with From Whom All Blessings Flow. Nah, something more. Something much more.

I was doing kitchen duty one day. I worked as a porter, an inmate employee, on mop up detail. Last one up in the kitchen, I thought. I took my dirty water bucket around a bend, back where the paper items were stored. Paper plates, cups, napkins, things of that nature. I heard a low moan as I rounded the bend—somebody sucking for air, cursing in Spanish.

"*A Dios mío.*" Gasp for breath.

"*Maricón.*" Gurgling something in their throat.

"*Hijoputa.*" Followed by an F-word in English that I knew too well. "*Pendejo.*"

Silence.

I came up on Luck, standing over an inmate known affectionately as Lipstick. "She" was a Hispanic with a pock-marked face and deep red lips she painted with dry Kool-Aid powder—cherry flavor, of course. "She" kept her green shirt unbuttoned at the bottom so she could knot it and keep it up under her breasts. And yes, she had them. I didn't know if they were real or balled-up socks. They were round, all I'd allow myself to overstand. Her real name was Jose or Javier, maybe even Jesus. *Hay zoos.* Anyway, some name that started with a *J* that I no longer recalled. I'd remember our J-boy, Miss Lipstick, for something else altogether after that moment in the kitchen: the crimson patch growing where a pocket would have been if she/he/it had been wearing a Perry Ellis dress shirt.

Luck turned to me. Didn't even blink. Didn't try to hide the shank in his hand behind his back. Just looked at me.

I took a step backward, foolishly, in my haste, leaving the mop bucket in front of me, my eyes on that sharpened piece of Plexiglas in Luck's hand. Then my gaze drifted up. Luck had on two shirts. Double clothing. A no-no inside. COs were supposed to check for that. Inmates usually doubled up when they were expecting to stab someone or, in some cases, when they were trying to ward off a stabbing.

"Hole up," Luck said to me. I did. He nodded at the dead J-boy at his feet. "Man was meant to be with woman," he said, his mouth turned up in a snarl. He nodded again at Lipstick. "He tried to get in my ass. A no-no. Leviticus 18:22. *Thou shalt not lie with mankind as with womankind: it is abomination.* You overstand me, young breed?" Luck always called me young breed when he was deadly serious about something.

I did and nodded as such because my mouth wouldn't form words.

"Cross man, cross woman," Luck went on, "but don't cross the Good Book. That'll get you dead. Spiritually or in the physical. Sometimes both. You hear me, young breed?"

I heard him and nodded again, to let him know I was on his side.

Luck took his prison-made blade and wiped it across J-boy's forehead. Shank clean, a streak of Lipstick's O-positive or whatever blood type he was just above his, um her, unblinking eyes. "Lipstick," Luck muttered, shaking his head. "You *were* a man. Too bad you didn't realize it."

Boy, did I overstand.

Then Luck turned back to me, took off his prison-issued green shirt, and slid off his pants. He'd doubled them, too. He tossed the clothes in a nearby plastic garbage can, which was big enough to allow Luck to kill at least our entire block of inmates and trash the evidence. He rinsed his shank in one of the kitchen's three bay sinks. Kept the shank, I realized, and didn't trash it with the other evidence. That was significant to me. Meant he planned to use that shank again some day, had probably used it in the past. I wondered how many bodies were on the shank, and then quickly shut out those thoughts.

"The COs here don't care about what happens to some batty boy," Luck told me, letting me know this was a sanctioned retaliation. It wouldn't do me any good if I were thinking about telling someone what I'd seen. I wasn't.

"Let's go pray," he said, taking me firmly by the arm. "And grab your mop bucket. Don't want them pinning you to this."

I clumsily grabbed my mop bucket, set it in its designated area at the front of the kitchen, and followed Luck out into the hall. A CO nodded conspiratorially at Luck as we passed through the hall. The CO's eyes flashed on me.

Luck shook his head. "He's cool. He's one of God's sons."

The CO nodded in appreciation.

I started seriously studying Scriptures with Luck that very day. Been reading at least a chapter a day since.

Thoughts of J-boy on that cold kitchen tile and me later that night with my head in the Book of Genesis scrolled through my mind as I stood outside Reverend G.H. Walker's office door at Fellowship Baptist Church. I'd taken the seed Aloe-slash-Diane had planted in my mind and come here to see if it could possibly flower. I wanted to knock at Reverend Walker's door, but was paralyzed by the sounds coming from inside.

Swoop…swoop. Swoop…swoop.

Inhaling.

The sign out front said Fellowship was "Organized in The Year of Grace, Eighteen Hundred and Ninety-Six." I thought about Aloe-slash-Diane, the trouble she said the church had been having.

Swoop…swoop. Swoop…swoop.

Maybe the grace Fellowship had had in its founding year had run out now.

The swoops left my ears. I was happy for that because I didn't want to be coming up on no Marion Barry-type foolishness. Didn't want to see Reverend Walker sucking on a glass dick, getting his crack smoke on.

I raised my hand to knock.

Sobs took over, loud, hard, long. I halted my knock again.

I dropped my hand. Maybe the Father, the Son, and the Holy Ghost—all three of 'em—were trying to tell me to move tread, get up out the Lord's House with my ridiculous notions. My shoulders slumped. I grimaced and shook my head, embarrassed for coming. No longer feeling fortified in the faith, I needed to get back to my motel room and search my heart for the strength to connect with the address on those letters I had got in prison from my father.

I stepped back as the sobs coming from inside Reverend Walker's office grew even louder. I bumped something and turned to see I'd knocked over the lectern in the hall. Pieces of light bulb lay shattered, broken from the lectern's attached lamp. Pages in the tossed-aside Bible were askew. I bent to pick up the mess and noticed the sobs had stopped. Turned just in time to see the office door crack open. A man with an oversized head and enough chins for an entire board of deacons popped out into the hall. He was the color of a greasy brown paper lunch bag, one with greasy fried chicken inside. He'd applied his cologne heavily.

"May I help you, young man?" he asked. I thought of J-boy again, glad this man hadn't called me *young breed*. My mind flashed to Luck for a moment.

I stood, brought the lectern with me, and placed it back against the wall. "I was looking for Reverend G.H. Walker," I said.

"You found him in God's mercy," the man said, extending a hand.

I clasped it. He had a warm, comfortable, strong grip. Miss Ma'am had always told me you could find the worth of a man in a simple handshake. "Your Daddy's, for instance," she once let me in on, "is limp, cold, like trying to get hold of a catfish fresh out the water." She then waved her hand and said, "But I don't want to say anything wrong about the man you got swimming inside you."

"Nice to meet you, Reverend Walker," I said.

His gaze dropped behind me: the Bible on the floor, pieces of bulb beside it. He turned his eyes back on me.

"I backed into it," I explained. "Knocked it over. I apologize."

"Backed?" He hunched his eyes.

I looked away, bent and picked up the Bible, and placed it on the lectern. Then I started to get those pieces of glass to hold in my hand.

"I'll sweep that up later," Reverend Walker said to me.

I stood again. "I really do apologize for the mess."

"You heard me crying," he said.

I started to lie, to say I hadn't heard anything. I nodded instead.

He looked off to something in the distance, something

too fast for him, something he couldn't catch—a blur far beyond his reach. His arms too short to box with God...or corral that blur. I knew that look. It had been mine on many a day.

"Eleanor," he said after a while.

"Excuse me, Reverend?"

"My wife, Eleanor. Passed away seven months ago today. On the dot." He swallowed so hard I could see his Adam's apple do a bob. Then he turned his gaze back on me. "I'm sixty-four, you see. Eleanor and the Lord are all I've known since I was twenty-four. Forty years...symbolic."

"The Great Flood," I said, then added, "Moses and the Israelites wandering in the desert before finding the Promised Land. Jesus on his knees daily, fasting, before he went on his Mission. All symbolized by that number, forty. Only number that occurs more in the Bible is the number seven." I cleared my throat. "You said your wife passed seven months ago?"

Reverend Walker cocked his head to the side, touched fingers to his chin, and rubbed the day-old gray-and-black stubble. "I hadn't thought of that, young man."

"The Bible...I've studied it religiously," I told him.

We both laughed at my unintentional choice of word. *Religiously.*

"Well, young man, I—"

"I heard you puffing on something, too," I cut him off. I liked him. I wanted that bit of four-one-one out on the floor for discussion. What was he puffing? I had to know.

His eyes narrowed. "My nebulizer. You heard me taking my albuterol treatment."

I thought of Miss Ma'am sneaking cigarettes in the bathroom, dropping the charred butts down in the toilet, same toilet she'd puke auburn-tinged vomit in one day. "You smoke?" I asked Reverend Walker.

"No. Oh, no." He smiled sadly.

"Asthma?"

He nodded. "Yes." Then he touched my shoulder. I could feel the electricity run through my body.

Reverend Walker asked, "So what can I do for you?"

I could hear my heartbeat all of a sudden, in my ears, throbbing like a church bell. I stood there, wordless. Could I do this?

"But I am poor and needy," Reverend Walker said in response to my hesitation. "Make haste unto me, O God. Thou art my help and my deliverer."

"Psalm Seventy. Final verse," I heard myself say. I could remember verses as long as Aloe-slash-Diane wasn't lying naked beside me.

"I'm impressed." Walker patted my shoulder. "Now, what can I do for you?"

I swallowed. "Someone I know was telling me about your problems holding on to an associate pastor."

Walker frowned. "Thorns," he said. "Thorns find themselves in the midst of God's goodness every so often."

"I was wondering what I'd have to do to…" I couldn't finish, or look him in the eyes.

"The Lord is your shepherd?" he asked me.

I looked up. "My strength and my redeemer," I answered, nodding.

"Come," he said.

"To your office?"

"Yes."

"You're going to help me?"

"Yes."

"Why?"

He looked at me, but I could feel his gaze passing through my body, off chasing some unreachable blur again. For the moment, I was translucent to him.

"Reverend?"

"My son," he said, catching glimpse of me again. "Johnny. Eleanor wanted to name him that. Johnny Walker. Same as that liquor that's the monkey on some folks' backs. I saw it as a problem from the beginning. Very unfortunate name." He shook his head and smiled.

I smiled, too.

"Anyway," he went on, "you remind me of my Johnny."

"Do I? Is he a pastor as well? I mean, like you?"

Walker threw his prodigious head back and laughed from deep in the gut.

I stood quiet.

He looked back to me and said, "Johnny's in prison."

My mouth dropped open, legs stiffened, heart pounded in my chest like the drums in a hip-hop song, louder than a church bell. I managed a feeble, "Prison?"

"Armed robbery," he added. "Has that posture you have. Only place you get it is in prison. He didn't have it before he went in."

I didn't, either.

"That look on your face," he went on. "Even when you smile, it falls short of a true expression of happiness. Tight around the mouth, as if your face is intent on running roughshod over your soul, won't let your soul's happiness touch it. That's Johnny. That's you."

I still hadn't said anything. Walker took my elbow and moved me with him. His cologne was so strong.

I stopped at the threshold of his office. "You sure about this? I mean, my past…"

"Only one judge," he intoned. "Only one judge. And His name isn't George Henry Walker. Let's go talk. We'll let the Lord order our steps."

Those words soothed me. There was a chance for me, a born sinner, still struggling with demons. Demons. My prison time, for one. The crime that had sent me there. Lying with women like Aloe-slash-Diane. My one judge could wash it all as white as snow. I was in His hands, He's Sweet I Know's hands.

"Where you staying?" Walker asked me.

"Ramada over on—"

"The church has housing for the pastor," Walker cut in. "I don't use it. I stay in the house where Eleanor and I started a family, started our marriage. The church's house is empty."

"I don't know what to say, Reverend Walker."

He nodded. "I'm forgetting my advice. We'll let the Lord order our steps. Now come." He reached for me again. This time I moved forward.

I went inside Reverend Walker's office.

If this became a reality, this crazy notion of mine actually took shape and I became a preacher, Fellowship Baptist's associate pastor, then I would truly believe that old adage I'd heard for years.

God worked in mysterious ways.

Reverend Walker popped two sticks of Doublemint gum in his mouth and looked at me. I could tell by the look on Reverend Walker's face that He did. God worked in mysterious ways.

6

Afeni Muhammad had seen her mother down on her knees in front of a man she didn't love, sucking him off so hard his eyes watered and rolled up into his head as his legs jerked in spasms. She'd seen her mother in the alley between their building and that equally crumpled piece of shit building next to it, her mother's panties and velour sweatpants pooled by her ankles, another man she didn't love pounding the shit out of her from the back as her hands found purchase on the side of a Dumpster. She'd seen her mother bouncing on top of yet another man she didn't love, the man rubbing her mother's booby nipples much too hard, her mother not saying shit in protest, but doing her best to mask the pain with a faux smile.

She'd seen her mother dance and heard men say nasty shit to her mother.

"Aloe, I'd love to plug a couple shots in that ass of yours."

Heard her mother respond, "Pay your token and you've got an E-ZPass to this ass, baby."

And Afeni had known, way before age fourteen, that she didn't want a similar life for herself. No way, Jose. She'd be a poet. She'd have the name on her poems

spelled out in all lowercase letters—*afeni muhammad.*
Some cool-ass shit like that. And the poems that got her
known would be clean, too; she wouldn't use the "shit"
word. Art. She wouldn't peddle sex in any of them, either.
Little black girls would admire her. They'd be writing
their own haiku poems. A lesson for young black girls so
different from the tutorial Aloe had given her. That's
right, Afeni called her mother Aloe, because "Diane"
didn't seem to fit. A "Diane" would know how to raise a
daughter. But an "Aloe"…she wouldn't know shit about
parenting.

And Afeni's mother didn't. So Aloe it was.

Yet the poor lessons learned from Aloe were snapshots
in Afeni's mind, pictures that didn't fade, whose corners
didn't curl up, whose images never blurred.

"You saw me deep-throating that brother?" Aloe had
asked her daughter once. Earlier that day Afeni had spotted her mother on her knees, as if worshipping the man
before her, the man she didn't love.

"Huh?" Afeni looked up from her issue of *Vibe* magazine, keeping her finger in place to hold her spot. Her
manicured and red-colored nail rested right in Snoop
Dogg's eye on the page.

"Deep-throating," Aloe clarified, and spotting Snoop
Dogg on the page, added, "Sucking his diznick?" She
smiled.

Afeni didn't return the smile, but dropped her eyes and
her voice, too. "Yeah. I saw you."

Aloe touched her daughter, gently raising Afeni's
head by the chin. It could have been a tender moment—
one of those television commercial moments with a soft
piano playing in the background, and Aloe and Afeni at
their kitchen table sipping from mugs filled with steaming coffee.

Shit, no.

Instead, Aloe looked Afeni dead in the eyes and espoused some real stupid shit the overworked folks at DYFS should put on a poster, in a circle, marked over with an X. "I'm glad you saw," Aloe said. "Know this... the harder you suck, the bigger the buck. Now, don't suck him 'cause you want money. That'd make you a hooker. Suck him like you love him and he'll hit you off with some cash for spending money, to buy yourself a little something. Anyway, the harder the suck, the bigger the buck."

"I figure on staying poor," Afeni had replied. "Or else I'll find another way to make money."

"That's right. You got your poems," Aloe had snickered. "I forgot. Scratch what I said. Don't shake your ass. Shake your spear." Aloe laughed deeply. "You get it? Didn't know your Mama was up on that, huh? Shake your spear. Shakespeare. You get it?"

"I get it, Aloe." And Afeni did. Got it good. Enough so that the hate for her mother, manifested at that moment, burned inside her like molten lava. Afeni, an emotional embodiment of Mauna Loa, a volcano bubbling over with hate, her circumstances making her wonder why God would take his grit sander and carve out *this* life for her?

Hate and questions filled Afeni's heart from that moment. Until...

The day she came upon her mother on the floor in the center of the living room, shaking, sweating, and rocking herself gently. The television was on, loud, stereo blasting, too. Aloe hadn't gone out to dance at the G-spot in two weeks; she'd broken her ankle three months back and, even after it healed, grew more listless with each passing day. It had been more than a minute since she'd deep-throated any man she didn't love for a few dollars, too. As far as Afeni knew.

"What's up, Aloe?" Afeni had asked. She figured it had something to do with money. The root of all evil. All that jazz. So true when it came to Aloe.

Aloe had shot around, her eyes wide. She touched a shaky hand to her chest and shook her head. "You and footsteps need to introduce yourselves to each other. I never knew anyone who moved around so quietly."

"Light on my feet," Afeni agreed. "Could probably be a dancer."

Aloe laughed at that as she wiped the sweat from her face.

"Not an exotic," Afeni added.

Aloe nodded. "No, not an exotic. Not my Afeni."

Afeni narrowed her eyes, took in Aloe, and didn't like what she saw. Aloe had dropped some weight. She noticed this now, in the dark of their living room, ironically, for the first time. But that wasn't all. Aloe also had bruises, like a single footstep in the snow running a trail up her arm.

"You okay, Aloe?"

"Will be."

"When's that?"

Aloe propped herself on her elbows, slid her diminishing frame over by the couch, leaned back against it, and patted a spot next to her on the floor. Afeni moved to the spot and sat.

"I've given you some bad advice," Aloe began.

"Which?"

Aloe sighed. "All of it. Messed your head up, confused you about sex."

"I'm okay," Afeni said. "I know not to heed the stuff you told me."

"Heed?" Aloe smiled. "You are a smart girl, Afeni. I'm proud of how you've turned out, despite me."

"You did the best you could."

"I'm sending you away," Aloe quickly said. "For just a little while."

Afeni wasn't surprised. Wasn't anxious or nervous. "Where to?"

Aloe told Afeni. A nice family. The woman who'd serve as Afeni's mother-guardian was a Christian woman who had done Aloe a solid, a favor, in the past.

Afeni touched her mother's shoulder. "You just get yourself better, Aloe. Do that for me. Okay?"

Aloe bit back tears. "Do me a favor, too?"

"What's that?"

Aloe opened her mouth several times before the words came. "Call me Mama," she said in a whisper when they finally did. Then repeating them, stronger, "Call me Mama."

Afeni thought it through. A mother gave her child chances, put her child in the best position for success. Aloe was trying to do that now by sending her only daughter to a better place, a better situation. Mauna Loa cooled. The hate was gone, the threat of an eruption thwarted by the promise of hope.

"I love you…Mama," Afeni said.

Aloe smiled in return, tears streaming down her cheeks. Afeni touched a hand to her mother's face and wiped the tear tracks away, hoping the tracks on her mother's arms would disappear, too.

But those thoughts of the past were just a tunnel to the "now" of Afeni's life. A tunnel, not a bridge. Afeni was too poetic to rely on a cliché of her past life having been "troubled waters" and her new life with the Sykeses a "bridge" over those troubled waters. Her time with Aloe, though difficult, had taught her lessons that she'd carry with her for the rest of her life. She hadn't gone "over" anything; she'd gone "through" plenty, and was better for the journey.

Still, Afeni missed Aloe. Especially in times like now, with Bevolyn Sykes ushering her to the church for a heart-to-heart with Reverend Walker, Bevolyn convinced that Afeni's fashion choices spelled out something sinister about Afeni's inner character, and Bevolyn trying to be Afeni's mother and shit.

"Do we have to do this?" Afeni was saying as they climbed the church steps.

Bevolyn didn't answer. When she reached the top step, she moved to the wide set of doors and held one side open for Afeni to cross through. Another tunnel to something.

Afeni paused. "I get the silent treatment because why," she asked, "I'm a child? That it? Speak only when spoken to?"

Bevolyn scanned her eyes over Afeni. A beautiful girl, she had to admit, with skin the dark brown of a Snickers bar wrapper, large, inquisitive eyes, and long, curly black hair. But she had to mess up those tresses with blond highlights. Wore too much makeup, too. Maroon-colored glossy lipstick that brought unnecessary attention to those lips of hers. Bevolyn saw how men stared at Afeni's lips. She knew that Afeni had learned all kinds of nasty things to do with her lips from her trifling mother. Hmph. And clothes—Lord have mercy! Don't even go there. A camouflaged hat, one you'd expect on some lance corporal or something or other. And Afeni had the nerve to wear it cocked to the side on her head. Aerobic tights under a gray jumpsuit she let hang off one shoulder. Sneakers, or when she felt like dressing up, some Steve Madden boots. The Devil was alive and well: Afeni's personal shopper, evidently.

"This ain't right, *Maji*," Afeni said. Bevolyn frowned, the response Afeni had been looking for. Afeni placed her hands on her hips. "What if I refuse to go in, *Maji*? Then what? You gonna drag me in…*Maji*?"

"Don't tempt me," Bevolyn's first words through clenched teeth. She was ready to use the rod on Afeni for all that *Maji* nonsense.

Afeni understood the implication of Bevolyn's three words. She saw the narrowed focus of Bevolyn's eyes, the hard-set jaw, the way she was manhandling the door's pull handle. Afeni decided to concede this battle and wage on in war another day. She moved inside.

"Wise choice," Bevolyn said. "I'll collect your gold, incense, and myrrh later." She invoked the story of the Bible's Three Wise Men for Afeni's benefit, always trying to find a way to pass along some biblical learning to this child God had put it on her heart to take in.

"The Three Wise Men, right?" Afeni asked. "We learned about them in Sunday school."

Bevolyn smiled. God had to be pleased. She was doing her best with a difficult situation, a girl tossed about by a difficult life. Now, the girl in her difficult teen years. Difficult: the word for everything. God: the only means of getting through difficulties.

Bevolyn led the way to Reverend Walker's office. Walker kept hours during the week so he could offer counsel to those gone astray. And Afeni, with her military cap and moist-looking lips, definitely fit the definition.

"Oh, boy," Afeni said, sighing heavily as they reached the office. Her hands were a pool of sweat, her heart a drum, and her mouth a cotton field.

Bevolyn knocked at the reverend's door.

Afeni took a couple deep breaths. "We got time to change our minds," she said.

But then Reverend Walker appeared in the doorway out of breath, his cologne overpowering, and chewing hard on gum. But he smiled grandly. "Sister Sykes, young Ms. Afeni, what a blessing it is to see you both."

"How are you, Reverend?" Bevolyn asked.

"In God's tender care and mercy," he replied. "What can I do for you?"

Bevolyn touched Afeni's shoulder and pulled the child forward. "We'd like to have a word with you, Reverend," Bevolyn said. "My foster daughter has some issues that need addressing. Are you busy?"

Reverend Walker looked to Afeni. Afeni's gaze dropped and her shoulders sagged. He then looked over Bevolyn's shoulder, down the hall, and finally returned his glance to Bevolyn and Afeni. "Sure, come on in."

They moved inside.

"So," Reverend Walker said after they all had found their seating.

Bevolyn cleared her throat. "Tell the reverend why we're here, Afeni."

"You tell him," Afeni said, adding, "*Maji.*"

"You're going to watch that," Bevolyn said.

"Watch what?" Afeni innocently replied.

Before Bevolyn could answer, the door of the office swept open.

"Oh, excuse me, Reverend," came the voice that fluttered into the room. "I didn't know you had company."

The man filling the doorway eyed everyone inside, in appreciation for the company, particularly the woman sitting like a debutante in the seat in front of Reverend Walker's desk.

Bevolyn felt something in her chest as she appraised him in kind. Heavily muscled, with deep brown skin, a wispy mustache and goatee, thick eyebrows…

She caught herself and touched her wedding finger, slid that thin gold band around on her finger. It symbolized a precious union. Was supposed to symbolize a precious union.

Fade haircut, dimples as thick as one of her fingers…

She focused on Russell Byron Sykes. Russell Byron Sykes. Her husband. *Husband.*

Briefly flustered, Bevolyn looked to Afeni and saw the gleam in her foster daughter's eyes, staring at this man as if he were that rapper in the pictures that wallpapered her room, 50 Cent. No *s* at the end, as Afeni pointed out to Bevolyn every time Bevolyn said his name wrong.

"This is Minister LeVar Path," Bevolyn heard Reverend Walker say. "He's going to be the new associate pastor."

Minister? Associate pastor? He didn't look like anything of the sort to Bevolyn. Too young, too muscled, too, (dare she say it?) sexy. She was already running down a list of the morally corrupt women in the church whom she could imagine propositioning this pastor to lay hands on them. Sally Gabriel. Donna Williamson. Oh, can't forget Tracey Whitfield. She'd be on him like white on rice.

"Minister Path," Reverend Walker went on, "this is Sister Bevolyn Sykes and her foster daughter, Afeni."

Bevolyn noticed the minister's head cock a couple degrees to the side, some kind of recognition flashing in his eyes. Why? She'd never seen him before. From the looks of him, they definitely didn't run in the same circles. Why did he glance at her, then, as if this moment were a reunion?

He padded across the floor, Bevolyn's eyes on him the entire way, and reached a hand forward for Afeni. "Pleased to meet you, Afeni."

Hmmph, Bevolyn thought, another one enthralled by this child's moist lips.

Afeni took his hand as if it were a new 50 Cent CD. "Pleasure's all mine."

Bevolyn shot her a glance. Little fast ass. Hold your horses.

Then Path turned to Bevolyn and extended his hand. "Sister Sykes."

She reluctantly took it, not liking the look in this so-called minister's eyes, studying her. "And where did you say you received your theological training?" she asked. She held on to his hand as she asked.

Path smiled, keeping the grip on her slender fingers. "I didn't."

"Didn't receive any?" Her small womanly hand under the tent of his large manly hand.

"Didn't say," he said.

"And still haven't," she noted.

"Umm," Reverend Walker cut in. "Sister Sykes was here to discuss some things regarding Afeni, Minister Path."

"Is that so?" he said, finally releasing Bevolyn's hand. She let her hand drop back to her side, slowly.

"Would it be okay if the minister stayed with us, Sister Sykes?" Walker went on. "He might have some counsel to offer."

"I'd prefer not," Bevolyn said. "How did this all happen? Associate pastor. Did the deacons approve this? No church meeting."

"I've talked to the deacons," Reverend Walker said. "Now, is it okay if the minister stays?"

"I'd prefer he did," Afeni said. "It is my life we're talking about. I think Minister Path would offer an interesting perspective."

Path turned to Afeni, his ever-present smile still a candle that lit the room. "You speak very well, Afeni. Not many young folk do, unfortunately."

"I'm very mature for my age," Afeni said, batting her eyes.

Path let that thought drift.

"Sister Sykes?" Reverend Walker asked.

"I'll defer to Afeni's wish," Bevolyn said. What hurt could come from his being here? She glanced at his wide shoulders. Plenty.

"Thanks for your belief, Sister Sykes," Path said.

"Afeni's wish, Minister Path," she told him. "I can't take credit for believing in you."

Path smirked. Spunky, spunky. Very, well, sexy in a woman.

Reverend Walker cleared his throat. "Shall we get started? What seems to be your concern, Sister Sykes?"

"She doesn't like the way I dress. How I style myself," Afeni said. "Thinks my lipstick and highlights point to a serious character flaw."

"They do," Bevolyn said.

"Maybe in Li'l Kim," Path said. "And even that is debatable. Afeni is a young woman, dressing in the manner in which young women dress. I think her style is understated, nice, if today's dress is any indication of her usual."

"It is," Afeni said. "I also have a banging denim jumpsuit."

"Li'l Kim?" Bevolyn asked.

Path answered, "Big Mama Queen Bee," and winked at Afeni.

"Reverend Walker, I haven't heard your opinion," Bevolyn said, turning disgustedly from the hip-hop, wide-shouldered, ain't-hardly-anybody's minister.

"I think I'd tend to agree with Minister Path, Sister Sykes. I know Afeni. She's a brilliant young woman. I still remember the poem she wrote for Youth Day. *Winter cool snow, falling fresh like God's grace that smiled upon a sinner's face.*" He grunted. Eleanor had loved the snow. Even at her age that last winter they had together, she would stick out her tongue and let snowflakes fall there to melt. "No," he said. "I don't see any problem with the way she's dressed, Sister Sykes."

Bevolyn sighed.

Path moved to Reverend Walker's desk and took a casual seat on the corner. "We spend too much time criticizing and discouraging our youth, Sister Sykes. We need to spend more time talking with them and trying to understand them."

"Amen," Afeni said.

"You learned that wherever you *didn't* say you studied theology?" Bevolyn asked Path. She kept her head rigid, held high, refusing to go scavenger hunting for a bulge in the minister's khakis.

"You're about what? Thirty-one, thirty-two, Sister Sykes? Around my age," Path said.

"Thirty-seven," Afeni answered.

Bevolyn cut her a look. "How do you know that?"

"I Googled you," Afeni said.

"You what-ed me?" Bevolyn asked.

"Googled. On the computer. It's a search engine."

"We'll talk about that later," Bevolyn promised.

"I needed to know what I was getting into, moving into your home," Afeni defended. "I came across an article. You were the president of some sorority, Kappa Alpha Delta, or something like that. At some anti-abortion rally. The—"

"Shut your mouth," Bevolyn snapped.

Afeni frowned. "Consider it shut. *Maji.*"

The room grew quiet.

"I was going to say," Path said after some time, "that I'd bet we could find a leather 8-ball jacket, some Reeboks, and doorknocker earrings in your closet, Sister Sykes. Your Salt-N-Pepa phase." He coughed into his hand. "But, now that Afeni has divulged your um, age, um, maybe some bell-bottoms and an Afro pick would be more appropriate. After all, you were around in the sixties." He held the smile that wanted to follow.

"I was a baby in the sixties," Bevolyn said, her tone biting.

Minister Path smiled.

"Your point, *Minister*?" Bevolyn asked, perturbed and angry with Afeni. Why? Because the child had violated her privacy? Or because the child had told her age in front of him?

Path leaned forward. "The fashion peccadilloes of your past didn't diminish you whatsoever. They didn't hinder you from becoming a sophisticated, beautiful, seemingly caring, and devout woman of God."

"Imagine you turning out as all of that, *Maji*," Afeni said. "Go figure."

Bevolyn sat wordless. Even Afeni mocking her, calling her that name she so hated—*Maji*—didn't matter. The so-called minister had called her a woman of God, which pleased her.

Beautiful.

And that, concernedly, pleased her even more.

7

I could close my eyes and imagine her as clear as if she were really standing before me. Long, maroon-brown curls that flowed to her shoulders. Skin the color of a blend of hot chocolate, an equal mixture of cream and syrup. African-bush-woman cheekbones, prominent enough to pull you away from her mesmerizing eyes for a moment. And yeah, those eyes. Light, light brown, almost golden. They stood out, like my cousin Lita's eyes. Large, too, just the way I like them. Full lips, a cute little cleft chin, and a tiny scar by the underside of her lips. I hoped one day that we'd be close enough that I could ask her about the scar. It added something to her beauty and intrigue. That scar interested me for personal reasons as well: I had a similar scar etched in the skin behind my left eyebrow.

Bevolyn Sykes interested me.

She was more than a milkshake. More like a gallon of Breyer's. Scratch that, Häagen-Dazs.

Tight body, too, with all the necessary features to pull in a black man's devotion: thick thighs; bubbled round butt that sat high, a "chumpy," as my boys and I used to call that particular delight; and breasts that could rival

Aloe-slash-Diane or any of the other women in the G-spot riding life's fast lane in pole position.

There were a couple of problems with my desire for Bevolyn Sykes, though.

One. she was a married woman. And He's Sweet I Know has definite words of caution against anyone throwing that asunder, or even trying. I knew that was a BIG problem if I continued to walk the straight and narrow, continued to try to follow the road From Whom All Blessings Flow laid out. And I did.

I skipped past that for a second, though, and looked at the other problems.

Two: she was older. Probably a tad bit more sophisticated than all the women I'd been with, combined. Imagine her and Aloe-slash-Diane playing a round of Jeopardy. Aloe-slash-Diane couldn't compete unless the category was "Songs with a Fast Beat." But Bevolyn, she was a whole 'nother other. I'd seen that the other day. She carried herself like the Black Jackie O.

Okay. Lastly: Bevolyn wasn't feeling me.

Hard to overcome that. That's like eating the forbidden fruit against From Whom All Blessings Flow's wishes and thinking you could run from His disappointed gaze. Not happening. I got the feeling Bevolyn Sykes made an initial decision on whether she liked a person, and if that initial perspective was a negative one...it stayed negative.

I so wanted to change that.

"Come have a word with the congregation."

My reverie of Bevolyn crashed when I noticed Reverend Walker, turned from his spot in the pulpit, stretching a hand toward me.

"Now?" I thought.

He nodded, which embarrassed me. I hadn't realized I'd said it aloud.

Sweat pooled in my armpits, my heart did a pitter-patter in my chest, and my mouth went dry on me. I gulped down a quick sip of water and stood, forcing myself not to look at the far right corner of the congregation as I took my place by the microphone. If you guessed that Bevolyn sat in that part of the church, you'd win the prize. A big, fat, anybody-could-have-guessed-that shrug of my shoulders.

"I'm pleased that God has seen fit to bring me here," were my first words as I settled before the congregation. I knew there had been a slight uproar with my appointment, from the caught-off-guard deacons to the parishioners. Reverend Walker, thankfully, had stood firm in my corner. Still, I needed the church's vote to make it official.

I paused for an "amen" or a "hallelujah," something to spur me on. When I didn't get one from the skeptical church members, I pressed on. They'd been through a lot, I knew. They wondered how long it would be before I sank in a sea of scandal. I wondered myself.

I put a fist to my lips and coughed in it, scanning the sea. It looked like a violent, thrashing, angry sea to me. Ye of little faith.

I pressed on.

"I pray my time here is of glory to His name."

Still not a peep from anyone. I glanced at the deacons for support. Not one of them met my eyes. They didn't want that guilt-by-association tag to stick to them if I eventually sank in that sea.

I considered Luck. Thought about his jokes and light-hearted manner of feeding me He's Sweet I Know's words. Thought about him standing over that J-boy with the dead eyes, Lipstick, in the prison kitchen. I had two choices as far as I was concerned in order to gather some kind of bond with this tough crowd. Tell a joke or stab somebody with a homemade shank. I spotted a woman way up front to my left who would be good for a stabbing. She had on an extra large hat with what looked like fruit sitting atop it. Real plastic-looking fruit. Yeah, I should shank her for wearing that monstrosity into the Lord's house. But that was just the Devil speaking, his deadly influence flooding my ears. Instead, I decided on the joke.

"Preachers are in great need of the support of the people," I said. "The people's hearts and minds. We need that to be successful shepherds." *We*, I'd said, as if saying it would make it so. As if I'd be a preacher in someone's eyes other than Reverend Walker, who had a son with whom I could trade prison stories. Me, a real preacher. Just because I said *we*. Was it possible? I prayed it so.

I noticed a young mother of two near the front of the church. She kept glancing at her watch, wanting this over so she could get home and put her roast in the oven, I supposed. Someone once said if you get the most ambivalent person in the crowd to follow you, everyone else would as well.

I focused on the woman and raised my voice a notch. She looked up at the change in my inflection. I locked eyes with her and went on.

"Which reminds me of this one preacher," I said to the sister with the two children, "who was new to town and went around to all of the parishioners' houses and spoke to all of them. Young and old. He introduced himself to everyone."

I fought the silence of the church, prayed as I talked, and asked Him for traveling mercy as I started this journey.

"All went well with the preacher's visits," I went on, "until he came to this one house. He knocked, knocked, knocked, and knocked some more. No one answered.

He walked to the edge of the porch and saw a car in the driveway. Came back and knocked at the door yet again."

Against better judgment, I looked to the far right corner of the church and saw that Bevolyn's eyes were on me. This buoyed my spirit. Afeni and some others sat next to Bevolyn. They all had their heads facing in my direction. I couldn't disappoint her, I mean, them.

"Now this preacher was discouraged because he could hear a television playing softly inside," I went on. "So he knocked harder. Really whacked that door. Still no answer."

I paused to wipe at my brow and smile. I noticed a few of the parishioners' postures stiffening, waiting for the punchline. I was on my way. I gave a quick thanks to He's Sweet I Know. He'd granted me traveling mercy.

"So the preacher pulled out one of his business cards and a pen. Wrote on the back of one of the cards, Revelation 3:20." I paused again and wiped my brow. "Now I know you good church folk know that Revelation 3:20 states His word as: 'Behold, I stand at the door, and knock: if any man hear my voice, and open the door, I will come in to him, and will sup with him, and he with me.' "

Pause. Wipe.

"The preacher left the card in the mailbox and, though disappointed, he moved on. Well, come Sunday morning after service as he counted the offertory monies with the trustees, he noticed his white business card mixed in among the money. He quickly pulled it out and flipped it over."

Pause. Wipe. Smile.

"Below his scribbling of Revelation 3:20 was another scribbling. Genesis 3:10. Which of course reads: 'And he said, I heard thy voice in the garden, and I was afraid, because I was naked; and I hid myself.' "

The congregation broke out into raucous laughter. I got my "amen" and "hallelujah" from more than one parishioner. I dared a look in Bevolyn's direction. Her smile was wider than anyone else's was. That fact was like a key into the gates of heaven. I would have had the patience of Job, if need be, waiting for that smile. But I was glad to get it this early in the game. Maybe there was a chance for something—I didn't know what—with her.

"I thank you," I finished, "for opening your arms to me. I pray our journey together will be a blessing unto His name."

I turned back to Reverend Walker, applause warming my back like August sun. He simply nodded, a cologne cloud around him as he stood and patted my shoulder.

"I can't tell a joke like he can," he said when he reached the microphone, "but I thank God I turned out better looking."

More laughter. He called for a vote. I received a strong majority. I was in.

"Stand for the benediction," he said after the vote, raising his arms.

A few minutes later I stood at the front of the church, Reverend Walker beside me, as members formed a line to come greet me. It was the best feeling I'd ever had in my life, the best feeling, in part, because I imagined Sister Sykes as being somewhere on that line. Though I'd yet, despite several attempts, to spot her.

"Blessings, Reverend Walker, and God bless you, Minister Path," said an elderly woman. She offered her hand. "I'm Sister Bernice Stokely."

"Ah, Mother Stokely," I said, smiling. "So nice to make your acquaintance. The deacons have told me so much about you. Mother of the church. Your late husband helped found it years ago, correct?"

Mother Stokely waved off my comment, seemingly embarrassed by the fuss I'd made over her. I'd been told so much about her, including the fact that she feigned embarrassment when folk doted on her, but also could get feisty as an alley cat when they didn't. People loved to watch her make her way down the center aisle for morning service. Her hair was a soft kittenish white, her skin a deep chocolate contrast. It was hard not to look at Mother Stokely; she was so pleasant to the eye. She was wearing a lavish "church hat" that looked like a miniature boat. Nice looking hat, though. You wouldn't find a bowl of plastic fruit on Mother Stokely's head.

"Yes, Minister Path, my Herbert did play a part in Little Fellowship's founding…that's what they called it then, Little Fellowship. Back when it was on Apple Street 'round the corner." She pointed her arthritic hand in the direction. "But anyway, you did a proud job today. I hope and pray that you'll stay a while."

"I plan on staying for quite some time," I told her.

Crow's feet tapped at the corners of her eyes as she smiled with her mouth shut, making me shift my weight from one foot to the other. I felt like a glass of clear liquid, a Sprite, as if she looked directly through me to the other side—same as I'd felt in that diner when I'd encountered that crazy woman, Swizz. Exact same feeling, only thing missing was the strong aroma of chocolate in my nostrils.

"I hope so, Reverend," she said. "You'll see that there is plenty of work to be done here. Stay a while and you'll see. God bless ya."

She gingerly made her way on so the folks behind her could get a close-up with me. I couldn't help but follow her movement down the center aisle. *Stay a while,* she had said, emphasizing it as if she could read my inner soul and see the doubts that made me question every move, motive, and future action. As if she knew I'd never stayed in one place for too long as an adult. And the only time I had, I had no choice. Had to stay.

"She's a striking presence," Reverend Walker offered.

"Yes," I acknowledged, "she sure is."

The watch-watching mother I'd noticed earlier pressed forward with her two youngsters, commandeering my attention, even though I kept glancing down the line looking for Bevolyn. I didn't see her.

"So good to have you here, Minister Path," the mother said. She nodded at Walker. "Reverend."

I moved to my politician's greeting: wide smile, a handshake at the ready, willing to kiss a baby so ugly, I couldn't tell if I was putting my lips on his face or his butt. "Thank you…Sister?"

"Marcia Gamble."

I leaned down to the two youngsters glued to her sides. "And what might I call you two beautiful children?" Luckily, they were. Like angels had made them from light brown-colored dust. The sight of beautiful children made me somewhat sad ever since my time in prison. Life on the inside had taught me that the world was a dark place. Children, to me, were too innocent to live in this world.

The oldest, a boy, stuttered, "I'm…I'm Nate. D-Dis here's my little sister, Latrece."

"Nate and Latrece. See you two in Sunday school, right?"

"Yes, sir," they replied in tandem as their mother looked on with surprise.

I turned my gaze back to the mother. "Ham, turkey, or chicken?"

"Excuse me?"

"Dinner today. I saw you looking at your watch earlier."

She blushed and covered her mouth with a slender hand, the nails of which needed a manicure and fresh polish. "Ham," she admitted.

"With pineapples?" I asked.

"Mmmm-hmm."

"God is good," I told her. She smiled and moved on.

The worshippers, and the line, continued moving forward slowly. I spent a comfortable amount of time with each parishioner, reciting his or her name for memory's sake. I still hadn't caught sight of Bevolyn. Looked like my joke, and her subsequent smile, hadn't been enough for her to come shake my hand.

On inched the line.

"Okay, Brother Gaines, God bless you," I said to one man. "And yes, I'll be sure to offer up a prayer for the Nets. You're right, by the way. It would be a sin if Jason Kidd left." Brother Gaines nodded appreciatively and wrapped my hands in his. I hoped the Nets made the playoffs this year because if they didn't, Brother Gaines just might stop coming to church. That would be a shame. He patted my shoulder and moved on, a bounce in his steps.

Then it happened. An explosion like the fourth day in July.

Three women and one on the brink of womanhood inched forward. They were the last of the line, and I could tell by their postures and demeanors that they had intended it that way. The last woman, shielded by the others, was Ms. Breyer's/Häagen-Dazs herself. I immediately smiled, seeing her. She immediately averted her eyes. But that was okay. She'd gotten on the line to greet me. She'd laughed at my joke. All was good in my world.

Reverend Walker tapped me on the shoulder. "I'm going to head on back and gather some items to take Sister Healy. She's home from the hospital."

"Okay, good, good, Reverend Walker." He left but his cologne lingered.

The women reached me.

"Sela Wheeler," one of the women told me. Her black hair was tied up in a bun and streaked with red highlights. She was a bit heavy-handed with the makeup, various hues of maroon, but had real nice features—features so familiar that I wondered where I'd seen her before. Then she said, "I'm Bevolyn's sister. I understand you've already met." Bevolyn hit her in the back. Sela lurched forward a foot.

I ignored that and said, "Yes, I had the pleasure of meeting your sister." I kept my eyes on Bevolyn as I said it. Again, she looked away.

"Pleasure," Sela said with fake shock. "Wow. You are a man of God."

I laughed. Sela did as well. A beautiful smile on a beautiful woman. It mesmerized me for the briefest of moments. Sela seemed to notice, for she turned her gaze away uncomfortably and stepped aside with her head down.

Another woman stepped forward.

"Zelda Overton," she said, extending a hand. She was the anomaly of the women, with her high yellow skin tone, where the rest of them were deep browns; angular nose and pointed chin—the sharp features of a female newscaster. Purple and white flowers were pinned in her hair. Lavender-colored makeup—very little in comparison to Sela—painted her eyes and lips.

"Nice to meet you, Zelda."

She nodded and quickly moved aside, catching up with Sela, whispering something in Sela's ear. Sela gave her a professional nod in response, one with no emotion or feeling in it.

Afeni took my hand and held it. I eased mine away after an uncomfortable amount of time had passed.

"Nice to see you again, Afeni," I said, when she hadn't said a word.

"You remembered me," she gushed.

"How could I not."

Her eyes widened. "Name of my next poem," she said.

"What's that?"

"I'm gonna name my next poem," she informed me, " 'How Could I Not?' "

"I hope to read it," I told her.

She moved away, looking as if I'd dropped the weight of the world on her shoulders. I could just see her, up all night for several days, even weeks, hunched over a table trying to pen the words to the poem. She had a crush on me, I could tell. I wondered what would happen to that crush if she knew the things I'd done with her mother, Aloe slash Diane. I shook that sin aside quickly.

Bevolyn.

"Sister Sykes," I said.

"*Minister.*"

I didn't bother extending my hand. Didn't need it. My eyes *held* her.

"I see you're still holding something against me," I said.

"Something about you I don't"—she paused—"I shouldn't say, 'I don't like.' But. Well. I don't like something about you."

"You haven't tried," I shot back.

"Sure I have. But that nagging dislike is there."

I touched my chest, feigned hurt. She rolled her eyes.

"You enjoyed my joke," I said.

"No, I didn't," she lied.

"I saw you. You laughed."

Her eyes fluttered briefly. She smirked.

"Denying it?" I said.

"Yes, I am."

"Explain the laughter."

"I didn't laugh," she said. "I smiled."

"Same thing."

"Not exactly, Minister. I smiled because of what I'd told the girls." She turned to see them. They'd begun walking down the center aisle toward the vestibule. Afeni brought up the rear. Zelda moved next to Sela, her hands bounding about in great expression, gripping Sela's jacket sleeve every few seconds. Sela walked stiffly on, saying nothing. She was most definitely Bevolyn's sister.

It was just Bevolyn and I, then, alone at the front of the church.

"What did you tell the girls?" I asked her when she turned her gaze back to me.

I saw a spark of sadness ignite in her eyes.

"What?" I pressed.

"Told them I thought you were a fake. And…" Her lips turned up; cheeks, too. You couldn't exactly call it a smile. It was something, though.

"And?" I asked.

"I told them I thought you were a fake," she said. "And that you'd get up there and tell a joke."

"Oh."

"Yes, *Minister*. Oh. And you didn't disappoint. You have a blessed day."

She turned and walked away. I said nothing. Many words crossed my mind, though, but they wouldn't matter to her. She'd made her decision. I was a fake. I'd never be any more than that in her eyes. That hurt. I wanted to be more. Her approval meant almost as much as He's Sweet I Know's acceptance. She slinked down the aisle. I watched her go.

8

Bevolyn had a favorite T-shirt, tan-colored, the material thinning from overuse. On the front it read—Seven Days Without God. The reply on the back—Makes One Weak. The words were a message, a reminder, a compass of sorts, guiding her in the proper direction: to live a life pleasing unto the Lord, and to live that life *daily*.

But this week she'd veered off course. Last Sunday she'd moved from the altar, leaving Minister Path's eyes darkened by a shadow of sadness, her legs feeling unsteady as she walked down the aisle knowing the minister's shadowy gaze was at her back.

Fake.

What she'd called him.

Disappointment.

What she'd felt in herself, seeing how much her words had hurt him. And what had he done to her? What had he done to warrant her ire? Nothing.

The days since had moved slowly for Bevolyn.

Monday. Rinsing dirty dishes in the sink before placing them in the dishwasher. A habit Russell had long ago given up on breaking her of. "So wasteful," he'd told her numerous times, to no avail. Then, after the quick rinse of the dishes, Bevolyn, bent, placing cups on the top rack and plates on the bottom, her thoughts elsewhere—on the shadow that had darkened Minister Path's eyes. That dark, dark shadow. The hurt she'd caused him. And for what?

Tuesday. On her porch, purportedly reading a romance paperback, but stuck on the same sentence, unfocused, the quest for love on the pages mattering little. A black-headed, gray-and-white bodied Sabine's gull flying overhead toward Sandy Hook, the face-warming heat of an orange sun, and a tall glass of perfectly sweetened lemonade at an arm's reach—things Bevolyn usually appreciated—having no effect whatsoever.

Wednesday. Bevolyn searching for a can of the Allens' Southern style collard greens at Acme, something flashing through her as she traveled the unfamiliar aisles: a feeling of foolishness for choosing this Acme instead of her usual grocer, Pathmark. It had been her hope that avoiding that place, with its suggestive name, would ease her mind from thoughts of the minister. *Path*mark. Minister Path. It hadn't.

Thursday. The worst day of the week. Making love to Russell that night, attempting to get back in the groove with her husband. Their bedroom lit by a candle, Jamaica Spice incense perfuming the air as Teddy Pendergrass implored them to turn out the lights, which they'd done before his velvet caressed their ears. Their shadows undulating on the walls, Russell trying so hard to please Bevolyn: flicking his tongue, made tingly courtesy of a mentholated cough drop, across her clitoris, gripping her buttocks with firm hands, stroking his fist-hard penis in and out of her. But instead of ecstasy, sadness had found Bevolyn, had tracked her down. Her breathless release, her drawn-out moan, her fingernails biting into Russell's back—all of it, what she'd accused the new minister of being. Fake.

"Something was missing," Russell had said afterward.

She hadn't replied, but yes, something was definitely missing.

Then he'd grinned and said, "I know. Let's do it again and I'll show you."

She did it.

Faked it. Again.

After the second time, Russell drifted off into sleep, his soft snore fluttering his lips. Bevolyn had gone into the bathroom to shower. That way she could pretend she wasn't crying. That her mind wasn't doing funky things to her. That the week hadn't been seconds, minutes, hours, days, marked by thoughts of the new minister.

She prayed.

But Friday had turned out to be much of the same.

Now, it was Saturday night; tomorrow would be Sunday.

A new beginning. Another encounter with the minister.

Church wasn't the place for any thought that didn't encompass God or his son Jesus. And yet, during Reverend G.H. Walker's morning prayer, Bevolyn found herself thinking about the horrible dream she'd had last evening. The dream was like déjà vu, a scene of Bevolyn at church, Reverend Walker, yes, praying. In the dream, Bevolyn had squeezed her thighs tight together, balled her hands into fists, and tried to focus, with her head bowed and eyes closed, on Reverend's talk with God.

"We thank You, Lord, for the blessings seen and unseen, heard and unheard, that You have bestowed upon us," Walker had prayed.

Bevolyn moved her neck in circles, trying to chase away

the prickly feel of her skin that came courtesy of her fantasy man's lips traveling up her spine.

"You've been better to us than we've been to ourselves," Walker went on.

Bevolyn's panties dampened and her middle throbbed as the man kissed her the way she had always wanted a man to kiss her, so different from the way Russell did. Forcing his warm tongue in her mouth, swirling it with hers as they shared each other's flavor: mint for him, butterscotch for her.

Bevolyn bit into her lip, Reverend Walker's words drifting to the background as she fell deeper into her fantasy. The guilt gone as this imaginary lover did things to her that made her swoon. His hands fondling her breasts, making her nipples harden. His tongue licking at her earlobe. How did he know she was so sensitive there?

So many words she could use to describe him: erotic, stimulating, sensual.

And what she felt enjoying this fantasy of him: sinful, dirty, oooh…no use denying it—moved, shaken, satisfied.

She ran her fingers over the scar by the underside of his lip, bent and kissed it, then licked it, then kissed it again. She felt as if she were kissing and licking herself, for she had a similar scar on her lip. She hoped he hadn't felt the pain she'd felt when she got hers.

She unbuttoned his shirt, ran her hands across his chest, and touched her lips to his nipples. He moaned and gripped her by the shoulders.

She was falling. Falling. Real. The real thing. A trip to the shower afterward, to cry, unnecessary. Falling. The real thing.

Gasping for breath. Her eyes open. Everyone's eyes around her still closed. Her forehead moist with sweat, her thighs sticking together.

She was about to close her eyes again, pretending she was deep in prayer, but the church organ blared loud through the speakers, Mrs. Percival heavy-handed on the ivories.

The congregation around Bevolyn stood to its feet. She did the same, singing, "Standing in the Need of Prayer," as boisterously as the rest. She tried to ignore the material of her blouse matted by perspiration to her skin, the sweat pooling under her arms and on the back of her neck, her damp panties cutting into her waist and clinging to her middle. She cursed the scarred man for invading her thoughts. Where had he come from? Who'd given him the right to kidnap her mind? Fearful and upset now as the realization of what had happened hit, Bevolyn halted her singing and asked God for forgiveness and mercy, asked Him to disregard the indiscretion she'd committed in His house.

Headed to hell with gasoline drawers on. She was no different from Russell, even though she tried hard to deny it, to live a life that made it not so.

Sunday. A new beginning, turned into a new low.

"—forever and ever. Amen," Reverend Walker said now, during this real service.

Morning worship was over and Bevolyn hadn't even heard the message, couldn't tell a soul what Scripture was the basis for Reverend Walker's sermon. No, she'd spent the past two hours thinking about her dream. That horrible dream.

Upset with herself, Bevolyn quickly gathered her things and moved down the center aisle. She slowed, though, as she eyed Minister Path up ahead, the last person she needed to meet now. Should she turn around?

Alone, she wished Afeni or Sela were with her. Or Russell.

But Minister Path didn't move. He held his spot. Bevolyn decided to continue in his direction. Nothing to fear.

She held her head high as she neared him and tried to move past. He reached forward and gripped her arm.

"Are you okay, Sister Sykes?"

She glanced around; no one appeared to be watching them.

"Fine. Blessed. Why do you ask?"

"I noticed you during the service," Path admitted. He let his hand drop from her arm. "You looked a little out of it."

Embarrassed, Bevolyn shook her head, denying the physical something that had happened to her last night as she dreamed, and still held her in its clutches today. "Why were you looking at me during service, *Minister*?" she said. Going on the offensive.

Path shrugged his shoulders and concentrated a deep gaze on her. "I don't know," he said softly. "Where's Afeni? Your sister?" Changing the subject.

"Afeni is away," Bevolyn said. Visiting her birth mother, a fact Bevolyn, oddly, didn't like. "Sela is…I don't know where." Up to her usual flaky self. Uncommitted to making a connection with the Father.

"I saw the other woman that was with you last week, the one with the flowers pinned in her hair," Path said.

"Zelda. You did? I bet you were glad to see her. She's very beautiful." Beautiful, and kind, as far as Bevolyn could tell, and sincerely in search of answers. Zelda wouldn't find them with Sela as her friend; Sela wasn't anything but a great big weight that would hold Zelda back. Again, Bevolyn wondered how those two had ever become friends, wondered why she herself shut people off, why she had never had a friend like Zelda of her own. Shaking those thoughts aside, she continued. "Zelda. Very beautiful, huh, *Minister*? Bet you're hoping to get on your knees with her." She paused and then added, as an after-thought, "To pray of course." Why was she so hateful, so angry? For some reason Minister Path brought out the worst in Bevolyn. She couldn't fight the edge that came to her every time she was in his presence.

"She came in late," Path said, ignoring her innuendo. "Sat in the back. Left a bit early."

"I'm sorry I missed her," Bevolyn said, settling down. He hadn't taken the bait, hadn't come back at her. He'd taken the high road. She needed to, as well. "Zelda seems to be a good person. Not many of them left."

"What is it about me that you so dislike, Sister Sykes?" Path asked. Changing tracks again. A glutton for punishment, going in this direction.

Bevolyn simply smiled.

"I thought you'd be good to know," Path said. "Thought you'd be open to...friendship." He shrugged. "I guess I read you wrong, *Sister*."

"That you did."

"It's a shame," he went on. "I think we have much in common. Maybe I'm grasping, though."

"Definitely," Bevolyn said. "No *maybe*. I can't see anything we have in common."

"You're a daydreamer," Path said. "I saw you during service, off somewhere. I am, too. Just like that. A daydreamer."

Bevolyn didn't answer.

"We both love God," he continued.

She rolled her eyes, something she never did, except around him.

"Both have scars," he said. "Real and imagined, I would assume."

That caught her attention. Particularly after her erotic dream of last evening, the man in it, scarred. "Scars?" she asked, frowning.

Path nodded. "Yours by your mouth, small, almost unnoticeable. But *I* noticed." He pointed a hand toward her mouth. Then he touched his face. "Mine subtle as well, hidden by my eyebrow." He showed her the thin scar just above his left eye.

Bevolyn clutched her pocketbook and Bible to her chest, trying to settle herself, feeling her body trembling like a leaf on a tree. "I better get going," she managed.

"You're not staying for brunch and the afternoon service?" Path asked her.

Bevolyn shook her head. "Can't." She backed away from him, ignoring his voice calling after her, and moved outside. Once she'd descended the steps, she trotted to her car, needing to get away from this place, that man.

Both have scars. Real and imagined.

Bevolyn drove in a daze. Before long, her key was in the lock at her front door, her hand on the doorknob. But she didn't want to enter. Another beautiful day the Lord had given, an unseasonably cool Sunday afternoon in August. A strong breeze had kicked up just before the eleven A.M. service and lasted through the benediction. It beat down on her now as she paused on her porch. She closed her eyes and let the comforting air paint her face, lick at her ears, and finger through her hair. It felt like the touch of a lover, felt like her dream sequence becoming a reality. Her hand slipped from the doorknob. Had she unconsciously been fantasizing about Path in her dream? That couldn't be, could it? She'd never seen the scar in his eyebrow, didn't know it was there, had she?

A loud child's laughter broke Bevolyn's daydreaming. Just as Minister Path had said—Bevolyn, a daydreamer.

On the other side of the Way, she noticed the Edwardses—Stephen and Tammy—tying the laces on little Samuel's roller blades. Samuel could barely sit still, the excitement making him jittery, making him laugh.

The sight of the boy saddened Bevolyn, reminding her of the void in her life: children, something she and Russell had talked about at length when they were first married, a subject they seldom broached any longer. They had Afeni, but that wasn't the same. Actually, Afeni's presence made their childlessness worse. She was the reminder of where they, as a couple, had failed.

Bevolyn sighed and turned back to her door. She was about to twist the knob when she caught a glimpse of something black in her driveway. She moved to the edge of her porch and looked over the rail. Her sister Sela's Honda Civic was pushed up against Russell's SUV in the alley.

"What the heck?"

Bevolyn stomped to her door and tugged at the knob. Realizing she had to turn it, she did. The door clicked open. She pushed it in and retrieved her keys, stepped inside, and somehow found the strength to calmly ease the door shut behind her and tiptoe across the thick carpet.

Naked. In each other's arms. Her husband. Her sister. All Bevolyn could imagine as she took tentative steps down the hall that led from foyer to living room.

Russell wouldn't stoop that low. Would he? Sela wasn't that stupid and selfish. Was she? Was this payback, a lesson from on high, for the indiscretion Bevolyn had committed at church? Thinking about that dream instead of the Lord's message.

God, please don't do this to me, she found herself praying as she moved down the hall, hands gliding across the wall for support.

Bevolyn crinkled her nose. A strong scent harassed her nostrils as she moved further into her marital home, the scent pungent, sharp. She tried to place it. Was it the scent of sex, that lusty, hot odor? Her legs wobbled at the possibility. She pressed on.

As she neared the living room, she could hear voices.

Bevolyn paused, leaned against the wall, and steeled her legs for the remaining few feet. She deserved this. She had brought this further heartbreak into her life when she sat in church with her eyes closed and her head bowed, wicked thoughts swimming in her head like sharks looking to eat away at her soul. She fought for a breath, felt her chest tightening, sent up a quick prayer, and moved into the living room.

No Sela, no Russell. Television on. Women of various races, but one shape in common—voluptuous—walking across a stage in bikinis.

Bevolyn huffed and stomped from the living room. They were here somewhere. She paused at the steps. Bedroom.

Again, she prayed, and then climbed.

She heard their muffled voices as she reached the top. She gripped the banister and prayed again, like her fourth short prayer in the last five minutes. Each day in the life of a person of faith consists of many small prayers: at stoplights, during showers, before eating, at the top of the stairs.

She climbed the last step and came to the first door. Bedroom.

They weren't there.

She looked toward the bathroom and saw the door cracked, the light leaking into the hallway. She heard the continuous flow of water, Sela's voice, then Russell's voice, then mingled laughter.

Bevolyn moved toward the door and softly pushed it in. Inside, the sink faucet was running. The medicine cabinet's mirror was fogged. One of them had fingered in

Highway to Heaven in the blur of the mirror. Russell was off to the side, his back to Bevolyn. Sela hunkered over the sink, her back to Bevolyn, too. Both of them were clothed, thank God.

"What's going on with you two?" Bevolyn blurted.

Russell wheeled. Sela calmly turned.

"Hey, Sis," Sela said as a slow smile broke out across her face.

"What's happening?" Bevolyn asked. Her gaze dashed to the running sink water, the mound of what looked like potting soil on the sink counter, and the box cutter in Sela's hand.

"Prepping for a little smoke," Sela said. Her voice was steady. She held up a crinkled swath of brown paper, cigar skin. "Want a toke when I finish this? I burned earlier and Russell tried to act as if he didn't want to get down. But now he does. So off again I go."

"In my bathroom?" Bevolyn said.

"Needed the steam." Sela nodded her head to the running faucet. "This cigar paper is dry as wood. I might have to switch up brands or something. I can't be having this."

Bevolyn sighed and looked to her husband. His shoulders immediately sagged, and his head dropped.

"You know how I feel about tobacco," she told Russell. He didn't look up.

"Not tobacco," Sela offered. "Weed. Mary-Juana. Greenery."

Bevolyn focused her gaze on Russell still. "Tell me this isn't so, Russell."

"Oh, it's so," Sela said. "And I'm hooking it up good, too. Sealing it with honey. Makes it sweet. The smoke is hard that way, though. But what the heck."

Bevolyn looked at her sister. "Leave. Take your *greenery* with you."

Sela eyed Bevolyn and saw something that backed her down.

"Oh, I'm taking it, don't you worry," she replied. She quickly gathered her items—the cigar, the tobacco innards, her box cutter, her weed—and dropped them into a big sandwich bag. She turned to Russell. "We'll get your head up some other time."

Then she turned to Bevolyn. "You need some cats and a broom. Witch."

"Leave," Bevolyn repeated through clenched teeth.

"You lucky you didn't come up in here and find him sticking his thing in me. Lucky I wouldn't get down like that." Sela paused. "That I wouldn't do you like that. Just a little harmless smoke, that's all, and you're tripping like this."

"Get out!"

"Nuh uh, no, you didn't just yell at me," Sela said.

Bevolyn balled her hand into a fist and moved toward Sela.

Sela put a hand up. "Leaving." And she left.

"What if Afeni had been with me, Russell?" Bevolyn asked when she heard the door slam downstairs.

He didn't answer. The Honda fired up in the driveway below the bathroom's window, that busted muffler cranking loud.

"You can't go to church but you can smoke dope, Russell?"

"Weed is hardly dope," he ventured. "And why are you home? Thought you were staying for afternoon service."

The Honda backed out of the driveway, the muffler still cranking loud, then softer, then invisible to the ear.

"Why are you home?" Russell repeated.

Bevolyn then remembered the television screen, the volume down low, the women prancing across a stage wearing little more than skimpy bikinis. "What was that crap on the TV downstairs, Russell?"

"Boxing," he said.

"Women boxing in bikinis? Funny, I didn't see them wearing any boxing gloves. Wearing hardly anything as a fact."

"Oh." His eyes flashed something. "They're having a competition of the ring card girls between bouts."

"You like watching that stuff?" Bevolyn asked. Smoking. Naked women prancing around on television. The women, busty, a mix of Asians, Caucasians, Latinas, and Blacks—a darn menagerie—infuriating. "You like that stuff?" Bevolyn repeated, her voice notched up a bit more. She shook her head and sighed. "There is so much about you that disgusts me. I can't believe I married you."

"I can't believe that I've *stayed* married to you," Russell shot back angrily.

Bevolyn was quiet.

"Say something to that?" Russell challenged her.

"Explain all of this, Russell," Bevolyn whispered.

"I don't know that I can," he said.

"Back in the doghouse, buddy," Bevolyn said. She plopped down on the toilet, took off her heels, tossed them halfway across the bathroom's linoleum floor, and then massaged her feet.

"I'm sorry," Russell said.

"Why are you home? No pressing work that you had to do with Rachel? You didn't have any papers to read today…at the bank?" Bevolyn dropped her foot from her grasp and let it hit the floor.

"No," Russell said. "Not today, for a change."

"I can't believe I'm in this. Through sickness and through health," Bevolyn said. "Richer or for poorer."

Russell looked at Bevolyn. "What would worry you

more? Losing me, or having the church folk gossip about your divorce?"

Bevolyn opened her mouth to say something. Nothing came out.

Russell nodded. "Thanks a lot, Bevolyn. Thanks."

"I've been understanding, about many things, Russell. You *know* that."

"Don't kid yourself, Bevolyn," he spat. "You've been understanding because you'd be a hypocrite not to."

She didn't reply.

"Hardly ever give me sex," Russell continued. "It's so good when we do it; I don't know why you cut us both out of that pleasure."

If only he knew.

"All of this is about sex," Bevolyn said. "Go on out there on the couch and watch your naked television whores. Have all the sex you want. I'll even bring you the cocoa butter lotion."

Russell made a turn to leave but turned back, fuming. "See. Totally condescending and cold toward me. I can't talk to you. Can't touch you."

"Sex again."

"Brought that child up in our house to…" He threw his hands up, sighed, and plopped down on the lip of the bathtub, squeezing his eyes shut tight.

Bevolyn sat quiet and still.

Russell looked up after a moment. "Nothing to say?"

Bevolyn shrugged.

He got up and left. Bevolyn let him go.

Rachel Sosa leaned against the frame of Russell's idling SUV in the parking lot of their office complex. She was slightly out of breath, having rushed, after Russell's earlier call, to arrive at the building in the thirty minutes he'd asked for. "Okay," she said, "What's the big emergency? And why are you out here looking like Will Smith and Martin Lawrence doing a stakeout in *Bad Boys*?"

"Get in," Russell told her.

"In?"

"Going for a ride," he said.

"A ride? You do know the computers, files, and other odds and ends we use to conduct business are in that building?" She nodded toward the complex behind them.

Russell clicked the power lock button, unlocking the SUV. He also hit the power window button, rolling his driver side window up, leaving Rachel standing outside. She got the hint, moved around the back of the SUV, opened the passenger side door, and got in.

"Somebody has PMS," she said as she eased inside and clicked herself in the seat belt. "Predictable Male Stupidity. So, where we headed?"

Russell looked at her. "Wherever you want to, Ray." The tone of his voice was rich, deep, not his usual. Isaac Hayes getting his mack game on.

Rachel cocked her head. A smile darted across her face. "Let me guess. Fight with wifey?"

Russell touched his neck in the front, massaged it, and looked away from Rachel. A grimace contorted his features. "Pretty much, yeah, I'd say so."

"Your marriage isn't as strong and happy as you make it out to be, is it?"

Russell continued to look away, surveying the empty lot, the cars blurring by on the highway. A minivan passed and he imagined the husband, wife, and two-point-five kids headed to some family gathering. His stomach churned. "No, it isn't," he said, so softly Rachel had to strain to hear it.

"I knew it," she said, exuberantly, then noticing Russell's dour expression, quieting some to add, "How long? Your problems. Recent?"

"Years," Russell admitted.

"Well, okay now," Rachel said in surprise. The inflection of those three words made them a short song.

"Yeah," was Russell's simple reply.

They sat quiet for a bit.

"I'm really sorry," Rachel said after some time had passed.

"You are?"

"Yeah. I mean, I know I make plays on you all the time, but, well, it's hard to explain."

"Try to," Russell said, his tone flat.

Rachel sank her body into the plush leather seat. "You're a good brother, boss. I see that. You're handsome, sexy, all of that. You've just never seemed married to me."

"I don't follow," Russell said.

"Hard to explain," Rachel said. She repositioned herself. "Okay. Check this. Some married guys have that aura of just like being strictly family men. You don't have that. You *seem* single to me. Sad almost. All the hours you spend at the office, always seemed like it was an escape to me. Refuge, you know?"

"Probably was, Ray," Russell said.

"So what happened? You said, 'years.' "

Russell swallowed. "We had a problem early in our marriage. I never quite settled that. I compounded the problem a few years later. We've been a squeaky wheel for as long as I can remember, to be honest. Our entire marriage, really."

"Wow," all Rachel could say.

"Can we go now?" Russell asked. "I need to get somewhere with you."

Rachel frowned. "You love your wife, boss? I mean, problems aside, you love her?"

"Define love," Russell said bitterly.

Now Rachel looked off, her gaze drifting. "Love is hurt, boss. You look at your wife sometimes, when things are going well, and you hurt because you can't hold her, make love to her, every moment of the day. You look at her sometimes, when things *aren't* going well, and you hurt because you won't hold her, make love to her, and are too stubborn to settle the disagreement. Hurt, boss. Love."

"Yeah," Russell said, sadly. "I love her."

Rachel unbuckled her seat belt, reached over, and touched Russell's knee. He looked at her hand, then her. Her eyes were pure liquid. He could drink them. She smiled in response to his wanting look, and his stomach did flips. He loved Bevolyn, yes, but Bevolyn wasn't returning the emotion. Now, Rachel, he lusted for her, and she'd made it clear, more times than Carter had liver pills, that she was down for whatever. So why had she unbuckled her seat belt?

"I'm gonna fall back this time, boss. But let's make things clear. I like you, a lot. An awful lot. That's no secret. And if you come to me like this again, tail between your legs, ready to jump my bones, it's going to be an archaeological dig, for sure. Lotta bone jumping. And—trust me on this—your marriage *will not survive that.* You make sure you're ready for that if you come my way again. Okay?"

Rachel didn't wait for him to answer. Instead, she eased out of the SUV, walked across the front of it, and headed toward her compact car. Russell watched the sway of her hips as she moved. He thought about what she said, equating love to hurt. He was glad she'd been wise and hadn't let him further damage his marriage. He tapped the steering wheel and made a promise he'd never get himself in this kind of predicament again.

He watched her slide into her car, saw her skirt hitch

up, her golden leg visible for one quick moment. *Promise,* he told himself a second time, *never to get in this predicament again.*

He drove off knowing promises were often broken.

Knowing that love, indeed, was hurt.

Knowing plenty of hurt remained for him and Bevolyn. Plenty.

9

I flanked Reverend Walker as we walked down the hospital's corridor strutting shoulder to shoulder, our heads held high, toward a mission placed upon us by From Whom All Blessings Flow. Like most hospitals, this one had that antiseptic smell, too-bright lights, and a mixture of bustling nurses and aides and techs versus muted family members of the sick and shut-in. One such family member, a worn-looking black woman who I imagined got Social Security checks direct-deposited into her bank account, stood outside a room with a man I presumed to be her son consoling her.

"He doesn't know you," the son told her. "Don't mind the things he says. It's the Alzheimer's talking."

"Washed crap stains out that Negro's drawers for forty-three years," I heard the woman say. "He conveniently stopped knowing me once he started wearing diapers."

I shook my head. Love was a bee-eye-tee-see-aitch with PMS twenty-four seven, three sixty-five. The heat from it could melt metal, was murder on ice cream milkshakes. And yet, a part of me still wanted love, the love of a special woman, a woman who would love me in return.

"Brother Braxton is having a hard time with this," Reverend Walker told me as we moved on.

"How old is his wife?"

"Thirty-three."

I shook my head. "Too young."

"Even if she were one hundred and thirty-three, it'd be too young," Walker replied, his eyes glazing already.

His deceased wife. Forever on his mind.

"Doctors offer her no hope?" I asked.

"In the hands of the Lord," Walker stated. "Best place to be, too. He can fix what the doctors can't."

Cancer of the brain that had spread to other organs in Brother Braxton's young wife. God would have to *fix* Brother Braxton, I found myself thinking. Prepare him for the challenges of being a widower. Not that I doubted He's Sweet I Know. If He decided to spare Braxton's wife, she'd be singing in the choir again. I just didn't think He'd brought them this far, through all this, for a miraculous cure to occur. No. This was one of He's Sweet I Know's lessons, a test of Brother Braxton's faith. I hoped he was up for the challenge. It was hard when it happened. Very hard. This much I knew.

"I hope something we say to Brother Braxton helps," I told Reverend Walker.

"Might," he said. "Might. You never know. You never know."

We moved on, silent the rest of the way. I had the feeling that even if I'd said something to Reverend Walker, he wouldn't have replied. His focus, I could see, was most clearly on his dearly departed wife.

We arrived finally at the hospital room of Brother Braxton's wife.

It was a single occupancy unit at the end of the hall. A placard with Sandra Braxton's initials—S.B.—rested in a clear plastic casing that hung by the room number. Reverend and I paused outside of the room gathering our wits. I considered what my mentor, good ol' Luck, had told me about grief. "It's hard to lose someone," he'd said. "Harder because we don't focus on the right thing. We don't focus hard enough on the things they did, but rather on the things they didn't. The things they never will. Young breed, when you lose someone, focus on what they did, you hear?"

I'd nodded. Thought about my mother smoking her cigarettes in the bathroom. Making my brother and me call her Miss Ma'am. The look in her eyes before her last few breaths. Love. The disappointment from not being Lady Day or Ella was gone from her eyes during those final moments. The happiness of being the mother to two boys was there instead. And she knew in those last moments she'd soon reunite with one of her boys for all of eternity. She'd be singing, "He's Sweet I Know" to my brother forever. I could see the expectation in her face. I stood over her that day, just a few before I'd stand over her again, numb, watching her heart rate plummet on a heart monitor. And for a brief moment, I wanted to go with her and reunite with my brother, too.

Luck was dead-on, though. I was glad of those things Miss Ma'am had done. The things she hadn't done, I accepted, were things He's Sweet I Know had never intended for her to do.

I thought of toy trains, G.I. Joe action figures, Transformers. Then, a silver-dollar-size hole that bled despite my fingers pressed against it. My brother. I was mostly glad for the things he'd done. Sad, though, for the things he never got the chance to do. He was too young when he left. Much too young.

I was glad the both of them didn't see what I eventually became.

Hadn't seen me handcuffed and humiliated.

Hadn't seen the tight jaw of that judge that looked down on me before announcing my sentence.

Hadn't seen me vomit and my eyes stung by tears in the back of the gray bus as it transported me to prison.

"You go on and lead," Reverend Walker said, breaking my thoughts outside Sandra Braxton's hospital room. His voice jarred me. I'd been so deep in thought.

"Lead?" I asked.

He touched my shoulder. "I'm right behind you."

I paused and said aloud, "God pass something down from on high to help this brother. Help his wife."

"That's right," Walker said. "Pass something down to help us."

Us, he'd said. I took notice of that.

Then I walked in. And just as quickly forgot about Brother Braxton and his troubles. Forgot the frail woman with the bald scalp, surgical staples where long black hair once was. Reverend Walker had shown me a picture of Sister Braxton. She'd had hair that would make an Indian proud, a thick ponytail knot of it falling past her shoulders. But I forgot all of that as I stepped in the room. I took one quick glance at Sister Braxton in the hospital bed. That's all I gave her.

Then I focused my eyes on the woman standing at the foot of the bed.

Bevolyn Sykes. Clad in a beige-colored skirt that began just above her knees and hugged her round behind like a mother clutching her however-many-pounds-and-ounces of newborn. She also had on a white blouse. I could see the imprint of her nipples in the material. Then I realized for the first time that the air was frigid and thanked the Alpha and Omega that it was.

I stood just steps inside the room, quiet, unannounced. Reverend Walker was by the entrance behind me, not pressing me to move forward.

"I have my moments of wanting to die with her," Brother Braxton told Bevolyn. She frowned and shook her head. He went on, "But I'm gonna do my best to let this go and let God do what it is He needs to do."

"That's for the best," Bevolyn said.

I licked my lips. Her voice was more beautiful than the praise songs of Psalms.

"So much I wish I could tell her," Braxton said of his wife who lay before him in a coma. He rubbed his wife's silent fingers. His voice didn't have the rich baritone I'd known from church, was bereft of its usual weight and vigor. "So many things I did that I wish I could take back," he added. "The stupid little arguments. Football games that I watched instead of holding her."

Bevolyn wiped at her eyes. Instinctively I touched mine as well.

Braxton leaned over his wife. "All those times, baby, I swore I'd gotten everything on your list and came home from the grocery store with items missing. I'd blow you off when you asked me to go back. If you come out of this I swear…" He choked on his words and slumped his head against his wife's lap. Bevolyn moved around the bed and patted his back.

Braxton gathered himself and turned to Bevolyn. "You're married, Sister Sykes. Can you imagine your husband gone?"

I noticed her back stiffen. She shot up like a jack-in-the-box. She didn't say anything, though.

"I shouldn't have asked you that; it's bad karma to even

think about it," Braxton said. He reached a hand forward in apology. Bevolyn took it. He told her, "I'm sorry. I just want to know how I'm going to survive this."

I moved forward. "I'll tell you something I've never shared with anyone," came out of my mouth. Call it divine intervention. I hadn't said those words as much as relayed them. He's Sweet I Know was working through me.

Brother Braxton and Bevolyn turned to me. Braxton smiled and offered a hand. Bevolyn moved past me and found herself a spot on the other side of the bed. I looked at her. She held my stare for a moment before turning away.

I peeked over my shoulder. Reverend Walker hadn't come in behind me. I imagined him down in the lobby, shaking and crying, remembering his love who had slipped away. I prayed he was thinking of the things they'd done and not the things they never would.

"What were you saying, Minister Path?" Braxton asked me.

"What?" I still hadn't reconciled my new title. Minister.

"About something you've never told anyone before?"

I cleared my throat, moved over by Braxton's side, and looked down on his wife. The cliché is to say she looked as if she were sleeping, and she did, but add to that she also looked as if she were dreaming, about her husband, their children, God. That's how pleasant her face was despite the sunken eyes, protruding cheekbones, the effects of the cancer eating her away. I looked at Brother Braxton. "May I touch her?"

" 'Course, Minister Path."

I walked my fingers to her lips and traced the outline around them. "Think about the first time you kissed," I told Braxton.

He closed his eyes He looked as if *he* were now in a coma, sleeping and dreaming.

I looked toward Bevolyn. She had her eyes squinted, her head at an inquisitive angle, cocked to the side like a curious dog.

I turned my focus back to Braxton.

"I lost my brother when I was just twelve," I said as I reached out to Brother Braxton's hand. He gripped it tight. "He hadn't yet turned ten. Loved toy trains. G.I. Joe. Transformers."

I took a breath.

I went on. From Whom All Blessings Flow pushed me on. "Gun accident. I was the one that found him. Hole in his chest. Blood seeping through. I didn't know what to do. I moved to him. He was still breathing. He looked up at me and smiled. His teeth and gums were red, looked like he'd been drinking Kool-Aid." I paused to collect my thoughts. Think through where I was headed, if I wanted to open the door to the room I knew was dark, no light switch or light bulbs anywhere inside.

Braxton's tight grip answered my internal questions. I had to go on.

"I bent down and pressed my fingers over the hole in my brother's chest, Brother Braxton." I coughed away a crumb of grief that had caught in my throat as I told Brother Braxton of my worst moment in a life of worst moments. "My brother found the strength to raise his arm. Put his hand over top of mine. Both of our hands on his chest."

"Praise the Lord," Brother Braxton replied.

"I knew he wasn't gonna make it. I was thinking about how I would. How I would make it without my brother."

"Go on, Minister. Go on," Brother Braxton implored me.

I closed my eyes.

"My brother said something. His voice was weak at that point. I bent closer to his ear, asked him to repeat it if he could. He said, 'AC.' I knew what he meant. Apollo Creed. *Rocky IV* was about to come out that weekend. We'd been talking all week about going to see it together. He was telling me to keep on keeping on. For him. Go see Rocky IV. And I did." I cleared something else from my throat. "You can find strength, Brother Braxton, in even the most trying times if you lean on the Lord. He was gracious enough to share your loved one with you. This wonderful person He created. And He didn't hoard them. He shared them. Remember that. Thank Him for that. Rejoice in that."

"I know it, Minister Path. I know it," Brother Braxton said. He released my grip and moved as close as he could to his wife. I left him whispering in her ear. I moved out into the hallway and started walking, past medicine carts, the nurse's station, a hallway loaded down with broken wheelchairs. Walking. Walking. Probably mumbling to myself as well.

"Minister Path?"

I turned to her voice. Sweet, soft, musical. "Yes, Sister Sykes?"

She was slightly out of breath from chasing after me. "Thought you might like this," she said, handing me a Kleenex.

"For what?"

"You're crying."

"What?" I touched my face. Wet. I hadn't even known. I took her Kleenex and thanked her as I dabbed at my eyes.

"That was nice," she said, "the things you said in there."

"Just words on my heart."

"I might have misread you," she admitted. "I was hard

on you earlier today, at church. Seems you have a pretty good heart."

"Would love to share it with you," I ventured. "God says, 'freely ye have received, freely give.' I think we have something we can offer one another. A sharing of spirits."

She touched the second finger on her left hand, twirled her wedding ring. Didn't say anything.

"I know we didn't get off on the best of terms, Sister Sykes, but—"

"Sixteen years, my husband and I," she cut me off.

"Haven't seen him in church with you," I said back.

She grimaced and I immediately felt bad for that low blow.

"Look," I told her, "I don't want to upset you. I'd like to get to know you, on the up-and-up. You seem like a good person to know."

"The way you look at me, Minister." She shook her head.

"You're an attractive woman: I admit it. But I respect that you're married. If *you* respect it."

"I do," she said.

"Then it'd just be two Christian soldiers trying to develop strategy for the war."

"Can't see myself in a ditch with you, Minister."

"Why'd you chase me down, Sister Sykes? For this? You want to lie to yourself, pretend you're so happy in your marriage and that you don't feel anything towards me, fine. Suit yourself. But I know the truth. I see it in your eyes when you look at me." I was grasping. Truthfully, I didn't know much about her marriage. I knew her husband didn't come to church with her. For a faithful sister like Bevolyn, I assumed this had to be a source of discontent in their marriage. And the thing about seeing some kind of desire for me in her eyes, well, I did. Maybe it was a strong dose of hope on my part. Maybe it was real. I couldn't say.

"That's more like it," she said. "Allow that pompousness to shine. All the women want the handsome new minister."

I smiled. "I'm handsome, eh?"

"My sister thinks so."

"Sela?"

"Only sister I have."

"But you don't think so?" I asked her.

"I won't go into that."

"You answered my question by not answering it."

"Sure I did," she said.

"Sure."

"I knew I made a mistake coming out here," she huffed. "Knew you were going to take this somewhere it didn't need to go." She started to backtrack and turned to move away.

"Sister Sykes?"

She wheeled to face me. "What?"

"You think I can have your sister Sela's number? Or give you mine to give her. I'd like to share my good heart with someone open to receiving it."

I wanted her jealous.

She paused, what I'd hoped for, and opened her pocketbook. She pulled out a pad and pen, uncapped the pen, scribbled on the pad and handed me a slip of paper with her sister's name and phone number on it. This response hadn't been part of my hope.

Still, I took it. "Thanks."

"You two deserve one another," she said. "Good luck."

She moved off with extra sway in her hips, the sashay, beauty, and hypnotic effect of her walk unexplainable. Unexplainable that one woman could have all that perfection. Unexplainable, like feeding thousands with a few loaves of bread and some small fish.

I started to follow her. She kept on. I kept on. She turned the corner and walked down the corridor to Sister Braxton's room. I turned the corner and walked that same corridor.

I didn't know what I would do, or why I was following.

When Bevolyn reached the door of Sister Braxton's room, she turned back to me briefly. She knew I'd followed. I could see the tightness of her jaw, the fire in her eyes. She shook her head and moved inside.

Jealous after all.

I pocketed the slip of paper with Sela's number on it, turned, and walked back to go find Reverend Walker. Okay, I had a hand to play. I'd call her sister. But what would I say to Sela when I called? And what would that play do except complicate this already-complicated situation?

I knew then, I needed to pray.

10

There it was: the stand, marble top and oak wood body. Resting on it, the telephone. Bevolyn had passed it several times, stolen shy glances in its direction, even moved a few steps that way a couple of times, but hadn't gone all the way, hadn't made that final commitment. Hadn't picked up the phone and dialed the digits that would connect her to the person who could end her personal torment. No, she'd quickly turned, pretended she needed something off the bookcase built in the wall. That Toni Morrison novel she'd yet to read, though she'd had it for five years. Or that Anne Rice novel she'd put down when she came to the first sex scene. After reading the sex scene, though.

Bevolyn stopped now, stood in the center of the living room, a feathered duster in hand that she wouldn't use, and looked at it again. The stand, marble top and oak wood body. Resting on it, the telephone. She took a deep breath and tossed the duster on the couch. She moved toward it. The stand, marble top and oak wood body. Resting on it, the telephone.

Hands shaking, she picked up the phone receiver and quickly dialed. After a few rings, a voice on the other end flooded her ears.

"What do you want, Bev?"

Bevolyn paused.

"I've got Caller ID. I know it's you," the voice said. "Say something or I'm hanging up."

"I was rough on you," Bevolyn said.

"Only way you know to be," was the reply from the other end.

"Let me finish," Bevolyn said. "I'm trying."

"An apology this stubborn coming out isn't really an apology, Bev."

"I'm sorry," Bevolyn said. "I was hurt. Confused. I want the best for you. I do."

"I know it." Soft, understanding.

"So I'm sorry, Sela. Okay?"

"Okay." Sela's smile came through in her voice.

"So what's going on?"

"Nothing," Sela said. "Thinking about a lot of things. I've got some heavy thoughts on my mind."

"Anything you want to talk about?"

"Nuh uh."

"I'm here if you ever do," Bevolyn said.

Sela repeated, "Nuh uh."

Awkward silence.

Then Sela. "You know, I owe you an apology, too. I shouldn't have brought the smoke into your home. Or offered it to your husband. I hope I haven't damaged things further between you two."

"Further?"

"Come on, Bev."

"We're fine," Bevolyn snapped.

Sela nodded on her end. "Right. Okay. You're fine. But anyway, I'm sorry, like I said."

"It's time for you to center yourself. Move on to better things." Bevolyn cleared her throat. "I passed your number along to the pastor this afternoon. He—he hasn't called yet, has he?" The real reason she'd called—needing that information, needing it so badly.

"Come on, Bev," Sela whined. "Why would you do that? Reverend Walker's an all right man, I guess. Of the cloth and all that. But dating him? Nuh uh."

Bevolyn laughed. "You're being silly. I'm talking about Minister Path."

"Minister Path? Oh." Sela paused. "I thought *you'd* go in that direction. The looks that passed between you two."

"Cut it, Sela. You know better than that. You know me."

Sela said, "Yes. I do know you."

Silence again.

"He probably won't call you, anyway," Bevolyn said after a while.

"And why is that?"

Bevolyn smirked. "I wouldn't exactly say you were his ideal type."

"You know him so much," Sela said. "What, are *you* more his type?"

"Me?" Bevolyn pointed at herself even though Sela couldn't see the gesture. "I wouldn't know. But guessing, I'd say yes. I would be more Minister Path's type."

"Well, we'll just have to wait and see," Sela fumed. "See if he calls me. See if in fact I am his type. I'll be sure and give you all the details. I'm sure you're dying to know them. Buh-bye."

"Sela."

Click.

She'd hung up.

Bevolyn slammed the phone down in its cradle, sighed, and ran her fingers through her hair.

"Minister Path."

Startled, Bevolyn turned to the deep voice: Russell standing at the edge of the room.

"Russell," Bevolyn said. "God, you scared me. When did you get back in? How long have you been standing there?"

Russell smiled. A smirk, really. "Somehow I knew you were going to say that. A line out of a bad book or a weak movie." He deepened his look. "I've been standing here long enough." He thought of Rachel's words from earlier: love is hurt. He thought of the crumb of conversation he'd heard from his wife on the phone. She seemed overly concerned with what was happening with the new minister. Love is hurt, indeed.

"That was Sela," Bevolyn offered.

"I gathered."

"I wanted to apologize to her for earlier. So I called her."

"Sure," Russell said. "I gathered."

Bevolyn stood quiet.

"Minister Path," Russell said again.

"What about him?"

"Forget it," he said. "Christian woman."

After a long pause, Bevolyn weakly shot back, "You doubt my faith?"

"No," Russell said, "I believe you're very faithful to what you believe in."

"Like our marriage."

He shook his head. "Too late for this. I'm turning in."

Bevolyn let him go.

11

Seconds.

All the time it takes a life to move from an unthinkable good to an unimaginable bad.

Luck had schooled me on the thin line that separated us all from life-altering tragedy, had told me the importance, with this realization hanging over our heads like a stratus cloud graying the sky, of finding our spiritual grounding in He's Sweet I Know. When those planes crashed into the World Trade Towers, Luck had seen me at the edge of the rec room, my eyes tearing, and mouthed, "God, young breed," while pressing a finger to his temple.

I'd quickly left the rec room and headed back to my cell. One of the "keeplock" inmates reached a hand through the bars of his six-by-nine as I traveled that corridor in a daze. Keeplock inmates are the ones on disciplinary restriction. They'd be in the Hole, the Box, Solitary Confinement—what you always see in movies— if there were space. But truthfully, Solitary was overcrowded. So keeplock inmates stayed with the general population, but locked in their cells, except for one mandatory hour allowed out per day.

This particular keeplock, a man by the name of Sandpaper—everybody in prison had nicknames—doing his bid for a botched armed robbery that had turned to murder in the first degree, gestured me aside.

"What's all the commotion out there, Juice?" Juice, my nickname to some, because I drank as many glasses of the stuff as they allowed during morning chow. And, to my dislike, because I had one of those big 'ol O.J. Simpson heads.

"Up in New York City. They knocked down the World Trade Towers," I stammered. "Flew commercial airplanes into them. Both of the Towers fell. It was horrible, Sandpaper. People jumping from their windows because the heat of the fire was so overwhelming. All those people… gone."

"Who they did this?" he asked, his voice notched up, his knuckles whitened by his hard grip on the bars.

"Terrorists," I told him. "Some Afghanistan group, they're saying."

"Damn, what we gone do?"

I thought about Luck and all his lessons. For the first time one of his lessons had truly hit home, truly moved me. I knew where I was headed: to my six-by-nine. I'd get on my knees inside and tent my hands, close my eyes and pray.

"Juice?"

"What?"

"What we gone do?" His eyes were like mine, wet. People want to believe that inmates are cold, calculated, and unfeeling. Some are. But most, like Sandpaper and me, feel. Feel too much, in fact.

I touched my temple and mouthed, "God, Sandpaper," and continued up the corridor, Sandpaper's guttural cries behind me in rhythm with my steps.

I tucked the lesson of From Whom All Blessings Flow's

importance during trying times, as I did all Luck's lessons, away for a day I'd need it.

This day, I'd need it.

It started nicely, with me fantasizing about Bevolyn.

I'd tapped the green and beige bottle against the palm of my hand, popped the top, and squeezed out a generous amount of scented shampoo. Bevolyn smiled as the water from the shower head kissed her naked body, lapping at her brown skin with a fierceness I could understand. I was more than jealous of that H2O. You don't even know.

I placed the shampoo bottle back in the hanging organizer and moved forward in the slick-floored shower enclosure, rubbing my hands together, a thick white lather coming to life in my palms. Bevolyn smiled and my heart responded, beating more wildly than my first moments in prison, when I learned firsthand what a cavity search was.

When I reached her, I massaged the shampoo into her soaking wet hair. She purred and moaned. I rubbed a bit harder. Bevolyn oohed and ahed as my fingers tapped out a melody as sweet as any that Ray Charles, God bless his soul, ever played.

"Let it sit for a few minutes," I told her.

"Kiss me," she said.

I did. A soft touch of my mouth to hers, though, was not enough for her. She spread her lips, pulled me forward by the waist, and wrestled my tongue inside her mouth. She tasted like the chocolate bar she'd eaten earlier. I prayed I didn't taste like the shrimp fried rice I'd eaten. That wouldn't be a good look.

She broke the kiss moments later. "Rinse me."

I did, running the water through her hair with the steady hands and care of a surgeon. I was ready to apply a palm of conditioner, but she took me by the waist again, pulled me as close to her as I could get, and looked up at me with those hypnotizing, pretty brown eyes.

"Ever made love in the shower?" she asked.

"No," I said. My penis hardened at the thought, throbbed as sprinkles of water fell on Bevolyn and dripped down her naked body.

"Thought about it?" she asked.

"Not until just now," I told her. "But now I'm thinking about it a lot."

She smiled, turned her back to me, and bent forward, her butt a perfectly round globe that I wanted so desperately to explore. The back shot of her folds down there made my knees weak. She was a shaver, for only a wispy spray of hair covered those lips. I wanted to kiss them, stick my tongue inside them, just as I'd done with the lips of her mouth minutes before.

She peered over her shoulder and smiled. "Are you going to take this or what?" She wiggled her backside as she said the word *this*.

She didn't have to ask me twice. I moved to her and slid myself inside. I didn't hesitate at this. Even a blind man could see that she was moist, wet, and more than ready. Her body tightened at first, her sex a tight fist around me. Then she made a noise that gratified my ego: a soft, throaty moan. And then she slackened, her body losing its rigidity, taking in my thrusts. She moved her hips in rhythm, gyrating, her firm and round bottom slapping against my thighs. I did my best to follow her lead. Then I used a technique I once thought I'd originated, to learn later in a very informative *Men's Health* article, I hadn't. I gave her the tip of my penis and maybe an inch more, then pulled it out, but not all the way. Tip and inch. Out. Then, hard, gave her the entire shaft. Alternated a little. Then a lot. Women loved it. That small poke of the tip turned them greedy for the full inches.

"Ooh," she grunted. "Damn it to hell!"

I repeated my magic.

We slipped despite the bath mat. She grabbed the towel bar. I trusted her; Didn't grab anything myself. Well, her waist, but that's all. No, I left her the task of keeping both of us on our feet. I kept up my stroke. Only a dumb man doesn't know that it's all about the stroke. Lose it, you lose her.

So I concentrated on my rhythm. Tip and inch. Out. Tip and inch. Out. Then, hard, the entire thing.

"Ooh, baby," she moaned. "Keep doing what you're doing when you do that."

I smiled. I had her speaking in tongues, or as close to it as I'd ever probably come. Men like to think that we could DESTROY a woman with our magic stick. My brethren on the inside were forever looking at women on the tube or in magazines and bragging on how much damage they'd inflict on the woman in question if given the chance.

I'd break her back.

I'd kill that.

I'd put dents in her spine, have her lookin' like Freddy Sanford's truck.

Man, I'd get all up in her rib.

I'd heard it all. The truth is, it took an extraordinary mix of skill and plain old physical chemistry between the two puzzle pieces for a woman's toes to curl.

Bevolyn and I, we had it. I grabbed her breasts and massaged them as I plunged into her. The nipples felt like small stones in my hands. There was an extra bit of wiggle in her motions as my hands glided across her breasts.

Tip and inch. Out. Tip and inch. Out. Then, hard, the…

The phone rang, cutting into my daydream like a test from the Emergency Broadcasting System. I'd told Bevolyn I was a daydreamer. I wasn't cowdunging.

I quickly wiped the cocoa butter lotion from my hands onto my thighs and pulled my pants up from my ankles. My belt clacked loudly. I wiped my hands on my pants again for good measure and moved to pick up the receiver. Maybe Sela was returning the message I'd left her earlier. We'd been playing phone tag for over a week. My fingers shook at the possibility. I didn't know how I would speak to her knowing I'd just wiped my hands clean of cocoa butter lotion and pulled up my pants, masturbating as I fantasized of her sister.

"Hello?"

"The reverend has been hospitalized," were the words from the voice on the other end.

It wasn't Sela, which was good.

"Deacon Meeks?" I asked.

"Yes, it's me, Minister Path."

"What happened? His asthma?"

"Asthma?"

"Yeah, he's an asthmatic. You didn't know?"

"He's not," Deacon Meeks told me.

"He told me so," I told Deacon Meeks.

"We'll chalk that up as a little white lie."

"So what's up?" I asked.

"We're not sure. He collapsed. Thank God his brother was visiting. The doctors haven't told us much, except that he's experiencing common problems for a person with emphysema."

"Reverend has emphysema." I was incredulous. "Since when?" I thought about him puffing on that nebulizer.

"Your guess is as good as mine. We all found out today. His brother is here. He's back with the doctors. The staff isn't telling us much. His brother is disgusted. He found packs and packs of cigarettes in the reverend's bedroom when he went to gather some of the reverend's things. Packs, piled across the reverend's bed. One big mountain of 'em. Like a tobacco museum. It doesn't look like he slept in that bed. Just smoked packs and tossed them on the pile."

"My Lord! He was smoking, knowing he had emphysema?" I was talking mainly to myself, thinking aloud.

"Smoking a lot. An awful lot," Deacon Meeks said. "Smoking like he wanted to check out."

The cologne. The gum. Masking the scent. Trying to smoke his way to Eleanor.

Seconds.

All the time it takes a life to move from an unthinkable good to an unimaginable bad. I'd gone from jacking myself off to the vision of Bevolyn, to this.

In seconds.

"I'm on my way," I told Deacon Meeks.

He hung up without fanfare.

I left in the same manner.

I thought about my mother as I rode the streets without regard to my speed; I also thought about toy trains, G.I. Joe, Transformers, and prayed to God that He'd make this situation right. I wondered what *right* would be, considering how anxious Reverend Walker was to pluck a feather from one of his wife's angel wings.

I arrived at the hospital and walked through the main lobby. The girl at the Information Desk tapped a pencil against a spread-open book. It looked like a coloring book at first, but then I saw that she was busy trying to work out a fill-in puzzle. She had her eyeglasses propped on her forehead and her eyes narrowed as if she couldn't see the page. She'd figured out all the three- and four-letter words, I could see, but was now stuck on the larger words.

"Excuse me," I said, "I'm looking for Reverend G.H. Walker."

She looked up, seemingly surprised to see me hovering above her. I have to give it to her, though, because she quickly regrouped.

"Is he one of the hospital chaplains?" she asked without breaking stride.

I shook my head. "Patient. Just recently admitted, today." Deacon Meeks had been shell-shocked, hadn't told me very much of anything.

"HIPAA laws prevent me from giving you that information. I'm sorry." She dropped her head to gaze clueless at the puzzle book again.

"Excuse me?"

"Yes? Can I help you?" This time she didn't look up. Her finger, the paint of the nail chipping badly, walked a trail across the page, stopping at a stretch of blank blocks, then wavering and moving up the page again.

"I'm the associate pastor at Fellowship Baptist Church," I said to the top of her head. Her hair was wheat colored and dingy looking. Thinking of my fantasy with Bevolyn earlier, I almost offered the girl a good shampooing. Instead, I told her, "Reverend Walker is the senior pastor. I know he's here. One of our deacons called me. I need to find him. Please."

"HIPAA," she repeated. "Write your congressman and complain."

I started to press her but decided against it, and just moved past her. She didn't call for me, didn't object. I walked through the hospital and came upon a woman pushing a meal cart, dressed in burgundy-colored scrubs, a nylon cap covering her head. Looked like a shower cap. This, of course, made me think of Bevolyn.

"Where could I find the patients with emphysema?" I asked the woman. "Breathing problems."

"Respiratory unit's on the third floor. C-wing," she said with an accompanying shrug.

I thanked her and headed for the elevator.

From Whom All Blessings Flow is a miracle worker. He put that woman, literally, in my path to guide me. I thanked Him on the elevator ride up, then again as the doors of the elevator dinged open and I stepped out into the unknown.

I looked to the right and saw an empty hallway. Then to the left. The deacons, many of whom still hadn't warmed to me, stood at the end of the hall by a community of couches and pay phones. Deacon Meeks was the first to catch a glimpse of me. He waved me over.

I walked on liquid legs toward them.

"Deacons," I said when I reached their gathering.

"Minister," a couple of them responded. They seemed to hesitate, as if they didn't feel comfortable calling me "minister." I can't say I blamed them; I didn't feel comfortable being called it, either.

"Do we have any new information on the reverend?" I asked.

Deacon Meeks bit into his lip and shook his head. At first, I took that to mean no new information was available, but then I saw that his mouth was half open, and he was trying without success to speak.

"Deacon?" I managed.

"Passed away," another of the deacons informed me.

I blinked. Stumbled backwards. All my memories of Miss Ma'am flashed through my head. Then of my brother. Then, Reverend Walker. He'd made it to his wife.

I wasn't sure if I was happy for him. Thinking, contrary from what Luck had taught me, about all the things we, Reverend and I, wouldn't do together.

"How?" I asked. "He wasn't sick. I mean, the emphysema, but that was…" Slight, I'd wanted to say, but the words left me. In the earliest stages. We hadn't even known he was afflicted.

"Pulmonary embolism. Blood clot traveled from his leg to his lung. Killed him"—the deacon snapped a finger—"like that."

"Sweet Jesus," I said.

"Minister, we have to discuss the church's succession plan," the same deacon said to me.

I sucked in a breath and leaned against the wall. I didn't care about any succession plan. I cared about another man sent into my life from He's Sweet I Know who'd gone from me. My father, of his own free will, admittedly. Luck, when I received my release. Now Reverend Walker. Too much, just too, too much.

"Minister?" I heard the deacon say.

"What does the church constitution say? What's the plan? Who takes over?" I tossed the questions at him, sighed, hurting so badly I didn't care about the future of Fellowship Baptist. Sad to say, but true.

"You," the deacon replied. "You take over."

Me? Ex-con to Reverend. I'd come full circle. I wasn't anywhere near ready. I stumbled back another step. One of the deacons grabbed my hand, held me by the wrist.

"We're counting on you, *Reverend* Path." he told me. "To guide us through this and down the King's Highway."

That's when my mind faded to black.

12

She had two-toned eyes: sandy brown dominant, then, in bull's-eye position, a fleck of burnt-toast brown. Exotic eyes, made even more startling in contrast to her dark chocolate skin. Eyes that pulled you in, lulled you. They'd forever been her best feature—what set her apart, what folk talked about when they mentioned her. Fortunately, for her, those eyes were so clear in their view she could take in the things of the world with 20/20 focus and with the clarity of seeing black when it was black, white when it was white.

She stood by the sidewalk, a little bungalow house before her. A pickup truck took up most of the driveway. Blades of brownish green grass dotted the blacktop. The lawn had been recently cut. Someone had planted a flower garden—small but handsome looking, with its rows of red, white, and purple intermingling blossoms. The sky was turning dark, though the air was hot and thick, humid. Rain, it appeared, was on its way. The rain would be good for the garden.

Lita Grimes looked behind her. Her late-model, green-colored Acura Legend idled by the curb. Plumes of gray smoke swirled from the muffler pipe. The tinted back windows vibrated ever so gently from the music playing softly inside: Usher. "Confessions."

Suction-gripped to the side back window of the Acura was a yellow plastic sign with a black border, square shaped but turned with one of the pointed corners facing up: BABY ON BOARD. Lita hadn't removed it, even when Samantha outgrew her child seat. No, Samantha would always be her baby. And there, in the front seat, clearly visible because Lita had yet to have those windows tinted, was her daughter, Samantha. The child was smiling at Lita, bopping her head to the music, then closing her eyes and swaying, lip-synching the words to the song, oblivious to anything else. Her small world—carefree.

Lita attempted a smile as a warm wave crossed her chest. She loved her daughter. Would do anything for her daughter, for her family. Anything.

Dysfunctional families were the norm if you listened to the talk shows and read the newspapers. But that had never been Lita's experience. Family for her had always been a positive, always been a source of deep comfort.

She thought of her cousin just then. Memories of their childhood flooded her. Picking crab apples together. Finding fun in the simplest things—rolling worn tires through the secret dirt trails they'd discovered in the woods, playing cards under his bed blanket at night, lit only by a flashlight, pretending they were camping. So close, most thought they were brother and sister. But he'd had a brother and lost him. Then he'd bonded to Lita like some industrial-strength glue after that tragedy. And she'd helped him through that. She'd been a good cousin. A friend, really.

Thinking of him was something she had been doing a lot lately. Even longer than lately. In fact, every single day he'd spent in jail. Over two years she'd obsessed about his safety. Would she get a call that someone had stabbed him between the shoulder blades? And what about his sanity? Would he come home irreparably harmed? Mumbling aloud, angry for no apparent reason, caring little of his hygiene, of no use to anyone?

She couldn't imagine what he'd gone through inside, how much he'd suffered. She hated that show *Oz* on HBO, a drama about life inside a prison. It was horrible…terrible. And he'd gone through that. Unbelievable. Now, after having served his time, she felt that he deserved a reprieve, that he should go on with his life. Go on without her. Prison had destroyed so much between them. She knew this. They'd never be the same. He'd made it clear in their last phone conversation.

"I'm not looking you up when I get out," he'd said.

"Why? We're family. I've missed you. Samantha has missed you," she'd replied.

"That's why." He paused. "Samantha."

He hadn't said any more. Lita hadn't needed him to. Instead, she allowed that understanding to take hold. He was an ex-con. Samantha didn't need any ex-cons in her life. Seeing things in black and white let Lita know that bringing that dark and black reality into her child's innocent and white perspective wasn't the right thing to do.

But here Lita was. Despite that knowledge of black and white, trying to look her cousin up. At his ex's, Myshelle's house. Myshelle would know where he was, Lita hoped, with the greatest of hope that Myshelle knew, and that she would tell.

She looked back at Samantha once more. Her daughter was busy singing still, eyes closed. Lita took in some of the humid air, released it, then moved up the walkway to the bungalow and stepped on the porch. Without hesitation, she rapped her knuckles against the door frame. She could see the tiny living room through the screen door. Myshelle was good at bringing out the best in what little she had. Doilies covered the knots in her wood furniture, and magazines fanned out over the water bubbles in her fake wood coffee table. A ficus tree stood in a corner, the plastic pot at its base cracked along the top border, those cracks dressed up with wrapping paper Myshelle had taped around the edge.

Lita knocked again and heard the soft swish of footsteps, slippers.

Myshelle appeared in the doorway wearing an azure-colored T-shirt that fell to her ankles, long enough to be a dress. A smile crossed her face. "Lita, hey, girl."

"Hey, yourself, Meesh." Lita still liked Myshelle even though her cousin had come home to find that the love he'd left behind had now done the same to him.

"You want to come in?" Myshelle asked.

Lita shook her head. "I've got Samantha in the car. And it's running."

"In the car," Myshelle gasped, squinting and looking out front. "Girl, didn't you watch that show on *Oprah*? Never leave your child alone in the car. Even for a second. Especially with it running."

"She's okay," Lita said. She swallowed. "Come on out with me; say hello to her."

Myshelle frowned. "She's not going to ask me all those questions about why I don't love *him* any more, is she?"

Lita shrugged. "I don't know. She might. She doesn't understand what happened. She's young and—" Lita stopped. Innocent, she was thinking. So, so innocent.

"I think I'll pass," Myshelle said. "I don't need to feel guilty about moving on with my life."

"Please," Lita begged. Then quieted her tone a bit. "Samantha really wants to see you. You know she loves her Aunt Myshelle."

Myshelle's features softened. "I'm still her auntie?"

"She's holding out hope you two will fix things, get back together," Lita admitted. "But either way, she loves you, Meesh."

Myshelle sighed. Then she stepped through the screen door. "*You're* not going to ask me any questions about why I don't love *him* any more, either. Right?"

"Right," Lita said. "Your life. Live it how you see fit."

"Something is different about you," Myshelle said as they started to walk. "I can't place it." She looked Lita over. "Not your hair. Or makeup."

"I don't know what it could be," Lita said.

Myshelle stopped and snapped her fingers. "*Don't.* That's it. You haven't said 'ain't' once. Talking like you went to State College or something. Look at you."

Lita kept quiet, kept moving toward her Acura.

"We're all moving on," Myshelle mused as they began walking again. "I guess. Huh?"

Lita nodded.

"Moving on," Myshelle said in singsong.

Lita turned to Myshelle when they reached the Acura, took her wrist, and said, "Thanks," with a tinge of desperation.

"For what?" Myshelle asked.

The back door of the Acura opened. Lita moved to the side and hugged herself. Myshelle studied the man who stepped out, the cut of his suit, his shiny shoes. Handsome brother. Look at Lita, she thought. No wonder she was acting all funny. Creeping on Earl, probably. Picked a good one to creep with, too.

"Hello, Myshelle," the man said to her.

She smiled. "You say that like we know each other."

"Heard stories about you," he said. "Plus I've seen you in action."

Myshelle frowned. "In action?"

"I'm Dante Ruffin," he told her.

Myshelle gasped. She could hear Lita behind her, laboring to breathe, crying hard.

"Oh, Lita," Myshelle whispered. "Damn!"

Dante Ruffin stepped up on the curb, a foot in front of Myshelle, a ready smile in place. He extended a hand. Myshelle didn't take it. His smile deepened and he reined in his hand, adjusted his shirt, and shrugged off the dis. "Disappointing that you'd disregard my goodwill so blatantly. But so be it. This is about business, anyway. You understand, I'm sure, Myshelle Maxwell."

Myshelle looked at Lita. Lita played furiously with her hands and shifted weight from one foot to the other. Myshelle turned back to Dante Ruffin.

"What do you want?" she snapped.

"As I said, I've seen you in action. You're very gifted in subterfuge, Ms. Maxwell," Dante said. "Very neat trick slipping my brother's tail. Delivering that note to another address. Very neat trick. We've waited and watched you for as long as we can, waiting for your ex to contact you, or you him. It's become obvious to us that you aren't going to. Found yourself a new love. Congratulations. And he is some mechanic, too, I must admit. I'd personally have a little fear crawling up under cars. Imagine if the lift broke and all that weight fell on you." Dante shuddered.

"What. Do. You. Want?" Myshelle said.

Dante nodded. "I've come as a representative for my family, to encourage you into assisting us."

"Why don't you let him be?" Myshelle said.

Dante smiled. "You sound like our Lita Grimes. As I told her, we simply can't. I trust you'll understand."

"I won't."

"Fair enough," Dante said. "So we'll just agree to disagree."

"Do you know where he is, Meesh?" Lita asked.

Dante turned to Lita. "Please, allow me to ask the questions. Why don't you go inside the car and keep your little artiste company?"

Lita saw the calm in his eyes. She knew it could easily turn to something else. So she quickly shuffled off around the car, slid in the front seat, and hugged Samantha once inside.

Dante eyed the display for a moment and then turned back to Myshelle, smiling still. "What happens to women? You start out as children so calm, so carefree. I gave little Samantha a handheld video game; she's content. Lita, a ride on the long shaft—setting her up, albeit, but it was good—and yet she's been nothing but an aggravation to me since. What happens from five to thirty-five, Myshelle? I need to know."

"I'm not telling you anything," Myshelle said.

Dante's eyes narrowed. "Sure you are. You may not know it now. But you are."

"This is ridiculous."

"Nice. Ridiculous is an all-purpose word. Your vocabulary is impressive. But, alas, not enough to take my eyes off the ball. Where is he, Ms. Maxwell?"

"I. Don't. Know."

"Or won't tell, so you think."

"He was at a YMCA in Fayetteville. He's since left. I called. He isn't there."

"So where did he go?"

"I. Don't. Know."

"Let me rephrase," Dante said. "You know him as well as anyone. I believe Lita Grimes when she says she doesn't know where he is."

"Believe me, too," Myshelle said.

"As I was going to say," Dante went on. "You don't know where he is. Okay, with a little hesitation I'll accept that. But I do believe you'd know where he'd go. So, Ms. Maxwell, where would he go?"

Where would he go? Myshelle thought it through. She shot a glance at the Acura. Lita and Samantha were still in an embrace, the child squirming, but Lita refusing to let her go. Myshelle bit into her lip.

"Ms. Maxwell?" Dante said.

"Why won't you leave him alone? Why won't you leave us alone? Me. Lita. Samantha."

"Last time I ask," Dante said. He stepped back and placed one hand on the Acura's front door. Inside, Lita started to cry hysterically, rubbing her hands through Samantha's hair, kissing the child's head.

"New Jersey," Myshelle blurted. "His father is there somewhere. That's where he'd go, to find his father."

"What's his father's name?"

"Leonard Vernard Furlow. I don't know any more than that about him."

Dante nodded. "Leonard Furlow, of course. And how do you know he'd go to find his father?"

"Letters," Myshelle admitted.

"Letters?"

"His father sent him some, while he was in prison. They"—she paused—"affected him. He sent me one to read."

Dante smiled. "Still have it?"

"I've moved on with my life," Myshelle told him.

"Still have it?" he repeated.

She looked at him hard for a moment, then turned and slinked back toward the house. She emerged a few minutes later, a hair stylist's trade magazine in her hands. She handed the magazine to Dante Ruffin and told him to open it. He did. The letter was a bookmark in the center of the magazine. He pulled it out and scanned it over, then read the sender's information aloud.

"Leonard Vernard Furlow. Sixteen Hundred Throckmorton Boulevard. Colts Neck, New Jersey."

Dante looked up at Myshelle and nodded. "Thank you, Ms. Maxwell. That's sufficient. We'll find him. Should we send him your regards when we do?"

"Leave," Myshelle said. "And don't come back."

Dante nodded. "I believe that's doable. I have plans for a trip anyway. The Garden State, I do believe that's what they call New Jersey." He turned and opened the Acura's back door, settled into his seat, and tapped the back of Lita's seat. She immediately pulled the transmission tree to DRIVE and pushed away from the curb. Plumes of the gray smoke from her muffler pipe trailed behind. Myshelle watched the car. Watched it turn into a dot. Then, a memory.

13

Reverend Walker's funeral service had been nice. I'd preached the eulogy. Not so much a eulogy as a love letter to the man I'd known only for a short time, the man who'd taken me in, given me a new chance, a new hope for the future. Gave me that chance knowing who I really was, what I really was: an ex-con. A *black* ex-con in a nation where black men were Public Enemy #1 and black men who'd served prison time were… were…There wasn't any word to attribute to the kind of disdain that went to that unfortunate group, of which I was a part. If they ever came up with one, it would make us sound like dinosaurs or something along those lines, I'm sure.

"So take your wings, dear one," I'd said as I neared the end of my eulogy, "and fly. Soar high and soar wide. We will miss you as long as God grants us the breath of life. We will cherish you…forever."

I meant every word.

Bevolyn had sung a song. She'd come to the microphone in her understated way, leaned in, and said, "This is a new one from Yolanda Adams: 'I'm Gonna Be Ready.' I can't sing it like she can, but I'll do my best." She then looked down to where the coffin rested. "God bless you, Reverend Walker."

And sung.

Boy, did she sing. It caught me by surprise. I'd have never known she could get down like that. There was a lot I didn't know about her. A lot I wanted to find out. I couldn't imagine having a wife like Bevolyn, and not being at an arm's length of her at all times. What was her husband's problem?

After the funeral service, I stood by Reverend's gravesite for the interment thinking about the man. There was no doubt in my mind he was dancing with his wife at that very moment. I also thought of Bevolyn's song and the utterly breathtaking voice she'd used to deliver it. I let my gaze drift shamelessly in her direction as I delivered the last words over Reverend Walker's soul.

Drifted to her as I read from John 11:25-26. "I am the resurrection, and the life: he that believeth in me, though he were dead, yet shall he live: And whosoever liveth and believeth in me shall never die."

And then the service ended, with Bevolyn quickly making her way past the other mourners, including her sister Sela, over the grassy hill and down toward the parking area. I gave chase, called out for her. I knew she heard me because I saw a hitch in her step. But she didn't turn and acknowledge me. I kept on anyway. That had become our ritual. She ran. I chased.

As she neared the bottom of the hill she buckled, then stopped, and bent to touch her shoe. I moved faster. When I reached her, she had the shoe in one hand, the shoe's snapped heel in the other. If she had been a cussing woman, a four-letter word would have been on her tongue.

"Sister Sykes," I said. "Are you okay?" I reached to help her gather herself but she brushed my hand aside.

"I'm fine."

"Are you now?" I asked, smiling. My first smile in days. She was still spunky, broken shoe and all.

"What did you need, *Reverend?*" she barked.

"Wanted to tell you your song earlier"—I shook my head and grunted—"touched me. Moved me. I had no idea you could sing like that. It really helped me deal with all that's happened."

"You need all the help you can get," she said. "I saw you looking at me up there." She nodded up the hill, toward Reverend Walker's resting place. She shook her head. "Why must you look at me in that way, *Reverend?* I don't understand it. It's shameful."

I ignored that.

"You need all the help you can get, too," I said, looking down at her broken shoe heel, "and, strangely, I don't see your husband here holding your arm, offering you that help." I turned and looked around to amplify the point and caught a glimpse of Sela's profile. She was holding the back of one of the metal folding chairs we'd set up around Reverend Walker's gravesite for the service. It looked to me as if she were talking, vigorously.

"You need to be over there," Bevolyn said. "Instead of over here in my business."

"That's my concern," I said.

She narrowed her eyes and slightly parted her lips, but refused to pass the word or thought on her tongue my way. I was playing dirty, I knew, but she had the ability to bring out the dirt in my spirit. Truthfully, I was sick of our little tango. She looked too good for me to front-on her. I'm not a victim to vanity, but I like to believe I carried myself well, looked decent, too. Mix two attractive adults together and some kind of sexual energy is bound to generate. We had that, though she fought it. I, on the other hand, didn't. Couldn't. Two adults. Grown. Grown *and* sexy. But then that voice was in my head: the voice of morality, the voice that should guide a preacher. *Married woman. Married woman.*

I hated that voice at times like this. I ignored it and focused on Bevolyn instead.

"There you go again," she said, huffing, shaking her head.

I didn't have to ask what. I knew. I was checking her out, caught up in a dream as my gaze traveled over her.

Her dress clung to every twist and turn on her body. And there were plenty. She had her maroon-brown locks pulled back tight, pinned in a bunch by a diamond-encrusted pendant. A mahogany shade coated her lips. She looked like a wealthy socialite, some billionaire mogul's wife. Again, I couldn't understand why her husband didn't have his arms around her now, why he didn't have her hand engulfed in his own.

I studied her like a painting, hoping to find something in her beauty that could help me deal with the grief of yet another loss. She had a perfectly good shoulder, I noticed, and I wanted to lean on it, needed to lean on it.

"How'd you get that scar?" I asked her.

She touched her mouth, rubbed it with her finger, but said nothing. I noticed sadness in her eyes as she rubbed. I noticed the sparkle of her wedding ring, too.

"Your husband," I said.

She didn't answer.

I decided not to press it.

"Why would your husband let you come out here alone?" I asked her. "Looking so good. I'd be so proud of you. The way you sang earlier…"

"*Reverend,* please," she said. Even her chocolate skin couldn't hide the strawberry in her cheeks. I'd managed to take her from sadness to happiness, even though she was fighting the happiness, fighting my praise.

"I complimented your singing, Bevolyn. Several times. I do believe a 'thank you' would be in order," I said to her.

"Do you, now, *Reverend?*" She harrumphed. "And please, feel free to call me Sister Sykes. Only my friends call me Bevolyn."

"Why must we go through this back-and-forth every time we see one another?"

"I'm the one going back," she said. "You, *Reverend*, are steady going forth. I think it's highly inappropriate. I'm a—"

"Married woman," I cut in. "Heard that record already. It's been getting a lot of airplay. I'm wondering if I'll ever get to meet this wonderful man doing the duet with you. Ask him about your scar."

"Make that the last time," she said, manicured nails waving just inches from my eyeballs, "you make reference to my marriage or my husband. Do you understand, *Reverend?*"

"Sorry," I said. She was right. It wasn't the best way for me to go.

"Yes," she nodded. "Very sorry."

"I wish it could be different," I said. "I don't like how things are between us. I keep thinking of how things might have been if I'd met you before you got…" I left it hanging at that. I wasn't about to invoke the *M*-word again.

"Different?" She cackled. *Cackled.* Threw her head back and let me see her tonsils. All at my expense.

"Something funny?" I asked, setting myself up.

"You," she said.

"How so?"

"Your little theory of how things would have been different," she said. "They wouldn't have been. I won't fall for the likes of you now. And I wouldn't have when I was single, either. You have some nerve. Calling my sister up to set up a date, and yet you're over here in my face." She shook her head and added, "Only thing I could ever imagine you doing for me is changing my tire, fixing my toilet, or painting one of the rooms in *my* house. Be-cause I know, you'd never get yourself together enough to handle a mortgage payment. If I was with you, everything would fall on me."

"Oh," I said. My voice betrayed me. I wanted to sound unaffected, strong. I sounded deflated, hurt, that one syllable—"Oh"—a mirror to my shattered soul.

Bevolyn noticed. Her eyes softened. She raised her hand in my direction, to caress away the awful things she'd said, I imagined. But the hand stopped midair, just above her waist level. She didn't caress me. She just teased me with the hope of it.

"All right," I managed. "You know where I am if you ever want prayer counsel…or your toilet fixed."

"Reverend, I—"

I put my hand up, palm facing her. "It's okay. Really."

Bevolyn didn't say anything but stood anchored in place, as did I. Our silence was broken, thankfully, a short pause later. Sela had made her way over to us, done talking, vigorously, to Reverend Walker's grave.

"That man baptized me," Sela said, "just a few months ago. And now he's gone. I was hoping he'd be around to baptize me again when I got my stuff together for real." She laughed.

Bevolyn and I remained silent.

"Did I interrupt something?" Sela asked, looking from Bevolyn to myself.

"No," I told her. I placed a hand up to my brow, shielding away the glare of the sun. It was beating down extra hard today, one of the hottest days of the summer so far.

"Right," Bevolyn said. "I was just leaving. Are you following me home, Sela?"

Sela shook her head. "Nuh uh. I wanted to have a word with Reverend Path."

Bevolyn looked at me, and then Sela. She paused as if she didn't know what her next move should be. Finally, she nodded, turned, and did a one-legged march to her car, her posture angry. Angry like her words.

"She's got issues," Sela said, watching her sister stomp on. "But don't we all, though?"

"Yes," I said. "We all do. I can't figure out what your sister's angle is, though. She's so angry toward me."

"Me, too," Sela said. "Horse hogger."

"What?"

"When we were little," Sela said, "we went to this event where they let you pet the horses, sit on them. Bevolyn wouldn't let me get anywhere near the horses. And there were only a few. I never did get to pet one or sit on one. But she did. That's how she's always been toward me."

"Doesn't explain me," I said.

"You scare her," Sela said. "That's why she's flailing at you. Fear."

"What does she have to fear?"

Sela smirked and looked me over. "You are a good-looking brother."

I homed in on Sela, looked at her hard. She had her sister's same pretty features, but was pleasanter, easier to talk with, not so stuck in her own world. No anger was in her tone, her eyes, or showing up as lines around her lips.

"So what's up with you?" I asked her, very much looking forward to her answer.

She fanned herself with bright orange-colored nails.

Bevolyn went with dark burgundy. Always. Every time I'd seen her, dark burgundy. It was refreshing to see a different shade. I could grow to love orange.

"Hot?" I asked Sela.

"Yeah. It's hot as a popcorn fart," she said.

"What's that?"

She wiped a trickle of sweat from her forehead. "One of my mom's sayings. She's been on my mind a lot lately. I need to go visit her."

"She as beautiful as her daughter?" I asked, though I was thinking in the plural. "Does she have your—?"

"She was," she cut me off.

"Was?"

"Gone. An outta-control brain aneurysm. Wiped her out."

"I'm sorry," I told her. Paused. "Very sorry. I didn't know."

She said something else, which I didn't quite gather, for I was too busy muttering myself.

"What's that?" she asked, then giggled. "You and I are straight-up mysterious. You called me Miss. Then, Ma'am. Whassup wit' that?"

"Huh?"

She waved a hand in front of my face. "Earth to Reverend Path. Earth to Reverend Path. Holla at me."

I had to smile.

"You're something," I told her. "You know how they're always trying to define films for audiences? You would be…"—I put my hands up to mimic focusing on a big movie banner—"MC Lyte meets Star Jones. Very intelligent, but have that street, down-to-earth vibe. I like it."

More than liked. I loved interesting women. Like Bevolyn. Like Sela, it turned out. I probably would have tripped out over their mother, the source of their *interestingness*. I can only imagine how interesting and attractive the tree was where their apples bloomed. From Whom All Blessings Flow was on top of His game when He made this clan, let me tell you.

"Oh, yeah?" Sela said. "You like my vibe. That why you called me Miss and then Ma'am? Respectfully letting me know you liked my vibe? Cute. Very cute." She flipped her hair then, laughed again, and smiled hard, all full lips and cheeks: signals, I knew, that a woman was digging a man.

I glanced over my shoulder. I couldn't see Bevolyn's straight-shouldered prance or hear that one heel clicking against the pavement. Didn't care.

"By the way," I told Sela as I turned my attention back to her, "I actually said, 'Miss Ma'am.' That was my mother. Lost her, as you did your mother. Lung cancer. She preferred my brother and I call her that. Miss Ma'am."

I wanted to share with someone, needed to share. Was happy I'd found someone, in Sela, I felt comfortable opening up to.

"Oh. I'm sorry. Miss Ma'am. Your mother sounds… interesting."

That brought a smile to my face; a laugh tickled its way out of my throat. "That's an understatement."

Sela smiled and for the first time seemed at a lost for words. Her teeth were perfectly straight, though a bit off colored. A smoker, I took that to mean, and that realization made my insides churn just a bit. But I wouldn't let that deter me. I'd cross that bridge when I came to it, as Miss Ma'am would say.

"Been having a hard time catching up with you on the phone," I said. I accessorized my words by poking out my lip, pouting like a little boy. Some women found that sexy. I hoped Sela was such a woman.

"Don't dooo that," Sela cooed. "You have no idea what that sad little boy look does to me." She touched my arm.

She looked pleased that the awkward silence phase had passed.

She was feeling the poked-out lip bit. I was batting a thousand so far.

"What does it do?" I asked, my eyes narrowed, head cocked to the side, lip clinched between my teeth. Flirting. For real with it.

She dropped her head, playing coy.

"Sela? What does it do?" I pressed. I saw her swallow. Nervous all of a sudden. Cool. I knew how to calm a nervous woman. I had a long line of *thick* rope that could pull her in. But, then, I was a reverend. I shouldn't talk that way. It would be hard not to, though, with the stunning Sela before me. I was frustrated with myself for being so caught up in Bevolyn I hadn't taken a real notice in her younger and just as exquisite sister. I had to make up for lost time.

"What does my sad little boy look do to you, Sela?"

She raised her head and took a deep breath. Too deep—the kind boxers take before they go into the ring against someone looking to knock their head off. But that wasn't my aim. I didn't want to box Sela. Wrestle her, maybe. But that's a different story.

"Would you like to go somewhere?" she asked. She wrung her hands, and her voice cracked. "I mean to grab a bite to eat. Coffee. The park. Something. I'm not propositioning you for sex. Ain't trying to get you in trouble with"—she pointed up—"Him."

"Not propositioning me?" I poked my lip out again.

She laughed and hit my arm. Just the response I'd hoped for from her. Her sister wouldn't have gotten that I was joking. And if she did, Bevolyn wouldn't have loosened her collar enough to play along.

I liked Sela. A lot.

"You and your sister are so different," I ventured.

"That we are," she said. Then, "So are you down to chill or what?"

"See." I smiled. "Bevolyn would have said…"

". . . Reverend, would you be kind enough to escort me to Starbucks for a caffeine jolt?" Sela finished.

"She's not that bad," I said, laughing.

Then we both said, "But close," in unison, which brought us to titters.

"Yeah," I said, once we'd calmed. "I'd love to go somewhere with you, Interesting Lady. I want to find out what makes you tick."

"What makes *you* tick?" she asked.

"An interesting woman," I said, then eyeing her from head to toe, "with a beautiful body. Meat on her bones in the right places. In an outfit that's both stylish and complementing to her figure." I threw in, "She's gotta love God, too," shamed that I'd originally forgotten it. I noticed something pass across Sela's face. "You?" I asked her.

"Same thing," she said, and then quickly added, "Except make the woman a man."

"Whew!" I playfully ran my hand across my forehead. "Glad you clarified that. You have to be careful nowadays."

I expected a smile but instead Sela said, "So let's go," in a clipped business tone.

"Let's," I replied.

"You drive. We can come back for my ride later."

"Okay," I said tentatively. Her vibe had shifted. Had I said something to upset her? I thought back.

But she took my hand, breaking my thoughts, and guided it around her arm.

I left my dread behind, my mind on this new and interesting woman instead of Reverend Walker. Instead of Bevolyn.

Hope coursed through me as I reached my car and opened the door for her. She slid in, her chocolate leg peeking from beneath her skirt making me think things I'd have to pray on later.

"This should be an interesting ride," she said as I eased into the driver's seat. That word again, *interesting*. A neutral word to describe a situation bloated with possibilities, but an as-of-yet unknown outcome.

"I hope so," I replied.

Sela smiled, touched my shoulder. "Me, too."

14

Sela Wheeler knelt down with a handful of cut flowers and plant a few in the earth by their stems. The others she lay across the ground, crisscrossing them over each other in an elaborate manner. She dug in the soil with her hands and shoveled some dirt around the base of the flowers she had placed in the ground. The dirt fortified the flowers, made them stand up like soldiers, rigid, keeping guard over the cemetery headstone of Sela's mother.

Satisfied with her handiwork, Sela picked up her straw carryall and retrieved a multicolored shawl from inside the large bag. She unfolded the shawl, spread it across the ground, and smoothed all the edges. Then from inside her carryall she pulled a Zippo lighter and a perfectly rolled Dutch Master blunt. She quickly fired up the cigar, took a long hard pull, and closed her eyes to allow that medicine to soothe, to assuage her troubles. She held the smoke in for some time before finally letting a small puff of it escape from between her lips. Everything was right with her world at that moment. Honey on her lips, a good burn in her chest, her body starting its slow float heavenward. She was most definitely getting her head up *too-day*.

Sela settled down on the shawl and sat with her back against the headstone. She took another toke on her cigar, held it, and blew out a small puff of smoke—one of the nicest little rituals anyone could have. Legalize it, she found herself thinking. Legalize it. And then she giggled. Starting to feel silly already. Floating.

She gazed at a nearby headstone adorned with fresh flowers, a basket with ribbon woven around its handles, and small stuffed animals of some sort in the basket. A gift to the dead from the living, she supposed. Same type of nonsense Sela had found herself doing not long after her mother's passing. She'd written up a long letter, detailing her innermost thoughts, sealed it in a pink envelope with flowers around the borders, and placed it by her mother's grave. Came back a few weeks later to find the envelope crumbling because of the harsh elements. It had been a rough few weeks. Snow, rain, sleet—a weatherman's wet dream. The ink of the letter inside the envelope had bled through to a shade of purple. Stupid. Sela hadn't even considered the weather, just rashly wrote that letter and dropped it by her mother's grave. She hadn't even said hello to her mother that day, but had quickly dropped the letter, run back to her car, and sat there breathing heavy, trying to calm herself. Because she'd been running? Or because of what she'd been running from?

She shook her head now, thinking about that time. The recollection made her mouth tighten, her gaze wander to another grave as she took another drag on her cigar. This second grave had a marker from the funeral home, no headstone, even though the person had been gone, from what Sela could gather from the marker, for close to three years. Sela imagined a funeral for this person—this Selma Williamson—with few family and loved ones. A eulogy, sweet poetic remembrances of Selma

Williamson's goodness, even though the preacher, and no one else, could personally attest to the real Selma Williamson.

Would Sela's own life, and then death, follow a similar pattern?

She went back to her routine instead of dwelling on those dark thoughts. She pulled on her Dutchie, held in the smoke, and then casually let some escape from between her lips.

"Don't know what Bev's problem is," Sela said, turning around so she faced her mother's headstone. Comfort always found Sela here at Whitefalls Cemetery. She could sit, get her head up, and talk to Carmen Wheeler as if the hooded man in black had never kissed her mother's lips, sucked her last breath away. "She acts like *she* made God instead of the other way around," Sela went on. She took in another lungful, her hand shaky and dirty, caked with the dirt she'd used to plant the flowers around her mother's grave. She added, "Your daughter's working my last nerve," between coughs.

Your sister means well, Sela. She's made her share of mistakes. She doesn't want to see you go through the same. It's a vicious cycle that needs to end where you begin.

"I hear you, Mama," Sela answered. She had conversations with her mother now that were more meaningful than their conversations when her mother was still alive. In life, Bevolyn had always been Carmen's favorite, but in death, with Bevolyn seldom visiting the cemetery, Carmen had grown to cherish her relationship with the daughter who did visit: Sela. Or, at least that's the way Sela envisioned things. It was probably just the weed talking.

"Got the biggest, glassiest house in the neighborhood and always throwing stones at somebody else's place," Sela fumed. "She thinks she's better than me because she was born again. I was there before that. I know what the real deal is. I'm gonna tell her about herself one of these days. I'm trying not to go there but…" Another puff really had Sela floating. Close enough to feel the cotton texture of the clouds with her fingertips, to kiss the powder blue screen of sky. But then, Sela couldn't figure, would the clouds feel like cotton, and was that blue of the sky really a powder blue?

Tell me about this reverend, Sela.

"You know about that?" Sela crinkled her forehead and giggled. Damn, she was high. "Reverend LeVar Path," she said. "Seems nice enough. I'm just getting to know him. Now, Bevolyn, she's all up in his Kool-Aid, her tongue probably redder than a mug. Acts as if she isn't, but she can save that act for someone who doesn't know better. I ain't the one. You should see the way she looks at him." Sela paused. "Or, maybe you have seen?"

I asked you about the reverend and you're off talking about your sister again. Man like that, looks like he should be in a darn Kenneth Cole ad, and all you can think to say is some foolishness about Bevolyn. Something isn't right about that, daughter of mine.

Sela let the comment hang. She squinted against the sun's orange rays, hunched her shoulders, and took in the cemetery. She sat the lit Dutch Master on the ground, saw it trying to spark flame to a blade of grass, and tapped on the grass. Tapped out the cigar. Done smoking. No longer in the mood.

Nothing to say?

"She's got my whole vibe out of order." Sela sighed, eyeing the blunt beside her. "I mean, Reverend Path is fine with a capital *F*, Mama. All those muscles and stuff. I look at him and I want to—excuse me, Mama—I want to light that brotha up and smoke 'im."

You sure about that, Sela? Sounds like just words to me.

"Yeah, I'm sure, Mama. Yes."

Do what's right, Sela. Follow your heart. Wherever your heart leads you, that's where you need to go.

"Thought you always said to let the Lord order my steps."

The Lord is in your heart, child. Come on. You know that.

"Listen, Mama." Sela slowed, took a breath. She looked again at the sky, transfixed by the contrasting blue and white, how the clouds moved, the earth turning, Sela knew, but couldn't actually see. She could almost picture a hand reaching downward and giving her a thumbs-up signal.

"Mama, I need to tell you something about myself. I hope it doesn't disappoint you. I wrote you a letter on it, once. Don't know if you got it because you never said. Anyway, I've been thinking and—" She stopped, noticing a figure move in her direction—a woman. The woman's head was down as she made her way through the maze of the cemetery. Fair of skin, shapely, dressed in some jeans that fit snug against her childbearing hips. A tight lavender-colored T-shirt, lavender being her favorite color, with rhinestone butterflies engraved on the front. Her long hair pulled back from her face, flowers pinned in the tresses.

"You're out here smoking and talking," the woman said to Sela when she reached the grave. "That's why you're taking so long."

"Thought you were staying in the car," Sela said, looking at her mother's grave as she said it, instead of her friend, Zelda.

"Wendy Williams started talking all crazy," Zelda said of the disc jockey on WBLS. "Got stuck talking about that book that guy wrote. *Down Low* or something." She blew out air in frustration. Her full lips fluttered. Sela watched them, her gaze stuck on the color Zelda had chosen to paint her lips with today. Very nice, cute, would look good on her, too. She really needed to get herself together, buy some new clothes, or change her hairstyle, ooh, buy some shoes. Shopping, like smoking weed, could be therapeutic. Zelda understood this, was always fresh to death, crown to heel. Sela needed to get there, too.

"I got tired of the radio, anyway," Zelda went on. "The music on the other stations weren't worth a damn. I gave up trying to find something to shake my ass to, figured I'd come check on you." She paused. "You zoning out on me, Sela. Did you hear me?"

"You didn't have to get out the car," Sela said. "I know you're scared of the dead."

"Not scared," Zelda corrected. "Just prefer they stay in their lane, and I'll stay in mine."

Sela swiveled her head, taking in the expanse of the cemetery. "How many dead do you think are here?"

Zelda instinctively turned, made a move to guestimate how many grave markers to each row, how many rows, et cetera, but then she caught herself. She turned back to Sela, a wondrous smile on her smooth-as-a-pebble face. "All of 'em," she said. "Ha-ha."

"I almost got you," Sela said, smiling in turn.

"You've got a nice smile," Zelda told her friend. "You should use it more often. It softens you. Calls attention to your face."

"Don't do that," Sela said. She turned her gaze to her mother's headstone again. Why had she stomped out her Dutchie? She could use a pull on that bad boy right now.

Zelda moved close to the headstone, bent, and ran her fingers through the ridges of the lettering. CARMEN WHEELER, 1950-2002. BELOVED MOTHER. "You've been talking to your mother?" she asked Sela.

When Sela didn't answer, Zelda turned to her. Her face registered the kindness inherent in her. Her lips were slightly upturned; seeing her eyes was akin to watching the ripples in a calm stream. "You've been talking to your mother?" she repeated.

This time Sela nodded.

"You tell her what you've been going through?" Zelda wanted to know.

Sela frowned. "You need to go back to the car, relax yourself. You hear me?"

Zelda heard her friend, saw the seriousness in Sela's expression, but she held her ground. "You tell her about Reverend Path," she said, "and how you're so hot and bothered by just the sight of him? All those muscles." Zelda placed something extra in a smile and shiver-wiggled her shoulders. "How you'd like to smoke him like a Dutch Master."

"Shut up" was Sela's only reply.

Zelda squinted her eyes. "Did you?"

"I've had about enough of you," Sela said. "Go back to the car, Zelda."

"Zelda? No Zee-Zee? Damn, I'm in trouble." Zelda put her hands on her hips and smirked. "You're upset with me, Sela? Are you ready to beat the crap out of your best friend?"

Sela didn't answer. Instead, she stood and snatched up her blanket, then struggled to fit the unfolded shawl back in her straw carryall. She stuffed, pushed, and prodded, to no avail. Then she gave up, folded it neatly and still pushed it in hard, as if it didn't fit, couldn't fit. But it did now. It fit. Fit fine. Sela was good for that, messing up the natural order of things, stressing to push something that fit where it didn't, something that didn't where it did. Playing God.

Zelda moved to Sela and touched her friend's shoulder. Sela wheeled, her nostrils flaring, her hands balled in fists. Zelda let her hand drop, but clasped onto a piece of Sela's shirt instead.

"You might want to move your hand back," Sela said.

Zelda shook her head, but moved the hand. "I'm sorry, Sela. You're my friend. I worry about you. You have some issues you need to resolve before you get in a relationship. Two words for you. Elijah Turner. Did I need to mention his name? You don't want a repeat of that disaster."

"Shut up," Sela said.

Zelda pressed on. "I don't want the reverend to hurt you like Elijah did. I don't want you to hurt him as you hurt Elijah. You're going about this all wrong. Trying to prove something to your sister. To yourself. I'm worried about you. So kill me."

Don't tempt me, Sela thought. But she said nothing, just reached down and plucked her Dutchie from the dirt, wrapped it in a paper towel, and dropped it in her bag.

"I'm going to head on back to the car," Zelda said, "and let you have a last word with your mother. Okay?"

Sela turned her back to Zelda. She stood, bag in hand, and gazed at her mother's headstone, wordless. She hiked the bag up on her shoulder and shifted her weight. She could hear Zelda's soft steps behind her, becoming fainter as her friend moved farther away. Sela closed her eyes, bit into her lip, and gripped her bag handle hard. Still. Wordless. Where to begin?

"I'm going to head on, Mama. Okay?"

Follow your heart, child. God is in your heart.

Sela stepped forward and touched the headstone with her hand. It was warm to the touch because of the sun. She forced a smile to brighten her face and said, "Thanks, Mama. I love you."

And I love you right back.

Sela walked toward her car, gravel and dirt making sounds underfoot, drowning out the voices in her head. Elijah Turner, her last boyfriend—things had gone so terribly wrong with him. She doubted she'd ever encounter another person in life who had as much hate for her as he did. It had been her fault. She'd lied to him, presented herself as someone she wasn't entirely comfortable being. He'd punched her in her mouth for it. Cosmetic dentistry had hidden the evidence.

History. Old news. Didn't have a thing to do with the here and now. She'd learned so much from that experience. She'd never again repeat those mistakes. Nuh uh. She wanted to smoke the reverend with all those muscles, smoke him like a Dutchie, treat him well. Hopefully, he'd treat her well in kind. That's what she wanted. Really.

Sela reached the driver's side door of her car. She paused and looked off in the distance toward the plot of land where her mother now rested, she hoped, in peace. Her eyes grew hot, tears flooding them, as she remembered the last Christmas she'd shared with her mother.

Carmen Wheeler had sat on the couch, tearing open the carefully wrapped gifts with a child's reckless abandon. "My gifts," she'd said when her two daughters' eyebrows rose, "and I want to see them. Right yesterday." Then she'd laughed that thick laugh of hers, rich like coffee beans, the kind of laugh that echoed in your ears hours after hearing it.

That Christmas the lines around her eyes and mouth shortened briefly from the happiness of Carmen's smile.

"You like it, Mama?" Sela. Always the first to speak.

"Little jazzy for this old lady," Carmen Wheeler said, turning the cashmere sweater at every angle as she inspected it carefully. "But I'll reach back and get some of my old groove. Make it work." She looked up then. That vision, the liquid joy in her eyes something Sela would never forget. "It's lovely, girls. Thank you."

Bevolyn squeezed her mother's shoulder.

Sela—and she didn't know why—had to fan in front of her eyes, had to purse her lips with the extra emotion. Perhaps God in His infinite wisdom was letting her know that relationship, mother to daughter, would end soon. Perhaps.

Carmen shook her head and beckoned Sela to her. Sela moved close, sat next to her mother, and laid her head on her mother's shoulder. "Daughter of mine," Carmen said, shaking her head, making a *tsk* sound with her mouth. "Daughter of mine."

Later, Sela would joke about the emotions of that day.

"Me crying. You with the sweater, looking happier than a dog with two peters." One of her mother's expressions. Sela shook her head. "Something in the air, I guess."

"Don't know how long the Lord will keep me here," Carmen had replied. "Got to cherish every gift I get."

"You're not going anywhere, Mama. You better not," Sela said.

"Not for me to decide," Carmen said. "I hope I'm here. I pray so. I want to live to see one of my daughters stop holding out on me and give me a grandbaby. Maybe next Christmas."

There would be no next Christmas. And no grandbaby.

Sela wiped her eyes, blew her mother a kiss, got in the car, and drove. Zelda sat silent beside her. Sela silent beside Zelda.

"Russell in?"

"Mrs. Sykes?"

"Yes. Rachel?"

"Uh huh."

"How are you, Rachel?"

"Been good. Hold on, I'll get Russell."

Hold music flooded Bevolyn's ears. Then, dead air, then Rus-sell's voice.

"Bev?"

"Your secretary seemed a bit short with me, Russell. She's usually more talkative. She seemed uncomfortable. Any reason for that?"

"Administrative assistant," Russell said.

"What?"

"You said, 'secretary.' She's an administrative assistant. Secre-tary isn't politically correct."

"What are you," Bevolyn asked, "her publicist?"

"Just setting you straight."

"I'm straight, all right," Bevolyn said.

"Did you need something, Bev?"

"Thought maybe I could meet you somewhere. We could have lunch together. We haven't done that in some time."

"Up to my neck in work," Russell said. "I'll probably just have Rachel grab us some sandwiches from the deli and eat real quickly in here."

"Us?"

"Rachel's helping me. She is my administrative assistant."

Bevolyn nodded, though Russell couldn't see it. "Okay. I tried. That's it."

"When things settle down," Russell said.

"Sure."

"You okay with this?"

"Yes," Bevolyn said.

"I better get going," Russell said. "I'm glad you called. It's good to hear your voice."

Bevolyn bit into her lip. "See you at home?" She'd said it like a question.

"Yup. Love—"

Bevolyn had hung up. She didn't feel like saying, "I love you," back to Russell, or hearing him say it to her.

15

Love has its inconveniences. Real love can overcome them. I learned that on the inside, one of the many nuggets of wisdom I picked up during that time when the promise of three square meals and a job paying little more than a dime per hour were my blessings.

Picture yourself locked down, isolated from those you love. Picture that existence for over two years, being a man, craving a woman, but having nothing but testosterone, angry testosterone at that, around you on a daily basis. The movies paint a picture of inmates in the shower, afraid to bend for a bar of soap; an inmate sleeping in his cell, when the gate suddenly clicks open and a larger, meaner, sexually frustrated inmate blocks the bars, standing over the awakening inmate, prepared to steal away his dignity. Rape happens in prison, for sure, but not as often as most folks think. Most of the time the sexual relations between inmates is consensual. Lockdown turns many a man from craving breasts, to accepting pecs, pectorals; from desiring that nappy dugout, to accepting that hairy butthole.

I refused to be one of the turned.

So when my Milkshake, my Myshelle, my love, came to visit, all was right with my world. Conjugal visits weren't a reality in our prison, but just smelling her strawberry-scented hair, feeling her butter-soft skin, gazing at her pretty brown eyes—that was all I needed. It was love. It was inconvenient, but it was all I had.

The visiting room was just a large cafeteria—like high school all over again, which I could accept, because if you were in prison, you needed learning. You needed it bad.

The COs on duty had to wear blue instead of their normal gray. "For the public," one had told me when I asked. The COs sat at desks wider than the inmates' cells, on a raised platform with a good view of the entire scene. Vending machines lined the back of the expansive room, offering chips, soda, everything except cigarettes. A play area to the side was set up for kids. I for one am glad I didn't have a kid to visit me. The ones that came were usually extra aggressive, banging those building blocks, ripping arms off those dolls. They'd possibly have to endure watching their own children playing in a prison's playroom one day—a vicious cycle.

Behind the play area were small offices, one of which housed a photographer who'd snap a keepsake Polaroid for the inmates.

"Get a picture taken," was the first thing I said to Myshelle during what would be her last visit. Maybe I had a premonition. Maybe I saw the weariness in her eyes. Or maybe my lust made me want her picture so badly. She'd worn the outfit I'd asked her to wear: blue jeans tighter than Will and Jada, and a pink top with a plunging neckline that highlighted the highway between her breasts. "Damn, you look so good."

"Yeah," she replied. "I do."

We sat next to one another in chairs aligned in a row by a wall topped off with gated windows. None of that talking on a phone with glass separating us. That's movie stuff, like Denzel in *Hurricane*—unreal. The only time that happened was when a visitor requested it, usually a wifey looking to tag an *ex-* on her title. She'd need that glass to prevent her locked-down husband from wrapping his hands around her neck when she let him know the marriage wasn't working for her. That didn't fit my Milkshake, my Myshelle, my love, so we met in the normal visiting room.

"Still having trouble sleeping?" I asked her. She'd told me during one of our frequent collect calls that my bid was wearing on her.

"Having trouble with it all," she said. "I ain't Tish, that's for sure."

If Beale Street Could Talk, by James Baldwin—I'd had her check it out of the library—was about a pregnant girl, Tish, whose man was locked down. She was what the hip-hop kids call a "ride or die chick" because she held him down, refused to let their love wither—refused. I had Myshelle check the novel out because she was my Tish, my ride or die chick.

I looked at Myshelle's flat tummy. "You better not be a Tish. 'Cause I haven't planted any seeds up in you. You overstand?"

"Talk to me the way you talked before this," Myshelle said, craning her head to look around the cafeteria. "It was *understand* then, not *overstand*. You understand?"

"Not the same cat," I told her. "I wish I were, but I'm not."

"And I'm not the same sister," she said.

"Meaning?"

She pointed to the side of the room. "My Coach bag is over there. It has my wallet, my keys, some body spray, and yes, some tampons in it. See the guy with the bald head?" I sat forward for a view. She went on with, "He knows just as much about the contents of my bag as I do. Had to check inside it because the buckle set off the metal detector. I worked so hard for that bag, damn hard. And he has it over there piled next to pocketbooks from Target."

"Your point?"

"Coming here to see you makes me feel like I'm in prison, too."

I narrowed my eyes and swallowed while my heart started dancing in my chest like a white boy with no rhythm. "You're bailing out on me. You're dropping me."

"Baby, I'm not." She touched my hand, sandwiched it with her own. "Really, I'm not. I'm just trying to let you know how rough this is. I want to come here and lift you up, but I can't. I don't feel uplifted. I don't feel like *uplifting*."

"Myshelle, if there's some other dude—"

"No other dude," she quickly said. She rubbed my fingers, kissed my neck, moved and sat on my lap. I flicked my tongue at her neck, breathed in her scented hair, felt her butter-soft skin.

I hurriedly took her in because I knew my time would soon run out.

And it did.

"Ma'am." The CO was on us as if we were an electronics store during the LA riots. "Feet on the floor. No touching except for kisses. Don't tongue him down if you do kiss. Kisses, keep 'em close-mouthed."

Myshelle moved from my lap and slammed herself violently into her seat as the CO left us alone again. "What's my inmate number?" she barked. "Where the hell is my green prison-issued clothes? I want my shit in a pleated skirt. A halter top. Think they can hook that up for me, baby? Huh? Do you?" She smacked the wall with an open palm. "Do you?"

I sat wordless. What could I say?

"I'm gonna go," she said suddenly, and stood, hands on her hips.

I lurched forward, panicking, and grabbed her by the waist, my head resting on her side. "Don't go, baby. I thought you were staying until two forty-five."

Visiting hours were from 8:30 A.M. to 2:45 P.M. I could stay outside of my cell as long as I had a visitor. I cherished that time, looked forward to it, needed it.

"Can't do it today, baby," she told me. "This is stressing me out."

I winced. I could actually feel a knife blade type of pain in my chest.

"Don't do that," she said. "Come. I'll take a Polaroid for you."

She took me by the wrist to the photographer's office and smiled for the Polaroid, smiled as if we didn't have an inconvenient love, as if our love wasn't cracking at the seams. I fanned the picture, and when it developed and I saw that beautiful smile, I smiled too. You've heard of fool's gold? That was a fool's smile.

We kissed.

"I love you," I told her when she pulled away.

She nodded and went through a door to the right. I was ushered through a door to the left and led to a tiny cubicle where I reluctantly handed in my Polaroid.

"Short visit," the CO outside the cubicle said, grinning as he licked his lips and studied Myshelle's photo. "If I had a pretty gal like that, I'd be loaded to bear over a short visit like that."

"You had a pretty gal like that," I told him, looking at his gut ready to jump from the cliff of his belt loop, "you wouldn't look so much like a bear." A weak comeback but all I had just the same.

He smirked. "Empty your pockets, *inmate.*"

I pulled them inside out and showed him I didn't even have lint. Didn't have anything.

"Step on in for your close-up," he said, opening the cubicle door.

I did. He shut it tight behind me.

"Wardrobe change," I heard him say as I went about the business of disrobing. I handed him the clothing. He fingered each piece in a check for contraband and, satisfied I was clean, hung them on a wall peg, and then stepped inside with me. It was a tight fit.

"Run your hands through your hair, Chris Rock," he said. "Funny man."

"Sure thing, Chris Farley," I replied. "Or is it John Candy?" Fat white comics who were both dead, not that I was wishing that on him.

"Pull your ears forward," he said, thankfully ignoring my barb.

I pulled them.

"Open your mouth. Say ahh."

"Ahh."

"Stick out your tongue."

I stuck it out. He looked under it thoroughly.

"Arms up."

As he checked my armpits, he tugged on a tangle of hair and made me jump and squeal. That brought about a fit of laughter that had him snorting like a pig with asthma. I wasn't amused, though.

"Turn around. Bend over and spread those cheeks." He paused and snickered. "Say ahh."

His hands probed my anus. I closed my eyes and focused on Myshelle. Love. Inconvenient.

"Your screen test is complete," he said. "I do believe you'll get the part. Get dressed, *inmate.*"

I quickly dressed and stepped outside. "My Polaroid?" I asked, holding my hand up.

He frowned. "Polaroid? What Polaroid?" He turned and looked at another CO. "Seen a Polaroid?" The other CO shook his head. Fat boy turned back to me. "Don't know anything about any Polaroid. Sorry."

Anger didn't boil in me. A wisecrack didn't form on my tongue. My hands didn't ball into fists.

No, I turned humble—very humble. "All I got," I said to him, my lip quivering. I could feel my eyes watering. I blinked as if he'd sprayed me with tear gas, or chemical agents in CO-speak.

He studied me a moment and then produced the Polaroid. "She is a beautiful woman," he said. "Handle this with care."

I took the Polaroid, thanked him several times, and went back to my cell.

Cried into my pillow.

That would be Myshelle's last visit. It was the day I learned love has its inconveniences. Real love can overcome them. And my love, our love, wasn't real.

"You're mighty quiet," Sela said to me.

I turned to her, the swish of my windshield wipers having a hypnotic effect on me as I drove. Rain sluiced down on us as if I'd stolen something from its mama. "Thinking," I said, smiling.

"Pretty hard, too," she said. "I could actually see your brain. It isn't pretty to look at, either. About the only thing that isn't pretty on you, I imagine."

"Well, thanks, and for the record, I bet you have a beautiful brain."

She touched her chest, the area above her heart.

"It's true," I said.

"So what were you thinking on, so hard?"

Myshelle. Polaroid. Strip frisks. Prison. Love. Unreal.

The memories stained my thoughts. I couldn't clean them away with baking soda or some homemade concoction that included vinegar. I might as well face it. I felt I could with Sela.

"My last girlfriend, woman I thought loved me, she gave up on me when I went through a hard time," I said.

"Oh?"

"Yeah," I said, "Oh."

"All men aren't dogs," Sela said, "but some women are. Female dogs. Affectionately known as bitches. I'd say your ex fits into that category."

I smiled. "You think?"

"You're good people, LeVar. If she did you dirty, I don't think, I know she was a bitch."

"I'll take your word for it, Sela. No one would know a woman better than you."

"How you figure?" Her voice hitched up. Her posture changed.

"You are one," I said. "Right?"

She smiled and relaxed her shoulders. "Yes. Yes, I am."

"You have to be careful about that," I said. "What looks like one thing sometimes is another. Have you ever seen the ads at the back of the *Village Voice?*"

She frowned. "Nuh uh. What are they for?"

"Beautiful, gorgeous women. Available for dates. Until you realize they're chicks with sticks. She-males."

"What's a reverend doing reading the *Village Voice* if it got all that in it?" she asked.

I smiled. "The articles, Sister Sela. The articles."

"I think it's sick," she said, not smiling, and spitting the words out.

"To each his own."

"What's the Bible call that kind of stuff? Freaky sex. Same sex and whatnot."

"An abomination," I said. "But I'm not one to judge. Don't feel I'm in any place to. A born sinner, just like the next man."

"You should preach that sermon some Sunday," Sela said. "My sister needs to hear it. She's one for judging."

I didn't care to talk about Bevolyn. Moving on from that, my new creed.

"Have you ever done a man wrong?" I asked Sela. "Left him hanging? Broke his heart?"

She turned away and looked out the side window as raindrops cried tears down the glass. That was all the answer I needed. I focused in on my driving, my wipers swish-swishing me toward those dark memories again. I knew it would take a new love—a powerful, real new love to make them forever vanish. My chances of finding that seemed dim. First, I'd fallen for a forbidden love: Bevolyn. Then, that forbidden love's sister: Sela.

Neither appeared doable. Bevolyn was married. Sela was single, but from the sudden shift in her posture and the silence that followed, I could tell there was a man out there somewhere that would have changed that if she'd let him. She hadn't. She wasn't ride or die.

I needed ride or die.

I pulled up to her building sometime later and parked my Toy-yoda by the curb out front. I kept the engine warm, on. "So?" was the only thing I could think to say. We'd just endured about twenty minutes of the most deafening silence I'd ever known.

"You learn," she said softly. Her back still faced me.
"What?"
"You learn from those mistakes," she said. "I know I did."
"What did you learn?" I asked.

She turned to me, her eyes a mirror of the side window, glassy, wet. A smile graced her pretty face. Bevolyn's features, but so much warmer, so much kinder on Sela. Or at least I wanted this to be the case. I wanted a love that didn't die when inconvenienced.

"I could tell you," she said, "but it would take more time." She leaned forward and looked up through the windshield. "The rain is easing."

I looked out, too. "It is."

"Keep driving?" she asked. "So I can tell you what I learned."

"You want to continue our ride?"

She smiled. "Yep. Unless you have a sermon to write or a soul to save?"

Continue our ride. The words of a ride or die chick. Maybe she *was* what I was looking for.

I touched her shoulder. She leaned over and kissed my hand.

I pulled from the curb. We kept riding.

16

Afeni shifted her backpack to her left side as she started the tiring ascent up the six flights of stairs. The elevator was forever broken, and when it did work, the stench of urine and vomit kept most from using it. Her mother's apartment complex, an edifice crumbling on the outside, cracking on the inside, rested in the bowels of one of the worst sections of Newark. Capital enterprise in the neighborhood consisted of the liquor store, the fish and chicken fry restaurant, and the hourly rate motel. More than a handful of the neighborhood women plied their trade in eight-hour days at the fleabag motel up around Mulberry Street, doing an hour shift here, another hour shift there, scraping together rent money with other women's husbands. At least Afeni's mother didn't go that route; close, but not quite.

Despair grew in the neighborhood like weeds. Hope was water during a drought. When she'd lived here, Afeni's writing journal had served as a compass to guide her through the maze that was her daily ordeal. Each line of poetry had been a passageway to brighter days. She'd traveled those passageways with her words and her imagination, moved swiftly through her plight with the flourish of her pen. In cursive strokes, her poems made her shitty life seem less, well, shitty.

But the Sykeses had rescued her from that. And though it wasn't always milk and honey in their home, Afeni was thankful God had seen fit to bring them into her life. Mr. Sykes could be moody, probably because of the long hours he put in at work, but Afeni saw a special fondness in his eyes whenever he looked at her. And it wasn't some nasty old man leering at a budding young girl, either. It was pride, the look always flashing in his eyes when she did something special.

Bevolyn was a different challenge for Afeni. It was probably just their X-chromosomes doing battle, two strong, opinionated females going at it. But, despite their differences, Afeni respected and cared for her foster mother. It warmed Afeni that Bevolyn Sykes's eyes would water just a bit, and she'd hurriedly hug Afeni and disappear to her bedroom whenever the day came for Afeni to leave to visit Aloe. Today had followed that pattern, and Afeni had wondered about it during her bus ride. Where did that apparent love come from? And if Bevolyn Sykes was so open to loving a child, why hadn't she had one of her own? Afeni knew she could. She saw Bevolyn swallowing the Ortho Tri-Cyclen pills with a gulp of water every morning.

Shit, who knew why people acted the way they did? Afeni climbed another landing of steps, thoughts of the Sykeses diminishing as a familiar stink tickled the hairs in her nostrils.

Old man Kato, a human permeation of urine and cheap wine, camped out as usual on the bend between the stairwell for floors three and four. Just before she came upon him, Afeni checked her pocket to make sure she still had a dollar. She did. She clutched it in a fist as she moved near him. Kato burped in acknowledgement as she crossed his path and the air around his head filled with a smell worse than day-old vomit.

"Hey, Miss 'Feni," he said.

"Hey, Mr. Kato," she answered.

"Is good to see you wit' us again," he said.

"Good to be seen," she replied. She counted quietly to herself, knowing it was coming.

"Dollar?" Kato asked, his dirty hand outstretched, covered with an even dirtier glove absent of its fingers. Dirt lived under his fingernails. Most of the nails were chipped, yellowing, and covered with some dried brownish gunk. Afeni didn't dare venture a guess as to what the dried brownish gunk was.

Afeni smiled to herself and opened her hand to reveal the crumpled bill. She sat her backpack down on the step and moved closer to Kato. She closed in on him without flinching, squeezing her nostrils, or acknowledging in any way the stench that rose from his frame. Very few people could match that trick when it came to Kato. He was like a speed bump on the stairs—folks slowed to pass, but they never came to a full stop.

"You got any new poems for me, Kato?" Afeni asked as he shifted his position to try to get a glimpse of the Georgie in her hand.

"No, Miss 'Feni," he replied as she tortured him by unfolding the bill and rubbing out the creases by flattening it on her knee and running her fingers across the face of the dollar.

"No?" she said. "That's a shame because I sure do want to pass this money along to you. A tip. But only if you get your Def Poetry Jam on."

"Miss 'Feni, please," Kato begged as she continued working with a surgeon's precision on the bill. "This ain't right you always work me fo' dat money. I'm a vet'ren you know. 'Nam. Before your time, but I got medals. Got more 'an John Kerry. I could be your next Yessur Mister President."

Afeni held the bill up above her head, inspecting its authenticity in the light of the hallway, all the while refusing to so much as look in Kato's direction.

"Okay, okay," he broke down, "I got a dang line or two." Afeni smiled triumphantly and turned her attention to him.

He cleared his throat, shuffled his position on the floor, and aligned his back straight with the wall, postured like a concert pianist about to tickle out Chopin's "Waltz in F Minor."

"Though you may hear me holler…"

Afeni prodded him on with a look.

". . . And you may see me cry…"

She rubbed her hands together, nodded several times.

". . . I'll be dogged, sweet baby…"

She waved her hand. Shit, man, don't stop.

". . . If you gonna see me die."

She smiled.

"That d'ere's Lang-stain Hughes, Miss 'Feni."

That would be about it: a few lines, a few nibbles. Kato didn't give too much. 'Just enough to get by' had been his mission statement since returning from the ditches in that far land. Afeni clapped softly and handed Kato the dollar. He snatched it from her hand, eyeing it like a sirloin. His eagerness always warmed her.

"Keep the poetry in you alive, Kato," Afeni said as she retrieved her backpack. "It's the only shield in this ugly world."

As she stepped up the creaky stairs, Kato took his attention off the dollar long enough to call to her, "You too, Miss 'Feni. Poe'etry inside."

Afeni closed her eyes as she reached her mother's door on the fourth floor: 401B. When Afeni had lived between the four walls inside, it was this point, the doorway of her apartment, which had always held her up. No matter how bright the day or how illuminating its promise, crossing the threshold of 401B had always dimmed her life like a light bulb with a popped spring. Afeni scanned the hallway, thinking about all the scattered lives represented throughout the corridor. Toys littered the floor. Either the children or their mothers had been too lazy to discard them in the Dumpster behind the building once the Tonka trucks got down to only two wheels.

This had been Afeni's world, far removed from what she now had with the Sykeses. Afeni couldn't help wondering how far her popularity would nosedive at Ponce, the private school the Sykeses sent her to, if the other teens could see her now. Would they look past the rotten odor that lived on the stairwell with Kato? Would they delve beneath the garbage littering the halls? Would they withhold judgment on the women who left their young children unmonitored while they ran out in skirts that barely covered their hips? Would they look beyond all of this and still see Afeni as equal, as someone to enjoy, to converse with? There was *their* world, and there was *her* world. She participated in both actively, but this life actually fit. The Sykeses were her blessing. This was her reality. She could land back here at any time, back to reality.

Shit. That would suck the big one.

In this world once you opened your door and stepped in, you'd find a mother named Aloe, a woman who danced in what most would consider underwear at best, for strange men, but familiar money. Shit. And that was the least of it. Afeni thought of the discolored marks on her mother's arms and hoped they would be gone today.

Afeni took her deep cleansing breath—just as they'd told her to do it on *Oprah*—and twisted the doorknob open. Immediately the sounds of a Nat King Cole Christmas album blared in Afeni's eardrums. She sighed and fought the desire to turn right around and head back home. She took her key from the knob, closed the door behind her, went to the living room area, slung her backpack on the floor, and plopped down on the couch. The couch screamed, the few springs still in place popped, and Afeni dropped down an extra couple of inches. The back of her leg cut into the wood frame of the couch. Broken. Aloe would have a fit. Shit. Afeni got up and sat down carefully on the one chair in the room, a throw-up-brown-colored monstrosity that shared nothing in kind with the living room. Muted shades of green colored everything else.

Nat King Cole continued to croon.

"Why does she do this shit?"

Nat King Cole's voice, though melodic, was a nail driving into Afeni's eardrum. She rubbed her temples, then her eyes, blew out air in frustration, fumbled with her hands. She stood, then sat, then stood again. She paced the floor, turned on the television, and turned it off just as quickly when she saw the image on the screen: a Snoop Dogg video with scantily clad women dancing on a stripper's pole. Not watching that shit.

Nat King Cole continued to sing about chestnuts roasting on an open fire.

"Shit. This shit doesn't make sense." Afeni felt like moving to the stereo, pulling that album off the record player, and smashing Nat King Cole against the wall. But she didn't.

Instead, she sat back down on the chair, rifled through her backpack, and found her journal. She pulled it out, uncapped a pen, and stabbed a quick poem out on the page. Her words drifted off the lines, extending way into the margin, the heat of her emotions setting fire in words.

"Coming Home to Nat" was the title of her quickly written poem.

Afeni recapped her pen, placed her journal back in her backpack, and stood from the chair. Hungry, she walked the ten feet it took to reach the kitchen and scrounged through the cupboards. A half-full bottle of Jack Daniel's was in one, an empty cereal box in another. Canned peas. Shit, no. A box of Orville Redenbacher microwave popcorn, Butter Lover's style. Shit, yeah.

Afeni removed a pack and placed it in the microwave, Nat King Cole still in her ears, though she tried to tune him out. She couldn't, so she tapped her fingers against the Formica countertop and hummed something else, something to try to drown out Natalie's father.

"La-di-da-di-da. I can't hear you."

The popcorn started to sing with her, then, a couple of minutes in, its song ended and the microwave dinged. Afeni stuck her hands inside and carefully pulled out the popcorn bag by the right end. It felt hot to the touch and her fingers soaked up a coat of excess butter. Shit, yeah. Just the way she liked it.

She turned around to head back to the living room.

"Oh, shit!" she yelled, dropping the bag of popcorn.

"What the hell?" gasped the naked man standing in front of Afeni. His skin was light brown, but that thing Afeni noticed hanging between his legs was blacker than a VCR tape.

The man quickly covered himself with his hands and did a moonwalk out of the kitchen.

Aloe didn't have a kitchen table because the space was too small. In the corner was a bar stool, the foam of its cushion bleeding through the poor patch-up job of gray duct tape. Afeni picked the popcorn bag off the floor, moved to the chair, and sat on it. She opened the Orville Redenbacher and stuck her fingers inside. Her hands shook as she placed a kernel to her lips. Nat King Cole haunted her ears again.

Aloe stepped into the opening of the kitchen, a fuzz-laden robe on, the waist strap missing so it hung open and showed her sweaty, naked body. Her belly button ring had a chain that hung down and disappeared in the thatch of black hair between her thighs. A rose tattoo bloomed on the right side of her waist. A black panther roared on the other side.

"Why you here?" Aloe asked Afeni.

"My day to come," Afeni said. "You knew I'd be by."

Aloe moved into the kitchen, leaned against a counter, and pulled the robe closed around her. "I mean in the apartment," she said. "You heard the Nat King Cole playing. I got it blasting, too. You know if I got Nat on, that mean something is jumping off for me. Don't come in. Hang out in the hall until my jump-off leaves."

"Didn't feel like sitting out in the hall," Afeni said. "I don't have but a few hours to stay here." She narrowed her eyes. "You should have saved your 'jump-off' for some other time. Some time when your daughter wasn't coming by."

Aloe waved her daughter off. "You must be…" Crazy. She let it drift like aerosol spray. But this was her child, after all, so she rerouted. "I've been trying to get a swing on that dingaling for months, baby girl. Raul is hard to come by, Afeni. In heavy demand, as they say. Nigga with them curls in his hair and stuff. Always smelling good. It's hard to get down with him."

"Aren't you just the lucky one," Afeni said. "Your ticket number finally came up, huh?"

Aloe smiled. "True. Felt like I was waiting to get my hair touched up or for some honey ham." She looked toward her bedroom and smiled. "But it was worth the wait. Let me tell you."

"I'm happy for you, *Mama*."

Aloe spread her arms. "Come give Mama a hug, girl. And stop hating. Your time will come. You're gonna get to play Nat King Cole, too, one day. Your corny ass might actually try to screw to Nat, though."

Afeni moved to her mother's arms and disappeared in the warm embrace. In seconds she didn't hear Nat King Cole, didn't see Raul's long black penis, was Diane's daughter, not Aloe's mistake.

"How are things with them?" Aloe asked, still holding her.

"Kinda funky," Afeni said. She knew immediately what "them" her mother was speaking of—The Sykeses. "I think they're having problems. They don't say it. Try to act normal around me. But I can feel it."

Aloe smiled but said, "That's a shame. Bevolyn treating you okay, though?"

"Yeah."

Aloe hesitated. "Russell?"

"Mr. Sykes is cool, too," Afeni replied. "Bevolyn—Mrs. Sykes, does more. Takes more of an interest, but Russell, he's okay."

Aloe mumbled something.

Afeni leaned her head from her mother. "What did you say?"

Aloe shifted, then laughed. "Nothing. Just was saying that Russell sounds like your father." She moved away from Afeni and went to the sink, turned her back to her daughter, ran the faucet, and washed her hands under the stream of lukewarm water.

"You never mention my father," Afeni said. "Or hardly ever. Why is that?"

"Nothing to mention." Aloe's shoulders shrugged. "He left me high and dry. Went out to get cigarettes and that was it. Typical." She laughed. "Should have known that was a bullshit excuse. He never even smoked. That nigga would get a coughing fit if a car backfired near him." She turned to Afeni then and smiled…smiled to cover her lie.

"You know where he is?" Afeni wondered.

Aloe wiped her hands on her robe, moved over toward the refrigerator, opened it, and pulled out a half-full bottle of Heineken. She frowned as she took a long swallow of the beer, then tossed the empty in her recyclable garbage can.

"Are you going to answer me?" Afeni asked her mother.

"What did you ask?" Aloe said.

Raul stuck his head into the kitchen before Afeni could repeat the question.

"Aloe, that was some damn good"—he paused, looking at Afeni—"conversation. We need to, um, talk again soon."

Aloe frowned. "You're leaving? So soon?"

"Yeah," Raul said. "I got to go meet someone about something."

"I hope you don't have to *talk* to them," Aloe said. "I do believe you're about *talked* out."

He grinned. "Naw, I'm done talking for the day."

"Shit," Afeni said. "Y'all can stop this talk nonsense. I know you boned. Shit."

"I'll get up with you, Aloe," Raul said.

Aloe winked. "Talk to you later. Next time we have to talk longer."

Raul started to say something to Afeni but decided against it. Instead, he turned and padded across the thin carpet in the hall, then softly shut the door behind him.

"My father," Afeni said right away. "Do you know where he is?"

Aloe went back to the refrigerator, opened it, and cursed when she found it empty of any more Heinekens.

"Aloe. Mama. Shit, I'm talking to you."

"Your daddy? Yes, I know where he is. You ain't ever asked before."

"Well, I'm asking now. Where is he?"

"I can't tell you, Afeni. It's best right now that you don't know."

"Shit. That's nonsense. I want to know."

"Well, I can't tell you. I promised them I wouldn't."

"Them who?" Afeni asked.

"I tell you that and it's over," Aloe said.

"Well, is he close? Does he live in Jersey?" Afeni asked.

Aloe smiled. "He's close. Real close."

"You think I might have ever seen him?"

"Unless you see like Stevie Wonder, you have," Aloe confided.

Afeni fumbled with her lips. "Close. I've seen him." She looked up at Aloe. Her eyes widened. "Not Raul?"

"No." Aloe laughed. "I told you he was a new jump-off, that I've wanted to swing from that dingaling for some time now."

"Right," Afeni said. "How could I forget? You're so poetic."

"Just let it go," Aloe said. "Bevolyn Sykes doesn't want you messing up her nice little life." One side of Aloe's face tightened. She held a breath in.

"Bevolyn?" Afeni frowned. "What does she have to do with my father?"

"What?"

"Bevolyn," Afeni said, "you said she didn't want me messing up her..."

"What?"

"*Them.*" Afeni moved toward her mother, pointing a finger at her mother's chest. "When you said 'them.' You promised them you wouldn't tell me. You were talking about the Sykeses before, weren't you?"

"Let it go, Afeni."

"Russell. Oh my God! He's my father, isn't he?"

"If you like it there, you won't rock the boat," Aloe told her. "Trust me, you rock the boat and Bevolyn will have you out of her house quick, fast, and in a hurry. If you like it there, then you'll keep your little mouth shut tight."

"Shit. Shit. Shit. I don't believe this. What's going on here, Aloe?"

"It's real twisted up and complicated, baby girl."

Aloe tried to step forward to hug her daughter again. Afeni put a hand up and held her mother back. "Don't," she told her mother.

"Let me explain," Aloe begged.

"No," Afeni barked. She turned and ran off.

Aloe watched her daughter move to the living room, snatch up her backpack, and then prance across the floor toward the front door. She could see the weariness in the young girl's gait, the weight of more than just the contents of her backpack that seemed to ride her shoulders. Afeni stopped to drop her apartment key on the flower stand by the front door. She turned and looked at her mother, looking like a traveler at a bus stop preparing to go on a long trip. She blew her mother a kiss and left. Aloe slid down the wall to the floor after the door shut.

"Shit," she said. "Shit!" She drank too much. It impaired her thoughts and made her lips way too damn loose.

Afeni stepped outside of Aloe's building to an emotional sky crying its tears, its face lacking color, gray. She considered the several blocks' walk to the bus depot, but the raindrops were the size of mint cough drops. She dropped her backpack, let it settle at her feet, and pulled out her cellular phone. The cellular phone the Sykeses had gotten for her. She dialed.

"Sykes residence."

Afeni almost said, "Daddy," but caught herself.

"I need a ride" was all she said. She never did address Russell in any way, just went straight into what she needed to say. She realized now that some part of her subconscious must have known of the deep connection between them, the blood connection. Her subconscious in turn hadn't allowed her to call him Mr. Sykes or Mr. Russell. Her subconscious was waiting for the day she'd be able to call him what he was. Daddy.

"Where you at, Afeni?"

"My Mama's," she said. "You know where it's at?"

He hesitated. "Buses aren't working?"

"Have you looked outside?"

There was a lull. Afeni could hear his footsteps walking across the floor. Russell grunted, probably, Afeni realized, from reaching up and looking out of a window. He was older. Older than Bevolyn, older than Aloe. Afeni wondered how he'd come to these two very different women. She knew he loved Bevolyn. It was in his eyes. But what about Aloe? Had he ever loved her mother? Should she be angry with him? What? Shit!

"I see it," he said, his voice coming back into the phone's receiver.

"Please don't say it's raining cats and dogs," Afeni said.

Russell laughed. "That's not cool enough?"

"Totally uncool," Afeni said.

"I'm heading out the door now," Russell said. "You sit tight." He paused before adding, "The rain is off the hook."

Afeni smiled. Daddy.

★ ★ ★

Afeni moved from the lobby of Aloe's building with the slowness of thick gravy pouring from a ladle. Her backpack hung from her shoulders. Russell's SUV idled by the curb out front. Afeni could see him looking behind her, at the building, thinking on apartment 401B, probably. He reached over and pushed the passenger side door open as Afeni reached the vehicle.

"Get in," he said, as if she planned to stay out in the rain. Afeni smiled. Parents, shit, they were crazy.

"Thanks," Afeni said as she settled in.

"No problem. Buckle up."

Afeni connected her seat belt. Out of the corner of her eye she noticed Russell still looking at the building. "It's a piece of crap," she said. "I know."

"Not the outside that matters," Russell said. "It's the inside."

Maybe he had loved Aloe.

"You think?"

Russell gathered his wits, smiled, pulled the transmission tree to DRIVE, and did just that. His eyes found the rearview mirror a couple of times before they turned right at the end of the street.

"Had a good time at your mother's?" Russell asked.

"Not really," Afeni replied.

Russell looked at her. "No?"

"Uh-uh. She had company."

"Company?"

"Some man," Afeni said. She looked closely at Russell to see if this brought any reaction. It didn't. He hadn't loved Aloe. Afeni knew it.

"He didn't bother you, did he?" Russell asked.

"Who? The man?"

"Yeah."

"Nah. He was cool. Kinda embarrassed because I saw him naked."

"You"—Russell slammed on the brakes—"what?"

"He didn't know I was there," Afeni said. "I was in the kitchen. He stepped in there. Backed up right away."

Russell shook his head. "I don't like that."

"It's okay," Afeni assured him. "Man, you're being such a father."

Russell's face dropped. He said nothing.

"Why didn't y'all have kids?" Afeni asked.

Russell started to drive again. "Who?"

"Who. You and your wife."

Russell grimaced as he made a turn. "Wasn't in the cards."

"You would have been a good father," Afeni said.

Russell turned to her. His eyes danced. "You think?"

She nodded. "Mrs. Sykes, too."

"Yeah, I always thought so. But our lives never fit it. We got married young. She was in college. I was working. We were sure our lives would include children. But…"

"Oh, yeah, college. I ever show you that picture of her I got off the internet?" Afeni asked. "I Googled her. It's from when she was in college."

Russell seemed amused. "Googled?"

"Search engine," Afeni said. "Y'all sure ain't up on new stuff. I would expect you to know, though. I used it to check up on her. See what she was about." Curiously, she hadn't checked up on Russell.

"What was the picture?" Russell asked, laughing. "Did she have the Afro?"

Afeni giggled. "Yeah. A big one. She was at a protest."

Russell frowned. "Protest?"

"Against abortion. At a clinic."

Russell's grip on the steering wheel tightened. Afeni noticed. "Something wrong?" she asked.

"She wasn't protesting," Russell said.

"What was she doing there, then?"

Russell didn't answer.

17

I opened the passenger side door of the Toy-yoda and took Sela by the arm. She stepped out with her certain rhythm, like a leaf blowing in the wind, a wave lapping at the sand of a beach, unmistakable, and unique to her, her certain rhythm. There was music in her movements, the way her mouth crinkled in a smile, how her hips swayed under the fabric of her clothes…music. And though I'd spent the past little while entranced by Bevolyn's song, I realized at that moment that Sela's melody was just as good, or better.

Sela stepped up on the curb and turned, waiting for me as I closed the car door behind her. When I turned back to her from the Toy-yoda, Sela's smile serenaded me. I smiled at her in kind.

"Coming up?" she asked. "Or you just gonna walk a sister to the door and leave her hanging?"

"You want me to?" I cleared the hitch in my voice— nerves, something I didn't usually have with women. "Come up, I mean?"

"Would I have asked…?" She let that song fade out, yet its lyrics echoed in my ears. Would I have asked, she'd said; if I didn't want you to, left unsaid. *Want.* She wanted me. I wanted her, too.

I took her hand and was about to squeeze her thin fingers in the lover's gesture of happiness, but she squeezed mine first. "Come," she whispered as she turned and guided me down the path to her apartment tower.

We stopped at the doors to the lobby as she rifled through her small pocketbook for a key.

"Isn't it amazing?" I said to her.

"What?" She didn't look up but continued searching through the clutter of her pocketbook.

I thought of Myshelle briefly, her disgust with visiting me in prison, having some CO hold on to her pocketbook, searching it for contraband when the metal detector chimed. The inconvenience of love. All the scars of my life, my brother, Miss Ma'am. I thought of the Ruffin Brothers, my father, all the uncertainties of my future, and wondered if Sela would hang tough through the inconveniences.

"LeVar?"

"Huh?"

She had her keys in hand, that song of a smile on her face again. "Isn't what amazing?"

"How God just erased away the gray and colored over it with blue and orange."

"You're talking about the weather?" she asked. "The sky?"

"Yes," I said, nodding. "The sky."

She looked up. A blanket of dazzling blue and orange covered us from overhead. The only evidence of an earlier downpour was the slick grass surrounding Sela's apartment and the beads of water on the hoods of the cars in her building's lot.

Sela smiled. "You're right, LeVar. It's amazing."

I moved my gaze from the sky to Sela's smile.

"He's Him," I said. "A miracle worker. Every day is full of His tiny little miracles." As I said those words, I concentrated on her parted lips, her raised cheeks, thinking Sela was one of His big, giant miracles.

"You know," she said, "I don't really get into too much God talk. Bevolyn's more into it than I am, I have to admit."

"But?"

Sela looked at me with those pretty brown eyes, and for once, I didn't see Bevolyn in them. She touched my shoulder, a habit of hers I appreciated, and squeezed ever so slightly. "But you make me want to know Him," she said. "It goes down easier…hearing about God…from you. As opposed to Saint Bevolyn."

"Why is that?"

"You don't look like any pastor I've ever seen."

"No?"

She bit into her lip and her eyes flickered. She licked her lips. "Nope."

"That good or bad?"

"Come on, LeVar. You know you're fine." She reached for my hand. I gave it to her. She squeezed. "It doesn't get any better than this. Standing here with you."

"How about sitting up there with me?" I suggested, pointing upward, toward her apartment on the second floor.

"I stand corrected," she said.

"Let's go, then."

A shadow crossed her face. She hesitated.

"Something wrong?" I asked.

She smiled again. Different song, though. Where the other had been uptempo, this one was slow and sad. I'd heard it before: Miss Ma'am's last days, Myshelle's last visit, Bevolyn at the front of the church letting me know she thought I was a fake.

"Sela?"

She swallowed. "I meant it when I said I learned from my previous relationship."

"Okay. And I believed you; that's why I'm here."

"Things you should know about me." She squinted, did something with her face and shoulders I wasn't familiar with, her body language bad, her words to come probably worse, I feared.

"Go on."

"I'm being very careful how I speak to you," she said. "No cursing. Making sure I sound intelligent."

"Aiight," I said, "I'm feelin' that. True dat. True dat."

She laughed. I was glad she had. That had been my intention.

"I'm serious, LeVar."

"Go on."

"I like you. I don't want to disappoint you in the end. I want you to know who I really am. What I'm really about, so you can decide, fairly, if you want to do this with me."

"I want to do it with you," I said.

She smirked, shook her head. "You better be serious."

"I was."

"Anyway," she went on, "I've got this situation. I like…I like…" Scratches marred the album of her words—a broken record.

I nudged the needle over. "You like what, Sela?"

"Smoking," she blurted.

I frowned and crinkled my nose. "I figured as much." I wrung my hands. "You know, with what happened to my mother, I don't like cigarettes much."

She shook her head. "Not Newports or Kools, LeVar. Dutchies."

I smiled and raised an eyebrow. "You telling me you get high?"

She nodded. "A hella lot." She touched her mouth at the slip of her tongue. "Oops. I didn't mean to say 'hella.' Well, I did, but…"

I shrugged. *Hella* wasn't exactly my idea of profanity, but whatever.

"Anyway," she went on, "I wanted you to know I smoke blunts."

"Why not E-Z Widers?" I asked. "Rolling papers."

Now she frowned. "What? You asking me that?"

I nodded.

" 'Cause blunts burn slower," she said matter-of-factly.

I nodded and smiled. "Cool. You're a wise woman. Anything else? Any other secrets?"

"No." She paused. "That's it? You don't have anything else to say?"

I thought of Reverend Walker, his words to me that day outside his study. I'd come to him, an ex-con trying to find my way, trying to find my way to From Whom All Blessings Flow. Reverend Walker had said to me, "Only one judge. Only one judge. And his name isn't George Henry Walker."

It wasn't for me to judge, either. I was still trying to find my way. As was Sela. As were so many others. It would take those of us trying to find our way to band together, I believed, for us to get on the right course.

Sela helping me. Me helping her.

"That's something you have to figure out on your schedule," I told her. "I used to burn, myself. But I reached a point where the only way I wanted to get high was with Him." I pointed to the sky.

Sela nodded. "See. That's what I'm talking about, there. Saint Bevolyn doesn't have that. You do."

"Let's not talk about her," I said. "Let's concentrate on you and me."

"Let's do that," her words a ballad spoken softly.

I took her in my arms, pulled her close. "Anything else? Anything else I need to know about you?"

She shivered in my arms. I wrapped her tighter in my embrace. She laid her head on my chest. "No," she said, "that's it." She continued to shiver. I continued to hold her close.

"Good."

"I so want this to work," she whispered.

"Me too."

She raised her head off my chest. "You too, what?"

"You said, 'I so want this to work,'" I told her. "I do, too."

She touched her lips. "I didn't know I'd said that out loud. I didn't mean to."

"It was a prayer," I said. "God answers them. Don't worry."

She laid her head back on my chest and whispered, "God answers them. God answers them."

I went up with her and left a few hours later. We didn't make love, but held each other in the way sensitive lovers hold one another after they've made love. All was right with my world.

God answered prayers.

18

"Tell me you love me."

"What? No. I've never told—"

"There's a first time for everything. Now. Tell me."

"Can't. I'm sorry."

"If I kiss you in that special place, maybe you'll consider it?"

"Too fast. Too much." Words. Hesitation behind them. "Maybe I should go."

"No. No. Okay. Be still. I'll leave it alone. Let me finish your feet. Okay?"

"Fine. But stay below my ankles."

Ssshh-ssshh-ssshh-ssshh-ssshh.

A pumice stone glided across her foot, smoothing those rough edges. She closed her eyes as the tension in her body eased, a cool glass of ice water sliding down her parched throat. The questions swirled in her mind, those incessant thoughts in her head, doing likewise…easing.

Sounds were in her ears now…waves, hard, crashing, rushing waves. Gnashing…gnashing, but still so peaceful. Birds overhead, chirping out a song as beautiful as Luther, Teddy, Marvin. Soft sand between her toes. Nuh uh. Wait. Hands, smooth fingers, rubbing lotion on her feet. Ooh.

"Just like that," she said. "Feels…"

"Good, right? I have magic fingers. You should let me give you a massage."

"No quit in you, is there?"

"That's right. Not when I see something I want."

Silence, no response to that from her.

Hands, smooth fingers, rubbing lotion on her feet. Ooh. Her eyes closed. Ooh. Massaging the heel, the toes…magic fingers. Yep, that would be about right.

Then those smooth fingers moved. Her eyes jerked open. "Whoa! What are you doing?"

"Relax. Keep still."

"I don't—"

"Relax."

She did.

Magic fingers on her calves moved up her leg and massaged the inside of her thigh, kneaded those tense thigh muscles. Lips kissed her thighs. She couldn't open her eyes. Wanted the lips there. Nuh-uh. Didn't. Wait. Yes. Did.

Smooth, magic fingers hooked her panties and moved the material aside for easy access to her V. Her V, moist despite her best attempts to keep it anything but, pink-brown, prettier than most, she'd been told once. Shaved clean of hair and smooth like the fingers of before. Lips kissed the V. Ooh. Tongue traced the outline of it. Ooh. Hands grabbed her ass, propped her up, and brought her with just the right amount of force to a mouth. That tongue again. Ooh. Had her on a train to an impending explosion. Had her fingernails digging into the mattress. Digging deep into the mattress. Fingers. Smooth fingers. Ooh. Fingers inside her, two of them, walking her walls, searching for that spot most knew nothing of, and couldn't have found if they did. At the ceiling of her V, the skin there lumpy. Find it, rub it, and she couldn't con-

trol herself. Those fingers found it. Damn, she thought
only she knew that spot, thought she'd never experience
a lover's fingers there, that the tingle that convulsed her
body when it was touched would come from her hands
and her hands only. Wrong. It wasn't her fingers there
now. Nuh-uh. The smooth fingers of another. Ooh.

She bucked her hips. Floating. Without a Dutchie.
Didn't need a blunt for this out-of-body experience. All she
needed…smooth fingers inside her. And wait…a tongue.
Outside her. Warm against her clitoris. Doubled up—fingers inside, tongue outside. It took a special lover, with
special skills, to pull off such a stunt.

She moaned, screamed, and uttered indecipherable
words.

Her V throbbed. She moaned, scratched and clawed at
the mattress, embarrassed that she was unable to control
herself. Tears in her eyes. Good tears, no sadness behind
them. Well, maybe a little. Ooh.

The two fingers inside her went wild, rubbed her so
hard, so wonderfully, with just the right pressure, the friction unbelievable. Her panties were sopping wet because
of them, those smooth, magic fingers. Nuh-uh, this wasn't
happening. Ooh.

It *was* happening. Hard. She clenched her teeth and
bucked, a wild woman.

Finished.

Breathing out of control. Panting.

After she finally caught her breath, "I'm not a dyke" was
the first thing out of her mouth.

The other woman smiled, retrieved her bra from one
of the bed's antique-looking corner posts, and swiped the
soft material across her wet lips, then did the same with
her smooth, magic fingers, wiping them clean of love juice.

"You hear me? I'm not a dyke."

"Maybe not a *Dick* Van Dyke. But you're a dyke."

"Zee-Zee."

"Sela."

"No."

"Yes."

"No."

"I'll quote you from just a moment ago," Zelda said. "Yesssssssssss!"

"Not a joke," Sela said.

"Right," Zelda agreed. "Serious as a ban on gay marriages."

Sela frowned and grunted. "Fuck."

"You wanna?"

"Zee-Zee. Stop. I mean it. I'm not a dyke."

"You stepped into my life...wait, excuse me...you stepped into Lady Bar a year ago today—Happy Anniversary, by the way—for what?"

"Don't know," Sela admitted. "I was looking for something."

"And you found it," Zelda told her.

"Not a dyke!"

"Nature has already spoken for you, Sela. Sorry."

"Bullshit. Nature hasn't decided anything for me," Sela shot back.

"My tongue and fingers in your—"

"Stop! It!"

"Okay." Zelda calmed. "What are you, then?"

"Weak," Sela said.

"For me?" Zelda spread her legs and pointed to her own V. "For this? That makes you a dyke, honey."

Sela muttered to herself.

"If you can't tell me you love me, right now," Zelda said, "you can count our—whatever you want to call it—over. I'm serious."

"I." Sela paused, hesitated. "I do. In a way."

Zelda shook her head, slid from between Sela's thighs, and repositioned herself up on the bed. She was naked, just as Sela was naked now, her panties on the floor. A smile brushed across Zelda's face when Sela's gaze fell to her blackberry nipples and pressed down on them, hard enough, and long enough, to make blackberry juice.

Zelda pushed Sela back gently by the shoulders and straddled her friend, putting her V directly over Sela's mouth. "Hungry?"

"Get off," Sela said weakly.

"Eat," Zelda commanded.

"No."

Zelda gyrated, bringing her V to within an inch of Sela's mouth and then pulling it away, then back again. Sela closed her eyes, but she could feel the heat Zelda's V emanated. The scent of it tickled her nostrils.

"You're weakening, Sela," Zelda teased.

Sela opened her eyes. She grabbed Zelda by the ass and brought that hot, pleasant-scented V to her mouth and greedily devoured it, licked around it. In it. Deep, deep in it.

Zelda moaned and continued to rock her hips.

Sela moaned as well, like a child enjoying an ice cream sundae. It tasted so good. So very good.

"Easy," Zelda begged, "I'm about to…" She started to tremble, shake. "Coooome." Sounding like "comb" the way it came out of her mouth.

Zelda wiped her sweaty brow and looked down at Sela with a satisfied grin. "Now that was love," she said. "But I still want you to tell me."

"I told you," Sela said.

"Again."

"I…do."

Zelda eased off Sela's chest, down to her waist instead, and continued to straddle her friend.

"Love…" She kissed Sela's breasts.

"Doesn't…" She lifted Sela's head, flicked her tongue across Sela's neck.

"Hesitate…" She framed Sela's face with her hands, kissed her lips, forced her tongue in Sela's mouth, where it tapped against Sela's teeth, then Sela's tongue.

"When…" Zelda broke the kiss. Sela frowned. She looked Sela in the eyes.

"Called…" She traced the outline of Sela's nipple with one of her smooth, magic fingers as she kept her loving gaze on Sela.

"Upon." She leaned forward then and took the nipple in her mouth, pulled, sucked, and licked it. Sela's moans lent melody to the room as Zelda's free hand, with those smooth, magic fingers, plunged inside her again.

Sela Oed extra hard and then returned the favor, doing to Zelda what Zelda had done to her, inhibitions gone.

There was a severe passion between the two of them, an electrical something that made their bodies warm to the touch, made their skin wrinkle where a tongue glided, fingers caressed, kisses settled. The passion came with a sense of emergency. They rushed as if they'd never get this opportunity again.

"Play with my hair, Sela."

"How? What?"

"Twirl it around your fingers."

Sela considered the demand for a brief moment, and then ran her fingers through Zelda's lovely strands of re-laxed hair. She was glad she had. Zelda arched her back in pleasure, cooing "That's right, baby, just like that, twirl it." Her gyrations were so intense that Sela had to con-centrate on her movements, shadowing them with her hands so as not to stray too far away and pull out gobs of Zelda's hair. They continued their little dance on the soft mattress, meeting one another for pleasure at the little dip in the middle. Zelda wrapped her arms around Sela and massaged her back, sharing each other's heat, their breasts smashed together, their Vs similarly arranged.

"We need to stop this..." Sela couldn't finish the thought.

"You stop it."

"Nuh uh."

They cupped each other's breasts, squeezed, kissed, and fingered each nipple until they had four ramrod-straight nipples.

"You've got me twisted in knots," Sela exclaimed.

"Fingers," Zelda moaned. "Inside me. Please. Now!"

Sela obeyed, searched, and saw Zelda turn her head to the side, bite into her lip. It wasn't long before Zelda trembled, then settled, for about the umpteenth time today.

"Hold me, don't stop," Zelda begged. "I love you, don't you ever stop."

"I won't," Sela replied. "I won't."

They fell back on the bed, Zelda's head resting on Sela's shoulder. They both had their eyes open, staring at the rectangular tiles on the ceiling. They spoke of hopes and fears, mixing the two in a gumbo bowl of conversation.

"What did we just do?" Sela asked.

"We just made love. Two dykes without a care in the world except for finding our individual pleasure. No worry."

"Have to worry," Sela said. "Family. Friends. Jobs. Have to worry."

"You're thinking about your sister," Zelda said.

Sela nodded. "And mother. She wanted grandbabies. LeVar. He's special. I don't want to hurt him the way I hurt Elijah."

"Tell him the truth."

"Important in a relationship, right?" Sela asked.

"Of course," Zelda said. "You know that."

Sela sat up in the bed and hung her legs over the side. Zelda moved behind her, ran her fingers over Sela's back, traced the ridges of her spine. Sela didn't budge.

"What are you thinking about?" Zelda asked.

"The truth," Sela said.

"You're gonna tell it?"

"Yep."

"Good.'

"Zelda?"

"Yes, honey?"

"I don't love you…not in the way you want me to. I never will. I never could."

Zelda's fingers froze, inches from Sela's ass. "But you can love LeVar that way?" she sneered.

"Yes."

"What about us? What we did?"

"No us," Sela said as she got up and started to retrieve her clothes. "What we did is in the past as of this moment. Never happen again. 'Bout the only thing our lips will have in common again is the end of a blunt. I hope we can continue to be friends. Okay?"

"Mistake," Zelda said.

Sela shook her head. "Nuh-uh. *This* was the mistake."

19

Emotions are tricky.
Hard to handle.

Grief, for instance, can find you as it did me after Miss Ma'am's death, in the shower pretending the moisture on my face came from the showerhead and not my eyes. Or after my brother's death, trembling and sobbing outside the movie theater over that big Russian, Ivan Drago, sending Apollo Creed to a dirt nap in *Rocky IV*. Trembling and sobbing, while the other moviegoers exiting the theater sang, "Doo doo doo, doo doo doo", amped-for-a-fistfight excited over Sylvester Stallone's heroics as Rocky Balboa. Drago's words from the flick, "I must break you," rang in my head like a church bell that whole night. I went to sleep with dark thoughts: toy trains, G.I. Joe action figures, Transformers, blood I couldn't stanch with my little fingers.

Now, grief can shake you, but fear can cripple you.

I upchucked after every meal for the first week I spent inside those cold and hard prison walls. On the seventh day, my vomiting was so violent, so taxing on my chest, that I fell on the cool bathroom tile afterward. Sweat had broken out on my forehead, my ribs hurt, and my throat was scratchy sore. My heart was a downhill slalom skier, beating wildly, fast, jerking around in my chest. I lay there on the pissy bathroom floor for what must have been twenty minutes or more, unable, despite my best efforts, to pull myself up. I didn't have a personal relationship with From Whom All Blessings Flow at the time, but I like to call the silent talk I had, with whomever I had it, prayer. And it worked. Eventually my legs and arms came alive. I made it back to my six-by-nine, my breath smelling like spoiled chicken and rice. I collapsed on my cot and tried to think about the distant future...years off...my release. A CO stopped at my cell and asked me if I was okay, if I needed to go to the prison hospital. I shook him off. I needed my release. That's what I needed. That's what every prisoner needs. All every inmate thought about, I'd come to find out, was the day it would all be over. Thoughts of release were especially clear when those inevitable bouts of paralyzing fear took hold.

Okay, grief can shake you, and fear can cripple you, but what of joy, happiness? What effect did those emotions have?

I've had little experience with joy and happiness during my three dimes of existence. But Sela had me feeling it—feeling joy, love, and happiness. My life was an Al Green song. For clarification purposes, I'm talking about "Can I Get In Them Panties?" Al, not "Can I Get A Witness" Al.

But as I said, emotions are tricky, hard to handle. This is the only explanation for the colorful, fluttery winged insects that cut a rug in my gut when Bevolyn walked through my office door. Aiight, I was getting cute; Bevolyn brought out the poetry in me, I guess. Scratch the fluttery-winged-insects-cutting-a-rug-in-my-gut nonsense. Butterflies were dancing in my stomach when Bevolyn walked through my office door.

"You cut your hair," were my first words to her.

It looked to me as if an inch had been sheared from her auburn-tinted locks. She wore a sundress, white with pink flowers, which adhered to every curve on her body. Her sandals, pink, with straps that wrapped her ankles and a little heel I wasn't used to seeing on casual footwear, also caught my eye—stylish. She would have been the perfect solution to add some much-needed color to *Sex and the City*.

"Just my ends," she said.

"Looks nice," I replied.

There was a brief pause before a wicked smile crossed Bevolyn's face. "I'm sure Sela would be so happy you noticed, *Reverend*."

"I'm sure you would be so happy if your husband had," I quickly replied.

The color drained from her face, she narrowed her eyes, and her jaws sunk in. She couldn't be civil, and neither could I: those tricky emotions I mentioned. I have no doubt that if she had a knife, her future would have included a walk down a prison gallery, "Yea though I walk through the valley of the shadow of death," uttered by a chaplain in her last rites before the lethal injection.

Murder was in her eyes.

Afeni, thankfully, appeared in the doorway just then.

"Young Sister Afeni," I said, gesturing with my hands. "Come on in."

Bevolyn continued to glare at me, glared even when her foster daughter took her place in the office.

"I'm not interrupting anything?" Afeni asked, looking at Bevolyn and then me.

"No," I said.

Afeni focused her gaze on her foster mother, a smirk on her smooth young face. "Looks like you two are having a moment. You sure you don't want me to step out so you can finish?"

Bevolyn turned, finally, and shot daggers at Afeni. "Sit."

"Yes, *Maji*," Afeni's reply. "Be sure and join me, you hear, *Maji*?"

I watched them verbally spar.

"Don't start that," came from Bevolyn, hands on her hips—wide, childbearing hips, hips a man could hold for purchase during sex, hips that looked good in her sundress, and even better out of that sundress, I imagined.

"It's a term of endearment, *Maji*," from Afeni, batting her eyelashes, overplaying her innocence.

"Not the way you say it. It's ugly the way you say it."

"And how do I say it? *Maji*. It's a beautiful word; how can I say it ugly?"

Bevolyn shook her head and sat in the chair facing my desk, Reverend Walker's desk. Afeni snickered and sat next to her.

"I don't know why you're tripping," Afeni said.

"You know," Bevolyn replied. "You know you're saying it…" She stopped, sighed, and fanned herself demonstratively with a smooth chocolate hand with manicured nails, their shade of choice, burgundy. I thought, sadly, of Sela's orange-colored nails. What hope did Sela and I stand if I still could feel this, something, when Bevolyn walked in the room?

"Stand back, Satan," Bevolyn said, fanning.

"There you go," from Afeni in response to that.

I took that moment to cut in. "It is a beautiful word, Afeni. But Sister Sykes is correct. It loses its beauty how you say it. Like you're marking Sister Sykes guilty of something. Like a mother is the last thing you'd consider her."

Both of their eyes found me. Afeni's were wide, her mouth formed in a big O, Bevolyn's expression similar.

"Maji?" Bevolyn spat. "You know what that word means?"

I nodded. "Hindi for *mother*."

"Wow," Afeni said. "I guess I need to tighten my game. You're the first I've known to pick up on that. Wow."

Bevolyn looked at me with an unexplainable something in her eyes. I tried to read it. She had her head cocked and I was happy to notice that her hair still reached down to her shoulders despite the snip-snip to her ends.

I shouldn't have noticed that, I knew. Even more, I shouldn't have been happy about it. I had Sela. Bevolyn had a husband. And she couldn't stand me, to boot.

But again, emotions are tricky, hard to handle.

I tapped my temple and focused on Afeni instead of Bevolyn. I could feel Bevolyn's eyes on me, though, and my face flashed hot. "I've picked up a lot of useless information down through the years, young Sister Afeni."

I smiled. No need to mention I'd scoured the prison library one hopeless day looking up tidbits about mothers, trying to reconcile Miss Ma'am's death. I'd come upon a list of foreign words for mother: ammee, Urdu; majka, Serbian; mere, French; and on and on. Foreign words for brother, too: bruder, German; hermano, Spanish; broer, Dutch. I memorized all of them. None of them made the loss of Miss Ma'am and my brother lessen. No, it took He's Sweet I Know for that to happen. And still, it's an ongoing process.

"I'm impressed," Afeni said.

I glanced at Bevolyn. She didn't look impressed.

I turned back to Afeni, said, "When I was younger I called this kid—darker than me by like two shades—a Pendejo. Spanish word I'd picked up. Not a nice one, either. He punched me in the nose. Turned out he was Dominican. I'd never known there were other Spanish-speaking folks other than the Puerto Ricans I was used to. Yellow people, what I'd always saw. Never knew anything about black Spanish. He gave me, and my nose, a lesson."

"Moral of the story?" Afeni asked, to her credit, smiling.

"Be careful how you say things. Words are as dangerous as any weapon known to man. I meant to dis that boy, thought he wouldn't even know it, and he made me pay for it. You're doing the same to Sister Sykes. You might pay the price for that some day."

I closed the Bible I'd been reading before Bevolyn and Afeni's arrival and pushed it to the corner of my desk, Reverend Walker's desk. "Now, tell me," I asked Afeni, "why the obvious contempt for Sister Sykes?"

"Yes, why?" Bevolyn said, her tone soft, tender. I imagined it in my ears while we made love on a bamboo cot in some Caribbean hut…a hint of rum on her breath from the Mojita she drank as we held hands and walked the beach…that rum in my nostrils as she moaned with each of my strokes…as she gripped my back and I gripped her hips.

Emotions are tricky. Hard to handle.

Afeni sucked in air, but said nothing in reply to Bevolyn's question.

I said, "These counseling sessions are no good if you don't open up, Afeni. I'm on your side. You saw that last time. When…when Reverend Walker was still alive."

"I know," Afeni said. "It's just so hard."

"What?" Bevolyn and I said in unison. We glanced at each other. Okay, more than a glance, we stared at one another, taken by our tandem sentiment, our in-syncness.

I could see Afeni looking at Bevolyn, then at me. She passed the look between the two of us several more times.

I cleared my throat and pulled my gaze away from Bevolyn—pulled—it was a difficult task. Afeni had a knowing smile when my eyes met hers.

"Where were we?" I asked Afeni.

"I was talking," Afeni said, "but then y'all had another one of your moments. Looking like y'all want to get jiggy with each other."

"Afeni!" Bevolyn gasped.

Afeni paid her no mind. "You pass judgment on me, all the time, *Maji*. Over clothes and stuff. Stupid stuff. It's crazy. All the stuff *you* hiding."

"I'm not hiding anything," Bevolyn said, head up, chin firm. "And find another word, other than 'stuff,' for your vocabulary."

Afeni rolled her eyes. "Sure you aren't hiding anything, *Maji*. Sure. Aunt Sela and Russell wouldn't think so if they saw what just happened. If they saw the *stuff* I just saw."

"You've got a fresh mouth, child," Bevolyn said.

"That abortion rally," Afeni went on, "that I saw you at when I Googled you. You weren't there protesting."

Bevolyn gasped and held a hand to her chest. She looked as if she might faint any minute. I leaned forward slightly, ready to dash around the desk and catch her, perform mouth-to-mouth, perhaps.

Afeni turned to me. "I'm sorry, Reverend Path, because I like you. I really do. I think you're cool and all for a pastor. But I don't think you're the best person to fix this situation."

"Hear, hear," called out an intrusive fourth voice in our conversation.

I looked up at the man in my office doorway. Bevolyn found strength and turned to look as well. Afeni sat in her seat, facing me, perfectly still, with a smile on her face.

I was just about to ask the strange man, "Can I help you?"

But Bevolyn said, "Russell, what are you doing here?"

My stomach dropped. My pulse quickened.

Emotions are tricky and hard to handle, especially the emotions of anger and jealousy. Bevolyn's husband. My competition.

I was up to the challenge, too. Had been looking forward to it for some time.

"Russell Sykes," I said. "I've heard so much about you. Come on in."

"What is this?" he asked.

"This is a church," I said, sarcastically. "A church is a place where people come to worship God. God is—"

"I'd chill if I were you," he cut me off.

"Would you, now?"

Bevolyn touched a hand to her chest again. I could only imagine what her heart was doing—beating a mile a minute, as Miss Ma'am would say.

"Russell, what are you doing here?" Bevolyn asked her husband. It came out sounding strained, as if her tongue were too big for her mouth. I smiled at that because it meant she was flustered. Flustered, I imagined, because her husband was in the room with the man, namely me, she'd had secret desires of having.

Russell stepped into the office and was by his wife's side in two long steps. He put his hand on her shoulder, and though she'd asked him the question, he looked at me. "Afeni told me about these sessions," he said. "I wanted to come see what they were about. See what kind of voodoo was going on up in here."

I raised my hand to a vacant seat in the corner. "Pull up a chair. You can take the ouija board off it and set it against the wall. I keep the headless chickens in my desk, so you don't have to worry about them."

"I'll stand," he said, deadly serious, not making any facial expression in response to my attempt at humor.

"Sister Sykes has been concerned about Afeni's dress," I filled him in. "She'd been having counseling with Reverend Walker before his untimely death. I felt there were other issues between young Sister Afeni and Sister Sykes. I thought it a good idea that we continue the counseling sessions."

"And you're qualified how?" Russell asked.

I reached for the Bible on my desk, picked it up, and waved it like the sword it was—sword against evil. Russell, in my mind, was evil. "I stand on this," I told him.

"You look like you stand on a street corner," he said.

"Excuse me?"

"The guys I pass on the corner on my way to work," he said. "You got the same look. You look like you're two steps from the jailhouse, no offense."

I sat forward, could feel my body tightening. "You say something like that, and then tack on a 'no offense.' You're—"

"Please," Bevolyn cut in, "don't do this, you two."

I waved her off. "I'm a man of God, *Russell*. You won't find me on any street corner, unless I'm preaching His word to the unbelieving. You'll find me in the church. But you wouldn't know that, would you? When's the last time you came to this church, *Russell*? I'm surprised you were able to find it."

He smirked. "You still haven't told me your credentials. What theology school did you graduate from, brother? Where are you from? What church did you attend before landing here?"

I opened my mouth, but sat wordless. He had me.

"Mighty man of God," he said. "Don't tell me you have nothing to say?"

I didn't.

So he turned his attention to Afeni. "You don't have to stay for this."

She glanced at me. Sadness shadowed her face for a moment. "Sorry, Reverend Path," she said. "I don't want to do this. Well, not like this."

"I understand, Afeni." I offered a smile that seemed to comfort her.

She stood. Russell reached forward, took her hand, and pulled her to his side. She situated her head against his chest and squeezed him tight, looking as peaceful as Reverend Walker in the casket. I glanced at Bevolyn. Russell's hand was still on her shoulder, rubbing it lovingly. Sister Sykes had her head bowed, her hands resting dourly in her lap.

A family.

Me. The outsider.

"I'm gonna be honest with you, brother," Russell said. "I'm gonna check up on you. Check into your background."

"What? Why?" The words, I knew, left my throat, funny sounding, with a hitch. Bevolyn looked up at me suddenly. Afeni raised her head from Russell's chest and did the same.

"That's right," he said. "Something strange about how easily you slid in here. From what little Bevolyn has told me, you just appeared one day. The only one who could vouch for you was Reverend Walker. Well, brother, he's gone now."

"Reverend Walker served this church for over twenty years, Mr. Sykes," I said. My voice quavered a bit. I focused hard on settling it. "If he vouched for me, that means something. The people believe so, as well."

Russell smiled. "So now I'm Mr. Sykes?"

I hadn't swayed him. He'd cut through the cow dung and gotten straight to the matter. I'd acquiesced, softened, my hard shell gone. I'd addressed him with reverence. And why? Because I was hiding my past. Again, I sat, wordless.

"I don't like the hold you have on my family, brother. Dating my wife's sister. Messing with our…Afeni. And my wife." He shook his head. "I have to know more about you. What you're about, because something isn't clicking."

"Brother Sykes…" I didn't have anything beyond that. My voice trailed off. It was embarrassing to the tenth degree. I prayed to He's Sweet I Know for strength. A rebuttal.

"Not your brother," Russell told me. Then he looked away from me, to Bevolyn, and then to Afeni. "Come on."

Bevolyn rose without pause. I looked at her. She didn't look at me. I looked to Russell. He smiled. I looked to Afeni. She frowned but held close to Russell.

I had no allies. I waited on From Whom All Blessings Flow, waited patiently. I still had time. The Sykeses still had to cross the carpet of my office, Reverend Walker's office. They still had to pass through my office door, Reverend Walker's office door. After that, as serious as Russell seemed, I was in trouble.

"Umm," was the only word out of my mouth. And it wasn't even technically a word. It was the sound of a condemned man. Me.

"Be blessed," Russell said. He took Bevolyn's hand and turned away. They walked toward the door.

"Brother Sykes," I called out in a last-ditch effort to salvage this.

He ignored me, opened the door, and held up a hand for Afeni to pass under. She did. He repeated the courtesy for Bevolyn. She passed under, too. He moved through last. He shut it softly, but it sounded in my ears like a live heavy metal band had begun playing right there in my office.

I picked up the Bible for strength, but put it down in the same motion because my hand was shaking so fiercely.

20

Sela worked each leg into her faded indigo-colored Guess jeans, pulled them up over her womanly hips, and slid up the zipper. She hated the idea of dressing this way for her date with LeVar, but he'd made a specific request that she dress down. Real specific, in fact, asking for jeans and a T-shirt by name. This was probably for the better, anyway. It saved Sela from swaying with uncertainty between wearing a certain style of dress or a certain style of blouse. Instead, she stood at her closet with her jeans on, a black lace bra providing support to her two handfuls, trying to decide which T-shirt would best serve as a subdued complement to the jeans. She had close to thirty T-shirts to choose from, all of them embroidered with catchy sayings. She'd always been the active type, so her closet had almost as much sportswear as dressy clothes—jeans and T-shirts galore.

"Cute, cute," she said, holding up a sky blue-colored T-shirt, viewing it as if it were a framed piece of artwork. Then she turned it around and read the message lettered on the back: *sexy*…not exactly what she wanted to advertise with a pastor on her arm. She placed the hanger back on the closet's shelf bar and pulled another. *I ran into his ex, then backed up and ran her over again.* Nuh-uh. This one was from her Trevor Bryant period. Trevor had a hard body, a soft brain, and a girlfriend with a bad attitude and a switchblade. Sela had found out about the girlfriend only after she'd slept with Trevor herself. All of that drama and Sela wasn't even particularly attracted to Trevor. Now, the girlfriend, Dyanna, she was another story…brazen and beautiful, gutsy and gorgeous. Sela had developed a serious love/hate feeling toward Dyanna. Thus, the T-shirt.

Sela gripped the shirt for a moment before placing it back in the closet, too. She pulled another. *What Would Buffy Do?* Buffy the Vampire, a badass chick—what Sela considered herself, but Nuh-Uh, some other time, not appropriate, again, for a date with a pastor, even if that pastor was LeVar.

She rifled through the closet again. Then she found it.

A plain blue T with no lettering. Sela didn't know where it had come from at first, but then she brought it to her nose and inhaled that sweet aroma…a T-shirt she'd borrowed from Zelda. It still carried her friend's perfume. Perfect.

She snaked her body into the shirt and closed her closet door.

"All right, Mr. LeVar," she said. "You got me dressing down, but I still can dazzle your olfactory senses with some of my unique scentage." She thought briefly about the unique scentage of the shirt on her back, but quickly brushed that thought aside. Sela was sure "scentage" wasn't actually a word, but this evening, with this opportunity for the love God intended her to have before her, the made-up word would find its place in the King's English. She had to smile to herself: she'd taken Bevolyn's dream man, and now, talking all that 'olfactory' and 'scentage' crap, sounded like Bevolyn, too.

She moved from the closet and consulted her dresser, the four little alabaster vases that contained perfumes she'd made herself during a visit she and Zelda had taken to a perfume factory last summer. They'd spent hours at the factory, working on their perfumes, woman bonding, laughing, touching one another's arms without any implications in the gestures. They'd been friends, the way Sela wanted them to be. What she wanted them to be. Nothing more. Nuh-uh, just friends. Friends. She had to repeat it in her mind several times and still wasn't sure her heart accepted it. Just friends and nothing more.

The best part of that perfume factory visit had been naming the fragrances. Zelda created crazy names. Screaming Vulva and I Didn't Have Time To Shave My Legs were two that now came to mind.

Sela went the spiritual route and named her fragrances after periods in her life: Falling, Rising, Faltering, and Recovering. Falling, after that night she'd slinked into Lady Bar. Rising, the euphoria she'd experienced in the coming days as she learned Zelda and Zelda learned her. Faltering, after making love to Zelda the first time, then looking at herself in the mirror afterward, and catching a glimpse of a naked *woman* in the bed behind her. Recovering, what she hadn't experienced at that time but knew would come—LeVar and what he offered.

Sela picked the vase of her favorite, Rising, off the dresser. It contained the essential oils of lavender, chamomile, and valerian, as well as distilled water and vodka—a beautiful fragrance that she imagined driving LeVar wild, but not too wild; after all, he was a pastor. She sprayed a drop in the palm of each hand and rubbed the perfume over her neck and chest. It masked the scent from her T-shirt, Zelda's T-shirt, and Sela convinced herself that was a good thing.

LeVar had also requested she wear sneakers, so Sela put on her blue and white Puma Flow Clogs and laced them up tight.

LeVar had been so secretive, so soft-spoken during his inviting phone call. He sounded as if something heavy were weighing him down. Sela knew that sound as her own.

She was dressed and ready by noon, sitting on the couch reading one of her *Essence* magazines, when the telephone rang. The calm of her reading gave way to a newfound anxiety, and her heart raced. Don't let this be LeVar canceling. Nuh-uh, Sela needed to get on with her life, her recovery.

"Hello?" she said into the receiver, her voice tentative.

"Hey there," the reply, understated, quiet. Sad.

"Zee-Zee?"

"The one and only," Zelda said, a smile in her new tone of voice, happy Sela had called her by that nickname that always stirred something inside Zelda.

"What can I do for you, Zelda?"

Splat. For Zelda the euphoria was gone, just like that.

"You're not selling me lime for my lawn," Zelda said, noticeably upset, "so for one, cut that business tone. This is your girl. Zee-Zee. Regardless of what happens with us, it doesn't have to be like that. Okay?"

Sela found her couch, plopped down on it, and reclined against its soft cushions with her eyes closed. "You're right. I'm sorry."

"Better," Zelda said. "I've been missing you. Wondering if you were getting into anything today. Maybe we can get together."

"Have to be tonight, if that," Sela told her. "I've got a date."

Silence.

"Zee-Zee?"

"Zelda," Zelda corrected. Now her tone was cold, hard, all business.

"Who's selling lime now?" Sela asked.

"With who?" Zelda asked. "Your…date? LeVar? Somebody else?"

"LeVar," Sela said. She heard the sound of Zelda's loud sigh in her ear. She imagined the pained expression on Zelda's face. She immediately regretted spraying on Rising to mask Zelda's scent. "Don't be like that, Zee-Zee. This is how it has to be."

"Why?"

"Because."

"That's the word for someone with a weak argument," Zelda said. "Or no argument. *Because.*"

"Because," Sela said, "I want children. I want to walk in public holding hands without people staring."

"Worrying about what other folk say and think, still."

"Because…" And Sela let it hang in the air like the scent of *Rising* masking the scent of Zelda.

"Weak argument," Zelda said. "Or no argument."

Sela squeezed her eyes tighter and hugged herself with her free hand. "Because I hate myself when I'm with you. Not during, of course, but afterwards…I hate myself Zee—Zelda. That's not how I want to live."

"Hate," Zelda said. She sounded incredulous, drifting as if she'd smoked a Dutchie. "Hate. Man. Dayum. Hate. That's strong."

"Look," Sela said, "I don't want to hurt you. I don't want to hurt myself. I don't know what to do, Zee-Zee. Don't know if I'm coming or going. But I gotta do what I think is best. I gotta do it like this. I'm sorry."

"Me, too." Zelda's voice had grown, unbelievably, weaker. A notch below a whisper. "I made a mistake calling. Sorry, Sela."

"Don't do this," Sela said. "Tell you what. After my date, later we—"

"Have fun on your date," Zelda cut her off. "Make sure you kiss him, okay, Sela? Use your tongue, too. I can tell you from experience your tongue is the eighth wonder. Smoke him like a Dutchie."

"Zelda."

But it was too late. Zelda had hung up. Sela rose from the couch and moved back to the phone's set, placing the receiver back in the comforting arms of the cradle. The counter of her kitchen island proved to be the perfect surface on which to place her hand for balance. She did, feeling her legs go wobbly, and her stomach, a mash of rusty gears, churning, turning, and rolling. She took a seat on one of her high barstool-type chairs, and sat there, with her head resting on her hands, which rested on the countertop, until her doorbell cried out twenty minutes later.

She looked up wearily, rose in the same manner, and somehow found her way to the door. She stopped, brushed a hand over her clothes, and took a deep breath.

"LeVar" was the labored word that left her tongue when she answered the door. "You ready to go? Or coming in for a bit?" It didn't matter, at that moment, which option he chose. Her mind was elsewhere—on Zelda, the hurt she'd caused her friend, the hurt she felt herself because of it.

"Might as well go," her pastor-boyfriend said.

Sela grabbed her carryall purse from the nightstand next to the door, and a light little jacket in case it was bitter cold up in the mountains or wherever it was LeVar was taking her.

"Where we headed?" she asked as she turned her back to him to make sure her apartment's lock held tight.

"Out," he said.

She turned and eyed him. "You're acting hella funky.

What's up?" It seemed as if she used that word, "hella," only in his presence. Was she subconsciously trying to sabotage this relationship? Turn the pastor away with her potty mouth?

"Lot on my mind," he said. "Sorry."

"Don't be. Ish happens, right? You want to do this some other time?" Her feelings were mixed. In a way, she hoped he said yes to doing this date some other time; in another, she wanted to go on with this new phase of her life, do it now while she still had the courage.

"Been looking forward to some time with you," he said. "I'll shake this off."

She hooked her arm in his and they took the elevator down. They stepped outside into a cool September afternoon, the temperature taking a turn south with each passing day. Even the weather matched the demeanor of Sela and LeVar. The sun shone a quiet muted orange. A breeze whispered so softly you could miss it except for the stray pieces of trash that walked across the lot outside Sela's apartment. The blue of the sky looked as if some artist had painted it on his canvas, lightening the blue tones with splotches of white.

"You're not looking so upbeat yourself, Sela."

She didn't answer. They walked in silence. When they reached his Toyota, he opened Sela's door like a gentleman, saw her inside, and shut it softly behind her—too softly. He had to open it again and slam it tighter on the second go round. Then he walked around, got in on his side, sat back, and buckled up. He paused, rested his hands on the steering wheel, took a breath, and looked at her.

"So?" he said. "What's up with *you?*"

"Lot on my mind," she said. "Sorry."

"Don't be. Ish happens, right?"

Sela smiled, her first since opening her door to him. He smiled, too, his first since his office door closing with a thud behind Russell Sykes and his family. Doors weren't being too kind to either of them.

"Where you taking me, LeVar?"

"You sound nervous," he said. "What you worried about? You think I'm gonna take you to wade in the water or something?"

"Funny," she said. "I don't know. You were so specific about what you wanted me to wear. So secretive about where I'd be wearing it to." She shrugged.

He scanned her body. "And you are wearing it, Sister Sela. Wearing it well, I might add."

"Mind your soul, pastor," she said, fanning at him with a hand of slender, lavender-colored nails. Lavender. Zelda's favorite color.

"You're right. You're right," he agreed.

"So where we headed?" she asked again.

He smiled, those dimples of his having an effect on Sela's own face, making her pull her lips tight. He *was* a good-looking brother, no doubt about it. All those muscles…hmm. And yet, well, she wouldn't let her mind settle on the "yet" of this situation. Nuh-uh.

"The truth?" he said.

"I'd expect as much. Coming from you, pastor."

"I like how you say that…pastor. Your lips pucker on the *p*. Very…" He stopped. "Mind my soul, right?"

"Right!"

"Well," he said. "Truthfully, I hadn't really thought about where we would go. My mind, as I said, has been somewhere else. But sitting here, looking at you, something has come to mind. I hope you like it."

"Well, hop along, Cassidy."

He ignitioned the Toyota and pulled from the lot.

"Don't know many pastors would drive like that," Sela said, after they'd traveled a piece.

He turned to her. "Like what?"

She nodded to the steering wheel. "One hand on the wheel. Leaning to the side. Gangster lean."

"Being me," he said, smiling, straightening up as he said it. "You're definitely not looking at a gangster, though."

"Not a Bad Boy?"

"Who I look like, Mase?"

She laughed. "See what I mean. How many pastors know about rap music? Mase. Stuff like that."

"He did leave rap music for God," LeVar said.

"Came back, too. So what does that mean for God's mission if his followers leave Him to go back to their old life?"

"Don't know," LeVar said. "I can't search that brother's heart. Mase, I mean. I can't know if he still rolling for Jesus. If he ever was. That's a personal thing, inside. Only God knows. Only God can search a person's heart."

Sela arched a brow. "You think it's possible for Mase to rap and still love Jesus?"

He turned to her again, one hand on the wheel, that lean back. "Sure! God is an accepting God. He accepts all kinds."

Sela reached across and touched his knee, then squeezed it.

"What's that for?" LeVar asked.

"You," she replied. "You say the right words. I feel like I'm getting to know God. I'm hella happy about it, too."

They both laughed.

"We're here," LeVar said a few minutes later.

"Here is?"

"Monmouth Park."

"Which is?"

"The horse track," LeVar said.

"A gambling preacher," Sela said. "You do amaze me."

He shook his head. "Not here to gamble."

"What then?"

"Horses."

"Horses?"

"Yep." He nodded. "Remember that story you told me, about you and…your sister when you were younger? Her riding the horses and you never getting to? I'm gonna see that you get to at least touch one today. We'll go stand by the fence when they march the racehorses out. You can touch them. How does that sound?"

"You remembered that?"

"Sure."

Sela smiled. How did it sound? It sounded wonderful. Wonderful, and loud…loud enough to drown out Zelda's voice in her ears, loud enough to drown out the sound of dial tone after Zelda had hung up on her, loud enough to drown the other voices in her head, those voices that told her the curve of a woman's ass and breasts was the greatest gift to the world.

"You mind if I put a little something on a couple of the horses?" she asked.

He laughed. "No. I don't. You know how to bet?"

She shook her head. "I bet you do, though."

"I like the exotic bets," he said. "Exactas, Trifectas. But we'll keep it simple for the newbie."

She leaned over and kissed him, deep, her lips warm against his. A breath caught in her chest as he wrapped his arms around her. A want grew in her middle. Recovering, just like that perfume she'd made. Recovering.

Afeni was at her computer composing a poem when someone tapped at her bedroom door.

"S'open," she said.

Russell stepped inside and closed the door behind him. "What you up to?" he asked.

"Poem."

"Got a minute?"

Afeni held up a finger, clicked a few keys on her keyboard, then turned to Russell. "Had to save that. I learned my lesson during our last blackout. Wassup?"

"Show me how to Google?" he asked.

"Sure," Afeni said. "Pull up a seat."

Russell did, on a white chair with pink flowers etched in the wood. He sat next to Afeni, his hand around her shoulder as he leaned in and studied the computer monitor.

"Dubya, dubya, dubya, dot, Google, dot, com," Afeni said, typing as she spoke.

A dominantly white screen appeared, then a rainbow Google banner, followed by a blank box, and then a gray box with SEARCH on it.

"You type whatever it is you want info on in the blank box," Afeni instructed him. "Then hit SEARCH."

"LeVar Path," Russell said.

Afeni turned and looked at Russell. He repeated the name. Afeni typed it in.

"What's that?" Russell asked, squinting at the new info that came on the screen.

"Umm," Afeni said. She looked closer. "Just one return. Looks like…"

North Carolina, Haywood County — All Known Cemeteries These lists…
   … 22 JAN 1907 24 MAY 1996 6 RICHARD L 19 JAN 1920 16 FEB 1964 21 ROWENA BELLE C 30 SEP 1882 25 FEB 1956 1 RUSSELL B 10 MAR 1985 9 **LEVAR A PATH**…

   ftp.rootsweb.com/pub/usgenweb/ok/jefferson/

cemeteries/chucksimms/haywood-m.txt   -   92k   -
Supplemental Result - Cached - Similar pages

". . . a death notice," she finished.

"That's it?" Russell asked.

"Yep," Afeni said. "Only that one return showed up."

"Put in Reverend G. H. Walker," he said. She did.

"Ton of hits," she replied.

Russell patted her shoulder. "Thanks."

He got up and left. Afeni stayed in Google and continued to search different variations for information for LeVar Path. Nothing came up.

Bevolyn had her back to Russell as he walked into the kitchen, working over the oven.

"Nothing," Russell said.

She turned. "What?"

"Nothing came up when we checked on your Reverend Path."

She didn't say anything.

"Kind of odd nothing would show, don't you think?"

She shrugged.

"Checked Reverend Walker," he added, "got a grocery list of items."

She watched him, wordless.

"No more," Russell said. "No more going to that church."

She started to say something but stopped. "Okay," she said, nodding. "You win."

"Do I?" Russell asked. "Do I win?"

She didn't reply. He turned and left.

21

"Three-four-seven-two," Sela said.

I looked over at her, my one hand on the wheel, my lean in full effect. You could take some things out of the man, but other things, no matter how concerted the attempt to abolish them, would never go away: my driving style, for instance, and a few other things about myself I didn't care to think about.

"Three-four-seven-two," she repeated in a singsong voice.

I made a sound, accompanying it with a shake of my head.

"Don't hate. Participate," Sela said, noticing what had to be a look of jealousy and its cousin envy on my face. "Enjoy my joy."

"Participate?" I replied. "What? You plan on forking over some of your winnings?"

"Me?" She touched one of her manicured nails against her chest. They were pretty colored, nicely done—light purple to my eyes. But she'd made it a point to correct me earlier when I complimented her on them, in my male ignorance calling them light purple. Lavender, she'd said, repeating it several times. Whatever color it was, the nail made an indentation in her T-shirt and drew my eyes to the flesh beneath that cotton material: solid breasts on a solid woman. I wanted to *participate* in undressing Sela; that's what I wanted. I thought of Luck's words to me from long ago.

"A vacation is good, right?"

I'd nodded in the affirmative.

"Well, how bad can fornication be? It's got that 'cation' in it."

I smiled, but said, "The Bible says it's bad, Luck. Come on, now. You a Bible man."

He sighed and looked far off. "You're right, of course, young breed. But I'm gonna keep reading and looking. God's a merciful God. He had to have put a loophole in there somewhere."

The loophole was to sin, to break the covenant we have with He's Sweet I Know. I focused on Sela, her beauty. We were all sinners, anyway. So be it.

"Yeah, you," I said, pulling my gaze away from her assets, focusing on the road before me. "Are you planning on sharing your wealth? I'm a cheese man, you know. Love cheddar." Despite my banter, my attempt to focus on something other than my lust, I felt a stirring in my jeans, pressing hard, its gangster lean a bit to the left.

"I'm the one that hit on that Trifecta," Sela said. "You ain't do naythan and you got your hands in my pockets."

"Superfecta," I corrected her. "The top four horses in the order they finished. Trifecta is the top three horses. I keep telling you that."

She waved me off. "Superfecta, Wonderfulfecta, Fantabulous-fecta, whatever you wanna call it," she said. "All I care about is the two thousand, four hundred and twenty-eight dollars I scooped up. Oh, and thirty-eight cents."

I winced at the amount.

She reached over and touched my knee, a habit of hers that didn't take long to grow on me. The touch of her hand on my knee made my face soften. I wouldn't be surprised, with a quick glance in the rearview mirror, if I saw my teeth and happy wide eyes reflected back.

"You gave me some good tips," she said. "All that Beyer Speed Figures and this-and-that handicapping stuff. This one's a wonder on turf. This one's using Lasix. This one fades in any race over six furlongs. Real good stuff, LeVar."

I smiled, anticipating the punch line.

"But," she said. "My way worked really well, too. I'm satisfied with it."

"And what way was that?" I asked. I knew. I just wanted to hear her say it again. I liked the seriousness on her face when she said something amusing. I liked the laugh that came from me in response, the way her eyes seemed backlit with passion every time she brought me to a smile or a laugh.

"Their names," she said. "I figured a horse named Long and Vicious had to do some damage."

I smiled.

"Wasn't too sure about Upsy Daisy but that worked out well for me," she added.

"You had a good time?" I asked her.

"You know I did."

"Would you have even if you hadn't won that money?" I wanted to know.

"Money was just the icing," she said. "It was…you know, you remembering my story about Bevolyn and me when we were younger. That. Never dealt with a man with that kind of understanding of women. We women like you guys to think. Most of y'all don't. And when you do, it's with your third leg."

Now, I touched her knee. "You're sweet, Sela. My third leg and I both concur. You're very sweet."

"You're chocolate," she said. "With nuts."

She didn't blush, which I liked. She was keeping it real, as the hip-hoppers say.

I cleared my throat. "Can I come up when we get to your place, Sela? I mean, really come up." There, I'd put it out there, keeping it real myself, the implications heavy in the air.

I waited for her reply, tapping the fingers of my one hand against the steering wheel, leaning over in her direction, my vision straightaway, on the road ahead.

"Are you asking what I think you're asking, pastor?"

"What do you think I'm asking, Sela?" I gave her a soul-stirring glance, burned my gaze into her.

"If you can anoint me," she said.

"You've got oil?" I asked.

She bit into her lip and nodded. "Stuff called Song of the Heart. Has a blend of rose and lavender. Massage oil."

"You do like your lavender, don't you?" I asked.

She half smiled. "I do. Yes."

"So, do you *want* me to come up?" I said.

She smirked. "Are my pockets fatter than they were this morning? Is Long and Vicious the truth? Did Michael Jackson get 'a little work done'? Is—?"

"Gotcha, Sela. You want me to come up."

"Yup."

"It is done," I said.

"Isn't that in the Bible?" she asked.

I winced. "Don't mention the Bible now. Or today, in fact. Okay?"

She smiled knowingly. "You got it, pastor."

"Sela." My voice notched up.

"I meant to say, you got it, LeVar."

"Cool."

"Can you do me a favor, though?" she asked.

"Anything." And I meant it.

"If you lift me at any point today, and I'm thinking that is a good possibility, can you say Upsy Daisy?"

I smiled. "Got to rub it in, huh?"

"You'll get your chance to rub it in, LeVar. The massage oil, remember?" She looked at me, eyes narrowed, very sexy…made my Adam's apple bob in my throat. "Okay?" she said. Implications, as I said, heavy in the air.

I nodded. Okay was an understatement.

She nodded toward the Toy-yoda's stereo. "Why don't you turn up the music? Let me mellow out, get in my vibe."

I did. Urban Contemporary courtesy of Hot 97 in our ears, we rode the rest of the way, Usher and Alicia Keys singing about that one person who always had your heart, "My Boo." I hummed softly as Sela, my hoped-for boo, sat back with her eyes pressed closed. She sang softly, but I could tell from the inflection of her words, and the personal signature that she put on the song, she could *sang* just as strongly as her sister could.

I quickly passed that thought of Bevolyn. Sela was more than enough woman for me. Bevolyn wasn't an ally, wasn't a friend, wasn't a lover, wasn't anything but the wife of a man I knew would be a thorn in my side. Somehow, I would have to take care of that situation.

I moved from those dark thoughts.

"Here," I said as I pulled into the lot of Sela's building a few minutes later. Usher's song had ended. Nelly and the neo-Teddy Pendergrass, Jaheim, were imploring some grown and sexy woman to come over to, "My Place." These urban contemporary singers, it appeared, had a great affinity for the word *my*.

Sela opened her eyes, looked around, and then looked at me and smiled. "Here," she echoed.

"You're still okay with this?"

"Are you?" she asked in turn.

"Yes," I said.

She tapped the dashboard. "Let's go, then."

At the threshold of her door a moment later, she paused. "I have to ask you this. And please, be truthful. What's the deal with you and my sister? I'm not some consolation prize, am I?"

I frowned. "God, no."

She looked at me, deep, searching for a lie, a tic that would give me away, such as my eyes shifting away or a wringing of my hands. I gave her nothing because it was true: she was far from a consolation prize.

"You said, 'God,' " she offered. "If you're lying, He'll…"

"I'm not lying, Sela."

"Attracted to her, though?"

I nodded.

"That won't change?"

"No," I admitted. "A good-looking woman is a good-looking woman. You know that saying, 'look but don't touch'? That's my MO."

She hesitated.

"I'm with you, Sela," I assured her. "Where I want to be."

"Don't even know where you're from," she said.

"North Carolina."

"Brothers or sisters?"

"Had one," I said. "A brother."

"Had?"

"Died."

She looked in my eyes and let that rest without further comment.

"What brought you to Jersey?" she asked.

I thought of my father for a moment. I'd yet to gather the steam to find him. "Destiny, fate," I told Sela. "It was in the cards for me to meet this special, special woman. Fall in love with her. Make love to her." I added, with a smile of my own, "Not necessarily in that order."

Sela hit my arm. "Had to mess it up."

"You the only one allowed to joke?"

"No, LeVar." She paused. "How does a pastor get to this point? Ready to make love to some woman that isn't his wife?"

I shrugged. "I'm complex, Sela."

"You are," she agreed.

"You okay now?" I asked, wanting to change this subject. I didn't need any visions of From Whom All Blessings Flow in my head. Didn't need that at all.

"Big move for me," Sela said. She pulled her shoulders together, as if a chill had passed over us. "I want to make sure it's right."

"I can overstand that," I said.

"What?" She frowned.

"Something I say," I let her know. "Overstand instead of understand. *Under* implies that you don't fully know the details. *Over* that you know them as well as anyone. You know?"

"Hmm, pastor. You are complex, aren't you?"

"Very."

Her eyes flickered, I'd say like a candle, but they were brighter than any candle I'd ever seen. "You're tired of talking, aren't you?" she asked. "Ready to get this party started."

"Very."

She smiled devilishly. "You asked for this." She rummaged through her mess of a pocketbook, finally found her keys, pulled them out, and opened the door. We stepped inside.

Sela hit a light switch and bright light swathed the hall-way. A neat row of shoes hugged the base of the wall. A small round table, covered in linen, sat next to an empty coat tree. A photo book, *Essence's Wisdom of the Ages*, lay open on the table. The woman on the page opened was striking. I could picture Sela photographed in that book, her beauty immortalized in its pages.

"Mi casa es su casa," Sela said. "Make yourself comfortable. Sit on my couch and scratch yourself to your heart's content or whatever it is you men do. I gotta go water my plants."

I followed Sela into the living room. The color scheme was beige and burgundy...nice. A rack of CDs with a stereo behind it stood in a corner. There wasn't much furniture: the couch she mentioned, a loveseat, an ottoman. *JET* magazines were fanned on a glass coffee table. I thought of those *JET* Beauties inside and looked at Sela, my own *JET* Beauty, as she moved toward a wall of ceiling-to-floor Venetian blinds. She opened the blinds to a window. No, a balcony.

I padded across the carpet.

Sela kicked off her sneakers, opened the balcony door, and stepped outside.

I stopped in the doorway that led outside, watching as Sela poured water from one of those green plastic water jugs with the long spout on a rectangular-shaped pot of flowers. The flowers, I noticed, were purple. Sela would call them lavender.

I stepped outside. The air was a bit sticky but relatively cool. I closed the balcony door behind me. Sela turned, green plastic jug in hand. She jumped slightly.

"Didn't hear you step out," she said.

"Busy with your flowers," I offered, eyeing that jug she rested against her thigh.

"We should step back inside," she said.

"I'd rather stay out here a bit," I said. "If you don't mind."

"That's cool," she said. She went to place the water jug on a little white table she had catty-cornered at the balcony's wall bend.

"Let me get that," I said, reaching for the jug.

She crinkled her eyes but handed the jug over. I hefted it: almost full. Then I turned it just a bit, letting some of the water splash on my hands. Lukewarm.

"What are you thinking, LeVar?"

I smiled and stepped toward her. She backed up, hitting the balcony rails.

I licked my lips and eyed her T-shirt, then tapped my hand against the green jug. I was right up on her.

"Gonna get me wet?" she whispered.

"In more ways than one," I told her. Then I lifted the jug and slowly poured the water on Sela. She closed her eyes and shivered as her T-shirt turned to skin. Something earthquaky moved in me as well as I took in her nipples, hardened and poking through her wet, blue T-shirt skin.

I set the jug down, moved to Sela, and unzipped her jeans. I eased them down just below her hips. Pink panties, not purple. I wasn't the least bit disappointed.

I pulled her close, letting her soaked T-shirt get me wet. I kissed her neck. Her eyes remained closed.

"I have a condom in my bedroom," she said.

"Jumping the gun," I replied. Then, "Only one?"

I peeled the wet T-shirt off her and dropped it in a clump on her balcony's floor. Her bra was a black lacy number. Her breasts were a wonder, a miracle, strengthening my belief in He's Sweet I Know, Creator of everything, but most importantly, them. I reached around her and undid the loops on the first try. That put me in the exclusive one-percent club of men who could perform that daunting task. I slid the bra off. Her round breasts barely moved, didn't drop. I cupped them, leaned down, and drank them greedily. Drank—not sucked, not licked—drank, like wine.

"Not my breasts," Sela said after a while. "Don't like that too much."

"Tell me where to go," I said.

"Finger me," she whispered. She still had her eyes closed.

I slid her jeans down all the way, letting them pool at her ankles, and moved my hand inside her pink panties. She spread her legs as if she were mounting a horse. I let my fingers roam free. They found wetness akin to a pond, a smooth split of skin, for she'd shaved. I stuck two fingers inside her.

"Ooh," she moaned.

I continued my sawing motion, my fingers cutting her in half. Her legs wobbled. She put her hands on my shoulders and pushed herself up, trying to escape the joyous pain of my fingers. I wouldn't let her. I grabbed her by the waist with my free hand and held her, continuing to saw with my fingers.

She was chipped wood, ready to break apart.

Her hands dropped from my shoulders and wrapped around me.

"Take me in the bedroom," she said. "I want you inside of me."

"Still jumping the gun," I said.

She made an indecipherable noise and then moved to unbuckle my belt, her hands shaking as she got it loose and then fumbled to open my pants. She fumbled more as she got them open and pushed them down. I stepped out of them. She grabbed my hardness and massaged it as if it were clay. It wasn't. It had passed that stage and was now pottery.

I brushed her hand away and took my fingers out of her. She jumped up and wrapped her legs around my waist. I hoisted her, turned, and somehow opened the balcony door and carried her inside.

"Bedroom?"

"Left," she said. "First door."

I headed in that direction, kicked the slightly ajar door of her bedroom open, and eased her down on the bed.

"Condom?"

"Side table. Top drawer."

I opened the drawer, found the condom, and tore it open. I shrugged myself out of my boxers and glided the condom down my hardness.

Sela lay on the bed, her legs spread. The light from the hall offered just a bit of illumination.

"In me, now," she directed me. Her voice didn't waver one bit.

I did as told, finding my way in her easy. She was tight, wet, and warm. I started with the ugly faces right off the bat. It felt so good inside of her. I hadn't felt anything like it since Aloe-slash-Diane. And Aloe-slash-Diane hadn't even felt this good—like a soft warm towel wrapped around me.

"Just like that," Sela sang in my ears.

I pulled out.

Her eyes shot open. "You crazy?"

"Back on the balcony," I said.

"Nuh-uh. Right here."

I sucked my teeth, but then decided she was right. This wasn't some Harlequin romance. Neither one of us needed railing splinters in our ay-ess-ess. I pulled Sela to me.

Told her, "Turn over."

She did. And I plunged in that apple right off. From behind, I was able to cup her breasts as I pushed in and out.

She pushed my hands away from her breasts. So I found her waist, her stomach, and used that to pull her to me. Pounded it softly, then hard.

She came hard. I did, too. Spent, we lay side by side looking at the ceiling.

"You were right," she said.

"About?"

"Gonna need more condoms."

I smiled. "All I got to do is go get my pants."

"You came prepared?"

"I was prepared to come," I told her.

She smiled. "You forgot to say Upsy Daisy, you know that?"

I reached forward and took her hands, pulling her up from the mattress. "Upsy Daisy."

She licked her lips. I'm sorry, but that did something to me. I yanked her closer. Her breasts smashed against my chest. I could feel her nipples poking into my pectorals.

"We forgot the massage oil," I said.

"On my dresser," she told me.

"I'll go get the condom," I said. "You get the oil. We'll meet back here in thirty seconds."

"Sounds like a plan."

I jumped up from the bed and scurried down her hall, through her living room, and out on the balcony. I picked up my pants and searched through the pocket, found my condom, turned, and stopped.

"The balcony was a good idea," Sela said. "Wanna give it a try?"

I didn't answer her with words.

But we tried it—out on the balcony, the night sky watching us go at it long and hard.

It was, as Sela would say afterward, hella good.

All was right with my world.

22

"You say you love me, but what do you love about me?" Russell asked Bevolyn as the arms of their bedroom clock moved past midnight on a trek toward dawn. He'd just eased under the covers after a hot shower. Bevolyn was still awake. The small lamp atop the table on her side of the bed was on, casting light on her Bible as she studied Scripture.

She placed a finger in her Bible to hold the place, then, noticing the expression on Russell's face, she closed it altogether and placed it on the side table. "Why are you asking this?"

"Because," Russell said.

Bevolyn sighed. "Well…okay…you're hardworking, a good provider—"

"Beyond that, Bev."

"Beyond that?" Bevolyn asked. "Exactly what do you want to know?"

"Are you attracted to me?"

"Why are you asking me this?" Bevolyn asked.

"Things haven't been right between us," he said. "I haven't seen any interest in your eyes. How you look at me. And you're always accusing me of being with someone else, wanting someone else. Maybe that's because you yourself…"

"You're worrying about me cheating on you, Russell?"

He shook his head. "I'm not, no. Maybe a little. I mean…" He squeezed his eyes shut, quickly reopened them, and looked at his wife of sixteen years. "Just tell me, Bevolyn. I need to know."

She thought for a moment and came up with, "You're handsome."

"Damn, Bev, baby. That's generic."

"Strong hands," she went on. "And your arms, I love your arms."

Russell touched her shoulder and halted her now that she'd started to open up. Fear flashed in his eyes. "You promised you would never do that to me again. You wouldn't, would you? I feel like I'm losing you. Lost you."

Bevolyn realized then what this was about: he needed affirmation, loving words. He was fragile, wounded, still hadn't gotten over the past.

Long ago she'd made a mistake during her third year in college, the first of their marriage—she'd cheated on Russell with a basketball player. Every limb on that basketball player, Bevolyn was pleased to find out at the time, was lengthy. It had been a torrid affair of lust and sex, no love in it.

Somehow, Russell had found out. They made it through the affair, and everything the affair brought into their lives, but it had created a domino effect on their marriage, brought the whole thing crashing down, to the point they struggled through now, daily, it seemed. Every day they endured as husband and wife was another notch on their belt, another twenty-four hours they could attribute to the grace of God, and not the love of husband and wife. It was a sad state to be in, but better than the alternative—their lives forever mangled through a divorce.

"I was young," Bevolyn said, tossing back the covers and moving to rest on Russell's lap. The move surprised him, as evidenced by his arched eyebrows. She continued, "I was a wife. A student. You were talking kids. But I never saw you, too involved with your work, me with my studies. My entire life was pressure."

Russell's love had initially caressed Bevolyn's soul. This man, with so much going for him, wanted her. Her. It was something she'd never experienced or witnessed. Carmen had never married, had never talked about any man, and had never mentioned Sela and Bevolyn's father. They might not even have the same father—Bevolyn didn't know. But then, Bevolyn was married herself, and she'd found that the movies and books that portrayed it as gravy were heavy-handed in their artistic license to stretch the truth.

"I made a mistake, Russ," she said now. "I'd never make that mistake again, ever."

"I see it between you," Russell said. "That *something* between folks that leads to something more."

"Between who?" Bevolyn asked.

"You know who," Russell said. He sneered. "That so-called Man of God."

"So this is about the reverend?"

"It's about—"

But her finger was on his lip. She shushed him, reached back and grabbed around his neck, brought him closer, more snug, and nibbled at his lip as if it were her favorite indulgence—raw cookie dough.

And Russell let her eat him.

Then she stopped. Russell opened his eyes as her weight disappeared and air hugged him. She had bounded from under the covers, shuffled across the carpet, and found a spot on the antique chair in the corner of their bedroom. Ornately carved in wood, with a plush burgundy pillow seat reset in the frame, it was an expensive chair. Bevolyn sat in it, one leg dangling, the other crossed Indian-style under her. She knew, because Russell had told her on more than one occasion, that the sight of her sitting in that way stirred something animal inside of him, which meant only one thing, Russell now realized. She was trying to seduce him.

He flipped to her side of the bed and sat up in the pool of warmness her body had just recently vacated. "You're leaving me hanging, Bev?" He knew, again, by the way she was sitting that she wasn't. This was just part of the game—his part, the oblivious husband.

"I wouldn't do that. Now would I?"

"You never know," Russell said. "You been kinda stingy with it." He nodded at the V between her legs, the "it" she'd been stingy with.

"Guess I have to make that up to you," she cooed.

Russell stood, stretched, and moved over to her. He bent to one knee, leaned in, and laid his head on the stomach below her full breasts. She tenderly rubbed his head. "How can a grown man be such a baby?" she wondered.

"Dangle sex in front of a grown man and…"

Bevolyn's hands stopped. "Just sex?" she asked. "Not sex and love?"

Russell realized he'd made a mistake, said the wrong thing, possibly vanished this almost-encounter to that graveyard where all their not-even-close encounters rested in peace. He sat up and looked at his wife. "Of course sex and love, Bev." She didn't seem convinced. "I know how much an affair would hurt you. I know. I wouldn't bring that to your doorstep. I wouldn't."

He waited, said no more.

"Unbutton my shirt," were her words after it felt as if an eternity had passed.

Russell smiled. "Gladly."

Bevolyn covered his hands with hers. "Slowly, Russ. We have all night."

He nodded. And when he'd gotten the shirt open, he reached inside, pulled her breasts to his hungry lips, and sucked the nipples until he could feel them in his mouth like small marbles.

"Are they tasty?" Bevolyn asked, thinking of Russell's cookie dough lips.

"Very," he admitted.

"Sweet or sour?"

"Like blueberry muffins, Bev."

He moved to her stomach, licked her innie belly button clean, and said, "Sweet, too."

She knew where his journey would end, couldn't wait until he got there.

He moved down, kissing the inside of her thighs now. "Damn," he said, "You just one big ole lollypop."

And then his tongue was inside her, warm, wet.

She gripped his head and moved him, just a little, in the right direction. Once there, her hands fell from his head and gripped the seat of the antique chair. She moved her hips, gyrated.

But then his lips and his tongue were gone.

"You stir my soup, Bev. You stir my soup."

"Don't eat with your mouth open," she directed him, pushing him by the shoulders back to her chicken soup for the grown and sexy's soul.

He tongued her to a wrecking-ball climax. He got pillows from the bed, thick, solid ones. And he propped them up in front of the antique chair. "Gotta be able to reach," he told Bevolyn.

"Reach what?" she stupidly asked.

He smiled, knelt on the pillows, took one out because now he was too high, and then nodded triumphantly. "About right," he said.

"For?"

He moved to her, knelt on the pillows again, and slid himself inside her with a little effort. For that, Bev. For that.

She bit into her lip, wrapped her arms around his neck, locked her fingers, and moved her hips in rhythm with his thrusts. The antique chair slid a few inches; the pillows under Russell fell out of place, their awkward lovemaking falling apart.

But Russell was determined. He kept at it, in and out, holding her waist, flicking his tongue at her breasts as they swung to him, then away, then swung to him again. Got the rhythm of that down, too.

His orgasm was a lion's roar. He slumped on the floor, spent.

Bevolyn found a comforting spot atop of him. She rubbed his chest. "I love you, Russell. The whole of you. I have for sixteen years. You don't have to worry. I'd never cheat on you again. Never."

And she repositioned herself so she could lay her head on his chest.

"I love you, Bev. We gonna be okay? I want us to be."

"I love you, too, Russ. And yes, we'll be okay."

And she prayed, at that moment, that God would make it so, that her lust for the reverend would subside, and her jealousy toward her sister would, too. That, in the worst-case scenario, if those things didn't happen, Russell would never ask her about the reverend again. That she and Russell could go on, business as usual. That if she did break down and return to Fellowship Baptist Church against Russell's wishes, Russell wouldn't find out.

23

"Incontinent. Again. Shucks."

Shame darted across the old man's face at the sound of the CNA's voice. She was pleasant enough, but all he could do was nod his head and keep quiet as the young woman wiped the urine and loose bowel movement from his backside. A gag-inducing stench filled the air and he felt bad that the room didn't have a window. Well, it did, but a small one way up out of his or any of the nursing staff's reach. They worried about patients here...too much, as far as he was concerned. He wasn't about to jump out of any window—didn't have the strength. The room definitely needed a window. A window he'd have propped open as far as its hinges allowed. A window for ventilation. A window for his own dignity.

"What's that CNA mean? Cute nurse's ass?" he asked her, spying the lettering etched into the pocket of her scrubs.

"Certified Nurse Assistant," she said, smiling. "Remember?"

He shook his head. He didn't remember.

The CNA continued her work. "I know you were too tired to turn," she offered, "but I couldn't let you lay in this, get bedsores. Bedsores can kill you dead."

He was using his one good hand unaffected by the stroke to grip the side of the bed as he lay, turned, with the CNA wiping his butt.

Dying would be a good thing, he thought. There wasn't anything left of him, anyway. And even when he'd been of sound mind and body, he hadn't really contributed anything of value to the world. To his wife. To his sons.

"Okay, I'm almost done, Mr. Furlow," the CNA said. Her voice was soft, fluttery, and almost all of her words sounded like a song. His wife had been the same way, a song in everything she said. And when she really got down to actually singing, watch out, she was a little slice of heaven on earth. But that relationship with his wife, like everything else in his life, had gone to crap. That didn't stop him from thinking on it, though.

"Almost done," the CNA repeated. "Just wanna put a clean diaper on you."

He could feel her situating the diaper under his left side. In a minute, she'd ask him to turn the other way. She'd then pull the other side of the diaper under him, roll out the old one, and then tell him to settle on his back. She'd wrap him in the diaper then, fastening those sticky straps. Just like a baby. That was what he'd become now, a baby all over again. Full circle.

"Okay, turn the other way for me. I'll give you a little push for help."

He did. He turned, mostly because of her assistance.

"Good. Now, lay on your back."

He did, plopping on his back.

"Good."

What was good about it?

"All done," she said triumphantly. "You're good and clean now."

He offered her a disingenuous smile and nod. She

smiled in turn, a smile that briefly took away his depression. What a beautiful smile, a beautiful young lady, he noticed. But then the dark thoughts entered his head.

Wonder what she thought about my ol' shriveled up dick? She probably can't believe how ballooned my darn prostate is, I bet.

He watched her clean up, watched her drop the dirty disposable wipes in a small wastebasket by the side of his bed, watched her pull off her stained latex gloves and drop them in the same garbage can. The gloves had traces of his loose brown stool on the fingers. She pulled a fresh pair of gloves from a pocket sewn into her scrubs and wiggled her fingers inside. She took out the garbage bag, twirled it, tied it, and placed it by the foot of the bed. She took an empty bag from the bottom of the trash can, tied an end of it, and slid it over the lip of the can.

Doing everything for him, he thought. He was useless. Useless. Always had been, too.

She picked up the old garbage bag and moved to the side of his bed. That smile draped her face again. "Okay, Mr. Furlow," she said, touching one of his hands, "you be easy. Okay?"

"What was your name again, young lady? I ain't good with names."

She smiled. "You're getting stronger, Mr. Furlow. Speech therapy is working wonders." She squeezed his hand. "Pam. My name's Pam."

"I won't forget this time," Leonard Vernard Furlow told her.

She nodded, knowing he'd probably forgotten her name already, and left the room.

He clutched the bedrail with his arthritic left hand. He could see his toenails sticking out from under the bed sheet. They were long, hard, and crusted yellow. The staff wouldn't cut them for him because he was a diabetic. And the podiatrist had yet to come by and do the deed, despite several orders put in from the well-meaning staff. He blew out air in frustration. A mess, that's what he was, a mess.

Despite gargling earlier, and Patricia—was that her name?—brushing his teeth painstakingly, his breath smelled like an overflowing garbage can in the dead heat of a late July North Carolina day. His skin was dark chocolate, rough and ashy despite the gobs of Eucerin cream they lathered on him daily. His full head of gray hair was actually more yellow than white. Most of his underclothes had permanent brown stains in the pants. That's why he'd switched to diapers.

Plain and simple, he was a mess.

"Mr. Furlow?"

Paula again. Paula, right? Oh, heck, it didn't matter. He summoned the strength to sit up and look at her, craning his neck. "What's that, young lady?"

"You have a visitor," she informed him.

"Visitor?" He could feel his heart rate climb. "Who is it, young lady?"

"Says his name is Lincoln Rhyme, Mr. Furlow."

"Don't know him," he snapped.

"Says he's a friend of your son," she added.

He looked at her, trying to find a crumb of April Fool's on her mouth, but he didn't, so he told her, "Send him on in."

She disappeared from the doorway. He ran down a list of things he'd say, how he'd act, the apologies he'd offer. Then, he stopped himself. A *friend* of his son, not his son. Still, this offered a glimmer of hope like none he'd known since that day he awakened, his right side as dead as his wife and her second born.

"Mr. Furlow."

The man was standing by his bed, looking down on

him, smiling, and looking very dapper in his tailored suit. His son picked friends well, it seemed. Good.

"Shake my left," he told the nattily dressed young man who had his own right hand extended, hovering over Furlow's right. "My right's no good."

The young man did.

"Kinda do look like a young Denzel," Furlow said.

"Excuse me?"

"Denzel…Washington. He was in that movie, *The Bone Collector*. Name was Lincoln Rhyme. I seen it on TBS. They messed it up, though. Instead of saying, 'son of a bitch' or 'bullshit,' they'd have 'em say, 'son of a fish' or 'fizzle stick.' Stupid stuff like that."

"Okay," Dante said.

"You have to pardon me, young man. I remember movie stuff. Can't remember everyday things, like the name of that young lady that wipes…" He let it trail off. "Anyway, my stroke did something to me, to my memory. But I remember movie stuff just fine, so I blab on about it. Makes me feel like I still got something left. Lincoln Rhyme, as I said, Denzel played him in that movie, *The Bone Collector*. Had the white girl with the Negro lips in it, too."

Dante Ruffin smiled. "I get that a lot, the Lincoln Rhyme comments. That movie happened to have been a book adaptation, you know. Jeffery Deaver. Wonderful novelist."

"Learn something every day," Furlow said. He cleared the phlegm from his throat. "You say you know my son?"

Dante nodded. "Sure do."

"How about?"

"Met him in prison," Dante said without pause.

A shadow crossed Leonard Vernard Furlow's face.

"He served his time like a champ," Dante said, emotionless, "and I personally think he was railroaded, to be honest. Didn't seem like he belonged in jail."

"That's what they all say. Want to believe," Furlow said. "But I'm glad to hear you think that."

"I do."

"You seen him," Furlow asked, "since he got out?"

Now a shadow crossed Dante's face. "I was hoping you had."

The old man shook his head.

"He told me about the letters you sent him," Dante went on. "They seemed to have meant a lot to him. I wonder why he wouldn't come see you."

"History," Furlow said. "Practically all of it bad."

"Does he have any other family in Jersey?"

Furlow frowned. "What's your business with my son?"

"Business, actually. We talked about maybe starting one, doing something positive with ourselves when we got out," Dante said. "He beat me by a few months. I'm out now, though. I wanted to hook up. He told me before his release that he was coming here to Jersey. To catch up with you."

"He told you that?"

"Sure did."

"He hasn't."

"I'm sure he will, eventually."

"And when he does, you'd like to catch up with him yourself?"

"I would," Dante admitted.

"What's your business with my son, Lincoln?"

"Told you."

"Refresh for me," Furlow said. "And what kind of business you in, just out the slammer, lets you get all dressed up like that?"

Dante smiled. "It's legal business. I'm a promoter."

"Promoting what?"

"Musical acts."

"Rappers."

Dante shook his head. "R and B singers, Mr. Furlow. I promote acts that themselves promote love, happiness. I'm all for those things. I'd fight to my dying breath to be happy…for people to be happy."

"My boy's mother…my wife…she was a singer. Sang like a summer's breeze. Made you close your eyes when you heard her, I mean."

"He spoke of her, said she was better than the professionals."

Furlow shook his head, sadly. "She was. She sure was."

"What happened? How come she didn't cut any records?"

Furlow looked at him. "I happened. I stamped that dream out like a cigarette."

"You're being hard on yourself, Mr. Furlow."

"Just telling the truth, young man."

Dante thought of the envelope in his pocket, the letter Furlow had sent his son in prison. "Your son shared with me the letter you wrote him, Mr. Furlow. The part about you being sorry you never showed him how to throw a football with a spiral, the little areas where you feel you failed him."

"That right?" Furlow said, remembering. It had taken so much out of him to write those letters, that letter, his script shaky and undisciplined.

"He forgave you, Mr. Furlow," Dante went on. "At least he said he did."

The old man's eyes misted. He lay silent.

"Well, thanks for your time," Dante said. "I really appreciate you seeing me, Mr. Furlow."

Furlow looked up from his thoughts, deep thoughts of his sons, his wife. "Leaving so soon?"

"I'm afraid I have to, Mr. Furlow. I've got some other business to attend to."

"What you want me to tell my son, he stops by?"

"Nothing."

"Nothing?"

Dante shook his head. "Life on the inside makes you skeptical, guarded, Mr. Furlow. I don't think he believed me when I said we would hook up when I got out, do positive things. Well, I have. I want to surprise him. I have something real special in store for him."

"You want to leave your name, some contact info with me, just in case?" Furlow asked.

Dante shook his head again. "Haven't gotten myself situated here in Jersey just yet, Mr. Furlow. I'll be in touch, though, soon. I'll keep my eyes out for him to visit you."

Furlow reached up with his left hand. Dante took it with his right. They shook.

"Don't be a stranger," Furlow said.

"I won't, Mr. Furlow. You can count on that. I won't. Not at all."

Book II

Lamentations

24

I stood at the fringe of my large living room, a smile on my face, thanksgiving in my heart. Gospel music played just a notch above softly from the stereo on the opposite side of the room. The decorations were understated, regal. Purple and white streamers, twined elaborately, hung from the corner of one wall to its diagonal wall. A long line of folding card tables, like ones on which you'd play Bid Whist, centered the floor. A throw-away-after-one-use tablecloth covered the tables, lavender-colored, looking as if it were made of some fine linen instead of plastic you could cause a run in with a sharp fingernail. White swaths of real linen with frilly edges covered the tablecloth. A huge wheat-colored basket overflowing with purple and white impatiens served as the centerpiece of the table. A feast of food: deviled eggs, honey ham slices filled with cream cheese and speared with a toothpick, egg salad sandwiches, pigs-in-a-blanket, chicken wings.

Open House.

"Mighty proud job," Mother Stokely told me. She had a smidge of deviled egg on the corner of her lip. Her eyes danced to the music.

I told her what I'd told every member of Fellowship

Baptist Church who had come up to me and offered similar sentiment. "Sister Sela Wheeler handled everything."

"Don't know Sister Wheeler," Mother Stokely said.

"Sister Sykes's sister," I said.

Mother Stokely smiled. "That's a mouthful of 'sisters' in one sentence, Reverend Path."

I nodded and smiled.

"Point her out to me," Mother Stokely said.

I raised a hand, then a finger. "That beautiful young woman over there by the punch bowl."

Mother Stokely didn't even look, but trained her eyes on me instead. "Your new woman friend, Reverend?"

I nodded. "Absolutely."

"Keeping it clean?"

I was surprised she'd ask, at first. Then I thought about Fellow-ship's problems before I'd come.

"Very clean," I lied. Well, not exactly a lie; we did shower after sex.

"Good to hear it. Good to hear it."

"Good to be heard," I said.

Mother Stokely moved on. She moved to Sela, stopped, and shared a few words with her. Sela's cheeks pinked and she nodded. They broke apart, Mother Stokely back to the table for another helping of deviled eggs, Sela to me.

"What she say?" I asked.

Sela shook her head but answered, "Her and her late husband had sex before they married. It's okay long as you shower afterwards."

I laughed, hard, so hard a coughing spell clutched me. Sela patted my back.

"She's a trip," I said once the coughing stopped.

"To Australia," Sela agreed. "Way far away."

"They love what you've done," I whispered to Sela.

She crinkled her nose. "Music's kind of corny."

She'd picked it out. A good choice, I thought. Gospel singer Montage Pheloan knowing who holds tomorrow, knowing whose help he needed—He's Sweet I Know, of course. I liked it, liked it a lot, liked everything Sela had done to make my home inviting. Open House had been Sela's idea. Again, a good choice. I hadn't thought of it myself, and yet, when Sela suggested I invite the church folk into my home, the home they'd provided for me, it all made sense. Sela had the makings of Fellowship's first lady, even if she didn't know it.

"What would you have played," I asked her, "if all these church folk weren't around?"

"Pink Cookies in a Plastic Bag Getting Crushed by Buildings," she told me without hesitation. A mischievous smile clothed her face.

"Never heard that one," I admitted.

Her smile deepened. "It's an LL Cool J song."

"Oh," I said, my tone somber. I thought about LL's chiseled physique, and even though mine rivaled his, I still felt a tinge of jealousy. I wanted Sela's thoughts, eyes, ears, on me and only me. I was stingy when it came to her.

"His metaphor for the art of making love," she added. "Which I'd like to be doing now, with you."

"Oh," I repeated. Loud, more enthusiastic than the first.

She tapped my shoulder and smiled. "Thought you'd like that."

"You read me like a book, baby."

"Okay," she said, softly, "don't start with the 'baby' stuff. Otherwise, these good folks are gonna hafta get up out of here so you can crush my pink cookies."

"Crumbs," I said, shaking my head. "Gotta love 'em."

"Watch yourself, Reverend," she chastised. I needed the admonishment. My gaze had been riding her roller-coaster curves. I was ready to get back on an outrageously long line, ticket in hand, and ride again.

"You really did your thing, Sela. Again, thanks."

"I tried," she said.

"Succeeded, baby," I volleyed back to her.

"*Reverend.*" There was chastisement in her voice, but playfulness and sexy energy in her eyes and on her face.

I had to get these folks out of my home.

I moved from Sela.

"Everyone…"

They continued to chatter, laugh, smile, thoroughly enjoying the festivities "Everyone, please gather around," I said in as loud a voice as I could muster.

Heads started to turn in my direction. Eyes focused on me and conversations ended. Sela moved from me to the corner where the stereo was, and turned it down.

I thought of Luck and his jokes, as the attention of the room shifted to me.

"There was this young boy," I said, "new to a school in a new town. First day of class, he's sitting in the back of the room, tentative, afraid to make contact with any of the other students."

Eyes were on me, faces frozen in half smiles. They knew I was apt to start with a joke. They knew me well.

I continued on, "The teacher noticed the student in the back of the room and asked him to step forward. His heart started to pound, hands and armpits puddle with sweat. But, he gathered his courage from God and moved forward. Met the teacher in the front of the class."

They were spellbound. I could see it in their faces, the quiet of the room. I glanced at Sela, my heart warm with thoughts of her. She'd said I made religion more accessible for her. Well, she'd made me grow into a pastor, a pastor I could appreciate. I felt comfortable for the first time in my life, even if it was based on a lie. Again, He's Sweet I Know works in mysterious ways. I was Exhibit A.

"So," I went on, "the teacher has the student introduce himself to the rest of the class. He does, his voice barely above a whisper. 'Where are you from?' she asked him. He told his classmates. Again, his voice a whisper. 'Tell us all something about you that you're really proud of,' she asked. 'I'm a Christian,' he replied, proud, his voice strong for the first time."

I paused and looked around. Several members had proud looks themselves. I felt good about that.

"Well, the teacher didn't like that comment very much. She frowned. Took her hand off the student's shoulder. 'We're all atheists, here,' she said. 'Aren't we, class?' One by one, each head nodded."

The members of Fellowship frowned now.

"The boy remained strong, unashamed. The teacher asked him with a sneer why he wasn't an atheist. He told her his parents were Christians and so was he. She sighed. Asked him if his parents were morons, would he be a moron, too. He shook his head. Told her, 'nope, then I'd be an atheist.' "

Laughter filled my living room. I looked to Sela. Her laughter was the hardest. It filled my ears like good music. Montage Pheloan.

"I'm glad," I told my congregation, my voice choking, "to be among like-minded folk. Christians. Glad to know each one of you. Glad God saw fit to bring us into one another's lives."

A chorus of applause, hallelujahs, and amens followed. I waited for it to die down.

When it did, I said, "I also want to thank Sister Wheeler for her help in putting this together." I paused to let them turn and glance at her, nod their appreciation. "And I want to publicly tell Sister Wheeler that the love she's shown me, and hopefully I've shown her in return, is something I'll forever be grateful to God for."

Almost everyone smiled except for Sela. Tears welled in her eyes and she touched a hand to her mouth. Her lavender nails were a perfect complement to her rich chocolate skin tone. She dropped her head and shook it. A few members went to her and patted her back.

I'd moved her.

By letting her know, publicly, how much she'd moved me.

25

Bevolyn bent and peeked in the oven as Russell entered the kitchen. She'd heard him pull up in the driveway and quickly moved to the kitchen to check if the food was near finished. The heat of the stove warmed her face. Russell's presence warmed her back. She stamped down her excitement, though. She had had too many past letdowns to fall aimlessly in thrall to joy. Too many.

"Something smells good," Russell said.

Bevolyn eased from the heat of the oven, closed its door, and wiped her hands on her apron. She glanced at the electronic clock display above the stove: not even five yet. She hadn't expected Russell home for hours. Lately, though, he'd been coming from work at a decent hour. They'd been holding one another at night, taking showers together in the morning, talking in bed…doing other things in bed.

"Baking a cake," Bevolyn said. "And why are you home so early, handsome?"

"Family and work. Need to balance them. I see it, finally."

Either that, Bevolyn imagined, or his mistress had taken a liking to hamburgers and French fries instead of steak and potatoes—lunch instead of dinner. Bevolyn glanced at Russell, searching for some clues. His jacket hung over his shoulder, his tie loosened, his shirt wrinkled around the belt area. Was his dishevelment a clue, as if he'd undressed, then dressed again? Images flashed through her mind; voices screamed in her head. She tried to drown them out.

"I hope the cake is chocolate," Russell said.

"It is," Bevolyn said.

He placed his jacket over the back of a chair, eased closer to his wife, and wrapped his arms around her. "What's the special occasion?"

"Just thought I'd do something nice." Bevolyn could smell a sweet aroma on him, sweeter than his normal cologne. A woman's perfume, she decided. "That isn't a problem, is it?"

Russell kissed her forehead and smiled. "Do I look like I have a problem with it? Come. Sit. Share a slice with me."

"Ice cream?" Bevolyn asked. She'd steeled herself to ignore the voices, the images, the disheveled clothes, the perfume.

"Breyer's?"

"I don't buy anything but. I know you wouldn't eat anything else." She'd said it as if he were guilty of some great offense, her tone biting, bitterness running through her. Bitterness she had to control, she realized. Shut out the voices, the disheveled clothes, and the perfume.

"Real vanilla beans," Russell said, oblivious to the angered tone she'd taken with him. "Got to go with Breyer's."

Bevolyn gestured toward the table. "Grab us some napkins. Sit." She turned away.

Russell cleared his throat as Bevolyn gathered the gallon of Breyer's from the freezer, a bowl from the cupboard, and two spoons from the silverware organizer. He'd been thinking all day, and now the thoughts were about to take wings and fly. He couldn't avoid this. "I want to tell Afeni I'm her father."

Bevolyn heard him, and her heart started pounding, but she continued preparing the cake and ice cream, wordlessly.

"Bevolyn."

"Yes," she said as she slowly turned to face him. It took every ounce of strength she had to keep from falling. She held to the countertop for support.

"Did you hear me?'"

"I heard you."

"And?"

"I don't think so," she said.

"Why not?"

"You know why not, Russell."

"Church folk? You don't even go any more."

Bevolyn frowned. Not going to church was a fresh wound she'd yet to dress with a bandage. "Not church folk," she said. "Bevolyn. Bevolyn doesn't want to deal with that."

Russell nodded. "I know about not dealing with things."

"That situation was different," Bevolyn said.

"Please don't go there," Russell begged. "Please don't."

Bevolyn couldn't let it go. "It was."

"You were pregnant, Bev. By a man other than your husband."

Back to this again—her fling with the basketball player…the little point guard he'd planted in her belly.

"You had already graduated from college and had a job," she defended. "Working with all those women."

"None of which I wanted," he said.

"How could I know that?"

"I told you so; that's how."

She shook her head. "Wasn't enough for me; you know that. I was wrong. I made a mistake. Paid for it. Had an abortion that I think about, still, almost every day. I keep telling myself I did right. It was the best thing."

Russell had to agree with that. He couldn't fathom the idea of looking at that child every day, knowing it wasn't of his seed. And yet, he knew, if Bevolyn had kept it, he still would have kept her. He loved her that much.

Bevolyn moved to him, hugged him, and laid her head against his chest. "We've been doing so well. Why do we even have to discuss history?"

Because their history shaped their future, Russell wanted to say.

Instead, he said, "I feel like we've destroyed two young children's lives, Bev. The unborn and the born. Afeni needs to know I'm her father."

Bevolyn moved her head from Russell's chest. Fire was in her eyes. "I thought to have that child come into our home, Russell. To make up for the mistakes we've both made. Give her the chance my baby with Lewis never got."

The mention of Lewis made Russell blanch. Lewis, long with sinewy muscles, basketball star. Had Bevolyn pregnant, a feat Russell had yet to accomplish, and perhaps never would.

"Can't give any more than that," Bevolyn went on. "Just can't."

Russell nodded and slid from her embrace.

"The cake, Russ."

"Lost my appetite." He waved her off. His shoulders sagged. His steps from the kitchen were labored.

Bevolyn sat at the table alone, staring across the room, aimlessly.

She realized, then, that she should have asked him about the perfume and wrinkled clothes.

Afeni slid her key into her mother's lock. The door glided open easily. She stepped inside, half expecting to hear a Nat King Cole record playing. The apartment was dark, except for a light in the kitchen. The microwave was running. Afeni could hear it. The sink was running, too. She headed for the kitchen.

Her mother stood over the sink, her back to Afeni.

"Aloe."

Her mother jumped and spun around, a hand over her chest. "Girl!"

"Sorry," Afeni said. She moved into the kitchen and leaned against the refrigerator.

"What you doing here?" Aloe asked.

"Mrs. Sykes asked if I'd give her the night."

"For?"

"Shit, Aloe. Stuff, I guess."

"What stuff?" Aloe wanted to know. "I might not have been home. I might have had plans."

"You're my mother," Afeni said.

"What stuff?" Aloe repeated.

Afeni shook her head and looked her mother in the eyes. "She doesn't have the "Chestnuts Roasting on an Open Fire" record, Aloe. She couldn't put that on and have me wait in the hall. That stuff. Some time with her husband."

Aloe grinned and nodded. "Why ain't you just say so?

She wanna get her jump-off jumped off. I can understand that." She handed Afeni a knife and three potatoes. "Peel those. Help your mama with dinner."

Afeni took the knife. The shit she had to put up with.

"How'd you get in, anyway?" Aloe asked. "You left your key last time. I saw you take it off and leave it by the door."

Afeni smiled. "Had a duplicate."

"You get the items?"

Nate Ruffin shook his head to Dante's question. Anthony Ruffin stood behind him, silent.

Dante frowned. "And why not?"

"Problem with the credit card," Nate said.

Dante sighed. "Credit card's fine. I don't understand. What did the person at the store do?"

"Called the hotline," Nate said.

Dante frowned. "What happened?"

"They asked me all this information. Last four digits of the social. Mother's maiden name. I slipped out like I had to go get it from my car. We booked out of there. I was afraid they'd catch on that it was stolen."

Dante leaned back. "Yes, they need that information to prevent identity fraud. If you know a person's social security number and their mother's maiden…" He stopped and let his words evaporate as he sprang up in his seat. A wicked smile crossed his face.

"Wassup?" Nate asked.

"Mother's maiden name," Dante said.

"Yeah, so?"

"We've been looking for a Furlow. It never crossed my mind that he might not be a Furlow."

"What would he be?" Nate asked.

Dante held up a finger, pulled out his cell phone, and

dialed a number. That wicked smile on his face grew wider when someone answered on the other line. "Hey there, pretty eyes," he said. "How's our little artiste doing?"

It wasn't long before Dante's conversation ended. He flipped his cell closed, a smile on his face as his brothers looked on him with expectation. "He might just be a Path," Dante said.

"Come again?" Nate asked.

"If you'd spent time in jail, then went on the run to start a new life," Dante said, "would you do it using your real name?"

Nate smiled as an answer. Dante was smart like that, figuring out angles he would never have thought of.

Dante tapped a knuckle against his head. "This thought never crossed my mind. Let's explore that avenue and see if it bears us any fruit, shall we?"

"And who we looking for, again?" Nate asked.

"Path," Dante said.

Zelda placed her bags down on the porch of her apartment and lifted her head to allow her keys a release from the clamp of her chin against her chest. The yellow cab that had transported her home from the grocery store pulled off from the curb and moved up the street, but not before the flirty driver tooted his horn in two quick and successive bursts. Zelda turned and watched the cab morph from full-size sedan to matchbox. "Thank God, he's gone," she said aloud. Then she began to wonder if he'd ever have the audacity to return; after all, he knew where she lived. It was definitely time to stop relying on public transportation. "You Spanish?" he'd asked her soon after she'd boarded his cab.

Zelda had looked at his hot chocolate-colored skin,

his soft hair, the startling darkness of his eye color, and tried to work her way through the maze of ambiguity that was his ethnic background. He was good looking, for sure, what some women went for. And yet there was no sadness in Zelda that he didn't move her. She knew who she was and was comfortable in the knowing. The L-word. Latina, yeah, on some level, but more importantly, lesbian.

"No," she'd answered him, but then added in the same breath, "Well, yes, actually. My father was Cuban, but my mother raised me. I don't have too much recognition of my Spanish side." She stopped abruptly.

"I thought so," the driver said, running his tongue over his lips. His lips were full, the kind a straight woman could get lost kissing. That's if he knew how to kiss. Sadly, Zelda knew, few men really did. Fewer still even cared that they didn't. That's why Zelda had gravitated to women, she believed, because women were more giving sexually, more enterprising during the endeavor.

"I have an eye for that sort of thing. I'm Dominican, myself," the cab driver went on.

Hadn't he heard her say she wasn't too in touch with her Spanish side? So why was he blabbing on and on about that small part of her, that part she didn't know or understand? That was the problem with men: they were selective with what information they wanted to accept. They heard, but didn't listen. Women heard *and* listened. A big difference.

"*El Dios en el cielo* got it so right when He created Latinas."

"Really?" Zelda feigned interest.

"Yes, really. And I can pick out a *chica caliente* from a mile away. You speak Spanish?"

Zelda smiled, fighting the urge to stick her finger

down her throat and vomit on this idiot. "I'm afraid what they taught me in high school has left me."

"Too bad." He muttered something in Spanish laced with sexual thought. Zelda knew that much. It was all in the way he rolled his tongue over the *r*'s, and how his gaze rolled over her from the rearview mirror. "Yeah, I knew you were a Latina," he continued, "soon as I pulled up and saw those hips of yours. The colorful flowers in your hair. *A Dios mío*! Please don't take offense to this, but I wish I were the lucky *hombre* unpinning that flower at night, or, crushing it against your pillow. *A Dios mío*!"

If he only knew.

Life would be so much easier for her if she'd gone along with it: pretended his tight curly hair, rich dark skin and eyes, and accent were things that moved her; let him unpin the flowers from her hair, or crush them against her pillow.

But she couldn't. That was for some other woman.

Zelda shrugged aside thoughts of the exchange with the cab driver, placed her key in her front door, and turned the knob. She reached down and picked up her bags while she held the door open with her knee. Out of the corner of her eye, she could see a figure emerge from a car parked across the street and head her way. Zelda quickened her pace and stepped inside. The taxi driver had her on edge.

"Zelda, wait a minute," the figure called out just before the door closed.

Zelda looked up to see Sela, her ex-something, running toward her. She stopped the door from closing, holding it open with her elbow. She turned and placed the grocery bags on the floor of her foyer and willed her heart to slow its pitter-patter. She turned back and stood in the half-opened doorway with her hands on her hips, tapping her foot…no, that was overplay. She quickly stopped tapping her foot, although she kept her hands on her hips.

"What are you doing here?" she asked.

Sela casually reentered Zelda's life with a smile, a greeting-card moment, while she caught her breath from the mad dash across the street. The sun shone perfectly off her eyes, brought out the light brown, almost golden hue that had caused Zelda to become enamored of her that first night they'd met at Lady Bar. Sela looked around uneasily, fingering the rail that led up to Zelda's apartment as if it were a silk bed sheet. "Can I come in?"

"Oh." Zelda smirked. "I don't think so, seesaw."

"Just to talk," Sela said. Then she crossed her chest with her arms. "Have some things I need to say. To tell you. Need to get them out if we have any chance of continuing a life together."

Life together? Manipulation had always been one of Sela's strong points, that and a body that the Hollywood actresses would point their personal trainers to, saying, 'mold me into that.' You could go through a full box of tithing envelopes before you'd find a weak spot anywhere on Sela's body. Not that Zelda would be tithing anywhere, because, sadly, she'd given up on Fellowship Baptist Church. Maybe one day she'd return.

"So, can I come in?"

Zelda thought about how much she had enjoyed exploring Sela, searching for that elusive weak point, and how much she enjoyed Sela's own excavation in her treasure. To Zelda's way of thinking, love had two distinct chambers, the physical and the mental, and Sela had captured the physical, and made it her own. And, on top of that, Sela had her mental, too.

"Come on in," Zelda said as she widened her doorway,

"but only for a few minutes. I have somewhere to go later, and I need to start preparing."

"Lady Bar?" Sela asked.

Zelda didn't answer.

Sela shrugged. Her perfume caressed Zelda's nose as she moved to pass her and walk into the apartment. They brushed against each other slightly. Sela stopped in the hall and turned, facing Zelda. Zelda closed the door behind her. Her knees knocked. The distance between them was less than a foot. Their eyes clung to each other for a moment.

Zelda forced herself to break the eye contact. "Grab those bags for me and bring them to the kitchen; make yourself useful."

"Oh, it's like that?"

"Yes," Zelda said as she sashayed past Sela, "it's like that."

Sela watched Zelda move up the hallway, hips swaying. A low whistle left her mouth. She shook her head. She followed.

"Where do you want these?" Sela asked as she joined Zelda in the kitchen.

Zelda cleared a pile of recipe books and food magazines off her countertop. "Put them here. And be careful with that one; it has my eggs on top."

"Yes, Ma'am," Sela replied. She bowed her head and gently placed the bags on the counter. "Anything else I can do for Madame before I retire for the evening?"

"That the perfume we made together?" Zelda asked. She had no time for games with this woman, had endured too much hurt playing Sela's game in the past.

Sela nodded. "Rising. My favorite."

"Can I get you something to drink, seesaw?"

"You can stop calling me that."

"Something to drink?"

Sela sighed. "You have cola?"

"Sure." Zelda removed a glass from the cabinet, opened the refrigerator, and poured Sela a drink from a cold two-liter bottle. "Ice? I imagine a woman such as you would like it as cold as it can get."

"No, thanks," Sela said. She'd decided to ignore Zelda's barbs, to take the high road. After all, if placed in the same situation, Sela herself would probably come out kicking and looking to draw blood, too. She respected Zelda's spunk, appreciated it and, at the barest level, found it sexy as hell.

"Sure? No ice?"

"I want a full glass," Sela said, "no cheating with ice."

Zelda nodded in affirmation. and handed Sela the drink. "No cheating it is."

"You look good," Sela said after her first sip. "Got a glow."

"Don't know anything about a glow," Zelda scoffed. "I lost some weight. Some dead weight. A hundred and some-odd pounds of it."

"That's good, Zelda. You deserve happiness, and I truly mean that."

Zelda took a seat across from Sela. She couldn't help feeling a pull to Sela, despite all the pain and failure they'd been through together. Admit it or not, she knew now, at this moment, watching Sela sitting quietly within feet of her, that she loved her. Loved her hard.

"So, I hear Reverend Path's Open House was a smash. You were quite the hostess, I also heard."

Sela nodded. She clasped her hands together and rested them on the table. Zelda noticed the lavender color of Sela's nails. Something fluttered in her stomach. Lavender, her color. She looked at Sela. Sela returned the look unblinkingly.

"Look, Zelda, I want to apologize."

"For?" Zelda asked. "Can't be our relationship, or whatever you want to call what it was. That wasn't real. But this thing with the reverend, now that's real. That's what Sela wants. Hot and sweaty sex with a man. And has it been hot and sweaty, Sela? Tell me. I'm just dying to know." Each sentence brought her voice up a notch. She was getting angry, something she'd promised herself she wouldn't get.

A pained expression came across Sela's face. "Sometimes we try and hurt those we love the most," she replied. "Truth is, I can't tell you how much being without you hurts me, how scared I am about a future without you."

"I never even wanted a future with you, Sela." A lie, but one Zelda had to tell nonetheless.

Sela tapped her fingers against the tabletop. Zelda glanced at Sela's strong but feminine fingers, and she remembered the good nights, nights Sela could work away all of life's kinks from her body with her gentle but firm touch. She thought of their one true vacation together. They had gone to the Poconos and Sela had given her a full-body massage that thrust Zelda deep in the throes of sleep. When Zelda awakened, rose petals were ravishing her skin, strewn over her entire body. Sela sat in the corner of the room, silently watching her, and when Zelda noticed, and gasped from the immediate shock, Sela had risen, fully naked and exquisitely proportioned, and come and made beautiful love to her.

"No future, huh?" She heard Sela call to her from across the table, across her thoughts.

"Nope."

"I guess it goes back to that cliché, one of the oldest in the book. You have to love yourself before you can truly love another." Sela looked away; it was evident that this next thought caused her great pain. "I never loved myself, Zelda. So I couldn't give love, correctly. Couldn't have built a future with you even if I'd wanted."

"Damn right that's a cliché," Zelda said. She noticed the surprise in Sela's eyes at her tone. "Didn't have anything to do with loving yourself," she added. "You just didn't want people to know you liked to eat coochie."

Sela's eyes bore down on Zelda and touched her inner wiring. The expression of seriousness in Sela's eyes crushed through Zelda's consternation. "Yes, you got me, Zelda. I like to eat coochie. Would like some right now, as a matter of fact." She smiled at Zelda, a subdued smile.

"Don't even go there, Sela."

Sela's eyes hunched. "Why not? You did."

"I didn't."

"Told me what I like," Sela said. "And I agreed. Told you what I *want*."

"Want all you want," Zelda said. She could feel herself falling, inane stuff coming out of her mouth. Wanting Sela, knowing that giving herself to Sela was a pathway to more pain, but still, wanting Sela. Wanting to kiss her lips, have Sela twirl her hair, eat each other's coochies.

Sela reached across the table and took Zelda's face in her hands. She turned it toward her own face, holding Zelda's head so they could see one another's eyes. "You will always be my girl, Zelda. The things we did—I'll always be yours. We might as well admit it. Let's stop fronting and get together. Now. You know you want it. I know I do." Zelda's knees touched; she could feel a dampness emerging in her crotch. She pulled away from Sela.

"Get it from LeVar. Reverend Path."

"Not the same," Sela said. "You know that. A man can't move me like a woman can."

"Any woman?"

Sela paused. "Don't know. No. I do know. Only you, Zee-Zee."

"Wrong answer, seesaw. Wrong answer. You paused. Hesitated. I told you once before that love doesn't hesitate."

Sela bit her lip, remembering that day. The sex. It had been wonderful, the sex. "You're turning me away, Zee-Zee?" Sela's eyes were full of curiosity.

"No," Zelda said. It even surprised her to hear that word coming from her mouth. Wasn't she turning Sela away?

"What, then?"

"Clarifying my position," Zelda said. "Letting you know I can't have it the way it was. I won't stand for being a secret joy. You want to be with me, you have to accept me, parade me, have no fear of letting anyone know I'm your special someone."

"Can't. You know that. This thing with LeVar is taking on a life of its own."

"You love him?"

"As much as I can love a man. Yes. But I admit it now. A man can't give me what a woman can. I mean…what *you* can."

Zelda shook her head sadly. "There isn't any room for me in your life, Sela. Thank you for helping me with the groceries." She stood, strong in her posture and her legs. "You know the way out. Take it and never come back. Ever."

Sela stood as well. Her body ached with desire. "We always made beautiful love. I meant what I said, about wanting to have a life together. Just not together like that."

"Answer's no," Zelda told her. "Find yourself another down-low female."

Sela nodded and left without further word. Out on the street, sitting in her car, she watched the sky, watched it and willed the orange haze to fade, the sun to set. Wanting darkness to fall.

26

Sela wouldn't cop to it, but I could hear the hesitation in her voice. The distance between us, at that moment, was farther than the reach of even fiber optics, most definitely the opposite of what I wanted, needed. My days had become a tick of seconds, minutes, and hours until I could share my evenings with her. And that's what we'd been doing. Sela and I spent most nights huddled in one another's arms.

"Wassup?" I said. "You're acting kinda cold toward me. Chilly."

"No chill."

"You're not you," I so ineloquently told her.

She didn't even comment on the strained phrasing. In a monotone she said, "Who am I, then?"

"Kinda…I don't know…distracted."

"Distracted?"

"You're on the phone," I said, "but you're not on the phone. Does that make sense?"

" 'Bout as much as everything else you've said."

"Sela?"

"LeVar?"

"I care about you. A lot. I want to share my life's ambitions with you. Have you share yours with me. Man to woman, we need one another. Let's not do this dance. Something's wrong. Again, I have to say it: we need one another. God made it so when He created us."

"Aww. You'd give me your rib?" she said. She was trying to sound upbeat and jovial, but I heard it as forced, fake.

I played along anyway. "You know I would."

"That's hella cool, baby."

"You know how I do."

"Hella cool. I'm hella lucky."

"Know any word beside hella?"

"Effin' cool? Effin' lucky?"

"Aiight. Stick with hella."

She laughed finally, for real this time, the chill melting, I hoped. I chalked it up to the demands of life. Those demands could sometimes weigh you down.

"So," I said, knowing I should probably leave well enough alone, "you want to tell me what's wrong? I know something's up."

"Nothing, baby. Really. I'm rushin', that's all."

She didn't sound in any hurry.

"*Ti takAya krasIvaya*," I replied. Again, going along with whatever she told me.

I could practically hear her eyebrows furrow through the phone line. "Ta-what?"

"You said you were Russian. That's Russian for 'you're so beautiful.' " I'd picked up foreign phrases, too, during that time when I practically locked myself in JCI's library and looked up words for *mother* in other languages.

She paused. I waited.

"For a minute there I thought you messed up and called me some other female's name," she offered finally.

"I wouldn't do that."

"Tita-whatever you said," she went on. "Thought you

went and got yourself a figure skater or a tennis player girlfriend to replace me." Now she was joking. All was right with my world.

"Getting jealous?" I asked her.

"Hella."

I laughed. She didn't, which concerned me; something was up. She was blowing hot and cold, timing off.

"Sela—" A beep was in my ear: call waiting. "Hold a second, love. I have to get that."

"I guess I can hold," she said. "But keep it short, please. Don't be preaching a sermon. And if it's Tita-whatever…" She paused for effect before adding, "Tell her I can do a triple jump and hit a backhand with slice my damn self. She's got a fight on her hands if she thinks she's taking you from me."

I didn't reply. She was blowing hot again, but once more, forced. I could hear it, feel it. Fake.

I clicked over, my heart heavy with worry. I heard a soft sniffle.

"Fellowship Baptist Church," I announced.

"Reverend Walker?" a woman asked. She fought to get the words in. As soon as she'd said them, the sniffles returned.

"Unfortunately Reverend Walker passed. This is Reverend Path. How can I help you?"

She paused. The sniffles ceased. When she finally spoke, her voice cracked. "My name is Geneva Braintree, Reverend Path. My grandmother used to attend your church."

"Used to?"

I couldn't see her but I could tell she nodded. "Roberta Quivers."

I hadn't heard the name. "And what can I do for you, Mrs. Braintree."

"Miss," she said. Oddly, that admission made me feel good. Maybe I was seeing the shift in Sela, preparing myself to bury her and our relationship in the same graveyard where Myshelle rested. Maybe I'm just a sinner with sex issues as Aloe-slash-Diane once told me all Christian men had.

"Miss Braintree."

"My grandmother took ill a few years back," Geneva told me. "Dropped out of church."

I frowned. "Her name hasn't come up on the sick and shut-in list." I hesitated. "Is she still with us? Living?"

Geneva sighed. "She's still here. And her name isn't on the list because I'm afraid she wasn't very...nice... when Reverend Walker, the deacons, and missionaries tried to visit."

"How so?"

"Cursed them," she said. I could hear the embarrassment in her tone. "Spit at a few. Tried to hit Reverend Walker, I'm afraid."

"You'd like me to come and talk to her?"

"Please," Geneva said. "She doesn't have much time left. She's angry with God. I want to see that her soul gets right before...She was a good, faithful woman, Reverend Path."

"I'm sure she is."

"Was," she corrected. "Not any more. But maybe you can help with that."

"What happened to her, Miss Braintree? Her ailment, I mean."

"Diabetes, mainly. She never did stick to the diets they prescribed. Called them 'constricting.' She recently had both legs amputated." She paused and started with the sniffles again. "There's a problem with the amputations I should warn you about."

"Go ahead."

"She somehow pulled out the surgical staples. They don't know how. She must have spent the better part of a day working at it. Her stumps look like ground beef." She broke off into a painful cry, the kind with a hyper-ventilation fit dogging its tail.

"Sister Braintree. Sister Braintree."

She continued to cry. Soon she'd be gasping for breath if I didn't calm her.

"Where is she, Sister Braintree? I can help." I didn't know if I could. I'd pray for her, though. I also filed a mental sticky pad note to pray for Sela and myself before the day ended.

Geneva Braintree took a great deal of time to calm herself. I sat, wordlessly, waiting. When she finally did, she apologized. I told her, no need. She nodded again; I could just tell. She told me the name of the hospital. I knew it. It was the same hospital where Reverend Walker had died.

I thanked Geneva Braintree for the call and clicked over to handle the situation with Sela.

She'd hung up.

I dialed her house number, then cell, and got voice mail for both. I sighed, grabbed my Bible, car keys, and wallet, locked down the office, and headed out.

Moments later, LL Cool J was blaring from the Toy-yoda's speakers, imploring his honey to hush for a while. The music was soothing, typical Ladies Love Cool James fare, and had me thinking of Sela as I drove with one hand on the steering wheel, bent at an angle in my gangster lean. Thinking of her when I should have been thinking of some comforting words and relevant Scripture to offer Sister Roberta Quivers when I reached the hospital. I knew He's Sweet I

Know needed me to go blow His horn for a bit, tout all the good that He offered, let Sister Quivers know that diabetes and a resistance to changing her diet had taken her legs, not Him. Let her know that even though she ate more than the six peanuts and five grapes the nutritionists allowed her on a daily basis, He hadn't gotten upset and quieted her for good. He'd hadn't taken her last breath. He'd spared her, what I considered grace. I had to get her to consider it as the same.

Such was the work of a preacher.

As I drove on, LL Cool J had hushed himself. Kanye West came through and told me that Jesus walks. I smiled at that bit of information. I knew that for myself but was happy Kanye reinforced the knowing.

I bobbed my head as I listened to the music. But again, my thoughts had drifted to Sela. They stuck there as I slowed for a changing light, stuck there as I saw the young, sand-colored girl on a pink bicycle move from the sidewalk, stuck there as I saw the car coming from the other intersection, the driver on a cell phone talking animatedly, not the least bit mindful of his own changing light.

Or the young girl crossing the street on her little pink bicycle.

I tensed, sat up in my seat, and my mouth opened, but no words would come.

Sadly, his car smacked into the young girl on her little pink bicycle.

She spun around several times, as if doing some bicycle trick, and landed in a thwack on the pavement. I didn't hear the thwack. I thanked He's Sweet I Know that my windows were up because the sound, I'm sure, would have hurt my heart. I didn't hear it, but almost as bad, I felt the thwack, felt it in my entire body. It sickened me, made my stomach mush, my mouth salty with nausea.

The driver who hit her slammed to a stop. He looked back, then to either side of himself. He paused when he caught my gaze. Then he shook his head and took off. My instincts kicked in. I caught his tags: PGH 22R. I wondered why he ran. It was obvious I'd seen him. Then I thought of my own criminal experience, thought of the moment of crossing the line, knowing your life would be irreparably harmed by your actions, and taking them anyway.

I glanced to the little girl and kept repeating the hit-and-run driver's tag over in my mind. PGH 22R. Please God Help, twenty-two chapters in Revelation. Please God Help, twenty-two chapters in Revelation. I would remember.

I looked up to see the girl's bicycle was a crumpled mess, rear wheel spinning. I moved quickly from the Toyyoda and rushed toward her. Blood bubbles were on her lips when I reached her. Her body was a pretzel, bruising already. I could see bone, stressing portions of her skin. She gurgled on the blood, sounding almost like a child blowing through a straw, playing with its milk.

"You okay, honey?"

Her eyelids fluttered. I propped her head on my knee and fished for my cell phone. I had one of those pre-paid joints, the only kind I could safely use. I wouldn't pass the muster of a credit check to attain the traditional cellular phone. And even if I could, it wouldn't be smart to leave that trail.

Somehow, with one hand, I dialed 911. "I need help, quick!"

I was asked what the emergency was, where I was. I strained to read the street corner sign. Someone had scribbled graffiti across it. I made out the street address anyway and told the calm operator. She then asked for my name, which I hesitated to give, but did anyway.

"I'm going to stay on the line with you, LeVar."

"Okay," I said.

"How's she doing?"

I looked down at her. She was obviously of mixed ancestry, Caucasian and Black, it appeared. Her hair was a mess of tangled golden brown curls. A comb could work halfway through her locks before citing labor laws and giving up the ghost. I tried to keep my thoughts light, opposite of what the moment really was: dark.

"LeVar, how's she doing?"

"Don't know...she's...breathing. I moved her head, have it on my knee. Should I have done that?"

"Don't move her any more."

"Should I have done that?"

"An ambulance will be there shortly."

I stroked the girl's forehead. I probably shouldn't have moved her, shouldn't have touched her, but I couldn't leave her strewn in the street like an animal. She deserved to be in someone's arms. As I ran my fingers across her smooth skin, a black curtain came down over my eyes. An image flashed on the screen of my mind: toy trains, G.I. Joe, Transformers. My brother. Blood seeping through a hole in his chest. My fingers couldn't stanch the flow.

"He was a little peanut head," I said. "Not cool one bit. Tried awfully hard, though."

"Excuse me? I didn't catch that, LeVar. Is there a change in the young girl?"

"She's about the same, I guess."

"You said something about a brother? Is her brother there? Is he hurt as well?"

I cleared my throat. "*My* brother was a peanut head. Awkward. Had a hard time in school. The boys in his class were ahead of their time. Talking about what they did with girls. Lying nine-year-olds. My brother didn't know it. He had such a hard time in school." I thought of my father. "At home, too."

I needed to seek my father out, find out why he'd been so indifferent to my brother, find out how he felt about my brother's death. He hadn't come to the funeral. I needed to let him know how much that incident, my brother dying in my arms, had affected me. I needed to let him know I blamed him in many ways for what happened to my brother, and eventually, to me. The two most traveled paths in a black boy's life—early death and prison. My brother and I had pumped up the statistical numbers.

"LeVar?"

"He had the biggest crush on this girl, Stacey Kimble-Williams. Had her last name hyphenated like a married woman with a career, but just nine. The same as my brother."

"LeVar, please remain calm. Take a breath. Is the young girl the same?"

"They teased him. Stacey and her friends. Teased him mercilessly."

"LeVar…?"

"I let them. Didn't say anything to Valerie, Stacey's older sister. Not exactly my girl, but she wanted to be. She would have stopped them if I'd asked. I'm sure of it. I never asked, though."

"LeVar, the ambulance is two blocks away. They'll be there soon."

"One day, at school, Stacey and another friend, Tammy Ruffin,"—I choked on the name—"they played a cruel joke on him. Tammy liked me, too. Was always up in my face. I could have gotten her to leave him alone." I shook my head. "Anyway, they got him under the bleachers. Got him to undress. Took his clothes and wouldn't give them back. He had to come out eventually. Naked. Humiliated. The teachers and principal turned him into some kind of leper. A young boy, that age, getting naked around girls. He was a freak. A threat to the entire school. They expelled him, pending an investigation. Miss Ma'am was livid. She stopped talking to either of us for a time. Any time we tried to speak to her…she'd sing. Drown us out."

"LeVar?"

I ignored her. I had to talk. Not necessarily to her, but more so to myself.

"I came up on my brother, after school some time after his incident. He was in my mother's bedroom. Crying. Holding the only thing my father left behind. His gun. 'You're crying over some stupid girls?' I said to him. He nodded. 'Might as well go ahead and shoot yourself, then.' Me, talking out the side of my face, as Miss Ma'am would say. I didn't think it was loaded. Miss Ma'am always said it was for show. My brother pointed it at his chest. Looked at me so sadly. I'll never forget it. Squeezed. I jumped back from the loud pop. I…"

"The ambulance should be there, LeVar."

It was. Right up on us. Across the way, I also spied two police cruisers coming to a rest by the curb. I didn't particularly like that. I've come to despise law enforcement. Like many black men in this country, I'd come to hate the police. Why? Because they took me away. And they'd just been doing their jobs. I thought of Tammy Ruffin and the games I'd played with her head years after my brother's death, when we were both grown and should have been beyond games. Taking her in, making her love me, making her think I loved her, and then, turning on her as the final act in my elaborate revenge plans. I knew if Stacey Kimble-Williams hadn't died in a car accident right after college, my time in prison would have probably doubled. I'd have gotten to her, too.

I had so many issues.

I closed the flip of my cell phone and stepped back when EMS reached me. Let them do their thing.

"What happened here?" a police officer asked me as I retreated, slowly. I'd bumped into him as if he'd been a wall I'd forgotten was there. Not likely—I never forgot walls. Never.

I turned to him. His cheeks were red like Kris Kringle's, and peeling like a cheap paint job. His belly hanging over the loop of his belt buckle told me he was a veteran of the force. No way had he just gotten in: he couldn't have passed the physical. His eyes were on me, the blood staining my shirt as if a pen had exploded in the pocket of it.

"Hit-and-run," I said. My voice was decidedly calm. He's Sweet I Know, was the source of my strength. "Guy was busy talking on his cell phone."

"That your vehicle over there?" Officer Kringle asked me.

I looked back and said, "Yeah." I saw that another officer had quietly eased behind me.

Officer Kringle nodded at officer two, a small black guy with a lazy eye and stringy hair. He actually made Sammy Davis Jr. look handsome. I saw Officer Sammy make his way to the Toy-yoda, lean down and inspect the front bumper, then stand back to his full height, all five feet six inches of it, and nod at Officer Kringle.

"You catch the plates? Type of vehicle? What the

driver looked like? You said it was a guy?" Firing questions at me.

"Please God Help, twenty-two chapters in Revelation," I said.

Officer Kringle frowned. "Pardon?"

"PGH 22R. Blue. Looked like a Honda Accord. Could have been a Civic; they're building them bigger. Didn't see the guy too well." I narrowed my eyes at Officer Kringle. "He was white."

Officer Kringle pulled out a pad and wrote down the information I'd given him. Officer Sammy flanked me now. He didn't try to mask the distasteful look on his face, as he looked me up and down. I didn't like him; almost felt compelled to hit him or call him a name. Almost asked him who could take a sunrise and sprinkle it with dew. Decided against that, though.

"He got the plates," Officer Kringle told him.

"Good," Officer Sammy replied.

"Anything else you can add?" Officer Kringle asked me.

"Is she going to live?" I heard myself say. At that moment, I wanted Sela's arms wrapped around me. I wanted to lay my head on her chest, have her rub my scalp and whisper words of love to me. The seconds, minutes, and hours couldn't tick fast enough for me. I envisioned the love we'd make later, the passion, holding one another afterward. Tragedy brought that out, passion, emotion. I'd tell her about my history. My family. My father. She'd tell me to seek him out, and I would. I knew now I was ready to confront him, to ask my father the questions that had bubbled inside of me for years.

"They'll do their best with her," Officer Kringle offered. "She's in good hands."

"My brother didn't," I said. "Didn't live."

"Pardon? Your brother?"

I nodded. My fingers itched for my cell phone. I needed to call Sela. Needed to *see* Sela, have that talk with her, about my history, my family, my father. Let her know who I was, and what I'd come from. Pray she'd want to stay on the Love Boat with me. Pray she'd hold my hand as I walked up to the address on the envelopes I'd gotten in prison from my father: 1600 Throckmorton Blvd., Colts Neck, NJ.

"My brother, he was nine years old when he died," I told Officer Kringle. Much too young. I could relate to Reverend Walker's pain. You could never prepare adequately for loss.

"I'm sorry to hear about your brother," Officer Kringle said. Officer Sammy nodded beside him. They were okay, I realized at that moment.

"My brother's name," I told them, "was LeVar."

27

She leaned against a stop sign under a dull streetlight that barely kept the stretch of block from being dark as a cave. Someone had christened the stop sign with graffiti: Pussy Cat Ave. She didn't seem to mind, didn't care. Pussy Cat Ave. was about right, she figured. There were hardly any business enterprises on the stretch, just a couple of walk-in cookeries where they fried fish and chicken in the same grease and had only grape soda and root beer to drink. A bunch of alleys, Dumpsters, trash, cats…at nighttime, women, just like her.

She had a Newport tucked between her full lips; plumes of white smoke drifted around her head. A warm day had turned into a muggy night. It was September, but it felt like August still. She was dressed cool: long white fishnet stockings on strong and long brown legs; her skirt, water in a glass, clinging to the shape of her wide hips and round ass in the same manner as water would meld to the contours of a glass; and a tight halter top built for a shorter torso—it fell just an inch below her small but perky breasts, which were mostly nipple. They were awe-inspiring nipples, though, standing up like soldiers under the material of her shirt, ready for the war. Vera reporting for duty.

Half a block past Vera, closer to the corner, another woman, the color of coffee grounds, strutted impatiently from the curb to the boarded-up building behind her. Vera shook her head as she took in the woman. She said her name was Delilah, which made Vera chuckle but nod. Delilah had the game confused. She walked with too much sway in her hips, advertising the product too hard. She dressed okay, though, Vera had to admit—a lacy Victoria's Secret number. Her big-ass titties popped halfway out of the top. Vera could take a half of those titties for herself and leave Delilah with plenty left over. To whom much is given, much is required. Despite what folk might think of Vera, she read her Bible. Daily. How many of the so-called saved could boast the same thing? How many of them knew—as Vera did after today's reading—that John the Baptist had baptized Jesus, done a stint in prison, and had his life ended in a horrible death by beheading?

Delilah caught Vera's gaze. "Drought," Delilah called out. "Fish ain't biting."

Vera shrugged her shoulders and turned away. Out of the corner of her eye, she could see Delilah disappear into the shadows of the building again and pull out a cell phone. Once more, Vera had to chuckle. She took a final puff of her cigarette, and then tossed the spent butt into the street. It joined a pile of butts. This was Vera's corner. Nothing shook here without her knowing it. She noticed Delilah leaning against the building, cell phone to her ear. Nothing shook here without Vera knowing it.

Like, across the street, that car idling by the curb, way off in a spot absent of streetlight, trying to fool someone. Vera knew the john was watching her, maybe in there jacking off, getting his pleasure free. She'd caught a glimpse of *Oprah* in Janet's Beauty Waves earlier. Oprah had implored her audience, in the studio and at home, to be proactive in their lives, to cultivate their successes. Vera had sat under one of Janet's blow dryers, feeling empowered. Now, this john jacking his shit while watching her, Vera not getting a cut, that wasn't right. She was standing idly by, not cultivating her success. She quickly lit another Newport, took three drags off it, and tossed it into the street. She wiggled her hips in her skirt, pulled it up some, cleared her throat, and headed toward the john in the car. She knew Delilah was watching. *Just going to see if I can bum a ride, sugar.* She laughed.

Vera was within ten feet of the car when the headlights suddenly came on. She paused in the street, shot a hand up to cover her eyes, and pressed on anyhow. The car's engine turned a second time, the gears scraping. She had the john nervous: he must have forgotten he'd already ignitioned the car once. She walked on the last few feet, directly in front of the car. He couldn't pull off unless he wanted a vehicular manslaughter charge. Vera blocked his way. Delilah, she figured, had her back if anything funky went down.

"Trick or treatin,' sugar?" Vera called out as she neared the car. She smiled as she reached the driver's side window. The smile quickly faded. "Oh. Damn. Well, hello."

The john didn't answer.

"Not usually my thing," Vera said, "but I ain't sweating it if you got greenbacks."

She reached inside and touched the john's shoulder. That's how Vera had gotten so good: she made the johns feel as if they were the only thing in her world, made 'em comfortable. Once she got 'em comfortable, she'd discuss prices. A suck was fifty bucks. A fuck was one hundred. Reasonable prices, less than some charged. She thought of the prosties hooked on drugs, the ones with rotting teeth and ashy gray-colored skin. More than some others charged. Her prices, in the middle. Good business considering she had such a good product.

"You're trembling, sugar," Vera said. This john wasn't comfortable. She had to change that.

But at that moment, before Vera could work her magic, the john pulled the transmission tree into DRIVE and pulled off, tires squealing, and spewing rocks. Vera had to pull her arm back, as if she'd touched a hot oven, to keep it from being yanked from its socket. She watched the car hit the corner and turn hard around it, a black blur. Delilah came from the shadows of the building across the way, moved to the corner, and watched the car speed off. Vera shook her head. Delilah was right. It *was* a drought tonight. Fish *weren't* biting. She decided to move on, go get herself something to eat, read on her Bible some more. Tomorrow was another day. Delilah could have the block for now. Vera didn't mind. She knew the woman would have it only for one night.

Zelda dialed the familiar numbers. She'd been hard on Sela earlier. She could visualize the hurt and disappointment in her friend's eyes. Their conversation was a movie in her head she couldn't rewind or fast forward, couldn't press STOP and have it end. Could she blame Sela for hesitating about her sexuality? She'd been the same way, maybe to a bit lesser degree, before she was comfortable going to Lady Bar with no shame.

Sela's answering system picked up after four rings. Sela's voice came on. Zelda's heart fluttered. She closed her eyes. It beeped. She opened her eyes.

"Sela, it's me, Zee-Zee. Give me a call when you get this message. I want to work something out with you. I don't know what. But something. Need you in my life. Want you in my life." She stopped. Saying too much. "Okay, call me back."

LeVar dialed Sela's number for the fifth time in the last twenty minutes. Again, he got her voice mail. This time, unlike the other four times, he decided against leaving a message. Where was she? He needed her badly. He wanted to tell her about the girl whose head he'd laid on his lap. He wanted to lay his head on Sela's lap, have her stroke his face, massage his neck, trace her fingers over his lips. All the soft and gentle things Sela did.

Frustrated, he picked up the phone again and dialed. This time he left a message.

"I'm dying over here, Sela, baby. *Please*. Call me back as soon as you get this message."

He hung up. Prayed.

Russell adjusted his position on the couch, taking in the pleasant atmosphere of Rachel Sosa's apartment. She had an incense candle burning. A vanilla aroma perfumed the air with sweetness. Music played softly from Rachel's Bose stereo, a lush composition of violin that filled his ears and made his neck and shoulders loose. A neat fan of *Cosmopolitan*s covered the glass top of Rachel's coffee table. The writing on the cover of the magazines was in Spanish. The color scheme of her living room, dark blue and crème, appealed to Russell in some carnal way, made his skin crawl and his imagination enter that forbidden place it didn't need to go. He felt a certain passion bubbling inside him. The passion scared him. For the briefest of moments, he contemplated sneaking out while Rachel attended to her affairs in the other room, but instead he reclined on the couch and forced himself to get comfortable.

"I'll be out in a sec, boss," Rachel called from down the hall. Russell nodded as if she could hear his gestures.

The CD stopped, a gearlike sound coming from the player, and then it started again. He tapped his foot to the soft melody.

"Sorry," Rachel said as she reentered the room. She wore teal-colored velour shorts, cut so that they rode high on her thick thighs, a white wife-beater tee that displayed her excited nipples, that funky blond spiky hair, and no makeup. She didn't need any. "I had to take that call," she said. "My girlfriend is having man problems again. It's getting to be a daily thing with her. She must think I have a degree in crisis management."

"It's okay." Russell continued to tap his foot, nod his head.

"You like the music?"

"Yes. Who is this?"

"Miri Ben-Ari," Rachel said. "Hip-hop violinist. Chick is from Israel, grooved with Jay-Z, Kanye West, Wyclef."

"Wow," Russell said. "She's gotta be tight, 'cause all of them are." He had no idea who any of those people were. Afeni, his daughter, would. That realization sparked a bit of anger inside of him. Bevolyn couldn't do this to him. She had to understand how important it was for him to let Afeni know she was his daughter. She had to.

Rachel settled into a spot on the sofa, next to Russell, the cushion collapsing to allow for her frame. "You like that song Wyclef has out…? 'Overnight Celebrity'?"

"Oh, yeah," Russell said, still nodding to the music filling the small apartment. "Love that one."

Rachel smiled. "Not Wyclef's song, boss. Twista's."

Russell stopped nodding. A smile broke across his face. "You got me."

Rachel nodded. "I got you."

"Your girlfriend," he said, changing the subject after some time had passed. "What's her story?"

Rachel sighed. "Boyfriend. Will. Cheats on her, mainly. Puts his hands on her occasionally, and flirts with every one of her friends. A real scrub."

"Has he ever said anything to you? You know, ever make a pass at you?"

Rachel looked away. "I've done some things I'm not proud of, boss. Led a very wild life. Sex has always been something important to me. Something…"

"Uh-oh. Here comes a confession."

Rachel smiled and eased over closer to him, giving him the full benefit of eye contact, looking strong and determined.

Her scent was arresting, those eyes captivating, the way she held herself spellbinding.

It had been the same way, once, with Bevolyn, still was when she acted right. But most days her attitude trumped how pleasing she was to his eye.

"I slept with Will," Rachel confessed. "Well, not alone: we did a threesome. A menage a trois. It happened almost two years ago and I still feel the shame from that night. We'd all been drinking—Rochelle, Will, and myself—and he talked us into doing it. Rochelle never really talks about it, but I can tell there's a part of her that hates me for participating. We've been friends for close to seven years. I think she'd have preferred it if it had happened with someone else, but she loves me so she doesn't let it affect our relationship. I humor her daily calls for advice, because...because I feel indebted to her. I owe her that much."

Russell took it all in, pictured Rachel in the compromising situation, imagined the look on her face the morning after. He thought of Diane, Afeni's mother, and saw a common thread between the two women—fast, wild, exciting. So different from Bevolyn. So different from anything he'd ever really wanted. So what was his move?

"What are you thinking, boss?" Rachel asked. "How horrible a woman I am, and what a big mistake you made coming here tonight?"

"Thinking that you're beautiful, adventurous, exciting..."

Rachel hadn't expected that answer. Overwhelmed by his words and expression, she leaned in and kissed him on the cheek, then the lips. Russell touched his cheek as if he'd just shaven and his skin was irritated, touched his lips as if he'd slurped a steaming cup of coffee, without testing its heat, and scalded himself.

"You didn't let me finish, Ray," he said.

"I know where you're headed," Rachel said, smiling.

"I don't think you do."

"Go ahead, boss."

Russell reached over and touched Rachel's hand. A sad smile crossed his face, and Rachel's, too. A romantic bath for two, making love into the morning, in every room of her small apartment—none of that looked promising any more. Russell was about to let her down.

"You're beautiful, adventurous, and exciting, Rachel."

"But," she said.

"But I need to be getting on home. To my wife. I'm sorry I stepped your way again. Last time this will ever happen, I assure you."

Rachel leaned forward again and kissed him for a second time. "Might surprise you, but I do believe in God, boss. In my own way. I'm not exactly where I need to be, I admit. Not like your wife or anything." He frowned at that. Rachel moved past it. "Anyway, I'll pray for you, boss."

Russell shook his head. "Seriously, I won't come this way again, Rachel. No amount of praying will—"

"Not for that," Rachel cut him off. "Praying for you and your wife. Praying that you two work your way through this pain. I need to stay in my lane, I really do. I see that. Can't be having a repeat of the situation with my girlfriend, Rochelle."

"I don't know what to say."

"Nothing to me," Rachel said. "But plenty to your wife."

"Still want to share a slice of chocolate cake with me?"

"Russell?"

"Uh-huh."

Bevolyn switched the phone from her right ear to her left. "Where are you?"

"On my way home."

"Where you been?"

"At the line," he said, sadly.

"The line?"

"Yeah," he said. "Almost crossed it, too. But thankfully I didn't."

"Some woman?" Bevolyn wanted to know.

"Yes."

"And you didn't do anything with her?" she asked. Her tone was skeptical.

"No, I didn't."

"Why should I believe you?"

"I'm your husband. I've told you this much. No need to lie."

Bevolyn sighed. "Why didn't you…?"

"Cross the line?"

"Yes."

"I'll show you when I get home."

"Not sexing with you after all this," Bevolyn said.

"Not that. Something else. You just hang tight. Warm up that cake. See you in a bit."

"Russ?"

But he'd hung up already.

Bevolyn placed the phone back in the cradle.

"You put your foot in those mashed potatoes, Aloe."

"They was all right," Aloe said, going for modesty. "Where you get that talk from, though? Sound like some woman from Stone's Throw, Mississippi, or some shit."

"A woman at the church," Afeni admitted.

"Where she from?" Aloe pressed.

Serious, Afeni replied, "Somewhere in Georgia," and stuck her tongue out at her mother.

They shared laughter for a bit.

Then Afeni moved from the table to the sink and started washing off her plate. She spoke to Aloe, softly tossing words over her shoulder as the water ran. "Always wanted it like this, Aloe. You cooking, me washing dishes afterwards, us watching movies late into the night, wearing our pajamas, talking and laughing."

Aloe's gaze fell on the wall behind the oven. Grease and grime ran roughshod over the paint job. Grime… Aloe's life. On her own at sixteen, dancing at seventeen after a year of toiling without success, sleeping on a different couch practically every night. All her belongings in the world had been tucked in a shoebox. She hadn't even owned the shoes that had originally come in the box. Picked the shoebox from the trash behind a footwear store.

Afeni turned to see her mother staring at the wall. "Earth to Aloe. Earth to Aloe." Afeni smiled. "Not very original, huh? Earth to Aloe. I'm a poet. I should be able to come up with something more—" She stopped, noticing the trail of tears running down Aloe's cheek. "Aloe?"

Aloe raised her head and looked deeply at her daughter. "Mama. Please."

Afeni nodded. "Mama, what's wrong?"

"Be eating these mashed potatoes by my lonesome, after tomorrow night."

Afeni crinkled her brow. "What are you saying, Mama?"

"I ain't mean to hurt you that last time…getting my jump-off and neglecting you, having you leave early, hurt. I messed up. I want to earn the mama tag. I want you to come home so I can."

Afeni turned off the sink, wiped her hands on a dish towel, moved to the table, and sat. "Did you love him?"

"Raul? Told you he was just a jump-off."

Afeni shook her head. "Not him. Russell."

"Oh."

"Did you?"

"Yeah. He came in the club I was dancing in at the time. Spent big loot. He was *fine* as can be. I was interested from gate. We talked. It moved slowly from there. He kept coming, and bit by bit, he grew on me more and more, became a love thing for me. He made such a fuss over me. Made me feel like a queen. I still could feel that way back then." Aloe wiped her eyes. Smiled crookedly, halfhearted. "Insisted on doing it raw. Trying to get me pregnant, it turned out. I wasn't with no one else, so I went with it. I found out afterward he'd planned it all.

He didn't tell me he was married until I had you growing inside."

"Then?"

"Then when I got pregnant, he wanted me to abort. He'd done everything to get back at his wife. She'd hurt him some way. He never said how."

Afeni pinched her nose and blinked her eyes. An abortion would have meant no poems. Her poems were good. The world needed her poems. That's all she thought about, no poems. It was so difficult to hear Aloe tell this tale of the past, so difficult. "Go ahead," Afeni prodded her mother, despite the pain that had clutched her sides.

"I ain't know what to do," Aloe continued. "I was just nineteen myself, hardly a woman. I felt used. All I knew"—she smiled at Afeni—"was I wasn't having nobody's abortion. I was having that baby. You."

"You regret it?" Afeni asked.

"Lots of regrets," Aloe admitted.

Afeni's head slumped.

"Never regretted not having that abortion," Aloe continued, "Not once."

Afeni's head arched up. Aloe's smile was bright, strong. "You mean it?" Afeni asked her mother.

"Serious as a dude tucking tens in my G-string instead of ones," Aloe said.

"Colorful description," Afeni said, smiling. "Wordplay."

"Learned that and other lessons from my baby girl," Aloe said.

"What are the other lessons?" Afeni asked.

"About what love is and isn't," Aloe said. "That, in the long run, Nat King Cole ain't very necessary."

"I'll get my things tomorrow," Afeni said. "Then I'm coming home. Okay, Mama?"

Aloe nodded and wiped away her tears.

★ ★ ★

Bevolyn was in the living room standing by the bookshelf, fingering the spine of a book by T.D. Jakes: *Woman, Thou Art Loosed.* Donnie McClurkin's CD played "Great Is Your Mercy," Bevolyn's mood music.

"Bev."

She didn't turn to her husband's voice. Instead, she clutched the book to her chest and hummed along to the music with her eyes closed. She heard Russell's faint steps coming across the carpet. In time, she felt his strong hands on her shoulders, felt those hands gently turning her to him.

She opened her eyes and saw the tears in his. Something in her dropped. Plummeted, rather, a much deeper sensation than a normal drop. Russell didn't cry. Russell was a man's man.

"You lied on the phone?" she asked, almost breathless with fear. "You did something with that woman?"

"Never," Russell managed.

"Why are you...?" Bevolyn couldn't say the word. Crying.

Russell swallowed. "It all comes to a head today, Bev. All of it."

"What took you so long to get home?" She tried not to look at his eyes, which were wet, glistening. Those eyes would throw her off course and keep her from asking the probing questions that nestled in her heart.

"Had to stop at the bank," he said. "Get something from the safe-deposit box."

Bevolyn frowned. "We have a safe-deposit box?"

"*I* do," Russell said.

"What's in it?" Bevolyn hesitated, worried about the unknown.

Russell released his hold on Bevolyn's shoulders, stuck his hand inside his jacket, and produced an accordion-style expanding file envelope. He handed her the envelope and quickly moved to the couch, where he plopped down and looked away from her.

Bevolyn undid the envelope's clasp and pulled out the tangle of paper items inside. She touched her hand to her mouth right away. "Oh, Russell," she gasped.

Russell sat, wordless. Bevolyn riffled through the papers...newspaper clippings...photocopies of photos. Her heart sank with each new discovery. Tears welled in her eyes. She looked over at Russell as she reached the end of the papers. She could see his shoulders moving as he sobbed on the couch, imperceptibly to the ear. She moved to him.

"Why did you dig for these items, Russ?"

"Didn't dig," he said.

Bevolyn looked down at the items in her hands. "Photos of me and Lewis. Newspaper clippings of his basketball career. Box scores—that's what you call them, right?—from games. Clippings of his work with this internet company. I didn't even know he did that. What he'd turned out to be. I've never wondered, or cared. But you've kept up, obviously. How did you get the photos of us together? What have you done? Searched library archives for all this?"

"Filed it when it came to my office," Russell said.

"I don't follow."

"He sends it to me," Russell said. "Mails packages to me. I usually get one every few months. Whenever he does something exceptional. Rubbing my nose in his success. See what Bevolyn is missing out on?"

Bevolyn touched a hand to her chest. "Oh my Lord. Lewis?"

"That's him," Russell said bitterly.

"How long has he been doing this?"

"Sixteen years," Russell said.

Bevolyn's mouth dropped open into a capitalized *O*. She said nothing. Couldn't.

"Sent me a letter when you first got together."

That's how Russell had found out.

"Kept sending me things," Russell continued. "Even after you broke it off with him."

"And,"—she could barely get the words together, coherently spoken—"and you've, you've kept this stuff?"

"Yes."

"Why?"

"I don't know, Bev. A reminder."

"Why would you want to remember?"

Russell shook his head.

Bevolyn waved the papers. "He's sick, Russ. Why else would he send you this? All these years."

Russell looked at Bevolyn. "He got bit by the Bevolyn bug. Same as me, I guess. Notice he sent me photocopies of the pictures. He's holding on to the originals."

Bevolyn looked at the photos in her hand. Photocopies, correct.

"Hurt me like you wouldn't believe, Bev. I went out and found Diane, got her pregnant, all to get back at you. Messed up her life, my own, an innocent child's, and ours. Been muddling around all these years, treading, not swimming, not exactly sinking, just treading. Working long hours trying to give you what Lewis would have given you. I want it to stop. Need it to stop."

"How?" Bevolyn spoke softly.

"Need to let Afeni know I'm her father for one," Russell said. "Need you to know I love you, deeply. I'm willing to forgive you, finally, if you're willing to forgive me."

He waited. Bevolyn didn't say anything, didn't move, blinked only sparingly.

"It's time," Russell said. "I've held this inside for too long. Our entire marriage."

"Why, Russ?"

"It was rough in the beginning," he admitted. "But I loved you. So I tried my best to move past it all. I laughed off the mail from Lewis. But as they continued to arrive, my thoughts got darker." He looked at her, suddenly aware of his wet eyes. He wiped them with the back of his hand. "But I loved you. Love you. So here I am."

"You've been faithful?" Bevolyn asked. "I mean, since…"

"Diane? Yes. My one and only moment of faltering."

"What about the woman tonight?"

Russell frowned. "Just another Diane is what it would have been. Hurting myself instead of hurting you."

"I never wanted to hurt you, Russ."

"Same to you, Bev."

"I want the pain to end, too," she added.

"Forgive me?"

"Yes," she said, nodding. "Forgive me?"

He stood from the couch and took the papers from her hand. He moved from the living room, headed to the kitchen in a rush. Bevolyn followed him, walking through the kitchen archway just as flames from the oven's burner ate through the newspaper clippings, the pictures, and sixteen years of pain.

Russell turned to her. "Cake and ice cream?"

She nodded and moved to gather the items.

"Come on, love, help me out."

She smiled in response. "You're too much, Lincoln. You know I'm working. I could get in trouble."

"You're working now," Dante Ruffin said, "but I'll be working later. If you'll have me."

"You know I'll have you," she replied. She bit into her lips, rotated her neck.

"Somebody needs a deep tissue massage," Dante said.

"You're going to *help me out*, Lincoln?"

"Get that info for me, love."

"Why do you need to find this guy?"

"He took something from me. Ran. I'm thinking he's changed his name. Defrauded your agency."

"You came here, got my nose wide open, took me out, wined and dined me just so you could get this info, Lincoln?"

He smiled. "Love, you are a pessimist if I've ever seen one. What do I look like, Al-Qaeda? Calculating my moves? Life a big chess game? I've got an Uncle Othella, but no Uncle Osama, trust me."

She smiled. "You're lucky."

"For?"

"Your genes, sexy."

"You're lucky, too," he said.

"For?"

He nodded his head and looked down. "Your jeans, sexy. Any more room for me in them?"

"There you go."

He smiled. "You inspire me, love."

"Give me a few. I'll check the database and bring you a spreadsheet printout. Have a seat like everyone else."

"Last name, Path," Dante emphasized. "Anyone who's had a license issued under that name in the past few months. Preferably off of North Carolina ID."

"I know my job," she said.

"Of course," he said.

She looked up at him, the nice clothes, the arresting

scent, and the chiseled good looks. "Give me a few minutes."

"You got it."

Dante wheeled and found a seat in the DMV lobby. The crowd of people was amazing. A woman sat nearby, reading her newspaper, two toddler-age children crawling circles around her ankles. She didn't seem to notice. A teenager was off in the corner, looking through the driver's manual, his forehead furrowed in concentration.

"Lincoln?"

Dante looked up. "That was quick, love."

"Only three names came up," she said. She glanced at the sheet of paper. "Jeanette, Meredith, and LeVar. None by the name you gave, though."

LeVar. The younger brother who had died. Lita had mentioned him, once. Dante smiled.

"Did I do well?" she asked.

"Very."

She seemed pleased. "You better do well, too."

"You can count on it."

"Picking me up around…?"

"Eight. Wear those jeans, love."

"I will," she said, adding sexily, "for a little while."

"There you go."

The car idled, parked across the way. It was back again, away from the streetlights, car beams quieted, but engine still running, music playing softly—Avant: "Don't Take Your Love Away." The heat was on low, blowing barely noticeably warm air into the car's interior. Enough warm air, though, to chase away the coolness of the night. The driver was sweating, from nerves more than anything. This was a difficult move.

The hooker who'd come up to the car before was

gone. The other one with the big boobs, wearing that sexy-ass lacy piece, still walked the corner, talking on her cell phone every now and then, escaping to the shadows of the building behind her every so often, really shaking that creamy ass of hers with every step.

Take a deep breath. Drive over. Satisfy this burning urge.

The transmission tree glided from PARK to DRIVE. The car eased from the curb and headed across the way, beams still off, Avant replaced by Usher. Usher was everywhere, controlling the charts, 2004 his year. "Caught Up."

The car stopped by the curb. Ms. White Lace turned, smiled, and strolled over slowly, hips swaying. Caught up was right. It wasn't hard to imagine becoming caught up with her, for sure. Boobs bouncing, hips swaying, full lips upturned into a smile.

White Lace leaned down into the car. Like the other hooker, the smile that had been on her face disappeared once she saw inside the vehicle. "Wassup?" she asked, the slang sounding uncertain on her full lips.

"Seeing what was up with you."

White Lace crinkled her eyebrows. "You're lookin' to date?"

"Yeah."

"Hope you ain't got any snot noses at home. A mister waiting on you," the hooker replied.

"Neither."

"I ain't too certain how to flip this. Usually it's fucking or sucking. What you lookin' for?"

"Both."

White Lace smiled. "Gonna have to be my compass. This is a new one for me."

"Okay."

"One hundred for an hour. Buck a minute. You can swing that?"

"Buck a minute's sixty dollars."

"My math ain't too tight," White Lace said, "but my coochie is."

"Yes. I can swing it."

White Lace stuck her hand inside the car. Her nails were manicured, her hand smooth. "Up front. Case things get dicey and you try to book on me afterwards."

The money quickly changed hands. The power locks clicked open.

White Lace asked, "What's your name, by the way? Mine's Delilah."

"Sela."

White Lace's smile returned, sad, but a smile just the same. "You're under arrest, Sela, for soliciting prostitution. Please put your hands on the dashboard where I can see them."

Book III

Revelation

28

He shrugged himself into a sleeveless undershirt and sat up on the edge of the bed. From her angle, it looked as if he were standing on a bridge, contemplating a jump. She reached for his shoulder, but her arms were too short. He stood, giving her a view of strong round buttocks wet with sweat, the same as the cleavage between her breasts—wet with sweat. The sinewy muscles in his ass flexed and relaxed as he moved across the room. The lights were on. He was the only lover she'd ever had who insisted on doing it with the lights on.

He walked out into her living room. She sighed, knowing what he'd come back with. And, just as she'd predicted, he reappeared a few moments later, his boxers on, pants and shirt in his hands.

"Night doesn't have to end, Lincoln," she said, hating herself for the whine in her voice. She'd aimed for strong, firm, independent woman and had fallen well short of that mark.

"Long day ahead of me, love," he replied. She noticed the smile on his face. It made her stomach drop. She turned away and closed her eyes. The only sounds in the room were her heartbeat and Lincoln quietly rustling his clothes as he dressed.

He moved to her bedside and stood over her, wordless.

She opened her eyes. "What?" A little bite in it, but not enough.

The smile was back on his face, this one different— tender. "Just wanted to thank you, love."

"For?"

"You know."

The beautiful lovemaking, she wanted to believe. Her company, maybe. The wonderful evening they'd shared, until just now.

No.

The printout she'd given him, culled from the DMV's database.

"I'll be seeing you," he said.

"Sure, Lincoln."

"You say that like you don't believe it."

She didn't say a word.

Something flashed in his eyes. He leaned down and kissed her lips, stood again, and walked from her room. Moments later, hearing her front door shut, she fell back against her mattress, closed her eyes, and tried, unsuccessfully, to chase away the horrible visions in her head…visions of what Lincoln would do to the man on that printout sheet.

LeVar.

Aloe stood out in the lot behind her building, puffing on a Newport, creating artistic white swirls of smoke that lingered in the air. She smoked one down to the butt, stomped it out with her booted foot, and then lit another. Stale garbage overflowed from the Dumpster enclosure. Stray trash crawled across the empty lot, and puddles of stench formed on the ground in various places. Bundles of newspapers and magazines leaned along the back fence in a neat stack. The sun had receded much earlier in the evening, so the only visibility came from the two security lights on the corners of the building. Aloe liked the quiet at the back lot. Out in the front there was little opportunity for solitude and thought, with all the car horns, revved engines, wobbly neighbors juiced off booze, and raised voices constantly ringing through the air. She continued to smoke in solitude. She looked at the Dumpster and thought of the things she'd done in this lot, the men she'd done them with, and the poor example she'd set for her daughter.

The back door opened but Aloe paid it no mind. Afeni peeked out. "There you are. Why you out here for?" She spoke to her mother with the door cracked slightly, enough space to make herself apparent and still stay at arm's length from the depravity of the lot. She frowned, noticing the white and brown stick between Aloe's lips. "Since when you smoked, Aloe?"

"I quit," Aloe said.

Afeni stepped outside. She had to—couldn't hold a conversation otherwise. "Don't look like you quit. Looks like you started," Afeni said.

"Not talking about smoking. Shaking my spear," Aloe said, smiling slightly.

"You did?"

Aloe nodded. "Shakespeare is too tough for this sister. Done shaking my spear. I'm getting on in age." She looked away from Afeni. "Not a very motherly way to earn a buck, anyhow."

"Shit, Aloe."

"Mama."

"Shit, Mama. What are you going to do?"

"Something I ain't done in a long time," Aloe said. "The right thing."

Afeni waited a pause, then said, "The right thing... that pay well?"

Aloe chuckled. "Girl." She dragged the one word out with love.

"We'll figure something out," Afeni said. "When I come back tomorrow."

"You mean brainstorm?" Aloe wondered.

Afeni's eyes sparkled and a smile found her face. She'd learned more about her mother in the past few months than she'd learned in her first fourteen years. She'd learned that her mother was more than boobs and butt and some stinky pole. Her mother had a vocabulary.

"Brainstorm, Aloe, that's right."

"Brainstorm, Mama," Aloe corrected.

"Brainstorm, Mama," Afeni said.

They didn't talk about the photos, the newspaper clippings, or the past. They didn't talk, period. They held one another close, bubbles surrounding them as they reclined in a bathtub of warm, soothing water. Unscented candles burned. Music played: Shirley Caesar, remembering Mama.

Russell leaned down and kissed Bevolyn's neck. White soap foam coated his lips when he broke from her. She turned back and saw the soap foam, laughed, then wiped it away with the softest finger Russell had ever felt. She craned her neck and kissed his lips, long, hard.

"That's more like it," she said. "My lips on your lips, and nothing else."

"That *is* more like it," he agreed.

"Should have been like this a long time ago," Bevolyn said.

"Can't worry ourselves about the *shoulds*, Bev. Time to move on. Love one another. Find ourselves a nice church home. Try—"

"Did you say what I think you said?" Bevolyn cut him off.

"I did."

"You? Church?"

"My mama, God bless her soul, brought me up in the church, Bev. You know that. Somehow,"—he looked off for a bit, thoughts traveling through time; like Shirley Caesar, he was remembering his mama—"somehow I got lost. Worst thing to be. Lost."

Bevolyn nodded.

Russell continued, "I've got some apologizing to do, some sins to ask forgiveness for. It's time I stopped being mad at Him for the mistakes we've made. He brought us together. Gave us a chance. We messed it up. And, now, like us mere mortals tend to do, we'll lean on Him to fix things."

"Amen, Reverend Sykes."

"No more Sunday mourning, with a *u*, Bev. Sunday morning, instead."

"I need you."

"Sela? You finally got around to calling me, huh?"

"What?"

"My message. You got it?"

"No."

"What's wrong?"

"Oh, Zee-Zee, I messed up."

"What's wrong?"

"I need you to come get me."

"Me? How? From where?"

"See if your landlady will let you borrow her car."

Zelda hesitated. "This is serious."

"Yes, it is."

"Where?" Zelda said.

"I've been arrested," Sela admitted. Tears were in her eyes and voice.

"For?" Zelda swallowed.

"Soliciting a prostitute," Sela said. "A female under-cover nabbed me."

Zelda closed her eyes. "Tell me where you are."

"I hate to ask this of you, but, can I borrow your car, Mrs. Wakefield?"

"Zelda?"

"Yes, Mrs. Wakefield, it's me."

"You know what time it is, chile?"

"Little after twelve," Zelda replied. "I know. I'm sorry."

"Said you wanted to borrow my car?"

She wanted to say, *Yeah, that bucket you keep parked in the driveway and can't see up over the steering wheel when you do drive it, slowly of course. The one Mr. Wakefield, God bless his soul, wouldn't let you drive when he was still alive.*

Instead, she said, "If I could?"

"It ain't used to moving fast, cutting around no sharp turns."

"This I know."

"What was that?" Zelda's recently widowed landlady asked.

"I said, that's not how I go," Zelda lied.

"Pay your rent by the fourth of every month," Mrs. Wakefield said aloud, thinking this through properly. Zelda stood quietly, letting her. "Ain't never had no loud party I can recall. Even put out my trash, without me asking. Haven't had those cats rummaging through the yard since you moved in."

Many positives, Zelda figured. Now, hurry up and make your decision. Go get those car keys.

"Lemme go get my keys, chile."

"Thanks, Mrs. Wakefield," Zelda said, smiling. "I owe you one."

Mrs. Wakefield waved her off and went to get the car keys. Zelda stood in the hall, thinking about Sela.

Mrs. Wakefield returned to the doorway. "They were in the fish tank. Don't ask me how they got there. Luckily I ain't got any fish or water in it."

"Luckily," Zelda agreed.

"Now, chile," Mrs. Wakefield said, her hand extended, but the keys still tight in her grasp, "you better bring her back without a dink. She'd still better be blue. And, I don't want to smell none of the wacky stuff y'all young folks smoke inside, either. Have me driving all erratic on my way to church."

Zelda smiled. "Gave that up a long time ago, Mrs. Wakefield. The wacky stuff, I mean."

"Good to hear it, chile."

"Thanks again."

"Hold on to the keys until tomorrow. I was dreaming about Harry Belafonte. I'ma try and see if I can get back on that banana boat with him."

"You've been getting along okay without Mr. Wakefield?"

"Taking it day-o by day-o." She smiled.

Zelda did, too, then left in a hurry.

She arrived at the parking lot some time later. It was dark, just as Sela had told her it would be. The only tip-off that something was up was the police van parked along the back of the lot, up close to the fence. Zelda pulled in.

Should she toot her horn?

Turn the car off and walk inside?

She didn't have to think on it too long. Sela emerged from the van, walking slowly, and painfully, it appeared from the strain on her face, down the wooden steps they'd attached to the large-sized camper. Sela walked with her head bowed, eyes on her feet.

Zelda unlocked the car doors and leaned over, just as Sela reached Mrs. Wakefield's Buick, to push the passenger side door open. Sela eased in, buckled up, and said, "Drive. Please."

Zelda drove, unsure what to say, so she kept quiet.

"I'm sorry," Sela announced.

"For?"

"Tonight. Earlier. The entire time I've known you."

"I don't understand."

"I didn't, either," Sela admitted. "But I do now. I'm a lesbian. And"—she looked at Zelda for the first time—"this lesbian is tired of hiding the fact."

"What are you saying?"

Sela plopped back against the cushions of her seat. "Soliciting a prostitute is a city ordinance violation and a misdemeanor punishable by up to ninety days in jail and five hundred dollars in fines. They impounded my car."

"And?"

"All because I wanted you today," Sela said, "so very bad. And couldn't have you, because you rightfully wouldn't be my undercover"—she laughed at the word, thinking of Delilah—"because you wouldn't be my undercover lover. I'm in this mess."

"You're blaming me for all this?" Zelda said.

Sela shook her head. "God, no! Thanking you. You came out and got my sorry ass."

Zelda smiled and licked her lips. "Ain't a thing sorry about your ass, Sela."

Sela looked at her, deep. "You think we can…"

Zelda nodded. "We can. But first you have to tie up all the loose ends to this saga."

"Which are?"

"Bevolyn, your sister," Zelda said. "LeVar, your whatever."

Sela nodded and closed her eyes. Loose ends.

29

"Check out the metro section, third page. Read it carefully."

Prison had been about validating the rules, following them as closely as possible. You had to lock in when a CO directed. Listen to radios through headphones, not using speakers. Keep banned contraband out of the cells: cash, cassette players that could record, alcohol-based toiletries, sneakers worth more than Ulysses S. Grant could fetch. No more than fifteen newspapers. Fifteen appeared to be a number pulled from the air. I had always wondered what the significance was. It didn't matter, though, only that the rule was followed.

You jumped when told, walked when told, lay down when told.

Conformity, they called it. Inmates knew the consequences if they didn't conform.

Gerard, my cellmate at one time, was no exception. He was a beyond-pleasant guy, in for something to do with taxes and naïve enough to admit it. Nicknamed Balls by the other inmates because they said he had none, he was slight of build but strong of mind except where it came to street sense, prison survival tactics. He'd point out rule infractions to other inmates. He asked the COs for an inmate procedures manual and read it when he got it. Gerard jumped when told, walked when told, lay when told.

Until.

There always is a nasty *until* lurking.

His Earth—Gerard's description for his wife—visited one day, asking for the Plexiglas-separated cubicles instead of the general visiting room. I knew immediately what was to follow. Gerard, good 'ol Balls, never saw the punch coming.

"Wonder what that's about?" I recall him saying, adding a "hmm." I shrugged and waited for his downcast return to the cell.

It happened sooner than I'd anticipated, maybe twenty minutes later. Mrs. Earth didn't beat around the bush, apparently. She was too busy turning on her axis, I suppose, to sit with him long enough to appear tormented by her decision.

"Over," Gerard said, his eyes wet, body trembling. "Just like that."

"Just like that," I repeated.

A punch he never saw coming.

"Fuck it," I heard him say some time later, the clearest words he'd spoken since slumping in the corner of our cell and mumbling.

"Uh-oh," I said, jokingly, "Balls is mad."

He looked over toward me, a sick smile on his face. "Damn mad," he said.

"Women," I said, shrugging.

He shook his head. "Men. We take their shit. Sometimes we make them do their shit. But me, I didn't do shit."

I didn't have the heart to tell him his wife probably considered serving time in prison as shit.

"Not shit," he said.

I smiled. I hadn't heard one curse word from Gerard in all the time he'd shared the cell with me. Then, after Mrs. Earth's rejection, he'd turned into a Snoop Dogg album.

"What are you going to do?" I asked him. I meant it rhetorically, of course.

"Burn this motherfucker to the ground," he said, eerily calm.

I snickered.

He pulled out a matchbook and commenced to set flame to the small bundle of newspapers that cornered our cell. Luckily, it was less than fifteen. I stamped it out quickly. Gerard got himself an IMR, Inmate Misbehavior Report, and keeplock status.

I thought of that past as I pulled down the appropriate street in my Toy-yoda. The newspaper Sela's friend Zelda had called me earlier and told me to buy sat in my passenger seat, where Sela should have been.

"Check out the metro section, third page. Read it carefully."

Unfortunately, I had.

I pulled the Toy-yoda to a halt in front of a modest but elegantly appointed house. Bevolyn Sykes stood on the front lawn waving for me. I mustered a smile, cut the engine, and got out, even though I didn't want to. No, I wanted to pull out a Zippo lighter and set today's newspaper in flames.

"I see my directions didn't get you too lost," Bevolyn said.

"No, they were perfect."

"No such thing as perfect, Reverend." I could hear the hurt in her voice. I agreed with her.

"You have a beautiful neighborhood," I said.

Bevolyn looked around as if she were the visitor. "Yeah, the people are nice. Everyone pretty much keeps to themselves. Russell and I like that."

"How are things with you? You and your husband?"

She smiled. "Great."

I turned away, knowing from the strength in her voice that she meant it.

My eye caught a dazzling array of reddish flowers along the lawn and my attention no longer was on Bevolyn and her newfound happiness. "I love these," I said, pointing to a row of the flowery bushes enclosed in an elaborate brick circle of fence. "They'd be nice for the church. My place, too. What are they called?"

"Gypsy Music Hibiscus," Bevolyn said. "They're a tropical plant and will die pretty soon, but Russell and I plant them every year. They never last as long as the price dictates they should, but we don't give up on them." Her voice cracked a bit.

Our eyes met.

"As well you shouldn't," I told her. "Even if they only lasted a day, they're beautiful enough to justify."

She smiled. "Enough of this, Reverend." She held out her hand. "I'm ready to look. Let me see the newspaper."

I handed it to her, folded, but opened to the page in question. I knew the words as if I'd written them. I'd read it several times. Too many times.

CRIME STINGS NET 11 ARRESTS

By Curtis M. Lawson

Staff Writer

ASBURY PARK—Police arrested 11 people in two major sting operations yesterday: one to catch drug dealers, another to seize those trying to buy sex from female undercover officers.

Bevolyn looked up briefly. I knew which part had caught her attention. She hurriedly moved on to continue reading, shaking her head, grunting.

Dean Sampson wasn't a target of either bust, but still fell when he borrowed $20 from an undercover officer posing as a prostitute and used it to buy crack cocaine from another undercover officer he believed was a drug peddler.

"He's not a very bright criminal," said Police Chief William Butterfield.

"You borrow money off a cop to buy drugs from another cop? Candidate for "Stupid Criminals" on *DaySide with Linda Vester*," he added.

Sampson, 38, of 9 First Ave., Asbury Park, was one of the nearly dozen people caught yesterday in the police department's latest "better-quality-of-life" crime sweep.

"We wanted to continue to send the message that Asbury Park is not the place to deal drugs or solicit prostitutes," Butterfield said last evening.

Bevolyn looked up at me again and held her gaze this time. I looked away. I could still see her scan down, and I knew which part her eyes would settle on.

Those charged are:

Edwin Rivera, 18, 85 Main St., Asbury Park, distribution of marijuana.

Daniel Mahoney, 45, 6 Bangs Ave., Asbury Park, possession of cocaine.

Luis Cruz, 40, 27 Basswood St., Apt. 2, Asbury Park, soliciting a prostitute.

Sela Wheeler, 28, 2 Springdale Ave., Tinton Falls, soliciting a prostitute.

Bevolyn gasped and touched a hand to her mouth. The rest of the article, a long list of offending names, didn't matter.

"My sister," I heard her say. "Female undercover officer posing as a prostitute."

My stomach dropped. My lover, my future first lady soliciting prostitution from a female undercover officer. I'd caught that, too, and had had it stuck in my craw all morning. What was that about?

"Reverend?"

I dared to look at Bevolyn. "Yes?"

"We've had our differences, I know. But I'm sorry. Very sorry this had to happen to you...my sister. Obviously, she's going through something. Female undercover officer posing as a prostitute. That says it all."

In a different time, under different circumstances, I might have played the tough-guy role, pretended I wasn't wounded. Pretended my heart wasn't broken; my life, which finally had moved in a good direction, wasn't shattered. Pretended I'd seen the punch coming. But like good 'ol Balls in prison, I hadn't seen it coming. It hit me hard. I was unprepared for it. No, I didn't play the tough-guy role this time. I nodded and thanked Bevolyn.

She surprised me, reached over, and gave me a hug. I awkwardly patted her back. No sexual desire or thoughts passed through me, even though this had been my hope for a long time—to touch Bevolyn, to hold her.

She broke the embrace and nodded to her car.

"Follow me. Let's go see if we can find her. Find out what's going on."

"She's not at home, I know that much. Went by there. You know where Zelda lives?" I asked. "101 Willow Street. I'm not sure where that is. I pulled her address from the church files. That'd be the place to start, I suspect."

"I suspect," she said, adding, "I know it," before moving toward her car.

She sat in it for some time, praying, it appeared. Then I noticed the muffler pipe shivering, the brakelights coming on, and the car moving in reverse.

Bevolyn drove.

I followed, talking to He's Sweet I Know every step of the way.

30

As Afeni turned the corner of her street—well, the Sykeses street, actually—she thought of a poem: "Footprints." Bevolyn, Mrs. Sykes, had introduced it to her. Mrs. Sykes said it was a famous poem. Afeni had never heard of it, and why should she have, living where she lived, having the mother, no offense, she had? The poem was about a man's dream, seeing his life flash across the sky, and two sets of footprints in the sand, his and God's. During some of the man's most trying times, though, he noticed only one set of footprints. The man asked God why He'd abandoned him during these rough-water moments. God explained that the one set of footprints were His own. He hadn't abandoned the man, one of His dear children. No, God had picked him up and carried him, safely, to calm waters.

Deep, right?

Afeni hoped that one day she'd write a poem as powerful as that. She believed she would, given the opportunity. She wondered if leaving the Sykeses and moving back in with Aloe would cut down her opportunities.

She had to take the chance, though. She saw the sadness in Aloe's eyes, the slack of Aloe's shoulders. Aloe needed her. And, in a way, she needed Aloe. Mother and daughter. A very personal, special relationship. And no matter how much she appreciated Mrs. Sykes, she couldn't have that personal, special relationship with anyone except Aloe. Mama.

But what of the relationship between daughter and father? Didn't that matter, too? She'd grown to appreciate Mr. Sykes, Russell. She recalled catching him watching her, a smile on his face, fatherly pride; the times he came into her room, stood over her shoulder as she explained the computer to him; the times he tried to talk to her, using slang as the bridge between their divide of years, generations. Special moments she'd lose. But should she care? If it had been up to him, she'd never have existed. Aloe would have let them vacuum her away.

All Afeni's reverie had come crashing to a halt, though, as she neared home. A strange car hugged the curb in front of the Sykeses house. And there, in the driveway, was a strange man, talking to Bevolyn, Mrs. Sykes. Afeni retreated behind a thick growth of bushes in a neighbor's yard and tried to gather a closer look.

Shit! That wasn't a strange man. It was Reverend Path.

Not good, Afeni knew. Russell had made it clear that Mrs. Sykes was to stay away from Reverend Path and the church. She'd heard Russell demand it, Mrs. Sykes conceding quietly.

What was going on? Why would Mrs. Sykes be so foolish as to stand outside, in broad daylight, with this forbidden man?

Afeni moved around the edge of the bush and got a better view of the Sykeses' driveway. Mrs. Sykes, she could see, was reading something that looked like a newspaper. Reverend Path stood by impassively, not looking too strong in the legs. Then, Mrs. Sykes looked up. Something in her eyes, Afeni noticed. What, though? Lust? Shit!

Mrs. Sykes returned her gaze to the newspaper and read some more, shaking her head as she did. Again, she looked up. She was talking now, Reverend Path talking back, the two of them seeming close, like old friends. Uh-oh. Afeni's heart raced and her stomach dropped as she eyed Mrs. Sykes leaning forward to hug Reverend Path. Reverend Path ran a hand along Mrs. Sykes's back and patted it gently, probably imagining his hand gliding across her ass or boobs instead. Afeni frowned. Shit!

Mrs. Sykes broke the embrace and said a few more words before she moved down the driveway back toward the house. Reverend Path turned and headed toward his car in the street.

Good. Go. Shit, this was crazy.

But Mrs. Sykes got inside her car instead of walking through the front door of the house.

Uh-oh. Shit.

Afeni saw Mrs. Sykes slide into the driver's seat, then saw her talking to herself, her head bowed, and her mouth moving. Praying? For what? Getting a head start on asking forgiveness for the sin she was about to commit?

Shit.

Mrs. Sykes ended her prayer. The car lurched to life. She backed from the drive. Afeni moved farther behind the bushes, knelt, and watched Mrs. Sykes drive to the corner and turn right. She watched Reverend Path mimic the move.

Shit.

"Gotta eat something, Sela."

"No, I don't gotta do nothing but live, then die."

"You call this living?"

Sela moved from Zelda's living room, walking down the hall to nowhere in particular. Zelda followed with the bowl of chicken noodle soup in hand. They ended up in the kitchen, Sela by the back door, looking out on an unspectacular yard and a rickety shed. Zelda placed the soup bowl on the table and came up behind Sela, placing her hands on Sela's shoulders.

"Don't, Zee-Zee."

"Why not?"

"Don't deserve this," Sela said. "Why are you doing this?"

"I love you, Sela."

"You…?"

"Yes," Zelda said, nodding, "love you."

"Even though…?"

"Yes."

"You called LeVar?" Sela asked.

"Done."

"Told him what?"

"To read the newspaper," Zelda said.

Sela turned. "It's in there?"

Zelda nodded.

Sela closed her eyes and moaned, then opened them, briefly, when she felt Zelda's warm lips on her own. She quickly closed them again and took in Zelda's tongue. It tasted salty with a hint of chicken. It warmed her soul.

When they broke the kiss, Sela said, "I think I will have some of that soup."

Zelda smiled.

Sela stopped, a couple of spoonfuls in, and looked up at Zelda. "You know, I love you, too."

"I know," Zelda said. She had her back against the door that led to the backyard. She licked her lips every so often, which drove Sela wild.

"Told Bevolyn?" Sela asked.

"I left that to LeVar," Zelda said.

"They're coming here?"

"I told him you were safe," Zelda said. "Implying with me."

Sela managed a smile. "I am. Safe."

He walked down the sidewalk toward the home. The soles of his shoes squished on the pavement. He tossed aside a few stray rocks in a harmony that sounded like a percussion instrument. The lawn was a carpet of vibrant green with colorful flowers, beautifully arranged. It was an inviting home, to say the least—more than most deserved.

He climbed the three stairs of the small porch and pressed the doorbell, but heard no chime. So he tapped a few knocks out, waited, and then tapped a few more, louder. All the while, his mind replayed the past, a funeral, in particular.

"Nobody not there."

He turned sharply, taken by surprise by the voice from over his shoulder, the voice of a young boy on a bicycle that needed its seat adjusted to fit him comfortably.

"What was that?" he asked as he came down from the porch, closer to the young boy.

"Nobody not there," the boy repeated.

"A man lives here, correct?" He pulled out a photo and showed it to the boy.

"Yup. That's Reverend Path."

"Reverend Path?" He could hardly believe it.

"I live right across the street. Reverend Path saw to it my mother could get me this bicycle." The young boy tapped the handlebars and smiled. "He was supposed to help me get it set right, fit me. But he ran out of here in a hurry earlier. Like a bat out of hell, my mother would say, but I can't talk that way about the reverend. Least not to his face."

"Okay."

"You a relative or something, mister? I shouldn't be telling all of this to no stranger."

He smiled and placed his hand on the young boy's shoulder. "His cousin. My name's Lincoln. It's good you ask that question. You can never be too safe nowadays."

"That's what my mother says. You should come meet her. She's lonely. She's a sucker for a mister in a suit. She baked Reverend Path cookies a few times, started going to church services, but he got himself somebody, and the Lord won't let him have two, even though my daddy did. So she stopped."

"Baking cookies, or going to church?"

"Both," the young boy admitted.

Dante smiled. Kids were something.

"You gonna come meet her, Mister Lincoln?"

"Not at the moment," Dante said, "but I'll be back. Okay?"

"Okay. I understand." The young boy's head dropped; his voice had fallen down several octaves.

Dante pulled his head up, by the chin. "What's your name?"

"Julius."

"Like Dr. J?"

"Huh?"

"Nothing," Dante said. "Julius, what's your mother's name?"

"Ann."

"Is she nice looking?"

"Spit me out," Julius said. "The girls at school won't let me play kickball in peace. So I'd say yes, she nice looking."

"Take me to meet your mother, Julius."

"You mean it?" Julius's voice was a rollercoaster on the high loop.

Dante looked back at the house and then turned back to Julius, a smile on his face. "Yeah. I've got some time to kill."

Emphasis on the last word. *Kill.*

Afeni was on the computer at her desk hutch, searching through Google, typing in keywords in hopes of finding something.

LeVar Path. Reverend LeVar Path. Path. LeVar. Getting LeVar Burton of *Roots* fame as a hit when she put in that last keyword. Coming up with *nada* for everything else.

Shit.

"Where's Bevolyn, Afeni?"

Afeni turned suddenly, a hand against her chest. "You and footsteps need to introduce yourselves to each other. I never knew anyone who moved around so quietly."

"What?" Russell moved into the room.

Afeni smiled. "Something I heard someone say about someone, once."

"Oh. What are you doing?" He glanced at the screen.

It was too late for Afeni to click out.

He squinted his eyes as he leaned down. "Google?"

"Yeah."

Recognition flashed in his eyes. "Why are you searching for that?"

Afeni looked away.

"Afeni?"

She spider-walked her fingers across the desk.

Russell turned her toward him. "What's going on?"

"Nothing."

"Where's Bevolyn?"

"She went off with Reverend Path," Afeni blurted.

Russell's eyes widened. His mouth opened and stayed that way. He rocked back as if punched. "Say what?"

"I saw them outside when I was coming home. They hugged. Then she got in her car and drove off. He followed."

Russell struggled for a breath.

Afeni touched his hand. He snatched it away. Her eyes hunched in surprise.

"You're lying," he said, finally. "You. Are. Lying."

"I wish I were," she said, shaking her head.

"No. Way. No. Way."

"Why would I lie to you?"

"I don't know," he said, his mouth curled together. He looked at her, his eyes cutting like a slice of lemon dipped in vinegar…beyond bitter. "I don't know why you're doing this."

"Aloe told me," Afeni said.

"Who?"

"Cut it," she snapped. "I *know* you know her dancing name."

"What?"

"You're my father," Afeni said. Blurting things out was her thing today, it appeared.

"What? I…what?"

"Please, don't deny it. That would hurt me."

Russell slumped down on Afeni's bed. She turned to face him. Tears were in his eyes. She couldn't figure if they were for her or for Bevolyn.

"I'm sorry," he said after some time had passed.

"Me, too," Afeni replied. "I'm leaving. Going back home."

He looked up at her. "What about school? You can't

just drop out; you guys just started. Ponce isn't cheap, either. We can't get back tuition."

"Not gonna drop out," Afeni said. "Going to go to Malcolm X Shabazz. Aloe's working on getting me registered. The kids there don't eat with a pinkie extended, and I'll give you my 50 Cent CD if even one of the boys there has a handkerchief in his shirt pocket, but they're good people. Like me. I'm sorry about the tuition."

Russell opened his mouth to say something. Nothing came out.

"I think it's for the best," she said.

He nodded and frowned, his face a mask, monstrous in its contortion.

Afeni said, "Now, about the reverend and Bevolyn, Mrs. Sykes. I saw her leave with him. Well, like I said, he followed."

Russell nodded.

"I'm sorry," Afeni said.

"Me, too."

Afeni turned back to her computer and clicked off from Google. "I can stop this, I guess."

"When are you leaving?" he asked, so softly it was almost a whisper.

"Today," Afeni said, without turning back to face him.

"I—"

"Go track down your wife," Afeni cut him off. "It's too late to worry about you and me."

Russell sat still for a bit, but then he got up and walked out quietly.

Afeni turned and looked at the door he'd passed through, a lump in her throat, her eyes suddenly wet.

Russell left a simple message with the voice mail on Bevolyn's cell phone.

"Looking for you."

Then, he moved to leave the house, pausing to look back. Despite himself, despite what he was feeling about Bevolyn, he smiled.

As he left, there were tears in his eyes for Bevolyn, for Afeni, and for himself. For himself, mainly because he knew he wouldn't let another man slight him for a second time. No way.

He'd kill before he allowed that to happen again.

31

Bevolyn's car came to a stop along the curb up ahead. I pulled in behind her, exhausted both mentally and physically. It had been a struggle to keep up with her. Several times the lights of yellow that she passed through winked themselves red as I approached them. Mrs. Lead Foot was in a hurry. I wasn't. I still hadn't quenched the desire to take a Zippo lighter to the newspaper resting in my lap.

Bevolyn moved from her car and slammed her door. Its sound a jarring echo in my head. I moved from the Toy-yoda and eased my door shut, newspaper tucked under my arm. Bevolyn waited for me by her car. I moved toward her, the sun beating down on me, my heart beating wild in my chest. Me, beaten.

"Could have left that in the car," she said, nodding toward the newspaper.

"Can't seem to put it down," I answered truthfully.

She looked at me. I looked away, focusing up at the bright orange sun. Its glare made me frown. Today, of all days, the heat had returned.

It was hotter than a popcorn fart.

"Are you ready for this, Reverend?"

I returned my gaze to her and nodded. "She might not even be here."

Bevolyn smiled sadly. "We both know she is, Reverend. Are you ready for *that?*"

"Tried to get ready for it on the car ride over," I said. "But you drove so fast I didn't have much chance to prepare."

"I drove fast? Or you drove slow?"

"You drove fast."

She looked at her car, then at Zelda's place, then me. "Guess I've been headed this way for a long time, Reverend. I just wanted to hurry and get here. Have for a long time."

"You've suspected Sela was…?" I couldn't finish it.

"Different," Bevolyn said. "Not this, no, but different. Always seemed to be missing something."

"I noticed that, too," I admitted. I looked toward Zelda's place then. "Thought she'd found the missing piece in me. But I guess not."

"Your piece just didn't fit, Reverend. Just didn't fit."

We glanced at one another.

"You're happy," I noticed aloud.

"I am," she confirmed.

"Husband is—?"

She shook her head to let me know that conversation was off limits. I recognized it as such, and said, "Let's go ring this doorbell."

"Let's," was her response. It drifted to me as she wheeled and walked toward the house. I followed, not exactly on her heels, more like I'd followed in the car, way behind.

She waited for me on the porch. When I caught up, she turned and rang the doorbell. I was glad to have her support.

Zelda answered on the first ring. She wore one of those long shirts that extend almost to the ankles, as pajamas. I noticed her trademark flowers were missing from her hair. Then it dawned on me...lavender was Zelda's color...and Sela's latest fascination. Her nails, my Open House—were they subtle signals for the one she really wanted—Zelda?

"Looking for my sister," Bevolyn said. "May we come in?"

I studied Zelda's face, which was a blank canvas and searched it for some emotion, some crack in her strong façade. I couldn't find a crumb of anything. She stepped back from the door and held it open for us. Bevolyn stepped inside. I stepped in behind her.

Zelda closed the door behind me. "In the kitchen," she said. "End of the hall. Straightaway."

"Thanks," I said to Zelda.

"Nothing to thank me for, Reverend."

"The heads-up," I said. I held up the newspaper and waved it at her.

"She's in the kitchen," was her response, cooler than polar ice caps.

I turned to Bevolyn and arched my eyebrows.

"You first," Bevolyn said.

I looked at Bevolyn and Zelda. Bevolyn nodded; Zelda stared.

"Come with me," Zelda told Bevolyn. "I'll show you around." She seemed warmer with Bevolyn than she was with me.

I inched down the hall using the wall for support. The last time my legs felt this way was when I walked those few short feet, naked, to get my intake cavity search at JCI.

Sela sat at the kitchen table, a pitcher of what I took to

be lemonade in front of her, with two glasses. She looked up when I entered. I saw the light extinguish in her eyes. She looked over my shoulder.

"Looking for your sister? She's here," I said. "She thought it best I come first."

Sela raised a hand and pointed to the seat across from her. I moved to it and sat. Neither of us spoke a word. I held out the newspaper and dropped it with a thud on the table. Sela coolly pushed it aside, picked up the pitcher, poured herself a glass, and sipped. I did the same. I didn't sip it, though, just placed it in front of me, close by when I needed it, when my mouth turned cotton. I knew it would.

Sela's eyes were on the newspaper.

"Go ahead," I said, "read it. And weep, as they say. I know I did."

I expected an "I'm sorry." Instead, she picked up the paper, read it, sipped her lemonade, read some more, sipped her lemonade, and read some more, taking forever with the words.

"Short article, Sela. You got busted trying to get some pussy," I snapped.

She looked up at me, newspaper in hand, but didn't say anything.

"Pussy, Sela," I repeated.

She took another sip of her lemonade and went back to reading carefully. I'd had enough. I reached across the table and slapped the glass from her hand. It hit the floor, splintering into many tiny pieces. Sela didn't even look in that direction. She looked at me, wordless and unblinking.

"What's happening in here? Everything okay?"

I turned to find Zelda in the doorway. She eyed the broken chips of glass on the floor, Sela, and me. She turned away without a word. I was happy to avoid that confrontation. I had my hands full with the ongoing one.

But then Zelda stepped back in. "Any problems in here, Sela, and I'll be glad to call the police, or"—she looked at me—"handle things myself if need be."

Then she backed out again.

A perfect pair, I decided. Sela and Zelda. Both of 'em Ice Witches. I was ready to smack Sela's face in the same manner as the glass of lemonade, but she surprised me by reaching forward and touching my hand so gently. A lump formed in my throat. When I saw her eyes water, mine followed. I turned away, ashamed.

Her fingers glided across my hand. She squeezed. I responded by squeezing, too. My eyes, that is. I squeezed them shut tight. Water still poured from them.

"What's that one thing about yourself that hurts you so much?" Sela asked. "That one thing you wish wasn't you? That one thing you wish you could move away from? But you can't. It's you. No matter what you do. It's you."

"The time I served in prison," I said. I could barely hear myself say it. Sela's fingers stopped gliding across my hand. She'd heard me, just fine.

I opened my eyes and looked at Sela, expecting scorn, disdain, some other fancy word for hate. There wasn't any.

"Martha Stewart prison? *Prison* prison?" she asked.

I cleared my throat and shook my head. "Mike Tyson prison. *Prison* prison."

She smiled at me. Subtle, but a smile just the same.

"What?" I asked.

"God works in mysterious ways," she said.

I rolled my eyes.

"You can understand me," she added. "You know

about pain, wishing it weren't so. God, He meant for it to happen this way. He had you come into my life, to teach me so much. I haven't smoked in a long time, you know. That's what your purpose was. To help me grow."

"My purpose was to love you," I said, fuming. "For you to love me back. Not to have you go chasing down pussy in the middle of the night. Ready to pay for it, too. What happened? Zelda have a headache?"

Even He's Sweet I Know cringed at that one. I was sinking, fast.

"Zelda's very special to me," Sela admitted. I closed my eyes. "As are you," I heard her say. I opened my eyes again, in time to hear and see her say, "Hella special."

I pulled my hand away and stood from my seat.

"LeVar?"

"What do you want?"

"Same thing you do," she said. "But no matter how much you want it, you still did a bid. And I still am a…lesbian."

I sat again.

"What did you do?" she asked. "If you care to tell me."

"Tried to raise a ghost from the dead," I said.

Her eyebrow arched.

I told her my story about my brother, that burden I carried around with me all those years until the Ruffin girl came along and I became that line in one of Tupac's old songs. To paraphrase it, next to doing the do with some lovely, revenge is the sweetest joy. I told her how I'd gotten the Ruffin girl to love me, then turned on her in the worst way. Sela flinched as I relayed the details of how badly I'd turned on Tammy Ruffin. She flinched and took a deep breath. I did the same. I thought of that time and my double life, juggling Myshelle AND Tammy Ruffin.

I paused to gather myself.

Then I told her more about Miss Ma'am, and eventually, my father—how his piss came out in two streams, how he left us all, how I still loved him, missed him so much it made me ache inside. I'd never told anyone that before, hadn't even admitted it to myself. It surprised me. I told her of the little girl I'd held in my lap the other day. I told Sela I'd needed her with me so badly, called her so many times. And to think, the entire time I'd needed her, wanted her, had to have her, she was off thinking about pussy.

I was angry. Vile. Nasty.

From Whom All Blessings Flow was disappointed. Hurt. Heartbroken.

"Nothing you can do about prison," Sela said when I'd finished venting. "Served your time. It's over and done with. Nothing, obviously, you can do about your brother. And I'm sorry about the little girl. That must have been painful, a reminder of your brother."

"But," I said. I didn't care to hear all this mumbo jumbo from her.

"But you can look up your father. Talk to him. That might help, I believe."

She was right, of course. I'd been heading in this direction since I'd come to Dirty Jersey. I'd put it off, avoided it.

The tension left my shoulders. The anger inside moved away. She was so right.

"You've shifted this thing," I said.

"I'm hella good at that," she replied.

I actually smiled. She did, too.

"I won't offer a sorry," she said, "because it's too late for that. But I think you know I am. Really, LeVar."

I paused, waited, procrastinated, thought, considered,

delved, and finally asked, "Did you ever really care for me, Sela?" I needed to know. It mattered to me. Closure, as the prison psychologist Dr. Mendes had described it to me. I was in prison because of it, thinking I'd find closure with the Ruffin girl. I needed it to get out of the prison of hurt that Sela had sentenced me to. "Really, did you care for me?"

"If I wasn't doing my own bid," she said, speaking softly and with great consideration, "you and I could have gone a long way." The twinkle in her eyes told me it was so.

I leaned across the table and kissed her forehead. She closed her eyes. I stood and watched her as she paused, frozen, leaning forward, her eyes still closed…a statue. I turned and left the kitchen and found Bevolyn in the living room, Zelda showing her a vase of some sort, Bevolyn nodding at Zelda's history lesson.

"You're up," I said.

They both turned.

"How did it go?" Bevolyn asked. Zelda looked at me hard. She wanted to know, too.

"She served her time. Got her release," I said.

Bevolyn frowned and opened her mouth to say something, but I wheeled fast and moved away, leaving in more of a hurry than Bevolyn on the way over here.

I had a pressing date with my father.

The last piece to this puzzle called My Life.

32

Russell sat in the quiet of his SUV. He had no desire for music. The AC was off…didn't have the strength to turn it on. He cracked the knuckles of his hands several times, though, in a show of his masculinity, his strength. A cliché, cracking the knuckles before a fight. He might as well go ahead and roll his neck, fix a hard scowl on his handsome face, and punch the palm of one hand with the fist of the other.

The house before him was quiet as well. The drapes were drawn, but inside the lights were off; it was dark. The driveway was empty. On the corner of the porch an American flag hung, with no breeze to make it swing and sway. Lavender-colored ribbon wrapped the porch's poplar wood balusters. The lawn looked freshly cut, a carpet of vibrant green.

Russell consulted his watch. He'd been waiting for over an hour. He'd wait until the end of time, if need be. Eventually, the reverend would have to come home. And when he did, Russell would be waiting, ready for action.

Bevolyn walked into Zelda's kitchen, finding Sela sitting at the table with her eyes closed. A pitcher of lemonade centered the table—Bevolyn's favorite drink. There was a glass across from Sela and another glass shattered on the kitchen floor. Bevolyn looked at the dish rack by the sink. She moved to it, pulled a glass off one of the prongs, moved back to the table, poured a full glass of lemonade, and took a seat.

"Open your eyes," Bevolyn commanded.

Sela hesitated but eventually did. Her lashes were mashed together in moist disarray, the whites of her eyes, pink, close to full-blown red. Her skin was ashen, most of the hue gone from it.

"I'm listening," Bevolyn said. "Explain yourself."

"What can I say?"

"How you ended up on that street, late at night," Bevolyn said. "And how you reached inside your pocket-book to get out money so that prostitute would do… things to you. Or is it for you? I'm not exactly sure how all that works."

"Please don't be hateful," Sela begged.

"How long?"

"What?"

Bevolyn's mouth twisted, her lips curled. "How long have you lived this lifestyle?"

"Uh…"

"How long?"

Sela shrugged but answered, "Middle school, I thought it. High school, I knew it. Past year I've acted on it, for the first time."

"Zelda?"

"Yes."

"Where'd you two meet? I mean, how does one meet people like that?"

"People like that?"

"The Bible says—"

"I don't care what the Bible says," Sela cut her off.

Bevolyn's eyes widened. "You better care," she spat.

"I'll cross that bridge when I come to it," Sela said.

"Right over the edge into the water," Bevolyn said. "To drown."

They sat silent.

"I don't expect you to understand," Sela finally said. "*I* don't even understand. I've tried to fight it, believe me. Look how much I hurt LeVar, myself. Zelda."

Bevolyn waved her off, stood, and moved to the sink. She turned on the faucet and began rinsing her glass. Sela moved to her, turned the water off, and covered Bevolyn's hand with one of her own.

"Need you to hear me out," she told Bevolyn.

"I heard you," Bevolyn said. "You admitted to being weak-minded."

"I never said that."

"You tried to fight it," Bevolyn reminded her, "but weren't able in the end. That's the classic fight we all have, trying to measure up to God's expectations. We fall short in our moments of weakness."

"Like you with the basketball player," Sela noted.

Bevolyn gasped.

"Russell told me," Sela said. "Let all his hurt out, with me, because you were too stubborn to listen to him. Full of excuses. Never truly apologized."

"I did," Bevolyn whispered.

"You didn't."

They eyed one another.

"No one's perfect," Sela said. "I'm certainly not. *You're* not. I just want to know if you'll support me through all this."

"The Bible says, 'But what things were gain to me, those I counted loss for Christ.'"

Sela smiled. "Translate for a sinner girl, would you?"

"You often have to give up what is profit to you, for Christ," Bevolyn said.

"So you want me to give up this very real part of myself, for Christ? That it, Bevolyn?"

Bevolyn shook her head. "No. But I must give up you, Sela. I must. I don't approve of this lifestyle. My Bible gives me verse after verse of direction regarding this. It isn't right. It goes against what I believe. Stand for something, or fall for anything. You've heard that?"

Sela's voice cracked. "Heard, 'my brother's keeper,' too. I suppose that doesn't apply to sisters?"

"I'm afraid not," Bevolyn said.

Sela's lips tightened. "Then we're done here."

Bevolyn nodded and moved to leave.

"Hey, Bevolyn?"

Bevolyn turned. "Yes?"

"What does the Bible say about abortions?"

Bevolyn's jaw muscles tensed. "Goodbye, Sela Wheeler." She turned and left.

Zelda appeared in the kitchen's doorway a few minutes later. "You okay?"

Sela wiped the tears from her eyes with the back of her hand and shrugged. "Down one sister." Funny, she never had thought she'd care. But she did.

"Come sit with me, Lincoln. Stop looking out that window."

Dante turned to Ann, little Julius's mother, and flashed her one of his smiles, the one that made women's limbs go loose. "Give me a minute, baby."

"Hmm. Calling me 'baby' already. I like that."

Dante shrugged. "What can I say? Little Julius was on point with his appraisal."

"What?"

"He said you were attractive," Dante said. "And you are. He also said you were lonely. And if I have any say, you won't be any longer." Bullshit. All of it.

"You say the sweetest things. You ain't just trying to give my ear diabetes, are you?"

"I've got an injection for you, just in case," Dante said. "And it isn't insulin, baby."

"God, Lincoln. God."

"No more computer chat rooms," he went on.

Ann blushed. "I shouldn't have spoken on that. Told you too much. You make a woman open herself up, though. Nothing I could do."

Dante smiled. "I've heard that a time or two."

A car horn sounded outside. Dante quickly turned to look out the window again. Nothing. False alarm.

"Why are you so worried about Reverend Path?" Ann asked.

Dante squinted his eyes and spoke without turning back to face her. "Wondering about this Explorer parked out front of the reverend—my cousin's—place. What does this guy want?"

"Counseling or something, probably," Ann said.

"Well, he's messing up my plans," Dante said.

"Mine, too."

Dante turned to face her, smiling, of course. "You've got plans, baby?"

"Big ones," she said, looking down at his crotch.

Dante looked at her large breasts. Her face was a bit hardened, truthfully, but those breasts were definitely calling him. Dante. Dante. Lincoln. Lincoln.

"What are you grinning about?" Ann asked.

"Nothing, baby."

"Something."

Dante looked outside again. The Explorer still idled by the curb. He turned back to Ann. "Little Julius isn't coming back tonight?"

Ann shook her head. "Told you, my girl offered to watch him for me."

Dante moved to her. "Come on, then. Show me that bedroom. I've got some time to kill."

Russell dialed Bevolyn's number again. Voice mail, as usual. He left her an even angrier message than his prior ones, and then slammed the phone shut and tossed it on the seat next to him. He was getting angrier by the minute. He moved from the SUV, went to the trunk hatch, rummaged around, and pulled out his tire iron. He went back inside and sat, tire iron on his lap, ready and waiting.

"Rachel, this is Mrs. Sykes. Is Russell in?"

"He left early today, Mrs. Sykes."

"Did he? I tried at home; no one answered," Bevolyn said. That was strange, she knew. Where was Afeni?

"He packed up a little after three, Mrs. Sykes."

"Well, thanks. I'll try again."

"Okay, Mrs. Sykes—"

"Rachel, may I ask you a question?"

Rachel swallowed but said, "Sure, Mrs. Sykes."

"My husband is a handsome man, Rachel."

"Yes," was all Rachel could say in reply.

"Anything ever happen between you two?"

Rachel was quiet.

"Rachel."

"No, Mrs. Sykes. No," Rachel said.

"Almost?"

Rachel was silent again.

"Thanks," Bevolyn said.

"I'm sorry, Mrs. Sykes."

"Don't be," Bevolyn replied. "Our marriage."

Bevolyn disconnected the pay phone and went back to her booth. The waitress had refilled her coffee cup while she was gone. The check sat wedged under it. Bevolyn took two sips of the coffee before pushing the mug aside. She picked up the check, scanned it for accuracy, calculated a tip, and went in her pocketbook and pulled out her wallet. Her hand brushed against her cell phone, its battery dead as a doornail, as she placed her wallet back inside her pocketbook.

The hostess thanked her for the visit as she passed through the doors to outside. She started the engine but sat, unable to drive just yet, Sela on her mind. Why had Sela allowed herself to fall into this sordid lifestyle? What would their mother think if she were still alive? How many times had she probably turned over in her grave? How could anyone choose that sordid life? What was in store for Sela on the other side? Eternal damnation? Was there any loophole whatsoever that would allow her to still pass through the Golden Gates?

Bevolyn didn't know the answer.

Reverend Path might, though.

She needed to talk to him. She decided now was as good a time as ever. She would go by his place. Knowing what she now knew about Russell, his almost slipup with Rachel, she would do her best not to wrap her arms around the reverend and press her lips against his. She'd do her best. But Russell had some explaining to do, some serious explaining. She should call his cell phone this moment, and get that explanation. But…she would stop by the reverend's first.

★ ★ ★

"Lincoln?"

"Just a minute," Dante called from Ann's bathroom.

"I'm sitting on this," she responded. "It's nice and warm for you."

"Keep it warm, baby. Just one minute."

"It ain't wine," she yelled. "It doesn't get better with time."

"Couple minutes isn't going to hurt it, baby."

"True. But it's impatient."

"Don't stand for its impatience. Be assertive, baby. Take charge. Give it the finger," Dante said, his voice laced with the tone of sex.

"The finger?"

"Finger it," he said.

"Oooh."

"Oooh," he echoed.

Her voice was gone. In a moment's time, he heard her low, soft, moan. He shook his head, smiled, and dialed the number on his cell phone. The other end picked up after several rings.

"This, En."

"Nate."

"Wassup?"

"Are you and Anthony ready?"

"Yeah."

"Good. This is definitely the place. I wanted to take him to our designated cleansing area and handle it there, but things aren't going according to my plans. You and Anthony move in, take him here at his house. He's not here yet, but he will be—I can feel it."

"Aiight. So this is the part where I get to use—"

"Your gun, yes."

"Aiight. Whatchu up to? Whatchu gonna do with this?"

Dante laughed. "Me? I'm doing some undercover work."

Nate gritted his teeth. "What, you hanging with some bird?"

"Ann," Dante admitted. "She lives right across the street. Gives me a good view of our boy's house."

"So me and Anthony handle this, while you getting butt from some bird?"

Dante didn't hear the anger in his brother's tone, or didn't care. He said, "Her son came up to me—and get this—did the soft sell for his mother. She has a body on her; face isn't ever going to be on a magazine cover. But the body is—"

"How you wanna handle this?" Nate cut him off.

"Just make sure you guys aren't noticeable. Wear those masks we picked up."

"The *two* masks," Nate said.

"Yeah."

"Why we gotta wear masks? Masks are wack."

"Because I said so," Dante replied. "Masks aren't wack. This isn't the movies; you can't just walk in there and say, 'break yourself, fool' and start shooting. People would see you, remember you. You don't want that. Hit him hard and vamoose. You got it. Oh, there's an Explorer parked out front. Guy inside. I don't know what he wants. If he gets in the way, hit him hard, too."

"You'll be hitting that bird hard while we do this," Nate sneered.

Dante ignored the comment. "Nate?" He paused. "Nice and clean on this one, okay?"

"Of course."

They disconnected. Dante pocketed the cell phone and walked into the bedroom.

"Candles?" he said.

"Too much?" Ann asked.

"No. Nice touch."

"I gave it the finger," Ann said. "Just like you said."

"And what happened?"

"It cried," she said.

Dante looked down at her spread legs. "Look at that—you're right. It's all wet."

He moved to her and got on top.

33

I sat in the Toy-yoda, engine running, my focus on letters. And not the kind that my father and the Ruffins had sent me in prison—no, alphabet letters, in particular, AISBI. AISBI floated through my mind screen, a movie I couldn't fast-forward, would never want to rewind, but one I'd unfortunately starred in nonetheless. AISBI... sounds so unassuming, so innocent, but isn't.

I shook aside those thoughts and looked at the building again. I glanced at the building sign. Big, block, red-colored letters stood out from the tan stucco. REHABILITATION AND LONG-TERM CARE, the letters read.

A nurse wheeled a man across the patch of sidewalk out front. I could see her talking to him. She had a pleasant and unyielding smile on her face. I'd say she was Filipino, small in stature but moved the wheelchair with ease. The man, far as I could tell, had yet to move his lips. He looked dazed, confused, a bit frightened, even. His knuckles were white from gripping the wheelchair's handrails so tightly. His pajamas hung off him. The nurse, every so often, would rub his shoulders to calm him. It seemed to work.

It dawned on me that my father was a sick man. I strained to imagine him, broken, a shell of his old self. I thought of the years since I'd last seen him, thought about his letters to me in prison...my letters...AISBI.

So this was what it had come to?

I so wished Sela were by my side, for support, strength. Then I thought of my real strength. He's Sweet I Know. I could do all things in Him but fail.

AISBI.

Again, I could do all things in Him but fail.

I cut the Toy-yoda's engine and slid out. My steps were strong as I made my way to the main entrance. The doors slid open for me. I moved through them, a sea of thin, hard, gray carpet with red freckles awaiting me. The woman at the information desk smiled. I smiled back.

"Leonard Vernard Furlow," I said to her. "He's a patient, I believe."

"Your name?" she asked.

I told her.

She consulted her computer for a moment, then tapped the monitor and turned to smile at me again. "First visit," she said. "I'm sure he'll be happy to see you."

"How long has he been here?" I asked her.

"Little over a year," she said. "Nice man. He always speaks to me so nicely when they wheel him outside. Gets my name wrong every time, but, nice man."

"You think?"

She nodded. "Elevators at the end of this long hall behind me. On the left. We only have the one floor for patients. Second floor. He's in Room 213. Private room. They'll show you to it once you get upstairs."

I thanked her and moved down the hall to the elevators. I was on and then moving up. AISBI. Thoughts of those letters made my face flash hot. The elevator dinged for the second floor just as sweat dripped down from my armpits.

I said a few quick and silent words to He's Sweet I Know and stepped off.

The nurse's station sat to my right.

"Leonard Vernard Furlow," I said to a woman sitting there. "Room 213."

"He's in feeding group now," she said, not missing a beat.

"Feeding group?"

She nodded. "Cafeteria's end of that hall." She pointed. I turned to see. A woman with flame-red hair was coming up the hall. I turned back to the nurse. "He's being fed dinner," she added as an afterthought.

"Being fed?" I asked.

Her eyes homed in on me. "You're his son." It was a statement more than a question, but there was a hint of wonder in it.

I nodded.

Her gaze left me and moved to the woman with flame-red hair. "Dr. Summers," she said to the woman, "this is Mr. Furlow's son."

The redhead stopped and looked at me, hard.

"Dr. Summers," I said. It was the only thing I could think to say.

"Wilhemina, please."

I told her what to call me. She did. She ushered me aside, against a wall in a quiet part of the hall.

"Your father suffered a stroke," she told me. "I wanted to warn you ahead of time. We all had hoped you would come eventually. I've been working with him regarding the day-to-day aspects of life. He's progressing as well as can be expected."

"My father has quite the fan base," I said.

"He's a wonderful man," Wilhemina replied. She looked off somewhere. "Wonderful, wonderful man."

I focused deeper on her. Flame red shocks of long hair, deep blue eyes. An anomaly, more so because she thought my father a wonderful man than for her hair and eyes.

"Your father speaks of you often," she said, back to me.

"Does he?"

"Yes. And your mother. Lovey this and Lovey that," she said, chuckling.

I didn't chuckle. There wasn't humor in it. Instead, I frowned.

"Something wrong?" she asked. Perceptive.

"Lovey wasn't my mother," I told her. "Some woman he messed with at one time." Miss Ma'am knew about it, spoke of it often, cried sometimes when she thought I wasn't around.

"Oh," was the only response from Wilhemina.

"Wonderful man," I said.

Dr. Summers pursed her lips "Let's head to the cafeteria."

We walked in silence.

"This is it," Wilhemina said, arms outstretched, once we reached the cafeteria.

"Thanks," I replied. We shook hands. She backed away gracefully.

The cafeteria was more of a recreation room. It boasted three sides of windows, three ways of looking at the outside world, yet most of the assembled patients congregated around the television set, playing cards, or sitting on sofas talking to one another, except for a small group sitting at tables. Workers were feeding them.

I noticed my father right away. He'd changed— shrunken, hair white, skin looked darker; his face sagged on one side. The young woman sitting with him wiped his mouth after every shovel of food. She had to.

I moved to my father, stood over him. He shakily raised a hand, gesturing for the woman with him to withhold the spoonful of food she was prepared to feed him. "Paula," he said to her, "could you excuse us for a sec? This is my son."

Something flashed in Paula's eyes. A smile broke across her face. She stood, handed me the spoon, and whispered, "He's so cute. My name's Pam," as she passed by me.

"Sit," my father said.

I sat.

"You can put that spoon down," he said. "I ain't expecting you to help me eat."

I put the spoon down.

"How you been, boy?"

"Fine," I managed.

"You got my letters?" he asked. He knew I had. And when I didn't answer, he nodded. "Of course, you got 'em."

I swallowed some spit and tried to wet my mouth. I wished I had some of Sela's lemonade.

"You did that thing they sent you to prison for?" he asked, getting right to it.

AISBI.

I nodded. "Assault inflicting serious bodily injury. Otherwise known as an AISBI. A class F felony. Nineteen to thirty-six months in weight. I did a little over thirty months. Eighty-five percent of my sentence."

"I look like Judge Joe Brown, boy? I don't need all that information."

"Just wanted you to know," I said. "You really need to know what happened to me. I have you to thank for it."

He frowned and cocked his head. "You blame me for that?"

"Yes."

He laughed, a fit that nearly choked him to death. I sat without moving. Pam came rushing over, patting his back, looking at me with sadness. I turned away from her gaze. I saw several other old folks looking at me, too. They had the same hint of disappointment in their eyes as Pam had. I turned away from their glares, too. When my father's coughing spell died down, I turned to face him again.

"Careful, Mr. Furlow," Pam said.

He coughed once more, but nodded. "I'm okay now, Paulette."

Pam looked at me. "I'm close by," she said.

I nodded.

"Where was we?" my father asked. I didn't answer. "Oh, you was blaming me for your time in prison. Right?"

"What did LeVar ever do to you?" I asked.

He shook slightly, I noticed. "Don't go talking about that, boy. Your brother is dead and gone. Leave 'im buried."

"You treated him like crap," I said.

"I treated him like a son."

"No, you didn't. You were okay with me, but him…"

"You don't know what you're talking about, boy."

"He never fit in, anywhere," I went on. "They treated him like crap at school. You treated him terribly at home. Why?"

"Did my best with him," he said.

"Not good enough. You didn't, either. You're lying to yourself."

He got awfully quiet. He drifted to one side, only half of his body strong. I didn't set him straight.

"It was good that you eventually left," I said. "Things were better for him at home. No more beatings with that belt. That sick game you played where you'd trap his head between your knees and force him to try to break loose. He'd try, couldn't, and then start to cry. You'd laugh. So merciless."

I could see I was getting to him. His eyes were shining wet; spit bubbled on his lips, bubbled like blood. I thought of LeVar, and the little girl broken to pieces by that hit-and-run driver.

"You proud of what you did to him?" I went on. "He never had anyone to stick up for him." My voice dropped. "Including me. And when I finally did…I ended up in prison for it."

My father's gaze was on the table, his food going cold. Food I wouldn't feed him. Food he couldn't feed himself. Food that dribbled out of his mouth even when Pam took her time feeding him.

"These girls played a cruel joke on LeVar in school," I said. "Stacey Kimble-Williams and Tammy Ruffin."

"Don't know 'em," my father cut in, "and I don't need to be hearing about 'em."

"You're gonna hear me out," I said, forcefully.

Our eyes met. We locked gazes and held them.

"The one girl, Stacey, she died in a car crash the summer she graduated from college," I went on.

"The other?" my father asked, into this now.

"She's the one I went to jail over," I said.

He made a gesture that resembled a shaking of his head.

"Years had passed, but I couldn't get over what Tammy Ruffin had done to LeVar," I continued. "Bumped into her one day. She looked good. We started talking, and she was digging me. I have to admit, I was attracted to her. Very." Even though I had Myshelle.

My father grunted.

"Initially, I was thinking 'hit it and quit it.' That would be the extent of my revenge. But I got more involved with her than I'd planned.

"She was unbalanced. Prone to arguments. Had a problem with her hands when she got upset. I made it a point to upset her as much as I could. It was a crazy situation. I didn't have any control over how I was acting, or what I was doing. We were poison for each other. Terrible. Then, one day, after one of our biggest fights, she punched me in my shoulder and I decided to hit back. And hit back. And hit back. I blacked out, truth be told."

My mind drifted. I was back in that moment. In her apartment, eating her food, food she'd spent all day preparing for me.

"What's wrong?" she'd asked me.

"Nothing."

"Nothing," she said, "but I saw you make a face."

"Beef is kind of tough. String beans could have stood some more cooking. And what did you use to mash these potatoes? Your foot? They taste funny and they're clumpy." I mentally abused her at every opportunity. The food wasn't nearly as bad as I made it out to be. If anyone else had cooked it, I would have doled out praise.

"Have to ruin everything, don't you?" she said. She tossed her fork on her plate and pushed back from the table, crossing her arms.

"You ruined it, baby. Not me."

She eyed me, her lips trembling, nostrils flaring.

"What?" I said, knowing my face had a huge smirk on it.

I didn't expect her to jump from her seat and practically leap across the table to get at me. And when she did, I didn't expect my hands to turn to fists and...

My father's voice halted my recollection of that day. "A boy of mine, doing that to a lady."

"Don't act as if you didn't do that and worse to Miss Ma'am. Don't even play that role."

"Never put my hands on her, boy."

"Beat her down just the same," I said.

He swallowed. "Your mama ain't ever had to call the cops on me, boy."

"Tammy didn't call the cops," I offered. I don't know why I mentioned that fact. It didn't really matter. "I turned myself in because I knew her brothers were looking for me. They were the wrong niggas to mess with. Tammy, she came to visit me at the jailhouse. She was willing to forgive me. Told me she loved me." As if that made what I did to her okay. Because she cared for me enough to forgive me. Because her mind was that fragile.

I started to tremble as I really thought about the situation.

"I mentioned LeVar's name to her and she didn't even remember him," I told my father. I was feeling so defensive. "I told her I had never loved her. That I just got close to her because I wanted to bring her harm. Told her I wished she were dead. She shook her head, refused to believe it. I kept at it. Told her about my real girl, Myshelle. My real love. Eventually, Tammy left on wobbly legs. Took some pills, an obscene amount, that night."

My father tried to shake his head. Tried to *tsk*.

"LeVar needed someone to stand up for him," I said. "Finally. You wouldn't. He shot himself because of them. He hurt inside so much, he shot himself because of those stupid girls. But truthfully, you'd put the bullet in the gun a long time before."

"You're misguided, boy," my father said. His voice was like the rest of him, broken. "Talking about that girl you killed—and yes, you killed her—with no feeling. I feel sad for you."

Sad for me?

"Dr. Summers told me you mention that whore's name sometimes. Lovey."

My father's lip trembled. Neither one of us was calm through this.

"Yeah, ain't that some crap. As much as Miss Ma'am stood by your sorry butt." I had cursed enough at Sela's; I wouldn't add to my sin with my father, especially since he was the biggest sinner of the two of us. I'd let him sink, while I swam, took the high road.

"Boy…"

"And you'd sit up in here, dying I might add, speaking on that whore. You should be praying to God, asking for forgiveness. For your dead wife. Dead son. But no." I should be praying to He's Sweet I Know, as well. Asking for forgiveness. I was walking across a shaky bridge, too, not even holding to the sides for balance and support. I'd been doing that since that day I put my hands on Tammy.

My father touched a shaky hand to his chest. That set me off.

"Don't even do that Fred Sanford bit," I said cruelly. "You're fine. Your heart is fine." I didn't know if it really was.

"Lovey was the biggest mistake of my life," he said.

"Sure was."

"Lashing out, but hurt myself," he went on. "Marriage weren't ever the same after that. Lashing out. Damn."

"Lashing out at who?"

"Your…." His voice trailed off.

"My…?"

"Mother," he spat.

I was incredulous. "You've got some nerve. You know that?"

"You don't know everything, boy."

"Enlighten me." I challenged him.

He shook his head.

"Didn't think you could." I smirked with the words.

"I could," he said. "But I don't want to bring your life crashing down on you any more than it already has."

I laughed at that one.

He reached forward and gripped the table with his good hand. "Boy…"

"I'm a man," I said. "You got something to say, say it. I can take anything."

"LeVar wa'n't my child," he blurted out. "Why you think he had your mother's maiden name?"

"Y'all divorced," I said. "She had it changed. I wouldn't let her change mine."

He shook his head. "Never divorced, boy. Never."

I thought of the day I came home and found Miss Ma'am crying hysterically. She'd told me she had gotten the divorce papers that day, that she was changing our names. I'd said no. LeVar hadn't cared. "I…" I couldn't think of anything to say.

"Had myself fixed after you," my father said. "Didn't tell your mother. Had my junior; I was done."

I couldn't speak.

"She came up pregnant," he said, sobbing softly. "I knew it wasn't mine."

"Those procedures don't always work," I managed.

"Mine did," he said, sadly. "I confronted your mother. She admitted cheating."

"Why?"

"That's my burden. Me and your mother's, boy. Grown folks' business."

I sat quietly.

"Anything else?" my father asked.

I shook my head.

"You best get going, then," he said. "You done came and stirred up everything I've been ashamed of, everything I've tried to move on from."

"Pop, I—"

"Some other time," he said. "I'm feeling weak."

"Pop—"

"Some other time, boy. You think on what I told you. Next time you come, if you do again, I hope you come the way I'd been praying you would."

"How's that?"

"With love," he said. "The way God comes at us. Forgiving us for our wrongs. With love. And I hope you've asked Him to forgive you for that girl…"

I nodded. A lesson in all this. Lessons in everything.

I stood and watched him. He'd turned his head away. He glanced across the room, out the window at the sky. A clear and sunny day had turned dark and gray, rain clouds on parade. I could see in my father's profile that tears ran down his face. They met at his chin, forming a large drop.

I started to say something else, but didn't. I just left.

Outside, the dark clouds colored the sky. I moved to the Toy-yoda on shaky legs. I'd thought I had life figured out…knew the bad guys, the good guys. I didn't know jack. I knew one thing only: it was time to go home. It would thankfully take me only fifteen minutes to get there. I'd fall in my bed, pray, and cry, probably. All this time, my father had been this close. So close, and yet, so far.

Misguided, he'd called me. I couldn't think of a better description.

34

The clouds opened up. A flash of violent rain dropped from the dark sky. Water sluiced down Russell's windshield. He cursed and turned on his wipers, frowned as the water and a fog surrounded him. Terrible weather, problems with the wife, and his stomach was growling on top of it all. Just as quickly as it had come, though, the hard downpour subsided, leaving a soft, yet steady drizzle of rain in its wake. Good, Russell decided. He could take a quick drive to Subway: he'd seen one of the sandwich shops around the corner.

He pulled the transmission tree from PARK to DRIVE and looked over his shoulder to make sure the blind spot in his rearview hadn't obscured any approaching vehicles. Verifying that the coast was clear, he eased away from the curb. He'd pick up one of Subway's melts: dijon turkey breast, ham and bacon—takeout. He'd bring it back to the house here and wait. He glanced down at the tire iron. Wait, and when the reverend returned home, get some answers. They'd better be the right answers, too.

The reverend eased his car down the slick road. Sprinkles of rain kissed his windshield before the rubber of his wipers pushed them aside. Anita Baker cooed softly from his sound system, her voice full and breathy, a nice contrast to the ugliness of the weather. Thoughts enveloped him.

Miss Ma'am hadn't been all he'd thought she was.

His father hadn't, either.

Life was funny like that, giving you some things in black and white, shading other things gray...confusing at times, so clear at others.

He turned into his driveway after a while, those thoughts heavy in his mind, his heart weighted down by them. He continued on to his backyard and hit the garage door opener. Its gate rose. He drove inside.

Home. But nothing sweet about it. No, a bitterness in his mouth instead.

Bevolyn parked in front of the reverend's home, steeled herself, and then moved from her car with steps of purpose. She struggled to close the gate to the front yard, but finally got it. She moved up the walkway toward the immaculate little house. Mums outlined the front porch. Lavender streamers still were in place from the Open House she'd heard had been such a success: Sela's grandest moment.

Bevolyn shook out her umbrella, closed it, snapped the straps that held it together, and climbed the steps.

She tapped on the door and waited, then tapped a second time and waited. She squinted her eyes and tried to see through the window. It was dark inside. She moved from the door to the edge of the porch, thought about her options, and then descended the stairs and headed up the side of the house, leaving the umbrella shut this time, letting the sprinkles of rain baptize her.

Firewood piled three logs high leaned against the stucco siding. Bevolyn thought briefly of the muscle and man-power it must have taken to pile the logs so neatly.

She came around the bend of the house. Reverend Path was in his garage, with the door up, his back to her. She paused for a moment, then adjusted her blouse and moved toward him.

Clearing her throat, she said, "Reverend," softly, so as not to alarm him.

He turned. His eyes were hard. The lines around his mouth weren't from a smile. "What did you need, Sister Sykes? It's been a long day."

"I know," she said. "Sela really threw us both for a loop, I'm sure."

His hard eyes pierced through her. "What did you need, Sister Sykes?" he repeated.

Bevolyn moved beside him, into the garage, and looked around while her shoulders quivered.

"You should take yourself home," the reverend said. "Get yourself a cup of hot chocolate. Snuggle with your husband. You have a fireplace?"

Bevolyn didn't answer. "I'm fine," she said.

"You're cold," the reverend replied.

Bevolyn could take that comment several ways.

"I need to talk to you," she said, "about my sister. I've got questions and concerns about her soul."

"Sounds like deep stuff," the reverend noted.

"Yes," Bevolyn admitted. "I need some biblical insight, Reverend. That would be your department, wouldn't it?"

"I usually only counsel *members*, Sister Sykes."

"I know, Reverend," she said. "But please."

Those pretty brown eyes he'd at one time thought of as God's greatest creation batted at him. Something moved inside him. Something shifted. They *were* God's greatest creation. Sela had them, too. But Bevolyn, she *owned* them. Pure and simple.

"Head on in, Sister Sykes." He handed her his keys. "This one's for the back door. I have to close up the garage."

"Thanks, Reverend."

"I'll only be a second. Make yourself comfortable." Emphasis on the word "comfortable."

"Okay," Bevolyn said.

She turned and headed toward the house. She didn't have to look back to know the reverend was watching her move. Her stride was strong and feminine. She could feel her heart doing a butterfly's dance in her chest. She didn't feel guilty, either. Not after her conversation with Russell's *administrative assistant*. Not one bit.

The back door led to the kitchen. The reverend looked to be neat: there weren't any dishes in the sink, the stovetop was clean, a small table adorned with pretty place mats centered the room, one chair sat back from the table, and a Bible sat in its lap. Bevolyn glanced in the Bible and saw the little sticky note the reverend had attached to the page. He'd scribbled *when in need of comfort* on the note.

That was something Bevolyn needed also. Comfort.

Russell took a bite of his sandwich as he drove. Mmmm, he murmured in approval. It hit the spot. He took a sip of his cola...ahhh, nice. He wiped his mouth with the back of his hand, burped, and excused himself even though he was alone. Good habits died hard. Bevolyn would be all over him, staring, waiting for him to excuse himself if she were around now. He'd learned to do it without thought, to act as if he had some home raising, as Bevolyn would say. She was a good wife.

Maybe he'd read this thing wrong. There had to be an explanation—a good one, too. Bevolyn wouldn't betray him again, after all they'd gone through. And after he'd just opened his heart to her, let her know the pain he'd carried around their entire marriage, showed her those hateful letters and pictures.

She wouldn't bring that kind of pain to him again. She was a good wife, a fine Christian woman.

But those positive thoughts of his wife disappeared as he pulled up to the reverend's house again and found his spot out front taken by Bevolyn's car, right out in the open. She didn't even have any shame. Russell brought his car to an erratic stop, parking it crookedly behind Bevolyn's, his front touching her bumper. He quickly leaned over, the Subway sandwich falling off his lap. He grabbed the tire iron.

It felt good in his hands. He hefted it, tapped it against his free palm. He jumped from the car, and without closing the door, headed for the house. He struggled with the yard's gate and kicked it in, stumbled up the path, and took the porch steps two at a time. He bypassed the doorbell and rapped his knuckles against the hard wood door—loud, hard, angry, insane knocks, thinking of photos and letters with each knock.

The door opened just as he was about to knock again.

"Russell, I—"

Russell didn't allow him to finish. He shoved the reverend inside and slammed the door behind him.

"Where is she?" Russell barked. "Where's my slut of a wife?"

"Back door?" Nate asked. The John Kerry mask he wore muffled his voice.

"What?" Anthony, George Bush mask on, asked.

"Back door?" Nate repeated.

Dubya's head nodded.

The senator from Massachusetts crouched down and followed the outline of the house, Dubya on his heels.

"Hear that?" Nate asked, turning back.

"Somebody shouting," Anthony said.

"More than one person inside," Nate said. "Turn back?"

"Negative," Dubya said. "No turning back now. Dante'd have a shit fit."

"Should crawl out of that bird's ass he's lounging in and come help us," Nate said.

"Keep moving," Anthony replied.

They moved toward the back of the house. The senator from Massachusetts went to elbow the glass and shatter it so he could unlock the door. Dubya grabbed his arm.

"You crazy? This ain't *Menace II Society,* the movie. Try the lock first."

Kerry did. He turned back. "S'open."

Dubya nodded. "Democrat first."

"Where is she?" Russell barked.

"Hold on, Russell. What's the problem?"

Russell shoved the reverend again. "Her car's out front. Where is my slut of a wife?"

"You have to talk like that, Russell?"

Russell raised his arm and stuck one of the tips of the tire iron in the reverend's chest. "Where. Is. She?"

"She stepped into the bathroom."

"Freshening up, huh?" Russell said. His mouth curled up in anger.

"I think you've got this all wrong," the reverend said. "Nothing is happening here. She came to talk about Sela."

"Where's the bathroom?" Russell asked.

"Off the kitchen," the reverend said.

"Take me to her."

The reverend turned and walked. He prayed God would watch his back, same as He'd watched it while he was in prison.

Bevolyn was backing from the bathroom door as they approached. "Did I hear somebody come in?" she asked in a soft, breathy tone. Then, turning and seeing her husband, her tone changed. "Russell...honey?"

"Save that act, bitch," Russell fumed.

She looked down at his hands, the tire iron, then at the reverend. "You don't think—?"

"Shut your mouth, bitch," Russell cut her off.

"That's two times you've called me out of my rightful name," she said.

Russell moved to her and smacked her with his free hand. "And once I smacked the shit out of you," he added.

The reverend shuffled to Russell and gripped his elbow. "Russell. Come on, man."

Russell pulled his arm loose and sank his elbow into the reverend's gut, and then sank the tire iron there, as well. The reverend doubled over, groaning.

Bevolyn started to sob, warm tears overwhelming her eyes. Her face burned from the pain of Russell's slap.

A line of spit hung from the reverend's mouth like a spiderweb. He took several deep breaths, righted his body, and looked up at Russell, still breathing deeply. He refused to put his hands on the man in retaliation. He'd traveled that road before. It hadn't gotten him anything but jail time.

"More where that came from," Russell told the reverend.

The two men locked eyes. Neither of them moved, though Russell grinned.

Bevolyn continued to sob.

"Shut up, slut," Russell told her. He turned to face her. His tone lowered some. "How could you do this to me, Bev? You have feelings for this guy?"

Bevolyn said, "Honey, please."

"Find him handsome?"

"Russ."

"Like his showy ass muscles?"

Bevolyn glanced at the reverend. His eyes had softened from earlier, in his garage. He looked as if he, too, wanted and needed an answer.

Russell chimed, "I'm not going to deal with a second stash of photos and letters or put up with your whoring on me again. Two times is two times too many. I don't deserve this."

The reverend looked deeper at Bevolyn. She dropped her gaze away from his inquisitive glare.

"Nothing to say?" Russell asked her.

Bevolyn looked up slowly. "I wouldn't put you through that a second time," she said. She focused hard to keep her gaze from drifting to the reverend. "I'd rather hurt myself than hurt you again, Russ."

Russell frowned. "Hurt yourself?" His grip tightened on the tire iron. "What are you saying, Bev?"

"I won't repeat it."

Russell's jaw muscles tensed. "So you not getting with this fake-ass Creflo Dollar," he said, "if you're being truthful and haven't. That's hurting you, Bev? Being with me instead of him is bringing you pain?"

Bevolyn opened her mouth to respond. No words came.

Russell closed his eyes and moaned. When he re-opened them, a fire blazed strong in the pupils. He turned the heat of his gaze toward the reverend and took a hard step in that direction, the tire iron swinging.

The reverend stood impassively. Bevolyn tried to grab Russell's arm, but he slapped her away.

Suddenly the back door exploded open, halting Russell's steps.

He turned to the commotion. "What the…?"

Bevolyn wheeled, then screamed.

The reverend saw—John Kerry?—raise his hand and move in Bevolyn's direction. Something was in his hand…a gun, the reverend realized. "Bevolyn, back up!" he yelled. He made a move to go and protect her, but Russell pushed him back.

"No," Russell growled. His mind was on pictures, letters, and betrayal, totally shut off from the other drama unfolding in the kitchen.

The reverend tried in vain to move around Russell.

Bevolyn's screams cut the air into blocks.

"Shut up," the John Kerry–masked man told her.

Bevolyn raised her hands, blinded by her curtain of tears, by fear. She reached absently for the gunman. He raised his own hand in response, his finger ready on the trigger.

"Bevolyn, no," the reverend called out. He took another hard step in her direction, barreling through Russell this time.

"Leave her be," Russell cried, his arms a belt around the reverend's waist.

Bevolyn continued to scream.

The reverend broke free of Russell. He moved to shield Bevolyn, Russell on his heels.

The gunman in the John Kerry mask squeezed his finger on the trigger.

Three shots fired.

Three bullets tore through flesh.

35

My stomach burns. I feel an odd pinch in it that makes my breathing painful. A blurry Bevolyn Sykes leans over me, talking to me in a calm voice. Tears are streaming down her face. She rocks back and forth, hugs herself, and tells me to hold on. Please hold on. Please. She's desperate.

I'm on my back, not sure if I'm lying on a bed or the ground. Bevolyn's eyes are odd like the pinch in my stomach. She says, "Pimp," I think, but I don't respond. Can't.

She grips my hand. I try to grip back but I can just tell my grip is limp, probably cold, the way Miss Ma'am described my father's grip. I narrow my eyes to force the two Bevolyns hovering over me to turn to one Bevolyn. It works for a brief moment, but then that second Bevolyn reappears.

"Oh, God," she says. "Jesus, Lord, please. No more. No more."

Her words turn to mumbling. I can't make them out.

He's Sweet I Know whispers in my ear. His voice is deep, authoritative, just as I've always imagined it would be. He's like an announcer on a game show, the guy that says, ". . . and now the host of *Jeopardy*—Alex Trebek."

Except He's announcing those from my life who have passed on already to the other side.

My brother, LeVar.

"Apollo Creed," my brother says. He gives me a thumbs-up, and when I smile, he excitedly throws punches and jabs at the air—quick punches, quick jabs. Too excited. He putters out quickly, spent.

My mother, Miss Ma'am.

"Strange fruit," she sings. Her voice is an early morning bird chirping, a melody only From Whom All Blessings Flow could create. She looks in my direction, notices me watching, I guess, and stops abruptly. "Your father's grip wasn't all that limp and cold," she tells me. I smile. She does, too. Then she's back singing again, "He's Sweet I Know" this time.

My mentor, Reverend G.H. Walker.

"God is good?" he asks me. I notice a woman behind him, a smallish woman wearing a pillbox hat, with eyeglasses hanging from a black cord around her neck. A smile is on her face, one arm is wrapped around Reverend Walker's ample waist.

"God is good?" Reverend Walker repeats.

I nod.

"Cigarettes are cheap here," he says. "You'd think I died and went to North Carolina."

I smile.

He turns to the woman. "Not that I need any cigarettes. Not any more, at least. Right, Eleanor?"

The dead J-boy. Jose, Javier, maybe even Jesus. *Hay zoos.*

"*Chocha no pinga, chocha no pinga, chocha no pinga,*" he chants as he skips by.

Then the two gunmen appear; unlike the others, they have a sinister red glow surrounding them. One wears a John Kerry mask, and the other, a George Bush mask.

"You are the hated L-word, Senator," the Bush-masked man says.

The gunman in the John Kerry mask turns quickly to Bush. "The people will in no way, shape, or form buy you selling me as a lesbian, President."

"Not a lesbian," the Bush mask proclaims, "a liberal."

The senator from Massachusetts waves a dismissive hand. "You've sold the people on falsehoods, President. Have them thinking toppling Sah-damn is a victory. Meanwhile, Osama bin Laden, the real enemy, is loose— putting out more videos than P. Diddy, I might add."

I hear Bevolyn again, mumbling, "Pimp." Her eyes are focused to my left. "Oh, God. Jesus, Lord. No more." She trembles as she continues to eye the spot beside me.

Bevolyn moves to me, pulls me close, wiping my mouth with my shirt collar. "No more, Lord," she says. "No more."

I wonder, *No more what?*

Bevolyn has me in her arms. I feel so comfortable there, at peace. She's still rocking, rocking me now, like a baby. Peace shields me.

The stage goes black. My stomach burns, an odd pinch in it that makes my breathing painful. As soon as I think this, the burn goes away, cooling instantly. My breathing is easy, unlabored, and most important, I feel no pain with it.

"Hold on," I hear Bevolyn say. "Please. Jesus, Lord. No more pain, Lord, please. No more."

No more, she says several more times.

I want to tell her my pain is gone, but can't. I close my eyes, thankful the burning and strange pinch in my stomach have subsided. Close my eyes. Sleep.

Book IV

Genesis